The Bird & The Bear
By Kate Vikki

The following product contains mild mentions of child abuse and attempted suicide, although not in any great detail. If either of these topics are triggering for you, please read with caution.

KATE VIKKI

*To Stephen, Sophie, and Daniel.
Thank you for being the best siblings an introvert could ask for.
This series is dedicated to each one of you.*

Playlist

1. WILLOW — TAYLOR SWIFT
2. TEARDROP — MASSIVE ATTACK
3. BONES OF RIBBON — LONDON GRAMMAR
4. 3,000 MILES — CHAMPS
5. PEOPLE — LIBIANCA
6. YOUTH — FOXES
7. DAYDREAMING — HARRY STYLES
8. GOOD TIMES — JUNGLE
9. ONE THING AT A TIME — MORGAN WALLEN
10. EVERYWHERE — FLEETWOOD MAC

Chapter One
A Study in Pink

MYLES

I keep asking myself if I made the right decision doing this.

I mean, sure, my entire degree was built on it, so I never had another path set out for me but this one. I got to where I wanted to be. I worked hard, I all but busted my precious balls and nearly fucked up my wrist—two separate incidents, only one of them involved a risky wank—in the process, but I made it. I did my four years to achieve a degree in Art History, followed by two years completing a PGCE, and I am finally here.

A high school art teacher.

I know what you're thinking. Really, Myles? *Art Teacher? That* was your dream job? And I can assure you that the answer is yes, it has always been my dream job, because I want to mould minds. Or something. I like kids enough, I guess, especially teenagers. I get to teach them at this wildly awkward age where they're completely split down the middle when it comes to art: they either have it or they don't. They think it sucks or they think it's the best thing since sliced bread. And I get to tell them why, even if they don't have a knack for art—the broad spectrum that it is—that it doesn't matter, because at least they got to be creative for an hour or two. They didn't have to worry about a maths test or reading a freaking Shakespeare play. They got to forget about it and got a bit dirty and a bit stupid. They got to have *fun*.

But all that aside, as I stare at the previous Year 9 group's display in the school canteen, I really do have to wonder if this was the right choice.

"Have you figured out what it is yet?"

I startle at the voice next to me; I had no idea I'd been approached. I look down and find a woman with straight dark hair cut in a bob standing beside me, her arms folded across her chest, lips pursed, head tilted to the side. She's about three inches shorter than me.

"Er, I think so. Unfortunately."

She snorts and turns to face me. "Opinion?"

I take a deep breath as I gaze back at the strange menagerie of canvases pinned to the wall. "Inappropriate?"

"Thank God. I thought I was going mad when they put it up and no one bat an eyelid. Myles, right? The new art teacher?"

"That's me," I hold a hand out.

"Emily." She gives it a loose shake. "French teacher."

"Nice to meet you."

"You too. Between you and me, I'm relieved I'm not the newbie anymore."

"You were the newbie?"

"For a whole year. Was a bit shit being the only new faculty member at the start of term, and the kids know it, too."

"Are they bastards?"

She shrugs. "They're teenagers, of course they're bastards. The boys are the worst, but fortunately I've grown up around a lot of men and know how to handle them. You, on the other hand…"

Emily gives me a slow once over, an interested perusal if I've ever seen one.

"What about me?" I ask when she doesn't say anything.

"The girls might eat you alive."

I clear my throat. "I'm sure I'll be fine."

"Yes, I'm sure."

We turn back to the display on the wall, and I have to scratch my face, still bewildered.

'A Study in Pink' they'd called it. And I wasn't sure what the curriculum for Year 9s last year entailed, but I hope it isn't the same this year. And if it is, I won't be teaching whatever my predecessor was.

"There's so many…"

Vaginas. I couldn't put it any other way. We are essentially looking at a wall of fucking vaginas in oils and watercolours and chalks and pencils. A study in pink is accurate, but I wish she'd chosen something that wasn't just various impressions of female genitalia.

"Who *authorised* this for the display?" I ask, rubbing at my chest and then crossing my arms.

"Paulson." The headteacher.

"Christ."

"Word on the street is that him and old Hilary were having an affair, so she could get away with shit like this."

"It's in the fucking canteen."

Emily laughs, and I rather enjoy the sound. "Just promise me come April when you're gearing up the poor sods for their final pieces you won't make them draw multiple abstract dicks."

I snort. "Yeah, no problem there."

"Well," she places a hand on my arm, and I swear I feel her squeeze it, as if testing the muscles there, "it was good meeting you, Myles." Given the way she purrs the last words, I can only assume she approves.

"You, too."

She walks away, a swish to her hips and an ethereal air about her.

I give the vagina wall one last look, grimacing at the thought of having to see it every day come the new term, and head back to my classroom.

Yes, I can say that now. *My* classroom. I've been spending the week getting myself up together—preparing for a form group; for my GCSE students; decorating—feathering the nest, as it were. It's Friday today, the last day before my own summer holiday. I won't come back after this until the last week of August—an entire month away—to settle in before the kids come back the first week of September.

While I'm packing my things up, my phone rings. *BEAU* lights up the screen with a photo of the two of us at his debut for the Coventry Rangers three years ago.

"Hey, man," I answer the call, wedging the phone between my ear and shoulder.

"Hey, Mr Wilson," he says in a teasing, sultry voice. I roll my eyes. "Still on for beers and pizza tonight?"

Beau Bennett has been my best friend since my first year of university. Granted, I didn't actually go to uni with him since he's been a professional football player since he was nineteen years old, but I was in halls with his twin brother, Nash, which is how we met, and immediately hit it off. While I found Nash to be a little arrogant and aloof, he and Beau spend a lot of their free time together, even now as adults, so Beau was around a lot when he was playing in the area.

Accidentally becoming friends with a professional football player also had many, *many* perks. He started his career playing for the local team in the National League the year we met and slowly worked his way into the Premier League with the Rangers main squad. Beau very quickly embraced the celebrity lifestyle and finds himself in gossip magazines more than he probably should, but I just joined him for the nights out and the occasional mischief. I don't always condone his bachelorhood antics.

"Yeah, of course. Just getting ready to leave—I'll head home and change and then pick it up on the way over."

"Cool. Have you seen Brinsley yet?"

Beau, I soon learnt, is actually not just a twin, but a quadruplet—two boys and two girls. According to him, he's the oldest because he came out first, but only by about a minute from the way his mum, Shirley, tells the story. Brinsley was next, followed by Sheridan another minute or so later, and finally Nash— who was apparently more comfortable in his mother's womb than he ever cares to admit—didn't come out until a full twenty minutes after the others. Brinsley, one of Beau's sisters, is also starting at Webster's School of Secondary Education as a faculty member this year. Shirley Bennett has been a teacher here for years and is now the Deputy Head. I've had lunch with her every day this week.

"Well, your mum said she's coming to set herself up next week, so no." I finally head out of the classroom, locking the door behind me.

"Oh, damn. Well, that's okay. You'll get to finally meet her and Shez at our birthday."

Yes, somehow, having known Beau and Nash going on five years, I've never met either of the Bennett sisters. For some reason, whenever there's been a get-together, either I've not been able to make it, or they haven't. From the boys' information, Brinsley has always been very studious and straightlaced, and Sheridan has social anxieties so barely leaves the house. It's safe to say, I am curious to meet both of them, having heard so much about them from Beau.

At the reminder of their birthday next week, I stall. It was in the back of my mind, but I'd forgotten about the whole event. And I say event because Beau is *making* it an event. Apparently, he, Nash and the girls all split the cost of a luxury cabin in a fancy holiday park in Lerwick Forest and invited six of their friends. I'm one of said friends. Shirley, and their dad, Brian, will also be joining the first weekend.

"That's true. I'm just heading out the door, so I'll see you in about an hour."

"Cool. Get me a meat feast!"

"Sure thing, Bionic Beau."

He preens at the fan-bestowed nickname. "Stop flirting or I'll be forced to snog you when you get here."

"You say that like it's a bad thing."

"You saucy minx. See you soon, Mr Wilson."

"Bye, mate." I chuckle and end the call.

I wander the halls towards the staff exit, peeking into each classroom and trying to familiarise myself with the layout so I'm not totally lost when I return next month. As far as I know, only me and Brinsley are new on the teaching staff this year, so most of the other classrooms are already broken in where decorating is involved. I can't wait to have that feeling of home inside mine.

Growing up in care, I never really knew what having a home was like until my second year of university when I moved into a house with Nash and a few guys from my course. I'm not from the area, either, but I fully intend to make Coventry my permanent home. I've lived here five years, I know all the local haunts, I've made some friends. Not having a family of my own actually made that transition easier for me. I'm never going back to London.

I live in my own flat now—I moved in just after my course ended in the spring. It's nothing special, but fine for me—a one-bedroom place in a converted waterworks just a short ten-minute drive from Webster's. I haven't done much decorating to the place, especially since it's not mine, but I will eventually. I want it to feel like home.

I pop my head into Shirley Bennett's office on my way past to see if she's around. Her door is wide open, as it has been all week whenever I've passed, and she's sitting behind her desk while she taps away on her keyboard.

The Bennett sibling's mother is without a doubt the best woman I've ever met. Petite, blonde and beautiful, the first time she met me she took me in for a hug that had a lasting effect on me for hours and proceeded to ply me with food and drinks while regaling me with stories about what it was like having a house filled with four children of the exact same age (give or take twenty minutes). Easily a woman teenage boys would hail as a MILF; Shirley is one of those people who just make life better.

"Knock, knock," I announce myself.

"Oh, Myles!" She beams up at me, blonde hair bouncing with each slight shake of her head. "Heading out early?"

"Yeah, I er, think I've done what I can for now, so I'm going to meet your eldest for beer and pizza."

"Doesn't he have a game tomorrow?"

Whoops. Nothing like dropping him in it with his own mother. "It's only a pre-season friendly. Plus, he never drinks the night before a game. Beer is for me. And you know he stopped eating gluten years ago."

"Oh," she tuts, smacking a palm to her forehead, "he has that cauliflower shit, doesn't he? Dur."

I can't help but grin. Shirley Bennett is like a walking sitcom character. "Yep, that cauliflower shit."

"That's good. How do you feel after this week? Feeling ready?"

"I think so," I say honestly. "I'm glad we've got a week beforehand to prep as well, otherwise I really might be worried."

"You've got some good kids, Myles. Your Year 9 group is a little tyrannical, but the Key Stage Four kids are great. And your form group are practical babies, so they'll be just as terrified as you."

"That's good. Can I just maybe get that in writing?" I joke. "Along with a promise that I won't have to make a bunch of fourteen-year-olds artistically interpret the female reproductive system?"

"God," Shirley whines and covers her face, "I'm going to kill Eric for that bloody display. How Hilary got away with it, I do not know."

"I heard a rumour." I shrug.

"Don't listen to it. Teachers are the worst gossips, Myles. Don't fall into the trap."

"Noted."

"Who were you talking to?"

"Er, Emily? I didn't get her surname. The pretty French teacher."

Shirley's face screws up. "Bloody harlot."

I practically choke on my own laugh.

"Sorry, that was unprofessional. I just don't like that woman—she's trouble."

"I'll try and keep my distance then?"

"Might be wise." She winks at me. "Anyway, don't let me keep you. Go have fun with my baby, and I'll see you next weekend."

"Yes, you will." I smile. "Bye, Shirl."

"Bye, sweetheart!"

I head out the door towards my car, checking my phone as I walk. No personal messages, which I'm not particularly surprised by, but I do have a Twitter alert announcing there's a new episode of my favourite web show being released tonight. That puts another smile on my face.

If I had enough talent, rather than Art History, I probably would've done an Art & Design degree instead. I can draw and paint well, don't get me wrong, but I never quite had the skill to make something of my own—to be truly original. I started watching animated web shows—web-toons if we're being specific—when I was fifteen and I never grew out of it. In uni I went through a phase where I'd watch multiple series at a time and avidly follow every creator, but now I tend to only look out for one or two. This one, *Goth Frogs*, is exactly as it sounds, and has become immensely popular in recent months. The storyline, script, and animation are all done by one person—well, woman—and posted to her YouTube channel.

There's a post about it on Instagram too—a screenshot of the episode and a second image of her workstation with the initial sketches, pencils neatly arranged and a Pokémon mug in the corner.

I say it every time she posts something, but I think this woman might be my soulmate. Knowing my luck, she's probably thirty years my senior with twenty cats and a foot fetish. I would be so lucky.

Chapter Two

WITCHY HOVEL

SHERIDAN

I blink at my laptop screen, and then I blink again. *Still there.* I try a third time just to be safe, but the email isn't going anywhere. It's really there, in all its terrifying glory.

Dear BennyBetty,

Congratulations!
We are delighted to inform you that your web series has been shortlisted for a Toonie Award. Please see the full list of Nominees at the bottom of this email.

We will be hosting an award ceremony on the 15th of December to announce the winners and we would love you to join us. If you would like to attend, please fill out the attached RSVP and return it to us before the 1st of December.

We hope to see you there!

Best wishes,
The Team @ ToonTime

An award? I've been nominated for an *award*?!

I hastily scroll down to the bottom of the email and start scanning the names. My mouth falls and I cover it with my hand. My heart is beating in my ears, *thump thump thump.*

There are so many incredible shows on this list and I'm in there amongst them. There's no way I'm as good as the others. No. Not a chance. But my web name is there, right next to my silly little animated show. *Goth Frogs* was always just supposed to be for me—a daft idea to get me out of a creative slump. To get the ball rolling. To get me *away* from the interior design hell I found myself in the very pit of. It was just for fun. It was never supposed to garner this type of attention—to get *award nominations.*

"Shit!" I squeal.

Hector, my little nervous ball of curly white canine, barks in response to my outburst. I blindly reach down to pat his head before he can break into the shakes.

Three nominations. *Three.* I'm in utter disbelief.

"Shez?!" My sister's voice rings through the house.

I'm comfortable enough with all my siblings—and parents—that they have a key for my cottage and can come and go as they please. A feat that I've only encouraged the past six months or so.

"In here!"

Brinsley, my twin, pops her head into the room. "What's all the shouting for?"

I spin in my chair to face her, and it's like looking in a mirror. Blonde hair, big blue eyes, and about half an inch taller than me, and slimmer in places that only I would notice. "I've been nominated for an award."

"Seriously?!" She squeals and starts jumping up and down. "Sheridan, that's amazing! Which house?"

I stand from my chair, wringing my hands. Only Brinsley and Beau know about my web show. Nash can be a judgemental prick at the best of times, and I just know he wouldn't get it. I spent years in school feeling like a weirdo for making drawings of things that made no logical sense. Frogs dressed as goths is tame compared to my overactive fifteen-year-old brain, and when some boys got hold of my little black sketchbook filled to the brim with animals in precarious costumes and abstract landscapes and creepy creatures formed out of dark shadows, Nash only jumped on the bandwagon to laud my weirdness for the entire school body to see. I love him, and we've grown closer since then, but he never understood me, and he never wanted to, and I've just learnt to accept that. Beau and Brin, on the other hand, while often cautious given my anxiety, are much better at accepting the things I do.

"Uh, no. Not for that. For the web show I've been doing."

"*Goth Frogs?*"

"Yeah."

Brin places her hands on my shoulders and squeezes. "That's *awesome.*"

"You think so?"

"Of course, I do, Shez! I've seen that show and I *know* it's funny. It's good! Your brain is weird and bright and complicated, and I love it. *We* love it."

I struggle to keep my smile away at that. "Thanks, Brin."

"So come on, what were you nominated for? How many?"

I pick up my laptop and show her. "Best Animator, Comedy, and Show of the Year," she reads aloud. "Wow. This is amazing—look at you!"

"I know, I'm a bit in shock, to be honest."

"Well, we need to celebrate! I bought some dye to refresh your tips," she scrunches a handful of my curls—the tips I've had dyed in various colours since I was sixteen, currently more pastel pink than the bright magenta it was the last time I touched it up, "and then we can open a bottle. Sound good?"

It did sound good.

After tidying up my home studio and putting all my art supplies back in their places, I huddle up to the bathroom where Brin has set up the box dye ready. While she gets to work, we talk about her, mostly, which I don't mind because her life tends to be much more interesting than mine. It doesn't matter what clothes I wear, or what I get tattooed on my body, or if I do add that cartilage piercing to my left ear; Brinsley isn't socially inept the way I am.

When my parents' friends ask about me, they call me a 'homebody'. I guess it's true in most senses—I do love being home and working on art and reading in my nook and watching comedy panel shows on the TV. I've never understood that crippling anxiety I get when I go out, but I've had it for as long as I can remember.

It has got better with age—I have a solid group around me, mostly including my siblings, where I can be myself. My *real* self. But I am that elusive Bennett sibling that people always ask about, simply because I'm never around to talk about myself. Maybe being called a 'homebody' is better than 'shy' or 'strange'. I know my parents love me and understand that it can't be helped. I know that Beau understands that a football game is too overwhelming for me to attend, even though he keeps a ticket aside for me just in case I do want to go. I know that it's strange for my family to have one member who seems to hide and thrive behind the scenes while the rest of them blossom in full view of the world, but that they get it. It took them a long time to, but they do *get* it.

"Andy asked after you today."

Andy, short for John Andrews, because there are too many people in this city with the first name John (and Steve, and Emma, and Sarah come to think of it) to be able to ever follow what anyone is talking about.

I snort, trying to mask my real feelings for my sister's piece of work boyfriend. "Did he ask if I was still content living my witchy life rolling around in mud in my little hovel?"

Hector barks, too attuned to my various tones of voice. He is *not* a fan of the mortgage advisor my sister shapes her life around.

Brin's hesitant pause tells me she is confused—that, little does she know, John Andrews asked me that very question a few months ago at family dinner. I try to keep my disdain for him under wraps, because everyone else seems to love him. Well, except Hector. "No, he asked if you were okay. I thought it was nice of him."

It's a polite social standard that she's trying to use to get me to like him more, because as much as I pretend otherwise, she can tell I don't.

Instead of saying what I really want to say, I settle on, "Yes, very nice."

She continues applying dye to the underside of my hair again, "Not everyone thinks you're weird, Shez." But John Andrews does.

"Is he coming next week?" I ask, if only to make conversation.

She sighs, a sad little sound. "No. He had planned to, but he's working now and can't get out of it."

"Can't he join for the weekend like Mum and Dad?" I don't really want him to do that, especially at the delightful news that I won't have to see his stupid face. But I want my sister to be happy, and for now, he seems to be the one doing that.

"Oh, I hadn't thought about that... I'll ask him when I get home."

"It's not far, is it? Where we're going? Lerwick is only a couple of hours at most."

"Not even that far, I don't think." She gives another happy sigh as she brushes dye onto the tips of my hair. "I don't see why he can't. At least it'll be another familiar face for you until you get used to the others."

I didn't want her to use that excuse. Part of the reason I agreed to go on this week away was to better cope with my anxieties with smaller groups. Yes, my siblings and our cousin are going, and two girlfriends I don't see nearly as much as I used to, but Nash and Beau have invited three of their friends that I've never met before. One of them is Beau's best friend, another is Nash's business partner. I should have met them by now.

"I'll be fine."

"Oh!" Brin gasps, remembering something. "I spoke to Mum just after lunch and she was *reeling*."

"Why?" I laugh, because when Mum gets going about something, she's hard to stop.

"So, you know Beau's friend Myles, who's coming next week, starting as a teacher at the school with me?"

"I might have heard him mentioned once or twice." Only all the fucking time.

Brin swats my arm at my sarcasm. "Well, she's been lunching with him all week while he sets his classroom up. *Apparently* that French teacher she hates has her sights set on him."

"Oh, God." I grin, I can't help it. "Not the 'frolicking tart from Toulon'?" Yes, that is really what Shirley Bennett had once called this French teacher she so despises. We don't know if she's from Toulon. "What is it about this woman that gets under her skin so much?"

"Fuck knows, but it's hilarious. I mean, she was going on and on about it, as if Myles was some helpless, dickless moron. *That harlot better stay away from our boy*. Like, I had to remind her at least twice that Myles is not related to us, no matter how much Beau might wish he is."

"I've never even met him."

"Neither have I, come to think of it."

"Really? Beau says he's always at the football."

"He sits in a different stand to me. I'm behind the home goal, I think he uses Beau's box."

"Oh. Someone new for both of us, then."

"I know! If this Emily woman is hitting on him—if that's actually true—then he must be halfway decent looking."

"I can't remember from any pictures the boys have shown us."

"Me neither. But Mum loves him which must mean he's at least a nice person."

"That means fuck all. He could be a complete dickhead when he's with his friends."

"True. I guess we'll find out next week."

Chapter Three
SOMETHING OF A WET DREAM

MYLES

"Trust it to be the girls late turning up. Honestly. Women."

Suppressing a sigh, I make that to be the sixth stupid thing Stavros has said in the ten minutes I've been around him. We're waiting at Beau's house ready to leave for our week away in the woods. I just pray to whoever I have to that I don't have to share a bed with that idiot.

"What's that supposed to mean?" Emma, a cousin of the Bennett siblings demands. It's the first time I've heard her speak all morning.

"Ignore him, Em." Beau slings an arm around her shoulders and gives her a little shake. "Steven here just hasn't had a woman in his bed for a while and it's turning him into a sexist pig."

"Don't call me that," Stavros snaps. I always forget that the idiot chose the name Stavros because there are too many Stevens in his lineage, and it was 'starting to get ridiculous'. As if *choosing* a name like Stavros isn't ridiculous at all when you have no Greek heritage whatsoever.

"Oops, sorry Steven," Beau taunts, then smacks a hand over his mouth. It's that little glittering in his eyes that gives him away. "I mean *Stavros*."

I lower my gaze to the floor and shake my head.

We are waiting for the twins I've yet to meet, but I wouldn't say they're late. I was already here with Beau—I'd gone to watch him at the game and ended up crashing in his spare room after a rather tough win. I wasn't surprised when I woke up in the morning to see an unfamiliar woman leaving the house. Nash turned up with Stavros in time for breakfast, and JP not long after him. Then the three girls—Emma, Bailey, and another I haven't caught the name of yet—had turned up only about five minutes ago, all together.

"Stop causing fights, Beau," Nash grumbles from where he stands by the boot of my car.

We've already decided on who's travelling in what car—except for the twins yet to arrive—and unfortunately, I've been lumped with the men. Hopefully whichever of the twins that decide to ride with me will behave as a kind of buffer if Stavros starts saying anything stupid, which is likely since he seems to be on a roll this morning with his idiocy. I'm regretting offering to drive, but Nash refused to have anyone in his car, Stavros drives like he's in *Grand Theft Auto,* and JP is currently banned after being caught drink driving back in June after the last football season ended and he went on a bit of a bender. Beau absolutely refuses to let any of the girls drive—for chivalry, not because he thinks they can't—although I heard that the twins especially put up a good fight about it.

"Tell your friend to not say stupid shit, then." Beau shrugs, leaning back against his car.

If we're in for a week of bickering, I might just dump them all in the forest and come back home. Brian and Shirley definitely won't tolerate it. At least I remembered to pack my earphones.

"Fuck off, Beau," Stavros practically hisses. "I mean, talk about an overreaction."

"If anyone's overreacting, it's you," Bailey says without a lick of interest in the faux-Greek.

Beau warned me last night, while drunk, that she can get a little close for comfort but that she's really just a harmless flirt. Apparently, she's not shy when it comes to men, but she's been relatively quiet so far. It is still quite early.

"This coming from the queen of gobshites."

I drag a hand down my face. A truly great start to a holiday when we're fighting before we've even started travelling.

"Just *shut. Up,*" Bailey hisses, and then proceeds to throw an empty water bottle at him. The cap end smacks Stavros right in the middle of his forehead, and I have to hold back a snort.

Thankfully, the last of our convoy pulls up in a little green Austin Mini, racing stripes and all.

"Hallelujah." Bailey sighs, skipping over to the Bennett sister's car. Emma, and the other girl I still can't remember the name of, follow suit with just as much eagerness.

I push away from the side of my car and walk to the boot, opening it ready for whichever twin's luggage I'll be carrying.

"Doggy!" Nash squeals, and I've never heard him sound more girly than in that very moment.

Following his delighted path, sure enough there's a little ball of pure white fluff on the ground, shaking like a goddamn leaf. It yaps once at Nash, who scoops it up and cradles it like a baby.

JP, a known dog lover, is immediately at Nash's side petting the small pup, who still looks like it is about to combust with how violently it's shaking.

"Please don't overwhelm him."

My gaze tracks that voice, finding two figures side by side, one with her hands on her hips and one clutching a dog bed to her chest like it's a lifeline. No need to guess who the dog's mother is.

"He's fine, Shez," Beau says, patting the head of the sister hugging the bed.

The Bennett sisters have exactly the same face, and yet everything else about them is so very different. Brinsley is somehow an inch taller, the slimmer of the two—not that it matters—with straight blonde hair practically down to her waist, and big blue eyes. She screams schoolteacher, from the dusty blue linen dress that just brushes her ankles, the straight-backed posture, all the way to the pinched smile.

Sheridan, on the other hand, looks something of a wet dream. Now that Beau has taken that dog bed away from her and the other girls have moved out of the way, I can see every glorious inch of her. She's short, her hair bounces with tight blonde curls, dip-dyed a vibrant pink at the ends. The eyes are the same blue as her sister's—big, and a vivid denim blue—with plump, heart-shaped lips. But she's curvier than Brinsley; an hourglass personified. The freckles on her nose and cheeks are more obvious than her sister's. Her paper bag-waist shorts are black cotton, and her form-fitting strappy vest shows her cleavage nicely, but not overly. And yet, the thing that gets me the most is her tattoos. She's covered in them—her left arm a sea of bright colours like splashes of ink or paint that make up images of birds. So many different birds. And then her right side is almost bare. *Almost*, if not for the twisting illustration of ivy, building up her leg, disappearing under her shorts and then reappearing over the back of her shoulder and twirling again all the way down her right arm to one of her fingers.

I realise I'm staring and promptly turn away, busying myself with making space in the boot again, even though there's plenty. Anything to keep my gaze away from that gorgeous woman.

"You know Hector isn't coming in my car, right?" Beau says, but it doesn't register with me who he's referring to until a moment later.

"Beau," someone hisses.

"What?"

The next time I turn around, the four Bennett's are huddled together having a hushed discussion, and everyone else has dispersed, splitting between the relevant cars.

"Myles!" Beau suddenly shouts across the car park, gesturing me over.

Trying not to look like a pathetic, tongue-wagging schoolboy, I wander over to the quadruplets with my hands shoved into my pockets.

"Myles," he gestures to me, then to the girls in turn, "Sheridan and Brinsley. Girls, this is Myles."

Brinsley sticks her hand out with a beaming smile. "Finally. Not sure how we've managed to go this long without meeting before."

I return her smile and her handshake but can't quite help but feel it's nowhere near as big. "You'll be fed up with me by October."

"Not if our mother's got anything to do with it."

"You mean *especially* if she does," Nash scoffs.

"That's true." Brinsley laughs.

I turn my attention on Sheridan, who manages to force a smile and a quiet, "Hi," before dropping my gaze again.

I clear my throat, "Hey."

Everything in her posture tells me that she's uncomfortable, and I remember that one of the twins has social anxiety, and that it clearly isn't Brinsley. I'll need to remember that—Sheridan isn't rude, she's just shy.

"So, we were just having a discussion," Beau starts, arms folded across his chest. "I'm not letting Hector in my car."

I'm confused. "Is that... like, a weird nickname for one of the twins?"

Sheridan snorts and quickly covers her mouth, cheeks dusting pink. Brinsley giggles, and Nash barks out a laugh.

"No, mate," he slaps my shoulder, "it's the dog."

"*Oh.* Well, that's okay. I don't mind taking the dog."

The four of them look at me as if I'm some kind of Martian.

"Hector is..." Brinsley starts, and then struggles to finish the sentence.

Sheridan's cheeks have gone even more pink, and I don't know how it's possible, but I swear her freckles are darker.

"Hector is what?" I ask.

"Nervous?" Beau offers.

"Is...that a big problem? Why do you all look so worried?"

"He's probably going to piss in your car," Nash supplies with no preamble. "Maybe even shit. Definitely fart a lot. And whine."

"You know what, I'll just drive myself," Sheridan blurts, complexion now that of a beetroot as she turns away.

"*No,*" Her brothers all but shout, halting her.

Brinsley rolls her eyes.

"Beau, you should really take Hector in your car."

"No. I love the boy, but no. Not in the Range Rover."

"Seriously? The whole thing's decked out in leather."

"Absolutely not. It's brand new and probably worth more than your new yearly teaching salary."

"Don't be a prick."

My gaze bounces between the siblings as they start bickering amongst themselves, and finally snap when I start getting a headache. I'm not a loud snapper, though—I learned to control my temper years ago. I just pick the dog bed up off the floor and carry it to the car, where I put it in the footwell of the front passenger side.

"What are you doing?" Stavros asks, drawing the attention of everyone else, including the bickering Bennetts.

I state the obvious, "Putting Hector's bed in the car."

"You can't be serious—that nervous wreck is not riding with us. Especially not shotgun."

"Please let me drive myself," I hear Sheridan plead behind me.

"Nope," Beau says.

Suddenly, a white ball of fluff appears at my feet, still shaking, but those brown doe eyes gaze up at me as if I'm the one who's been feeding and loving him all his life.

"You gonna ride with the lads, Hector?" I ask him, pointing at his bed.

He barks, a yappy sound, and then jumps into the car. Someone behind me gasps.

"I'm not riding shotgun with that thing," Stavros says, scowls, and folds his arms.

I'd like to say I'm not a violent person—not anymore, at least—but my fist is itching for a punch in this dickhead's mouth. "No, you're not."

"Thank you," he says with a huff.

"You're riding in the back." I give him a flat smile.

When I turn around, all the girls are staring at me. Bailey, of course, is the one to open her mouth:

"Damn. I think I just came."

Chapter Four
WATCH DIALS

SHERIDAN

Myles Wilson is quite possibly the sexiest motherfucker I have ever had the pleasure of looking at. And it's *really* hard to look at him without combusting. He's not just sexy because he's good-looking—which he most definitely, absolutely, completely is—but because he can handle a twat like Stavros without breaking a sweat. How Nash can work with that smarmy git, I do not know. *Why I signed myself up for a week with him,* I do not know.

All I do know right now, is that sitting shotgun to a driving Myles in his modest black VW Polo with Nash, Stavros and JP squashed in the back, is setting my anxiety levels at an all-time high. It's all shoulders, elbows, and knees in the back seat, with one of them grumbling every so often about how uncomfortable they are. Stavros has said at least five times that a man of his size shouldn't have to sit in the back of a Volkswagen—even though I'm really not sure what that has to do with anything—and we haven't even got on the A45 yet.

Hector jumped into my lap the second Myles started the engine, farted, and started his shaky legs ritual. He's panting so heavily that the windows are steaming up, and it smells like rotten eggs inside this little car.

I'm going to kill Beau and Nash for not letting me drive my damn self.

"I'm so sorry," I say for the second time, and open the window a crack to let some fresh air in. The heat definitely isn't helping. "I'll pay to get your car fumigated or something. I didn't know Hector was blacklisted from Beau's precious Range Rover."

Myles just laughs. "It's fine, Sheridan."

"Damn thing should be blacklisted from all cars, not just Beau's Range Rover," Stavros mutters.

I hear a sturdy *thump*, followed by an "Ow." I don't need to turn around to know who punched who.

I couldn't leave Hector at a shelter or with a reliable neighbour—he'd just never recover. He's nervous enough at home as it is without him being lumped with a practical stranger for a week. The only alternative to this was for me to just not come at all, which my siblings said wasn't actually an option. That's why I'm so irritated with Beau. The 'oldest' of us, who usually handles me much better than this, and Hector. He loves Hector, to the point they're inseparable when he comes to the cottage some evenings. He's just too damn fussy about his bloody car.

A doctor told me to get a dog to help with my anxieties. I decided to adopt rather than buy from an official breeder since purebreds are expensive and there are too many dogs in the world without good homes. Little did I know, I picked up the one puppy who had more anxiety than I did. *I've* never wet the bed multiple times. I think. I'd have to double check that with my mum, but I'd like to say that if anyone out of the four of us was a bedwetter, it was probably Nash.

"He'll be fine once we've been going for a little while," I say, more to remind myself than the rest of the passengers in the car. "I've given him tablets and spray to calm him down."

"I honestly don't mind. Lots of dogs get nervous in the car."

"If the David Beckham wannabe and GI Jobs in the back there" —someone, I think JP, starts cackling at my analogy— "had just let me drive myself, I could've saved everyone the trouble."

"Was never gonna happen, Shez." Nash sighs from the middle back seat. "You'd have followed us to the motorway and carried on back to Ansty instead of going to Lerwick Forest."

Damn it, he's not wrong. But I can't let him get the last word in. "We're not even going on that motorway."

"Deflection!"

Hector barks at the volume, stumbling in my lap to look over my shoulder into the back seat at the source of the shouting. How one dog can be so nervous yet so nosey all at the same time I have no idea. Nash gives his head a scratch for good measure.

Myles glances over his shoulder, "She's not wrong, though."

Ha. I don't get smug often, but I do like being right.

"A woman with a sense of direction..." Stavros muses, "who'd have thought it?"

I clench my teeth, clamping down on my own rebuttal.

"You know, Steven, I'm not opposed to pulling over and leaving you on the hard shoulder," Myles says through an equally strained jaw.

"I'd like to see you try, mate."

I'd like to see him try, too, actually. In fact, if this was a train with one of those emergency brake lever things, I'd be yanking on it so hard just to get a front row seat of Stavros's ejection.

"For the love of God, man," John Paul, who I have a serious suspicion is nursing a bad hangover, speaks for the first time all morning, "just shut the fuck up."

Turns out there's only one shitty man in this car, and it's the idiot who picked his own name.

"Here's a great idea," Nash leans forward, "how about some music?"

"Most sensible thing anyone's said all morning," JP mutters.

"I'm picking!" Stavros butts in, and Hector barks again. "I ain't listening to any of your lot's shit."

"And a woman *definitely* can't pick," I mutter.

Myles snorts, and it makes me blush. Again. I hadn't expected him to hear me over the bickering in the back, but apparently, he had. He adds to it when he quietly says, "Especially not one with a sense of direction who's already sitting in the front."

My chest heaves with a silent laugh, and I can't help looking over at him. He's grinning and it's absolutely beautiful. The apples of his cheeks bloom with it, and I want to poke one. His short choppy hair, which is somehow both light and dark blond all at the same time, ruffles in the breeze from the open window. His skin is pale, but he seems to tan well, the sun giving him a golden glow which stretches into his gorgeous hazel eyes. Shameless, my gaze trails down to his arms, held confidently at twelve and six rather than ten and two, the veins in both of them painfully visible. I'd never considered myself a forearms kind of girl, but I am right now. I also don't very often find myself hot for men I've only just met, but apparently Myles is the exception. I can see a peek of a tattoo on his left bicep, but I'm way too shy to even contemplate asking what it is.

While I've been gawking at my brothers' friend, the three in the back have been fighting over who's music is going on and what in particular we're going to be subjected to. I'd rather sit in silence at this point, but I know that's never going to happen, and opening a book would just be downright rude, as tempting as it is.

I feel my phone vibrate where it's wedged between my thighs, and I try and coax Hector's back legs up to reach it.

Brin
How's it going? Xxxx

Grateful for a distraction, I reply instantly.

Me
About as well as you might expect with that idiot in the back xxxx

Brin
Which idiot? Xxxx

Me
Steven Alfred Sinclair-King LXXXVII xxxx

Brin
Lol what number is that? Also yes, complete twat.
Do not envy you xxxx

Me
87. Fortunately the others also seem to be just as equally pissed off by his twattishness. Xxxx

Brin
I'm sorry.

I've snapped at Beau for lumping you with the boys. Xxxx

Me
It's fine. Nothing like throwing me in the deep end I guess xxxx

Brin
Have you managed to get your vagina under control yet? Xxxx

Me
Come again?????????????

Brin
Myles…

Me
What about Myles? Xxxx

Brin
Here, I wrote a poem:
Oh Myles
I really like your smiles
And those fancy watch dials
I bet you've got nice kitchen tiles
Which I one day hope to defile
With you

Trying not to laugh is proving to be really difficult, because yikes. *Where* did she come up with that? More importantly, *how* did she come up with it so completely off the cuff? My sister is nuts. She's about to become an English teacher to a bunch of teenagers and yet she's sending me limericks about…defiling kitchen tiles? At least I know I'm not the only Bennett sibling with a vivid imagination.

Me
… Wow. And people call you prude.

Brin
THEY DO NOT.

Me
Not anymore they don't. Xxxx

Brin
Are you just going to pretend that my poem wasn't instant genius? And that you obviously have the hots for Beau's insanely good-looking friend who just so happens to be your type to an absolute T? Xxxx

Me
I do not. Xxxx

Brin
Sure, Jan. xxxx

I sneak a peek at the *insanely good-looking* man beside me and find myself biting my lip. I'm perfectly fine to admit I *have the hots* for Myles to myself, but I'm not telling my sister. She'd only tell one of the girls in the other car, who would then tell the rest of them, and then one would mention it to Beau, or Nash, and finally it would come back to me, and probably Myles, leaving me to spend the rest of the holiday looking like some kind of fraught tomato.

Yeah, no thanks.

I realise that the boys have resorted to shouting at each other, only because Hector is suddenly barking like a maniac. I snuggle him to my chest and lower the window a little more, even though we're easily going sixty and the wind will probably irritate Stavros, but I don't care. I need to calm my dog down.

"Enough!" Myles suddenly yells, the carefree man I was admiring minutes ago long gone. "I'm putting the fucking radio on."

Which turns out to be, sadly, the worst decision he could make.

Chapter Five
Stoppage Time

MYLES

"Look on the bright side, man," Stavros claps a hand on my shoulder, and I desperately want to shove him right off, "at least the dog didn't piss on you."

I throw a look his way that has him removing his hand instantly.

This has been a disaster of epic proportions and we're not even at the holiday park yet.

I didn't think turning the radio on would result in Hector wetting himself all over my passenger seat, and conversely, Sheridan's lap. I hadn't expected the volume to be so loud when I turned it on, or a kind of death metal to be playing at such an insane volume. I'm not even that into death metal, especially not through the radio. Come to think of it, I can't even remember the last time I listened to the radio in this car—I usually play music through my phone.

The look of utter horror on Sheridan's face will be painted in my memory until the day I die. She didn't say a word after requesting that we pull into the first services we came across, just sat silently shivering and clenching her fists while the dog incessantly whined. As soon as we pulled into a space she shot out of the car and took Hector with her. That was half an hour ago.

"Good job they'd got something to clean your seats with," Beau says, joining me where I'm standing by a fence overlooking the motorway.

He can fuck off, too. "Imagine how much easier it would've been if Hector had pissed on your leather seats. It'd just wipe right off."

"Oh, come on, not you as well." Beau rolls his eyes.

"I'm just saying. You made your sister feel like a burden all because of your bloody car and now I've got a piss-stained seat and Sheridan has been awol for half an hour and is probably devastated. Hope that's worth it to keep your car clean."

Beau's gaze narrows, eyes dragging over me suspiciously. I've never felt more *seen*. Nash and Beau are both incredibly protective over their sisters, and I know I've just opened myself up to one of his lectures. How many times have I heard him reem out one of his teammates over an inappropriate comment towards one of the girls? Countless. If I remember rightly, Brinsley has a boyfriend—and I find it odd that he's not here to celebrate with her this week—so I doubt she'll apply to his incoming spiel, but I'm not bitching about his attitude toward the strait-laced sister. I'm talking about the one they all seem to coddle.

"Listen up Wilson, 'cause I'm only gonna say this once." Beau angles his body to face me fully, somehow managing to expand his shoulder breadth like I'm some sort of threat. "Stay away from Sheridan. She's too awkward and shy for someone like you, and she's got far too much going on in her own head to worry about your baggage as well."

"And what the hell is that supposed to mean?" I demand, folding my arms. I know what he's insinuating, but I want to hear him say it.

"You know exactly what I mean, Myles. Sheridan ain't the girl for you, no matter how cute you think she is." *Damn fucking cute.* "Leave her alone."

Beau and I have been friends for some time now, but for the first time ever, he's used my upbringing—or lack thereof—against me. Yes, I grew up in care. No, I don't have a family of my own to rely on. In fact, I'd go as far as saying that Beau and his brother *are* my family. I understand his need to protect his sister, but I suddenly feel incredibly alone.

"Nice to know how you really feel about me, man." I smack the top of his arm and turn away.

"Don't be like that." He catches my arm, but I swat his hand away.

"You know, in all the time I've known you, you've never once used my childhood against me. Until now."

He's following me as I stomp my way back to the car. "I'm not using it against you."

"That's *exactly* what you're doing, Beau. I'm too *broken* to even be considered for someone you care about. Right? Never mind the fact that I've known your sister all of *two hours*. Get your head out your arse."

"You're not broken, Jesus Christ!"

Something churns inside me—something I haven't felt for some time—that I locked away behind lead-lined walls with a combination code, safe, chain and padlock. I haven't felt it stir for a while, since before I met the Bennett brothers easily, but right now I can feel it scratching against steel and lead, taunting release.

It's easy to ignore it and use my words instead.

"Aren't I? So, you're telling me that my *baggage*—you know, not having my own family and growing up in the shitty system—isn't the exact reason you don't want me anywhere near your sister? Because I'm damaged?"

"You're not damaged, Myles."

"Then use your words better next time. And fuck you for letting me think I'm not good enough."

When we reach the car, JP is sitting in the back seat with his legs out the side and eating a sandwich. Stavros has disappeared somewhere with Nash, and the girls are all still inside the services waiting for Sheridan. I've had all the doors open in the hopes of airing out the smell of dog farts and urine and after dousing the front passenger seat with fabric cleaner and air freshener.

"Still no sign of the girls?" I ask in a tone more clipped than intended.

JP glances between Beau and I while mid-chew. He swallows and shakes his head. "Nope."

I give him a curt nod. "I'm going to get something to eat."

Before I have the chance to escape inside, I spot them—all five girls emerging from the front doors of this random Roadchef services like the freaking *Reservoir Dogs*, with Brinsley at the hilt. But obviously my gaze drifts to Sheridan, who's changed out of her shorts and vest and into a shapeless white and black pinstripe T-shirt dress with her white high-top Converse. She's pulled her hair up into a wild mess of pink and blonde on top of her head, and Hector is tucked under her arm.

God help me, I've got to spend a week with this girl and pretend I don't fancy the shit out of her just to appease her anal brother.

"Those Bennett genes are summat else," JP mutters and earns a swift punch from Beau. He's leaning over the car now with his arms resting on the roof and his chin on top. His reputation is almost as bad as Beau's is, except he's younger and more reckless. Hence the driving ban.

"Paws off, John," Beau practically hisses.

"Wouldn't dream of it. Plus, Brin's boyfriend scares me."

Beau snorts. "He's a teddy bear."

"So are you." JP winks at him.

Nash and Stavros appear behind the girls, each carrying a McDonalds takeaway bag. I sigh at the thought of my car stinking like grease for the next three days. My poor interior can't catch a break.

"Here," Nash says when they're all within reach of us, and tosses me a wrapped burger, "eat up."

I'm surprised either of them thought of me when they were buying food, but I'll take it. I'm hungry enough to eat anything at this point. "Cheers."

"Are we ready to get back on the road?" Beau rubs his hands together.

I quickly scarf down the double cheeseburger and toss the wrapper before sliding into the driver's seat. Everyone else piles in after me, including Sheridan and Hector.

"You alright, Shez?" Nash asks from the middle seat, leaning forward.

She clears her throat, giving a nervous wriggle in her seat. "Yeah, fine. I've given Hector tablets; he should doze off in a minute."

"Why didn't you give them to him before we left Cov?" Stavros scoffs. "Could've avoided this whole thing."

"They make him drowsy."

I turn a glance over my shoulder. "Maybe we should've given them to you instead, Steven."

Stavros glares at me, but I give him a noncommittal shrug and turn back to face the front. Sheridan seems to be fighting a smile when I glance her way.

We rejoin the motorway, following behind Beau and the girls in the Range Rover. The rest of the journey is silent, leaving me to overthink my conversation with Beau.

I'm mostly frustrated because I don't think he really means what he said about me—he's just very overprotective when it comes to Sheridan. We've never fought before about anything—not girls, not money, not his dumb car—and I'm irritated that he'd jump on me over one comment about his behaviour towards his twin. There was a time, when I was still in university, that we were so drunk so often that we'd share girls. Nash never joined in—he's got his own preferences when it comes to sexual partners, and I'm not nosey enough to ask.

Also, so what if I fancy his sister a little bit? She's pretty—anyone with working vision would be able to see that. JP is no doubt drooling over her in the backseat in broody silence, and Stavros is thinking inappropriate things about her—he's just better at behaving like a tit to cover it up than I am.

I glance over at Sheridan without making it obvious. Hector is curled up on her lap and snoring away, and her hand strokes over his head and neck in a soothing motion. With the dress she's wearing, most of her legs are on show and the hemline is dangerously close to being considered inappropriate. Not that I'm complaining. She's staring out the window, just watching the world go by.

I'm not like I was those first few years of studying—I don't go after women I don't know the instant that I meet them. I'd rather get to know them first, but if getting to know Sheridan is going to cause issues with Beau, then maybe I'll keep my distance.

I realise too late that Beau has sped off miles down the road, and I'm reminded of how much I hate driving. Beau drives like a lunatic and I'm the complete opposite, for no other reason than that I've never felt overly confident behind the wheel of a car. Growing up in London, I never had one, but I wanted to make sure I could drive in case the need arose. Moving to a different city where public transport is limited to buses and taxis, I'm glad I had the foresight because now I drive everywhere.

I let out a sigh and switch lanes, hoping to catch up with him a few miles down the road.

Chapter Six

ESCAPISM

SHERIDAN

"Looks like this is us…" Myles mumbles as we pull into a gravel driveway.

Tall trees line the road and open up to a small private car park. Atop the crest of a low hill sits a wide single-level structure, clad in silver wood and grey slate. Something about it reminds me of a 70s bungalow, even though it's much more modern and probably very minimal inside.

Myles pulls in beside Beau's car—he and the girls are already trailing up the long pathway to the front door.

Hector is like dead weight in my arms so there's little chance of him being able to walk by himself. I undo my seat belt and clutch him to my chest as I open the door and step out. I grab his dog bed out of the footwell and start making my way towards the cabin. I can hear the excitable sounds of my siblings and our friends around us now that we've arrived after a brief—yet rather tragic and unplanned—stop, but I can't find it in me to get animated about it yet.

Quite frankly, I'm regretting coming on this stupid trip and it's only been a couple of hours. I don't know if my tether is long enough to withstand a week of Stavros's idiocy, along with trying to keep my dog as calm as possible while in an unfamiliar environment. He's not used to going away overnight unless it's to Mum and Dad's. After the situation in the car, I'd be a liar if I said I wasn't worried about Hector.

I also can't quite bring myself to look Myles in the eye after my dog urinated all over his car seat—and my lap. It's not the first time he's lost his nerve, but it is the first time it's happened with someone who is essentially a stranger to us. I was upset when we got to the services and ran off. The bathrooms are always massive, so I found the cubicle furthest away from the door and hid in it while I got over a panic attack. It was embarrassment more than anything else—of course I would be the one to land myself in a sticky mess, literally, in a stranger's car because of a dog with a nervous disposition. Bloody typical.

The girls found me eventually after hearing what had happened and helped me shower and find me a change of clothes. I always wondered why there were showers in service stations and now I know.

"Okay," Beau says once the door is open to the huge cabin, "there's six rooms. Two are king beds and the rest are twins."

"Me and Sheridan can take a double," Brin says, saving me from having to wait to find out where I'm going to hide.

I dart off to locate one of the double rooms. It's a bit of a maze inside—the ceilings are low, and the hallways are narrow, kind of like a static caravan—and the bedrooms aren't all in one place, which is confusing. Once I find what I'm looking for, I drop the dog bed into a cosy spot by the radiator and tuck the dozing Hector into it.

I watch my pup for a moment and feel a stab of guilt. I wish I'd stayed home with him, birthday or not. He's not cut out for this kind of stress—the travelling, the people, the excitement. Much like me, he doesn't cope well with overwhelm. I can't believe I ended up getting a dog who's got worse anxiety than me. Who gets a dog to aid their mental health and ends up with a creature *more* nervous? Absolutely typical. He's only eighteen months old. I could never get rid of him now—he's comfortable with me.

I hate giving him medication because it takes him hours to come back around.

Brinsley finds me watching Hector and dumps her bags on the bed we'll be sharing. "Aw," she coos, standing beside me, "is he okay?"

"He's knocked out. He won't come around for a bit yet."

My sister strokes a hand down my back. "Don't worry too much about what happened. I think Beau feels appropriately guilty."

As he should, I think. I make a non-committal sound.

"So, according to the activity schedule Beau and I made," she continues, turning away to sit on the bed, and rummages through her stuff, "we're going bowling first before the parents get here, and that's at three o'clock. So, we've got time to settle in."

"Cool," my voice is still quiet, but I nod my head, "I'm gonna go get my stuff."

I turn to leave, but Brin stops me. "Shez. Are you alright?"

Without looking at her, I admit, "No, not really. I'm overwhelmed. But I'll get over it."

"Did Myles say anything to you in the car?"

"No. It was all quiet after we got back on the road."

Brin hums, contemplative. "I don't think he's mad. Not at you, anyway."

"He should be mad at me. If someone's dog pissed in my car, I'd be livid."

She scoffs. "You drive a vintage Mini, not a 2011 model VW Polo. Very different circumstances. Plus, none of what happened is your fault."

"I should've stayed at home."

"Nope. You are right where you need to be."

"I think some people disagree."

"If you're talking about Stavros, I will smack your face."

I bite back a smile. My demure twin has a vicious streak that only a select number of people know about, and I love seeing it rear its pretty head.

"I need to draw." Is all I say.

"Good idea. I'm gonna call Andy."

A scowl fights for control on my face, but I keep it away. As I make my way through the maze of halls in this ridiculous cabin, I try to ignore the excitable giggles and guffaws from my brothers and our friends as they explore our temporary home. I just want my sketchbook or my iPad—anything to quiet the noise in my head.

Drawing has always been my means of escape. When everything gets too loud, or I need mental preparation for literally anything, I will find a quiet corner, or bright open space, and just draw. I didn't have time this morning, even though my hands were itching to replicate the blur of the trees and mass of green fields while we were in the car, and it's scratching at my brain.

I manage to escape outside without being stopped. I suppose I'm lucky in that my brothers and the girls know to generally leave me be until I come to them. And I will go to them eventually. Right now, though, I need art.

I haul my two bags back inside and set them in the corner of the room out of the way. I'll unpack properly later. Brin is wandering around the cabin on a video call with Andy, so I have the room to myself again. I know she won't come back for a while.

I dig through my luggage for my iPad. The lighting in this room isn't spectacular for drawing on paper, so the digital landscape is where I'm going. I also scrounge for my headphones and put on some quiet music. I have a very specific playlist for drawing that my brothers and Dad call 'witch music'. Eh. Whatever. It works for me. Settling on the bed with my music playing—Willow by Taylor Swift my starting track—I disappear into a land of colour.

I start with my current surroundings. A primarily dark scene—greys and browns in vignette, drawing attention to a bright spot in the lower right-hand side. Hector. My blood sings as I bring him to life on the screen—red dog bed, light yellows and pinks streaming in from the window on the right, casting him in white and pale greys. I make him look like an angel.

It's only a rough sketch so once I'm done, I save it in my files and send a copy over to our family group chat. I do it every time I draw something on my iPad because I know my mother in particular likes to see them, even if she thinks my drawing is just a hobby. I'm pretty sure she's keeping them in a sort of portfolio, but she's never admitted it, and I'll never ask.

I start another one, completely oblivious to the time. I'm rarely a passenger in a car these days and getting to watch the scenery fly by while we were on the motorway really gave me some inspiration.

I don't know how long I'm sitting there, but I'm only vaguely aware when Brinsley returns to unpack, and she doesn't talk to me. She leaves again, and I'm not aware of anything else but my landscape until Beau flops down heavily on the bed.

"What are we doing now?" He asks casually, tucking his hands behind his head.

I finish the section I'm working on and then turn it to face him, taking my earphones out.

"Very green."

I stick my tongue out at him. "It's not finished yet."

"What's it gonna be?"

"Just a landscape—some fields, a little farm in the distance there." I indicate it on the screen.

"Cute. I think our Shirley will like this one."

"She always likes them. I just know that she doesn't believe being an artist is a sustainable career. Awards or no awards."

"Maybe if you told her about your awards she might come around to the idea."

I know he's only trying to help, but Beau doesn't get it. He was lucky. Scouts were looking at him to play professionally at seventeen and made his debut at nineteen. His career has been certain ever since he decided he wanted to play football for a living with a Premier League club. It's not that simple for me.

"I don't get paid for my web show, Beau. I post that shit because I enjoy it, no other reason."

"You could get paid, though. You've got fresh ideas; you're talented; you're different. I bet if you made a pilot and sent it to a bunch of platforms, one of them would offer you a deal."

"I highly doubt that." I scoff, continuing my drawing. The truth is, I'm actually too scared to even try.

"Shez, the longer you continue to doubt your talent, the harder you're going to make life for yourself. Because we all know—including Mum and Dad and Nash—that interior design is not for you. No matter how good you are at it."

I've paused in my drawing to turn over his words. I didn't know Beau could be so insightful, and the part I hate the most is that he's completely right. But I'm a chicken and it will take a miracle to change that.

I choose not to answer him and continue with my greenscape. Beau watches in fascinated silence for a moment, but it doesn't last long.

"I'm sorry about this morning, Sheridan. I should've put you in my car with Hector. I was a prick."

This is the thing about Beau. Sometimes I think he likes playing the villain just so he can apologise. The man is a golden retriever in human form. Whoever decides to marry him—although that seems like a pipe dream at this point—will be the luckiest girl in the world. I just hope she's spunky. I think he forgets to leave the persona the media have created for him on the pitch. He's not a bad person, he just doesn't think before he speaks and sometimes, he comes off looking like a dickhead.

"It's fine. But you owe me."

"Anything you want, baby sis. Tell me and it's yours."

"Anything?"

"Yep. New tablet? It's yours. Groomer for Hector? New tattoo? You name it, I'll get it for you."

"A new tablet seems excessive."

"I mean it, Shez. Tell me what you want,"

I purse my lips in thought. "Let me think about it. You know I don't cope well under pressure."

Beau snorts. "Fine. Anyway, put your talent away. It's time to go bowling."

I can't help but grimace as I tuck my iPad back into its case. "I suck balls at bowling."

"I mean, I'm no bowling expert, but I'm pretty sure there's no need to be sucking the balls."

I groan and shove at his shoulder. "Sod off."

* * *

I feel like I'm back in PE in high school all over again, and it's miserable. Inexplicably, everyone thought it would be a good idea to split our teams in two, but rather than doing boys vs girls, or Bennetts vs everyone else, someone thought it would be a genius idea to let the two oldest siblings pick the two teams. That's Beau and Brinsley, and if I don't get picked last, I'll eat my fucking hat.

Or JP's, since I'm not wearing one.

Nash, given his defensive posture and deep-set scowl, is equally livid with this decision, but he does somehow find a way to complain about everything. Youngest child and all that. Stavros, the massive dickhead, is only egging him on.

As always, I keep my mouth shut.

The bowling alley is glow-in-the-dark, which means really odd things are glowing when they normally wouldn't, like the stripes on Emma's trainers, or Stavros's veneers. But the thing that draws my attention the most is the word written across the chest of Myles's T-shirt. It's nothing obscene—unless you count a man's pectorals as such—but the white 'NO' against black fabric in big block capitals is very distracting.

Myles's T-shirt and Stavros's teeth aside, the other thing that is glaringly obvious is the amount of people gawking in our direction. No doubt because two Premier League footballers are gracing their presence, and one in particular is plastered all over newspapers at least once a month for some reason or other.

"Alright, I want JP," Beau declares once we've been set up at our parallel lanes.

Brin narrows her eyes at our eldest twin. "I want Nash."

"Myles," he says with a scratch of his jaw.

Nash whispers something in Brinsley's ear, and she nods in agreement. "Emma."

I stifle a sigh because I saw that one coming. Nash and Emma have always been unusually close for cousins, but it's never been cause for concern, so who cares, I guess.

"Bailey," Beau smirks, and Bailey pumps her fist in excitement.

"Gemma." Brin throws him the finger.

This leaves me and Stavros for the choosing, and at least my one relief is that I don't have to share a lane with that stupid prick.

Beau looks guilty when he meets my gaze. "Sorry, Shez. But I want to win."

I notice Myles's head snap in my brother's direction, but I'm not surprised in the slightest. Does it hurt to be boycotted by my own sibling? A bit, but I also don't really care about bowling.

I force a nonchalant shrug. "It's fine."

"Come on, Steven." Beau nods the idiot with false teeth over to his lane.

"Wait," Bailey scowls, "am I on an all-boys team?"

"No, mate," Beau throws an arm around her shoulder, "you're on the winning team."

I've never known bowling to be a team sport, but what the fuck do I know? Besides, he's probably not wrong. My hand-eye coordination is absolute trash, and I definitely won't be able to lob a ten-pound ball in a straight line without landing in the gutter every time. This is honestly a living nightmare.

We set up our names in the order we want to play. I am last, obviously, because I'm past the point of caring. Last to be picked, last to throw, and likely last on the scoreboard, too.

Whatever.

Chapter Seven
NUMBER ONE CHEERLEADER

MYLES

Sheridan is *terrible* at bowling.

We're not even on the same lane so I shouldn't be watching, but I can't help it. Every time she appears from the benches, straightens her T-shirt dress, and wanders over to the ball shelf, my gaze drifts to watch her. She's wildly clumsy and never bothers looking at how many pins she knocks over, apparently fully resigned to any effort. By her seventh throw, she has scored a grand total of twenty-eight points. That's not even half.

All I want to do is march over there and walk her through a good swing, but I'll probably be castrated by her brother, so I keep my thoughts and my hands to myself.

On the other hand, I'm somewhat smug to say that I'm leading overall on points, out of both teams. This has wound Beau up to no end, but I'm trying to remain as blasé as possible about it, because I know that'll rile him up more than boasting would.

By my ninth throw, I somehow end up strolling to collect a ball at the same time as Sheridan. I'm not sure if she's avoiding looking at me on purpose—I didn't see her for hours after we unloaded the car at the cabin—or if she's just that thoroughly checked out and she hasn't noticed a thing.

Sheridan picks up the same ball she has for every round—a light, green eight-pound ball—and routinely makes her way to the end of the lane. I get a waft of that same apple-y scent I had in the car and mirror her movements. We throw our balls at the same time, but while I watch mine roll to the end and knock every single skittle down with that satisfying clunking sound, Sheridan just ambles off once the ball hits the wood. She somehow bowls over a surprising seven pins, and her mask of indifference slips a little when she realises that she only has to knock down three more to get a spare.

"Go on, Shez," I say without thinking.

Her head whips my way, big blue eyes wide as if she wasn't expecting me to talk.

"Get the spare." I nod towards the end of the lane. The remaining skittles are in a clump together on the right-hand side of the alley, so she could easily do it if she concentrated hard enough. I'm not entirely sure why I'm so invested in her result. Maybe I want her to prove Beau wrong, even though it's a bit late for that.

Wordlessly, Sheridan turns back to the alley to size up the throw. Brinsley and the others on her team are shouting words of encouragement at her, which is more than they've done for any other throw. She takes a breath and swings her arm back, then forward, and for once she leans into the throw. This time she stays when the ball rolls down the lane, and watches it plough through all three pins.

A small, disbelieving laugh slips out of her. "Huh."

I give her a grin. "Nice."

The girls and Nash are clapping and hooting, and she walks back to the bench with pink cheeks.

Fortunately, Beau and JP had been too busy talking football strategy to notice my cheerleading efforts.

We finish up bowling with our team (if that's what we're really calling it) winning, and I have the most points overall. My prize, from a begrudging Beau, is as many sweets as I like from the pick 'n' mix in the sweet shop. It seems a little ridiculous, but I'm not one to turn down confectionery when it's free.

We struggle our way back to the cabin, a little livelier than we had been before. When we get there, Brian and Shirley have already arrived and settled in. Shirley is in the kitchen starting on our dinner, which I know from experience is going to be an absolute feast, and Brian is on the sofa in front of the giant TV watching the news. Hector has been relieved of slumber and is curled up at Brian's feet, watching the arrival scene unfold. Apparently, he's still a little drowsy.

"Mummy!" Beau shouts like a complete twat when he strolls into the cabin and spots his mother. He towers over her, as do most of us men. The Bennett women are notoriously tiny, and the men are not quite the opposite, but still on the taller side.

"Hello, my darling boy." Shirley welcomes her son in a hug that I've seen too many times. While the Bennett siblings reunite with their mother, I make my way over to Brian, who has since stood to take part in the welcome party.

He gives me a firm handshake by way of greeting. "Myles."

"Hey, Bri."

"Given any more thought to that Beach Boys tribute idea I proposed?"

I snort, failing at not laughing. Every time I see Mr. Bennett, he asks me if I want to start up a Beach Boys tribute act, because with his first name and my surname combined, we'd make Brian Wilson—aka the best songwriter ever born.

"God, you know, I haven't really had time."

The older man chortles and pats my shoulder. "If we can get the rest of the boys on board, I reckon Beau would make a really good Dennis Wilson."

"Beau would probably be quite good at the drums. Just don't tell him Dennis was the most popular with the ladies because it'll go straight to his head."

"Or that he was really good friends with Charles Manson," he deadpans.

I splutter out a laugh. "Jesus, Brian."

The Bennett patron cracks up and wanders off further into the throng of guests.

I greet Shirley when she's finally free with a peck on the cheek and an offer to help with dinner. I always offer to help, because it's the least I can do given the number of times she's fed my homeless ass.

I'm halfway through cooking off chicken breasts in a large skillet with lemon wedges and a white wine reduction when Sheridan appears.

"Can I do something?" She offers, again refusing to look my way.

"Sure, baby girl." Shirley gives her 'youngest' daughter a bright smile. "Potatoes need peeling and chopping. Into little cubes."

Sheridan nods silently and gets to work peeling potatoes. The telltale sign of metal against potato skin in a swift and regular motion tells me that if peeling potatoes isn't Sheridan's usual job when she's home with her family, she's still done it enough times to be confident at it. And *why* am I mentally congratulating her on *being good at peeling potatoes?*

Music is playing from a phone somewhere, a tinny quality to it, but I like having the background noise. Every so often I notice Sheridan and Shirley bobbing their heads along with it, from Harry Styles's Daydreaming to Jungle's Good Times to Fleetwood Mac's Everywhere. I'm sure, if I listen close enough, I can hear one of them singing. And I don't think it's Shirley.

I start pouring cream into the wine reduction just as Sheridan seasons the potatoes with salt, pepper, and dried thyme, and then shoves them in the oven in a baking dish. I can only assume Brian and Shirley brought all this food with them, because I know for a fact that Beau didn't.

Ten minutes before everything needs to be served, I boil off some tender stem broccoli and then toss it in with Sheridan's potatoes to crisp it up.

"Do you cook a lot, Myles?" Sheridan asks when I close the oven door.

We haven't said a word to each other the whole time she's been in the kitchen. I notice that Shirley has disappeared, and everyone else is spread out across the lounge watching old episodes of *Gavin & Stacey*. Sheridan leans against the sink where she's just finished washing the mess we created, a glass of the wine I used in hand. I don't know why, but my gaze drops to her feet, where she's now sporting a pair of black fluffy slipper booties in favour of her Converse. They look far too warm to be comfortable for the summer weather, and yet I find my lips upturning.

"Every day."

Growing up decent hot meals were few and far between. I lived off frozen dinners, ready meals, and tinned soup until I was about fourteen years old, so the second I could get in the kitchen and start cooking proper food, I didn't hesitate.

Sheridan smiles at me, and damn if it doesn't make me feel warm inside.

"Do you?" I ask, hoping to keep up a conversation with her.

"I always try to. I like being in the kitchen. It kind of feels like the *real* heart of the house. Know what I mean?"

"I know exactly what you mean. It's the room where the most activity happens."

"Precisely."

"Do you always help your mum in the kitchen when you're home?"

"Most times, yeah. It's not really even for the cooking. I just like being with my mum. The rest of 'em avoid the kitchen at all costs, so it was kind of the only time I ever got Mum to myself."

I couldn't exactly relate to her, but I understood the feeling. The *desire*. I don't even know who my mother is, and I've reached an age in my life where I don't particularly want to, either.

"I bet the boys hogged her."

"Oh, completely." Sheridan is grinning now, and it's utterly breathtaking. Christ, I don't think I've ever been this instantly attracted to a girl before. I feel a bit insane. "And even though Brin is a proper daddy's girl, she was never afraid to ask for attention the way I was."

I can only imagine it all too well. Three loud, demanding children, and then one who was just afraid to be vocal about anything. I understood the desire to keep quiet. In care, being quiet meant a quiet life. No one was looking at you if you weren't talking. Sometimes they'd forget you were even there.

"Are you not a daddy's girl?" I tease.

Sheridan looks over her shoulder to the open plan lounge. Sure enough, Brinsley is perched on the arm of the armchair Brian is sitting in, her head resting on his shoulder. When Shez looks back at me, the smile tells me all I need to know. "I love my dad, and I know he loves me. But I don't have that kind of relationship with him. I think we understand each other and that's enough."

I twist my body slightly to snatch the bottle of wine off the counter, fill up a glass of my own, and then top off Sheridan. "As long as that's enough, Shez."

We clink our glasses together, which for some reason makes her laugh. And then I'm laughing with her.

"Mr. Wilson!" Beau whines from his place on the corner sofa.

I take a deep breath, and Sheridan visibly smothers a snort. "What, Beau?"

"I need more beer!"

"Beau Bennett, you lazy bastard!" Shirley suddenly appears from one of the hallways. "Get your own sodding beer—you've got two working legs, ain't ya?!"

"But I'm comfortable." He pouts.

"Don't care. You want a beer; you get it your damn self. Myles has already made your dinner."

"I see no evidence of this dinner," he retorts.

Someone, I don't see who, throws a cushion at him.

* * *

"Can the four of you sit together on one side, please?" Shirley asks, rising from her seat and gesturing with her finger towards the end of the table.

Knowing better than to complain, the four siblings rise from their seats and congregate at the end of the dining table where Brian has just vacated.

Dinner went as smoothly as it could. Brian provided inappropriate jokes at the worst times imaginable, all the boys groaned good-naturedly; all the girls tried to stifle their tittering laughter; Shirley gave her husband a suitable shunning. No one fought, which was a freaking miracle, and I'm almost certain it's because Stavros is too chicken shit to say anything untoward around authority figures. Meaning he's barely opened his mouth all night.

Shirley busts out a giant birthday cake for the quadruplets, and when Brian starts singing, the rest of us join in. Trying to fit

'Beau, Brin, Shez and Nash' all together into the song ends up sounding utterly ridiculous but is a cause for a good laugh. In addition to this, Sheridan spends the entire song blushing like someone had been looking up her skirt.

"What the fuck is that?" Nash asks with a cringe as the siblings take a better look at their cake.

"*That*," Shirley grins, "is your worst photos, as voted by your friends here."

Ah.

I wondered why she'd asked me to send the least flattering picture of Beau that I could find.

"Mum, that's so mean," Brinsley whines, visibly disgusted by whichever one had been selected for her.

"It was your father's idea." She shrugs. "And, according to Bailey, you didn't have a bad photo."

"I mean, this one ain't great." She points at the cake with a frown.

"Anyway, blow your candles out before they melt all over it. And make good wishes."

The Bennett siblings take a deep breath in unison and blow out their candles in one go. Shirley then takes the cake back and starts dividing it between everyone. When I get handed a slice, I catch a glimpse of blonde curls dipped in pink.

Chapter Eight

CLITERATURE

SHERIDAN

"So…" Bailey flops down onto the bed Brin and I are sharing later that night. After polishing off our cake and opening a bottle of fizz—or five—and opening presents—I don't want to talk about it—we settled in the lounge and watched *Step Brothers*. I can't remember who chose it, but I wasn't surprised to learn that Stavros knew all the words and the idiot douchebag brother played by Adam Scott was his favourite character. "Can we talk about Myles?"

"What about him?" Gemma asks as she perches at the foot of the bed, legs crossed.

"Well, he's delicious," Bailey says simply.

The boys are all still in the living room and our parents have gone to bed. The girls weren't tired enough to go to sleep yet but also wanted to gossip a little, so we've locked ourselves away in our bedroom with another two bottles of white wine and a selection of snacks.

"He's not a piece of meat, Bailey." Gemma frowns.

"I don't know," Brin snuggles up next to me and rests her head on my shoulder, "his pecs say otherwise."

"Exactly!" Bailey exclaims with a click of her fingers. "And he can *cook*? Oof. I think I'm in love."

"Hey, I helped with dinner too," I retort with a scowl.

"No offence, Shez, but peeling some potatoes isn't that significant a contribution," Gemma tells me.

I give her my middle finger. Contrarian bitch. I struggle with Gemma the most out of our little group, and it's not because she's notoriously contradictory to everyone's statements. It's because she's fucking boring, and that's saying something considering I struggle to leave the house on a regular basis.

"I thought your potatoes were delicious," Emma finally speaks, quiet as a mouse, and I know she purposefully used the same word that Bailey did. If there's anything I've learned about our cousin Emma, it's that while she doesn't say much, when she does choose to speak it's usually with a reason.

"*Thank you*, Emma." I grin smugly.

"I agree with Em. Sheridan's potatoes were the best part of dinner," Brinsley says, always defensive of me.

"We're getting off track, here," Bailey complains. "I would like to call dibs on the twins' sexy friend."

"B, this isn't Year 9 and Myles isn't the shiny new kid. You can just call dibs on people." Brin frowns.

"But he's so pretty," she pouts. "And he gives off proper nerdy vibes and you know I love me a hot nerd."

I can't hold back my snort because she's right. He does seem kind of nerdy.

"He's going to be an art teacher, right?" Gemma seems sceptical. "If anything, he's trying too hard to be cool."

The urge to sigh is overwhelming, but I don't. I'm not a combative person and I'm not about to start being that way with one of my oldest friends just because she's being more difficult than usual. It must be the wine.

"Who cares?" Brinsley brushes her off. "Besides, let's not discount the fact that Myles is Sheridan's type to a T."

I take a big gulp of my wine so that I don't have to respond.

"Oh fuck, you're so right." Bailey sighs. "And she's got baby Hector." We all look at the pup curled up on his bed. His head is down but his brown eyes are watching us. "Major dick magnet."

Emma does something completely out of character and giggles. Gemma, the prude, just grimaces.

"Would you go there, Shez?" Emma nudges my foot with the tip of her index finger.

I decide to play dumb, "Go where?"

The four of them groan at me. "With Myles!" Bailey shouts, and Gemma slaps a hand to her mouth to shut her up.

"Oh, no, I don't think so." I can't believe how calm I sound.

Never mind the fact that I got to spend an hour in the kitchen with him earlier because I couldn't help myself. I *wanted* to be in his orbit somehow, even if we were practically silent and I still struggled to look at him after Pissgate. But watching him bowl from afar in the dark had fucked with my head—the way his forearms rippled when he swung; the way his neck muscles tensed when he cheered yet *another* strike; the way he showed support for me, who wasn't even on his team and had been fully resigned from the game from the very first swing. Yeah, I'd placed last just like I thought, but it didn't feel quite so significant a loss knowing that I'd had his support.

So yes, I'd looked for an excuse to be in the kitchen with him before eating, because he seemed just as comfortable at the oven as I would've been had I been the one cooking, and I find a man that knows his way around the kitchen to be a major turn on. It hasn't even been a full day yet, but I haven't found a single thing I don't like about Myles Wilson.

"Why not?"

I blink at Bailey's question, because I can't remember what I'd said. "Er,"

Brin chuckles, squeezing me in a hug. "I know why. It's because no girl wants to be a cliche that falls in love with her brother's best friend."

"Who said anything about falling in love? You could just bang him. I bet he's great in bed." Bailey lifts her eyebrows suggestively.

"How can you tell just by looking at him that he's good in bed?" Gemma scoffs.

"Do I *look* like someone who could ever manage casual sex?" I demand. It takes me a week to recover after going to a bloody pub. Casual sex would likely put me in the grave.

"This is why I called dibs." Bailey punctuates each word with a thump on the mattress with her fist. "Myles, the sexy soon-to-be art teacher, needs to be appreciated as often as possible as soon as possible."

Gemma rolls her eyes. "You are incorrigible."

"I take that as a compliment." Bailey grins. "My sister calls me a slut all the time, so I think incorrigible is much better."

"You are a slut," Brin says with a shrug. "It's just not slander."

"Amen," I agree.

"Myles isn't the only man here, you know," Emma reminds her.

"Yeah, but I don't wanna sleep with either of the Bennett boys 'cause we've known them since they were prepubescent and that's a bit weird. I'd rather fuck a dead horse before I let Stavros touch me—"

"Ew."

"Gross."

"—And JP avoids me like the plague. I think I scare him a bit, to be honest."

"You scare *me*," I tell her, and she beams at me.

"I think sex should be heavily avoided on this holiday," Brin says, ever the diplomat. "We're here to celebrate our birthdays and have fun, not partake in any coital marathons or orgies."

The four of us look at my sister, taken aback by her statement.

"Did you just seriously utter the phrase *partake in coital marathons and orgies*?"

"She is an English Lit teacher now," I say proudly. "Words and classic literature are Brin's specialty."

"Or, as I like to call it," Bailey's smirk is positively mischievous, "cliterature."

Gemma practically chokes on her Pinot Grigio.

* * *

I don't remember whose idea it was to sneak into the kitchen after 1 a.m. while the boys were passed out in the lounge to steal another bottle of wine, but my head is certainly giving me grief about it this morning. I'm also not sure whose genius idea it was to hire pedalos at the ripe hour of 10 a.m. the next morning, but I want to throw up just looking at the way they all rock from side to side where they're lined up on the dockside.

"I feel sick," Bailey groans as we stand shoulder to shoulder, and she looks especially green.

"Maybe you should sit this one out, B," Beau suggests as he gives her a once over.

"I think I might have to. Can someone stay with me?" She gives her best sad pout and throws it in Myles's direction, but he isn't paying attention to her.

He's gazing out over the lake, hands shoved in the pockets of his board shorts, life jacket covering a plain white T-shirt. He's been quiet this morning, ever since he saw me coming out of the bedroom looking like death warmed up to take Hector for his morning walk. He's got a tennis player's frame, and it's doing all sorts to my body temperature, in all areas. He's not hugely muscular like Beau and Nash, but I definitely spotted some definition on his abs. It makes my mouth water, and I don't even like tennis.

"I'll stay with you," Stavros offers, and Bailey looks enraged. But she keeps quiet. Of all the men, Stavros easily had the most to drink. I also get the distinct impression he doesn't want to go in a pedalo because he can't swim, and he's scared of falling in. This is just an assumption, though, and I could be wrong. But I doubt it.

There are smaller families dotted all along the beach waiting to get into their own pedalos. The dads, and some of the sons too, all seem to be taking notice of us—or rather, Beau and JP. The mums are all looking at Myles. I feel a kinship forming.

My mother, like a typical teacher, takes it upon herself to split our group in half now that we don't have two extra people, which is how I end up on a pedalo with Nash, Emma, my mother, and Myles.

"I think the boys should pedal," Shirley says with a wink as we hover around the floating vessel.

Nash sighs, but his subtle smirk says he saw it coming. Myles, who appears to want to do anything to please her, says, "I think I was born to chauffeur you in a pedalo, Shirley."

"Stop flirting, or Brian might get suspicious," she replies with *another* wink.

I throw her a baffled look, while Nash grumbles under his breath. I am aware that Myles has spent a significant amount of time at my parents' house after multiple invites from Beau turned into an expectation of him to just be there any time a gathering took place. How I managed to avoid him for so long—completely unintentionally, I might add—is beyond me.

Once we're all settled in our seats—the boys in the back pedalling and me, Mum, and Emma in the front with me sandwiched in the middle—Nash and Myles start moving us into the lake, following the other group. Of course, Beau seems to have completely misunderstood the point of a pedalo, because he's egging Dad and JP, who are pedalling, to go as fast as possible while he sits in the front seat like some sort of golden retriever dictator. We leave them to it and take it at our own leisure.

"Have you got much work coming up when you get back, baby?" Mum asks, patting my thigh.

"A bit, but nothing I can't handle. It's mostly site visits, and they're mainly in London, so I've booked an Airbnb in Camden for a week." I neglect to mention that I'm not looking forward to a week away from home or spending any time in London when I find it so suffocating.

"Oh, yes. We're having Hector, aren't we?"

I nod.

"What's going on in London?" Emma asks.

"Er," I try to think of the projects in chronological order, "a hotel in Mayfair going through a complete revamp. A restaurant refurb for a celebrity, but I've signed an NDA so I can't say much on that one. And just a few residentials. They're all in north London, and I've managed to get them in over two days, so I'm not traipsing around the city with all my stuff."

"Oh, that's good." Emma nods.

"Will you drive?" Mum says.

"No, not in London." I shake my head vehemently. "Too much hassle, I'll probably get the tube. Or a taxi if it's not convenient. The company will pay for everything anyway."

"Alright for some," Emma says playfully. "I need to get you over to my house—I need some ideas."

People always say this to me. *"Oh, I need some design tips—can you come see my house?"* And I never go because they never follow up.

"Sure. I can come the week after London? Your place isn't massive anyway, it won't take long," I say, just to placate her.

"That'd be cool."

Mum suddenly shifts in her seat to face Myles, who sits directly behind her. "Sheridan is an interior designer and she's *amazing.*"

I clamp my jaw tight. "I'm alright."

"Shut up." She scoffs. "She's won awards, Myles. *Actual*, noteworthy accolades."

"The *company* wins the awards," I correct her.

"Yeah, for the projects *you* work on. Stop downplaying your talent."

I always struggle with this type of praise because it feels conceited. They can congratulate me openly on my awards from work because interior design is a serious, well-paying job that almost everyone has an interest in and an opinion on. But what if I told them about my *other* award nominations? Because I don't think the excitement and the pride my mother shows now would be equal to those about my web show. But whatever. I'll take what I can get.

"Is there anything I'd know if you said you'd done it?" Myles asks, probably to try and derail Shirley's soapbox.

"My flat," Nash offers.

"Yes, your man cave of a flat." Emma scoffs, and I can't help my smirk. "A truly revered location by the interior design gods."

Mum snickers.

"Perhaps, but I *have* been there." Myles chuckles.

"Oh!" Mum gasps. "The player lounge at the Rangers ground."

I roll my eyes. "That hardly counts."

"Why not?"

"Because it's private."

"Oh, that fancy restaurant in town," Emma supplies.

"You mean the *only* fancy restaurant in town?" Nash mutters.

"Yeah. The one by the shopping centre on the corner. All turquoise and grey and gold. Turkish place"

"I think I know…" Myles mumbles. "Did Beau take us there with Steven once?"

"Yes!" Nash claps.

"That place is really jazzy."

"Jazzy," Mum repeats. "You're right, Myles. It is. And my baby girl designed the whole inside."

I stifle a sigh. I just want to go back to bed. Being the centre of attention while hungover is no fun. "Can we talk about something else now? Literally anything but me and interior design?"

There's a vacant pause, and then my mother cracks, "Your father and I want to buy a caravan."

I twist in my seat to look at Nash, who is shaking his head with an unreadable look on his face. I turn back to my mother. "A static caravan?"

"No. One you hook to the back of your car."

I blink at her, dumbfounded. "Why?"

"We thought it'd be fun."

"Please don't," Nash begs. "I don't think I could survive knowing my parents are the type of people to go on caravan holidays."

"And Dad *hates* caravans," I add.

"Well, he loves me more. And I want a caravan."

My parents, ladies and gentlemen. The epitome of true love.

Chapter Nine

LONERISM

MYLES

Shirley and Brian leave us to it after lunch, packing up their car to head back to Coventry. Is it weird to say that I'm somewhat sad to see them go? They're not *my* parents, so maybe that has something to do with why. Especially since Beau seems to think we're going to have *more* fun now they're gone.

Because Beau is on holiday and he has no shame, he takes the hair of the dog route and starts necking bottles of beer the second his parents are gone.

"Who's up for drunk Monopoly?" He grins from his throne—also known as the armchair—positioned perfectly to watch TV.

"Only if I can be the car," Stavros demands. From across the room, Sheridan rolls her eyes as she sits on the sofa in the very corner.

"How do you imagine us doing that when there's only seven pieces?" Emma points out.

Beau just shrugs. "We pair up." Like water off a duck's back. The man has an answer for everything. "I'm bagsying Sheridan, though."

"Of course, you'd pick Sheridan, she always wins Monopoly," Brinsley complains.

"I'm really good at Monopoly, too." Stavros winks at her.

"Er…" She wrinkles her nose right back. "No, thanks. I pick Em."

"Whatever. Nash is smarter than you, anyway." He shrugs.

Brinsley simply gives him her middle finger.

"Guess it's me and you then, Myles." JP nudges me from my left.

"As long as you're alright with losing, because I am utter shit at it."

"Eh," he simply shrugs, "can't be good at everything."

He makes a valid point. I won at bowling yesterday, so my pride is still intact.

"Alright, let's do it." Nash stands and leaves the room in search of the popular game.

* * *

We get absolutely demolished by Sheridan. I can't even include Beau in the narrative, because he has barely contributed all night, just sitting there nursing his next beer while occasionally whispering utter bollocks to his sister about what they should do next. And Sheridan usually ignores him because his ideas are stupid.

JP and I tapped out first because his attention span is abysmal—I honestly don't know how he plays football for ninety minutes professionally every weekend without getting bored—and I have the negotiating skills of the average candidate on *The Apprentice*.

I watch in fascination as Sheridan plays a beautifully tactical game that winds up with her bankrupting the other teams out due to a frankly obscene number of hotels positioned on the board, including on the dark blue properties.

"Well, I guess we know you're not a gold digger," Bailey jokes as she helps tidy away the pieces. "That was kinda beautiful to watch."

"I love watching women bring men to their proverbial financial knees," Brin agrees.

"And you should know how to play better, mate." Beau points a finger at his twin. "You've got a degree in business and hospitality."

"Oh, fuck off," Nash snaps. "You're the most financially responsible footballer known to man and yet you just made us play almost four hours of a stupid board game and forced yourself onto a team with Shez knowing you'd win!"

"And have to do fuck all in the process," I can't help but add, because Beau had fully checked out of the game by our second loop around the board.

"You can shut your face, you were pathetic." Beau scowls.

"I never said I was any good," I retort. "In fact, I told JP that I was crap at it right off the bat."

"A man who doesn't lie..." Bailey says in a tone that's almost contemplative. "I might be in love."

Someone sniggers, but I'm too busy focusing on the fact that Bailey was obviously talking about me—and how much that's weirded me out—to notice who. Don't get me wrong, Bailey is beautiful—naturally tanned skin, dark hair, deep brown eyes. She's sure of herself, too, which is never a negative thing, because she means what she says. But I like my women with a little more... mystery? Christ, what a stupid thing to say. The point is, I don't have a problem with Bailey. She's just not my type.

"And on that note..." Gemma says with wide eyes, and stands from her place, "I'm going to bed."

I check the time and it is getting quite late, but I'm not overly tired.

Now that Brian and Shirley have gone, we've all managed to get our own rooms, sort of. Brin and Sheridan are still going to share the double they were in last night, and Gemma is taking the other by herself. Beau and JP, Nash and Stavros, and Bailey and Emma are sharing the twin rooms, and I'm having the last one to myself. Even though the boys could have slept in their room last night, we all ended up passing out on the sectional after one too many whiskies. Our alarm clock had been Brian's booming laugh.

"I think I'm gonna go, too," Emma says around a yawn.

Sheridan mutters something to Brinsley, who nods, and then she's disappearing down the hall. She reappears less than a minute later with Hector's lead, and at her commanding whistle—which I find strangely, but immensely attractive—the pup leaps out of Nash's lap and runs for the door.

"Alright," Brin asks in what I imagine will be her 'teacher' voice, now standing behind the sofa, "which of you males is volunteering to chaperone Shez on her walk?"

It's on the tip of my tongue to offer myself up, but I know if I do, I'll get another verbal lashing from Beau, and maybe Nash, too.

Nash hauls himself to his feet. "I'll go. I think Beau has had one too many beers. Again."

"Maybe. But I'm still gonna wait up until you're both back."

That's how I end up in the living room with only Beau and Brin because both of them refused to go to bed until their siblings were home safe. I have to admit, I feel a little pang in my chest at the notion, because I've never had anyone look out for me that way. Simply because I *don't* have anyone.

Once again, a painful loneliness creeps in, even though I'm surrounded by people on all sides. I guess the truth is, I want to find my person, because this life of lonesome is becoming, simply put, fucking miserable.

The three of us don't speak while we watch a late-night rerun of *Peep Show* episodes, and I'll admit I find the whole thing unnerving. It brings me the realisation that Beau still hasn't apologised about his comments regarding my 'baggage' a day and a half later. Part of me thinks he never will. That same part of me recognises that he's probably forgotten all about it given the excitement of the past thirty-six hours. I suppose we haven't been alone together since we got here, but that doesn't mean he hasn't had the opportunity to pull me aside for thirty seconds just to say, "I'm sorry".

The reminder of the whole sorry affair has ignited a bad mood in me, and I suddenly don't *want* to be in the same room with him if he's going to be so self-centred. I get it—he's protective of his sisters, especially the one that's socially awkward most of the time—but he really didn't have to insult me in the process.

I don't know why I'm getting so precious about it. I barely know the girl—I just think she's pretty. And kinda cool. No, not just cool—damn awesome. But I *don't know her*. So, I really need to forget about it. But I also want Beau to apologise because apparently, I am also a stubborn prick. Maybe I'll give him the silent treatment until he works it out.

Right. Because that's super mature of me.

Fuck sake. I need to go to bed.

I'm about to excuse myself and do just that when something cracks, then thuds in the cabin somewhere. The noise is matched with a yelp and followed by a loud, "Ow!"

Beau is on high alert. "What was that?" He asks as he storms towards the source of the noise.

Brinsley and I follow him, and as we reach the hallway, the door to the other double room bursts open with a frustrated looking Gemma emerging.

"What happened, Gem?" Brin asks with a concerned frown.

"The bed broke. That's what."

"Aye?" Beau cocks his head.

"The bed broke?" Brin repeats.

"Yeah, it broke."

Beau blinks at her. "How?"

Gemma blows out a breath and points inside. "You wanna go and have a look?"

I really do. I didn't realise how nosey I am until right now, but I guess that's the territory that comes with being raised in a group home. Everyone else's business gets kinda fascinating.

Sure enough, inside the double room, the bed has completely caved in the centre, and one of the legs has snapped.

"What the fuck?" Beau splutters. "What you been doing in here? Some kind of vigorous masturbation?"

I fight the roll of my eyes, but Brinsley does me a solid by whacking him on the arm.

"Need I remind you that it was *your* parents who slept in here last night?" Gemma says pointedly.

Beau recoils then shudders. "An image I didn't need, thank you Gemma."

"Serves yourself right for saying dumb shit."

"You can't sleep in here," I say, before the conversation can get any more idiotic.

"Of course, she can't," Brin agrees.

"I'll call the office." Beau sighs and wanders back into the living room.

"You can sleep in the room I've got," I offer with a polite smile.

"Oh, I don't want to impose…"

"It's fine, I'll sleep on the sofa." I shrug. I've slept in worse places.

Gemma looks like she wants to say something else but chooses better of it. It seems silly discussing it further, so I start moving my stuff out of the room I was going to be in and swap it with Gemma's in the double. I might not be able to sleep in there, but my things can live there.

Nash and Sheridan return with Hector midway through our luggage swap. The dog—with no desire to see the unnecessary chaos through to the end—bolts to the girls' bedroom to hide.

"What's going on?" Nash asks, half-turned towards his room.

"The double bed in the other room has collapsed. Gemma is having the twin room and I'm gonna sleep on the sofa until it's fixed," I explain while hauling the last of my luggage across the hall.

Nash and Sheridan share a look. "Well, you're a better man than I am." I'd like to say I already knew that. He claps me on the shoulder and then disappears into his shared room with Stavros.

When I chance a look at Sheridan, she's already watching me with what I can only describe as a wistful expression. It makes me want to shiver.

Her lips lift in the smallest, gentlest of smiles, before she says ever so softly, "Good night, Myles."

"Night, Shez," I murmur back.

She turns away, and I can't tear my gaze away from her until she's out of sight. I don't know what it is about her that has me so intoxicated, but I do find the view to be ten times better when she's in the room. A crazy thought to have about someone I hardly know.

I dump the rest of my belongings in the now useless bedroom and close the door on it. Beau told us while we were swapping all our things over that someone should be coming to the cabin tomorrow while we're out, so hopefully I'll only be sleeping on the sofa one more night.

With the duvet off the unused twin bed, I settle onto the couch in the front room and stare up at the ceiling, feeling somewhat untethered. I'm not drunk like I was last night, so I don't have the luxury of just passing out. The room is loud in the silence. I can hear crickets outside; the whirring of the air-conditioning; the hum of the fridge behind me. And Beau and JP gossiping in the room close by.

There's something innately lonely about sleeping by yourself in a cabin with nine other people. I don't know how, but something has got to change.

Chapter Ten
MENTAL BLOCKS & DRY SPOTS

SHERIDAN

The next two days are so busy I sleep like the dead each night.

Beau, like some version of a military general, has planned out each day in meticulous detail, and my body can really feel it by the end of day four. Not only do I feel like I walked a million miles—which is ridiculous to some degree since we spent all of our third day either in the fancy pool area or in the spa (well, us girls did. After the fun of the so-called River Rapids wore off, the boys disappeared to do some inflatable football nonsense)—but I also feel like I've been dragged through a hedge backwards and sat every exam known to man- and womankind. I didn't realise my mental stamina was as weak as my physical. That needs fixing. Maybe Brin has got some book recommendations for me.

I had a massage for the first time in my entire life, too. I'd nearly binned off the idea given the fact that my comfort levels around strangers are next to zero. Plus, I wasn't entirely sure how I felt about said practical stranger all but feeling me up for an hour. But Brin reminded me—relentlessly—that therapists are professionals and basically paid *not* to talk. Safe to say, I am now a massage enthusiast. So long as they come from an Irish woman called Saoirse with strong hands and a soft voice.

We beat the boys home and decided to leave them to their own devices. Together the five of us—and Hector—walked down to the lake in the park and had a picnic dinner. I took my sketch pad with me and drew caricatures of everyone, then I tucked myself away and sketched the landscape around us while the sun set behind the trees.

When we finally decided to head back to the cabin, the boys were already drunk and fighting over a game of strip poker. Stavros was practically naked; Myles—the only one who seemed remotely sober—was the only one still *fully* dressed; Nash and JP were without their shirts; Beau was without his trousers. Bailey was delighted by this turn of events and decided to whip out the white wine and the popcorn just to watch them from the opposite end of the dining table. Gemma seemed disgusted and disappeared to her room, while Emma and Brin sat together on the sofa and put on a horror film. I debated joining them, but I wasn't done drawing yet, so I swapped my sketchbook for my iPad and started working on the next episode of *Goth Frogs*.

I was wrapping up the story with my silly little web show and needed to start planning something else if I wanted to keep posting my work online. I had a few ideas; I just didn't know if any of them had any merit or were even worth expanding on. But that was a problem for another day.

The following morning, we went for breakfast at the on-site pancake house, and then walked up to the large welcome building for our escape room booking. Being the most intelligent of the four of us, Nash and Brinsley were elected team captains since we couldn't go in more than groups of six. I ended up on Nash's team with Emma, Stavros, and Myles. Somehow, that was worse than bowling—being stuck in a room with a man I hated and a man I was irrevocably attracted to.

And Myles was a victim to his own case because whenever Steven said something ludicrous, his jaw would strain or his fists would clench, or his forearms would flex. Sometimes, it was all three, all at the same time. But whether it was one action or all three, my traitorous body, without fail, lit up like a struck match on a gas-doused pyre, and that hideous, slick desire shot straight between my legs. More than once, I watched Myles rub a hand over his scruffy jaw in an attempt to mask his irritation, and every time I would wonder what that stubble might feel like rubbing against my thighs.

I felt like a depraved slut.

This wasn't normal. I needed to get over myself, and this growing obsession with my brother's best friend. I was the walking cliche Brin said I wanted to avoid being, and I was really starting to hate myself a little bit because of it.

After the escape room—which our team *smashed through*—we had a quick lunch and then attacked the mini golf. This time we did boys versus girls, which gave me a welcome reprieve from Myles Wilson and his fiendish good looks.

Saved by my lack of aim—something I never thought I'd say.

Bailey was surprisingly good at mini golf and definitely helped us draw somewhat even with the boys most of the way around the course. We still lost, but she and Beau drew equal score-wise, which resulted in an obscene number of golf-related innuendos. I'm horrified to tell you that when we got back to the cabin, Beau and Bailey decided to go on a walk together and were gone for hours.

So much for not touching my brothers' genitalia.

* * *

On day five at Camp Bennett, I wake up when the sun does. Which means it's about half-past five. Curse my stupid body clock.

Brin is still fast asleep, and I know she will be for a while. After Bailey and Beau came back last night and disappeared into one of the twin rooms while sucking face, she produced a hip flask from out of nowhere and tried to force the image away with whisky. She'll be feeling the effects of that today.

Hector is wide awake, staring at me with his pretty doe eyes and expectant face. I roll out of bed and creep towards him, and his tail starts thumping excitedly.

I scratch him behind the ears and whisper, "Ready for a walk, puppy?"

He gives the softest ruff and stretches out of bed.

I quickly dress and clean my teeth, and then as quietly as we can manage, we slip out of the room and into the hallway.

The living room is bright in the early summer morning light. I hope Myles manages some form of lie-in each day, because this would drive me mad, and there's curtains in our room. Even though the front office at the welcome building said they'd send someone to replace the broken bed, no one has come yet. Beau and Brin get more irate about it each passing day. I'm surprised they haven't made a wordy formal complaint yet.

I'm trying to silently pull my trainers on by the back door when I hear Myles stir.

I pause in my movements, hoping that if I keep quiet, he'll go back to sleep.

But he doesn't.

Instead, he sits up and stretches his arms skyward. The duvet he's been using pools into his lap, revealing that glorious torso of his and the tattoos that go with it. Not massively ripped, not skinny, a little weight around the hips that poses no hindrance to the rest of his physique. His tattoos are abstract yet cohesive across his entire chest, from the line of his collarbones to his hips, and including the centrepiece—a large dot work bear on his abdomen.

He's mouthwatering, and I'm gaping at him like a damn fish. I'd seen his marvellous chest the other day when we were in the River Rapids, and it is no less special now than it was then. He's not moving around all the time now, either. It's just out there in the open for me to drool over like some weirdo nutter.

He yawns, drops his arms into his lap, and then looks straight at me. I fumble with my shoelaces while I give him a tight smile.

"Morning," I croak out.

Myles clears his throat and snatches a T-shirt off the ground. *Great, you've made him uncomfortable.* "Morning. What time is it?"

"Early," I manage to say in a normal person's voice. "Just before six."

"Christ," he grumbles and rubs his hands down his face. It musses his light beard up, and I'm thinking about his face between my legs again.

I clench my thighs together and shiver.

"Sheridan?"

"Huh?" I snap out of it and meet his gaze. Crap, he'd asked me a question and I'd completely missed it, too busy thinking about his damn mouth. "What, sorry?"

"How come you're up so early?" He repeats, and I can tell from the twitch of his lips that he's fighting off a smile. I don't know if he realises what I've been thinking about or if he's just entertained by how I can get easily distracted, but I really hope it's the latter.

"Probably the same reason you are." I shrug. "The sun is up."

He chuckles, nodding, but it seems more to himself than at me. "Want some company?" He asks, standing from the sofa. I force myself to look away from his legs. His *bare* legs.

"Where?"

Myles frowns and gestures at the lead in my hand, and a content Hector at my feet. "I assume you're taking him for his morning walk?"

God I am helpless around this man. "Oh. Right. Yes."

His lips twitch again, and I want to kiss them. *Bollocks.* "Yes, you're taking Hector for a walk, or yes, you want some company?"

Do I want Myles's undivided attention for an hour? What a terrifying notion. And yet… "Both?"

He grins in that beautiful way of his, and my heart all but collapses on itself. I am so well and truly fucked. "Give me five minutes and we can go."

Once he's disappeared down the hall with his duvet and pillow, I sink into the closest chair I can find and put my face in my hands.

I am a *mess*.

I don't think I've *ever* felt this way over a man before. Not a real one, anyway. Sometimes Bailey and Brin share books with me that err on the filthy side, and I find myself wondering if men like the ones in smutty romance novels exist, because *whew*, they're too good to be true. But Myles Wilson is very real, very handsome, and has this very incredible ability to make my knickers damp whenever he walks into a room. Not even my ex-boyfriend managed to do that before. I'm not sure if that says more about me than him, but he's in the past and Myles is in the here and now, about to take my dog on a damn walk.

Lord, give me strength to survive.

Myles reappears no more than three minutes later in a clean T-shirt, plain white, and blue jeans. I try to ignore the fact that such a simple outfit can look so good on a man, and hook Hector's lead onto his collar ready to leave.

We've done this walk enough times now that Hector knows we're going through the brush of trees at the back of the cabin to the nearby trail and turning left to take a shortcut to the lake. In the evenings we go out the front and around all the cabins where all the roads are lit.

I let the dog lead for a few minutes and stop when he does to relieve himself. Not the most romantic of things to do with a handsome man in one's company, but beggars can't be choosers, I suppose.

Neither of us have said a word by the time we reach the lake. The sun begins to crest the trees across the water, setting the view aglow in golden light. It's breathtaking, and I take a moment to commit it to memory, because I want to draw this.

After a moment I sneak a glance at Myles, and I have to suck in a breath. His hazel eyes are glowing like freaking Citrine. I think this man might be physical perfection, and that bugs me.

I start walking again thanks to a restless Hector. Myles follows behind me, still silent. I'm starting to wonder why he offered to come.

"Do you draw at all?" I ask, just to break this weird silence.

"Not nearly as much as I should."

I know Myles is going to be an art teacher at the same school Mum teaches at—the same that Brin has also joined the faculty of to be an English teacher. If I remember rightly from what Nash used to tell us, he's got a degree in Art History, which is way more interesting than me and my higher education college level vocation. I didn't go to university—the thought of suffering through another three years in education for a degree I didn't want makes me nauseous.

"But you enjoy it?" I push. I'm desperate for us to have something in common and being a teacher ain't it.

"Mostly. I have enough talent to get me through a degree, but I'm not very original. I never found my own style and, it turns out, I'm not creative enough to find constant inspiration and motivation like you do." He tops off his flattery with a polite smile.

"You give me an awful lot of credit for someone you hardly know," I tell him.

Myles shrugs. "Perhaps. But you've done a lot the past few days, and I have to admit that I'm envious."

"A change of scenery always helps," I admit. "Even though I don't like leaving the house too often."

He chuckles, the sound warming my chest. "You seem to be coping alright this week."

"Well then, you're misunderstanding my motivation. I draw a lot when I'm stressed or overwhelmed."

"As opposed to me who just *never* draws."

I watch him for a second, unable to help myself. If it was acceptable, I'd look at him all day. I know Brin especially would get a kick out of that. "I go through dry spots too, you know. Artist's block. It happens to everyone." I decide not to mention that I've only just come out of my most recent bout, which lasted a solid two months. I'm surprised the watchers of *Goth Frogs* still care about it.

"Yeah?" This seems to surprise him.

"Of course."

"What's your longest dry spot?"

I try to ignore the innuendo behind the question and answer honestly. "Six months."

His expression draws back with shock. "Wow. That's not what I thought you'd say."

"Why, what would your guess have been?"

"A couple of months."

I scoff. "You give me *way* too much credit, Mr. Wilson."

Myles pauses and gives me a funny look, and I regret opening my mouth. Then, thankfully, he laughs. "I don't think I'm ever gonna get used to that."

I know my face is on fire because I can feel it on my cheeks, but I do my best to pretend I didn't just call him by his new title. "Sure, you will. And at least you know you've got Brin going through exactly the same shit at the same time in the same place. She's a great listener."

"She does give off that impression," He agrees, nodding away. "Although she didn't seem delighted about the Bailey and Beau thing last night."

"She'll get over it. I think it was more shock at seeing them that way than anything—Bailey said to us the other night that it'd be weird sleeping with one of the twins, so it was a bit of a one-eighty. One minute they were flirting over golf puns and the next they were sneaking off into the bushes to finish the job. And they've never shown interest in each other before."

"It did happen very fast," he muses. "You don't seem too bothered by the whole thing."

I shrug. "I'm not. Honestly, I'm surprised they didn't fall into bed together years ago—they're both such massive flirts. I'm not particularly worried about it, either. I can guarantee you that the pair of them will behave like nothing happened today. Beau doesn't do serious, and Bailey is the type to keep count of all the men she sleeps with and then rank them from one to five. This will change absolutely nothing."

"Given the noises coming from that room last night, I think your brother might rank quite high. I'd say at least a four."

"I don't want to think about that, Myles."

He snickers, and I lightly shove him away.

It's the first time either of us have initiated contact with the other, and I can't quite believe it was me who started it. Being alone with Myles…it feels good. Normal. Safe. I'm comfortable with him and I like that, because I can't say that about a lot of the new people I meet. I might have to wait another five years before I see him again once the week is up, but something tells me that won't be the case. I have a feeling Myles is going to be around a lot more now.

Chapter Eleven
I'M NOT DRAWING YOU

MYLES

We decide to spend the day by the lake. No competition, no rivalry, no separation—just good old-fashioned sunbathing and open-water swimming.

In principle, it's a brilliant idea. Genius. Bonding without looking for a way to cause a rift. No team captains and picking sides. It's basically a day of napping.

Except it's so hot that the girls are all in bikinis, including Sheridan, and I'm like a man starved. I can see all too much and yet nowhere near enough. That ivy tattoo teases its way around her limbs in a way that has my mouth drooling—like the sole purpose of it is to make men (and women, and every fucker else) gaze at every inch of her spectacular body.

I have to make a conscious effort to look away before Beau can have another go at me for not being good enough for his sister. What-the-fuck-ever. I'm probably not good enough for her, but I'd treat Sheridan like a bloody queen if I was lucky enough for her to let me. I'd be worshipping that damn ivy and all those birds every night for the rest of eternity, and that's only the least she deserves.

Instead, I find myself sitting as far away as possible with my nose pushed up against the inner spine of a book that I'm not making any attempt to actually read.

In other non-Sheridan-related news, Beau, and Bailey—as Shez astutely predicted—are carrying on about their lives as if their evening of debauchery and loud sex never happened. I mean, sure, I've had my fair share of one-night stands, but I'd never been quite so…ambivalent towards them the next day. Kudos to them, I guess.

Sitting out in the open so obviously with Beau and JP has garnered the attention of pretty much anyone who pays attention to football, which seems to be most of the men—and boys—and at least a third of the women. Every now and then someone will notice and whisper to someone else. By the time we've been sitting down for thirty minutes there's a lot of people looking at us.

I'm still reading without taking in a single piece of information when Beau plops himself down beside me. *Oh good,* I think, *he can bring all that attention my way.* Although this next conversation has the potential to be awkward as shit, I'll take it over pretending to read any day. I close the book without keeping my page and set it down.

"What's your book about?" Beau asks.

"No idea," I admit.

He snorts, shaking his head. "Not like you."

I shrug, wondering if I can get away with a lie. "There's too much going on. Too noisy. I've never been able to concentrate when it's loud."

"You're about to become a teacher to a bunch of teenagers…"

"That's different. I won't be trying to read when I'm in a classroom."

"Perhaps," he muses, and then we're quiet again. This is, hands down, the most uncomfortable I've ever been around Beau, and that's a damn shame. "So…are we going to talk about it?"

I don't know why, but I decide to play dumb. "About what?"

"The fact that we haven't had a private bloody conversation since we got here." He scoffs, all tight features and tense shoulders.

"I think you know why that's happened, Beau."

He sighs, brow furrowed deeply. "I didn't mean to offend you, man."

"Well, you failed."

"Come on, don't be like that. If you *really* knew Shez the way I do, you'd know exactly where I was coming from. Not just because she's my sister. I love her to pieces, and I don't want anything to fuck her up. Not more than she already is."

"Wow, flattery is really not your strong suit."

He lets out a frustrated grunt. "You just don't get it, Myles."

"You're right. I don't." I stand up and brush any sand off my backside. "And this is a shitty apology attempt, by the way."

"I didn't come over here to apologise." Beau follows me as I start walking up the beach to the path. "I wanted to clear the air."

"You've failed at that, too. Solid nil-nil on the achievement front this week. Congrats."

"Fuck off." He catches my arm and turns me to face him. "I know you went out for a walk with her this morning."

"So what? You expect me to let her go out alone?"

"You could've asked me."

"And get an eyeful of your dick? No, thank you."

"Nothing you haven't seen before."

I roll my eyes and start walking away again. Dense bastard. "Bailey was there too, you know. It's impolite to walk into a woman's room unannounced. And that woman is your sister's best friend, which actually makes you a complete fucking hypocrite. Brinsley basically drank her weight in Laphroaig after seeing the two of you sucking face. So, I guess that takes the list of people you need to apologise to up to three."

"Who's the third?"

"Sheridan, for having such little faith in her." I stop my walking and whirl around to face him. We're far enough away from our group that they wouldn't be able to hear us anymore.

That taunting beast is scraping at the walls again, testing the hundred locks I buried it behind for any give. "You know what, Beau? I do fancy your sister. I think she's cute as hell and any fucker would be lucky to have her, but it would be all her choice. And maybe a few days ago I would've shoved the attraction I have to her down because I value our friendship enough to let it go. But since you've insulted both of us in the process, I actually just want to say a massive fuck you. I deserve better than that, and so does your sister."

"Don't fucking touch her, Wilson. I swear to Christ."

"I'd never go there if I knew she wasn't into it, Bennett. But if she decides she wants me? I'm not gonna say no."

I start stalking away again, needing to clear my head, to calm the raging savage in my head locked in its prison.

"Where are you going?!" Beau calls after me.

I don't have an answer to his question, so I just give him my middle finger instead.

* * *

I do two loops of the lake on the cycle path before I come back to the group. My mood is still shitty, and Beau outright refused to look at me. Coward. I don't want to look at him, either.

If Beau said anything about our disagreement while I was gone, no one mentions it, because when I start rummaging around everyone asks how my walk was. I play it down with a non-answer and head down to the water for a swim.

I'm so hot my balls are sweating, and the cold lake water does me wonders. After a couple of minutes, Brin, JP, and Emma decide to get in with me. We chat about nothing in particular while we tread water up and down the lake. It's nice. It feels more like a vacation than it had while storming a path around the open water.

Every so often my gaze trails to Sheridan. She's been sunbathing under an umbrella since I got back and has only moved to turn from her front to her back or top up her suncream. Bailey has been good at helping her with it, but fuck do I wish it was me. I'd find any excuse to touch her at this point, and not just to spite Beau. When she'd playfully knocked into me this morning my heart had soared. Pathetic, I know. But when everyone tells you the girl is socially awkward yet she's comfortable enough to touch *you...* Yeah, I was smug.

The next time I look over at her she's given up the sunbathing and is setting up her sketch pad. Beau and Nash have taken up residence on either side of her, so she's in a Bennett brother sandwich, and I have to stifle a frustrated growl. Overprotective prick.

We give it another fifteen minutes or so before we get out the water to feed ourselves. Turns out, an angry hike followed by an hour of open-water swimming can make a man hungry. I'm ravenous when we sit back down.

We eat lunch as a group before splitting off to do our own things again. I end up hijacking Gemma's sudoku book because I can't face the thought of opening that bloody book again.

Fortunately, it isn't long before someone else sits with me, and this time it isn't Beau, or anyone else looking for a fight.

Sheridan confiscates the puzzle book and leaves her sketch pad in my lap, turned to a new blank sheet. "Come on, Myles."

I turn to face her, and my breath gets stuck in my throat. She's caught the sun with all her sunbathing—her eyes are glittering denim, her skin is warmer in colour, but doused in a billion tiny freckles that spread across her nose, cheeks, and chest, it takes all the strength I have not to turn her over so I can inspect every inch of her. She's lovely on a normal day, but sun-kissed? She's fucking gorgeous.

"What's this?" I manage to ask, voice but a husk.

"I want you to draw me something." She taps the page with her index finger. And now I'm noticing her pretty painted nails. They look like pink marble.

"Isn't it bad luck to draw in another artist's sketchbook?"

Her nose turns up and I feel a strange urge to stroke my finger down the slope of it. "I think you're making shit up. Now, come on." She shoves a pencil in my hand. "This page isn't gonna fill itself."

I twiddle with the pencil in my hand. I'm more a charcoal and pastels king of guy, but I'm not going to complain, even if she is asking me to ruin her work with my own. "What do you want me to draw?"

"I dunno. The lake. A tree. Hector. You pick."

"Why don't you draw one of those things?"

"Because I draw them all the time." She huffs and starts turning back through the book to show me each of her drawings. Just as I expected it would be, Sheridan's work is freaking incredible.

Why she wants an amateur like me to spoil her portfolio I'll never know. I've seen some of her stuff before in Brian and Shirley's house but seeing it raw and unrefined like this makes me feel like a six-year-old next to Pablo Picasso.

"Wow," I mumble. "Sheridan, you're *really* good."

"Thank you," she says, and even though her cheeks dust with pink, it feels like a brush off. "Now show me what you've got, Mr. Art History."

Better than Mr. Wilson, I think to myself. Christ, my dick had stood to attention this morning when she addressed me like that. A terrible thing to happen mere weeks before my official start as a high school teacher.

"I don't know, Shez. I'm a bit rusty."

"Come on," she whines. "Anything you want, Myles. I *want* you to. I don't mind. Even just a little squiggle."

I study her face again—the line of her neck and the swell of her cheeks—and all I really want to draw is her, and the way her pink and blonde curls are piled on top of her head. That thought gives me pause.

And then I think, *fuck it.*

I twist in my spot to face her, getting the pad into a comfortable position. And I start drawing.

"What are you doing?" Sheridan demands after a couple of seconds of me throwing intentional glances her way.

"Drawing like you asked me to."

"You better not be drawing me."

I decide not to answer her, and she starts fidgeting. *"Myles."*

"What?"

"Tell me you're not drawing me."

"Okay. I'm not drawing you."

Sheridan leans over my knees where the sketch pad rests, blocking my view. She gasps. *"No.* Not me. Please?"

"You said anything I wanted," I retort, nudging her back so that I can carry on.

"Yeah, but I didn't mean me!"

"Well, you're the only thing I want to draw. So." I shrug. Then, because I can't help myself, I pinch her chin and angle her head the way I want it, displaying the smooth plain of her neck. "If you can keep looking that way for five minutes, that'd be great."

I return to my work for another moment. The next time I look up to take stock of another feature and translate it onto the paper, she's gawking at me like I said the Earth is flat. "What?"

"Nothing," she mutters, and settles back down.

Perhaps I was too forward, but I don't care. I want her to know I think she's beautiful, and I hope this stupid portrait proves it.

I don't force her to sit still for very long, because she's not very good at it. I've noticed she always needs to be doing something with her hands.

It starts with fiddling with the ties on her bikini bottoms—which is bright pink—and then twirling her fingers through the curls on top of her head. Then she buries her hands in the sand and sifts the grains through her fingers. Then she gives up completely and spends the rest of my drawing time on her phone.

It makes me smile—her little tick. I understand it, too. She doesn't like being looked at, which is a shame because I damn like looking at her all the same. If I could get away with doing this all day just to *keep* looking at her, I absolutely would. But she's more perceptive than that and would no doubt call me out on it the second she sussed me out.

"Are you done yet?" She asks, following it up with a sassy sigh.

"Can't rush perfection, Shez," I tell her with ridiculous nonchalance. She goes to open her mouth again, but I cut her off, failing to hide my smirk. "Two more minutes."

"If I'd known you'd take this long, I wouldn't have asked."

I can't help but laugh. "Who knew you were so impatient?"

"I get fidgety."

"Yeah, no shit." I grin. "Right, I think I'm done."

I turn the pad around to face her with a proud smile. Considering I don't use pencil and I haven't drawn for months; I think I did a pretty good job.

Sheridan stares at the page for a moment, then she blinks and snatches the whole book off me. "Oh my God. Myles!"

"What?" I try to look at the page again, feeling a jolt of dread through my chest. "Is it bad?"

"Bad?! No, it's not bad! It's—It's…" she struggles for words while I struggle for breath. *Please don't say hideous. Please don't say dreadful.* "Amazing. Seriously amazing."

I breathe a sigh of relief while she beams at me. "Oh, thank God."

"At least we know that degree of yours wasn't a complete waste," Sheridan jokes, and gives my knee a pat that sends my brain into overdrive. "Now my turn. And I'm giving this to my mum, by the way."

Feeling like a man close to the edge of his wits, I give her the biggest smile I can muster. "I think I can live with that."

Chapter Twelve

MIDNIGHT SNACK

SHERIDAN

"Do you mind if I stay with Gem tonight?"

I've just got out of the shower, hair wrapped in a T-shirt to keep the curls bouncing, and only a towel covering me. The day's heat finally got to me, and while I managed to keep from getting sunburn—a first, I will admit—I felt disgusting after sweating and baking all day.

"Sure, I don't mind." She's a better friend than I am. I love having a room to myself.

We've not long been back at the cabin. We went out for dinner rather than staying in for the first time since we got here, which was a welcome reprieve from cooking. As much as I enjoy it, cooking for ten people as opposed to just myself has started to become exhausting.

Having to share a bed every night when I usually get one to myself is also strange. My sister's desire to swap rooms for the night means I get to starfish in the middle again. If she told me she was staying in Gemma's room for the rest of the holiday, I still wouldn't be mad.

I change into the pyjamas I've been wearing—a thin vest and shorts combo that keeps the heat off me. I've always really struggled to sleep in the heat.

"What were you and Myles drawing earlier?" Brin asks when I perch next to her on the edge of the bed. "You were with each other for ages."

I try not to blush at the memory of sitting with Myles next to the lake. Fidgety as I might have been while he was drawing me—no one has ever chosen to draw my portrait before—I was still surprised to find myself so content. Plus, Myles is an incredible artist—all sharp lines and shading. I could tell by the way he held his pencil and twitched his fingers that he's probably better with charcoal, but his pencil skills were not lacking. I'd love to see what he could do with a bit of flint. I can just imagine him with dirty fingers and black smudges on his face and arms. The mental image alone turns me on something fierce. I think I need help.

"We did portraits."

"Of each other?"

"Yeah."

Brinsley visibly fights a smile and fails. "That's so fucking cute."

I give her a disgruntled nose wrinkle. "Whatever."

"It is! God, I so love this. Can you get together please?"

My retort comes out spluttered, "I barely know the guy!"

"So? You're on holiday together! That's one awkward milestone out of the way."

I shake my head at her and unwrap my hair. Brinsley, ever the mother hen, takes out my detangling brush and starts teasing it through my curls.

"I'm rooting for this, by the way. Myles is lovely. Smart. Handsome. And your type to a T."

"You keep saying that," I grumble. "What even is my type? I didn't know I had one."

"Sure, you do! He's got a tennis player's body. Tall, lithe but with a bit of muscle yet not *too* much. I think you favour fairer hair, too."

I can't help but frown as I think her words through, because fuck, she might be right.

"And his tattoos?" Brin continues to gush. "Not my thing entirely, but the fact that you don't know they're there unless he takes his top off? *Whew!* Tell me you don't fancy the pants off him."

I want to rebuke, I really do. I hate people knowing when I've got a crush, because the recipient of said crush finding out and rejecting me is one of my greatest fears. Even in adulthood. But denying that I 'fancy the pants off him', as my twin so eloquently put it, is difficult, because I really do. And it's not just because he's attractive, but because he's a nice person as well. Nice is such a shit word sometimes but being known as a nice person is one of the best attributes someone can have.

"He's not ugly," I finally admit.

"A ringing endorsement there, Shez." Brin snorts.

I shrug. "I try."

My sister sighs, finishing with my hair and wraps her arms around my chest. "I know you, Sheridan Bennett, we shared a womb and a freaking sack of water for nine months before we even saw daylight. I know when you like a boy, and you *like* Myles. *But* I know what you're like, so I'm gonna shut up. That being said, if you ever feel like talking shop, you know where to find me."

"Noted. Thanks Brin."

She unlatches from me with a kiss on my cheek and leaves me be, with only Hector for company.

I'm not overly tired yet, so I tuck myself under the covers and turn on the TV on a low volume. Apart from shitty morning television, I haven't properly put it on yet. According to the facilities booklet in the bedside table drawer, there's Netflix available to all guests, so I navigate my way to it and pick something easy to watch: *QI*.

Now that Brin is sleeping elsewhere, Hector decides it's okay to sleep with me again on the bed. He curls up at the bottom by my feet and starts snoring away.

I fiddle with my phone while only half paying attention to the facts Stephen Fry provides on screen. Did you know that right up until 1912, pottery and sculpting were actual Olympic events? Also, Olympic medals are not made of gold, silver, and bronze, but mostly silver.

I get through three episodes before I realise that I'm showing no signs of fatigue. I'm wide awake even though my body is exhausted.

Admittedly, I keep thinking back to earlier when I was drawing Myles. He'd just sat there, patient as a saint while I revelled in sketching his perfect face. I remember my mouth watering as I built on the lines of his stubble, and the shadow of his cheek bones, the hazel of his eyes. That was one aspect I wasn't happy with. Trying to capture the lushness of his eye colour with a monochrome pencil had been difficult, but when I'd turned the pad around to show him, he seemed thrilled with it.

Then he asked me if I was going to give that one to my mother as well, and I'd cracked up.

I love that he can make me laugh.

Some men didn't have a solid sense of humour, and others—like Brin's boyfriend Andy—didn't have one at all. My ex-boyfriend carried all his humour in his little finger, and that had nothing to do with why we broke up.

I realise now that I'm smiling thinking about my afternoon on the beach.

Something had clearly been bothering Myles in the morning because he disappeared after what looked to be a short but heated discussion with Beau. No, I couldn't help but look for him the whole time while pretending to be invested in a word search. When he'd come back an hour later and headed straight for the lake, I was relieved, and then at once horrified when he dunked his head in the water and re-emerged looking like the version of him that had existed in my dreams each night this week. That had been my cue to look away, and so I made Nash keep me topped up with suncream while I worked on my freckle tan and kept my eyes firmly *off* the blond Adonis.

I roll onto my back, *QI* forgotten, and spread my arms and legs wide while staring at the ceiling, but I'm thinking about Myles and what he looked like coming out of the water. A sigh escapes me, because those water droplets glistening down his torso and dripping off the tips of his hair and hem of his board shorts were practically pornographic.

If I was brave, I'd slip my hand into my shorts and get myself off to the image of him that way. But I'm not brave, and the thought of Brin deciding to come back, or one of my brothers barging in here for something makes the feat seem futile.

When the credits roll on yet another episode, I realise I won't be getting any sleep at all tonight without help.

I need a nightcap.

I didn't realise that turning twenty-five meant receiving the mantle of 'pensioner' at the same time. I've never needed a nightcap in my Goddamn life.

Hector is sound asleep when I sit up again, which makes it much easier to sneak out of the room without getting waylaid. I slip out the door and into the hall, and then walk on practical tiptoes to the kitchen. Knowing Myles is still having to sleep on the sofa, I'm conscious of waking him if he's asleep.

When I round the corner into the main cabin space, I halt.

In only his boxers and nothing else, Myles stands in front of the open fridge eating what looks to be a Babybel. I hope they're not from Brin's stash, because if she finds out she'll skin him alive.

He hasn't noticed me yet and I don't know what to do. Ideally, I should move, because if he catches me gawking at him in the dark, he's going to think I'm a complete freak. That is of course, if like most other people who meet me, he doesn't already think that.

But I'm enraptured by his damn body again. That broad chest decorated in tattoos that look sinister in the dim fridge light. His hairy calves and muscular thighs. My mouth waters. *Again.* I find myself wondering what his fitness regime is. He must have one if he looks this good, and yet I don't think I've seen him exercise all week, and he's here helping himself to a little midnight snack. *Cheese*, no less. The man must enjoy having nightmares.

No, wait…

QI taught me once that cheese before bed giving you nightmares is a myth.

Huh.

Alright, so he just really likes cheese in general. A man after my own heart.

He tosses the wax into the bin and turns back to study the contents of the fridge, all the while scratching his chest.

"You gonna stand there all night, Shez, or are you gonna do what you came out here to do?"

Bollocks.

Light on my feet, I may be, but I'd make a shit spy.

"Sorry," I mutter, finally stepping into the room.

He smiles over his shoulder at me, his gaze trailing down my body.

Maybe I should have put a T-shirt on, though it would have done nothing to hide how tight my nipples have become. Traitors. My face is on fire.

"And here I thought I was the only one who got midnight munchies," he jokes as he takes out a chocolate mousse—again, from Brinsley's collection—and knocks the fridge door shut.

"Technically you are." I slide my way around the counter. "I'm not hungry."

It's probably my overactive imagination, but I swear his eyes flare. "No?"

I shake my head. "Nope. I couldn't sleep."

"And..." he rips the foil lid off the plastic pot and discards it, "you thought I'd be better company?"

His tone is more curious than arrogant, if a little hopeful. Like he wants to believe it but doesn't.

"Yes, that was it, Myles." I give a patronising pat to his chest, and then instantly regret it, because *wow* this man is as solid as a brick fucking wall. "Not the two fingers of whisky that can get me to sleep."

"Are you an eighty-year-old man?"

I snort because that had basically been my earlier thought. "Apparently."

I can feel his gaze on me as I reach up into a high cupboard for a tumbler, set it on the counter and pour out a rough measure.

"How come you're still up?" Myles asks when I turn to face him. He eats his mousse with a teaspoon.

"Just couldn't sleep. I don't know why, just don't feel very tired."

"Well, you're on holiday. You don't have to get up in the morning."

"I know. But I'll hate myself tomorrow when I'm knackered because I let my body do whatever it wants. Watching the telly hasn't done anything for me so I thought a nightcap would work better."

Myles's gaze travels south again when I mention my body—a poor choice of words on my part—and I'd be lying if I said I didn't enjoy it. Knowing that there is a possibility the attraction is mutual, I feel a hell of a lot better about myself.

"You could try turning the telly off," he suggests, voice somewhat coarser than it was not fifteen seconds before.

Mutual, I think.

I stick my tongue out at him regardless, and he chuckles. I take a sip of whisky, if only to calm the sudden rapid beating of my heart. It doesn't help.

"Why are *you* awake?" I ask.

He shrugs. "Couldn't sleep either. Then I got hungry."

"What a pair we make." I raise my glass, and he clinks his mousse pot against it, which just makes me giggle.

God, I am pathetic.

"So, what riveting TV were you watching to keep you up so late?"

"*QI.*"

Myles studies me for a moment. "Why does that make *complete* sense?"

I scoff. "I'm actually missing the next episode, so can we wrap it up, please?"

He taps the end of his teaspoon to his lips. "Only if I can join you."

My stomach does an Olympic gymnast-worthy somersault, and I gawk at him a bit. "You want to watch *QI* with me?"

"Sure, why not? I'm about to become a teacher, and I won't be a very good one if I'm not a font of mostly useless knowledge, will I?"

Fuck, I want this man.

That desire strikes me across the face like a well-placed slap. If he's not careful, I might end up falling in love with him.

Because I don't want to look like a besotted moron, I pretend to think it over, even if I only manage a second. "Fine, but I don't do snacks in bed, so eat up."

"You don't do snacks in bed?" He asks, as if I just confessed to a cardinal sin.

"No, ew."

"Why not?"

"I don't want crumbs in my sheets! I'm sleeping there." I finally neck my glass of whisky and leave the glass in the sink.

His gaze narrows in on me. "You're weird."

"Dur."

Myles drags a hand down his face. "That was insulting, I'm sorry."

I make a washy noise. "I'm not insulted."

We head for the bedroom, Myles close behind me. I can feel his warmth at my back, even though we're not touching. I realise he doesn't bother to put a T-shirt, or even jogging bottoms on. Just follows me into the room in his pants and nothing else.

Fuck.

He doesn't speak again until we're in the bedroom with the door closed. "I do actually like your weird, you know."

"Good to know. I like your weird, too."

"And what about me is weird?"

I get comfortable under the quilt again, being careful not to disturb Hector who hasn't moved an inch since I left the room.

"I don't know yet," I admit. "But when I figure it out, I know I'll like it."

Myles settles down beside me on Brinsley's usual side, except he sticks to the top of the covers like a freaking gent. I'm not ashamed to say I wish he'd get under the covers with me, but this is nice all the same. He tucks his hands behind his head, stretching out his body, and the urge to nestle against him is instantaneous and overwhelming. All that lean muscle on his chest and arms and thighs on display for me like a sexy-limbed buffet. A real feast for the eyes.

"You put an awful lot of faith in me, Birdie."

I blink up at him, tearing my gaze away from his assets. "Birdie?"

He seems surprised at his own remark, then recovers. "Yeah, Birdie. 'Cause of your tattoos."

I am *not* swooning. I'm not. "Sure she's not an ex of yours?"

He meets my gaze, expression soft yet confident. "I'd never get you mixed up with anyone, Sheridan."

Welp. "Not even my own twin?"

Myles grins. "Nope."

"What if we dressed up exactly the same and I covered all my tattoos up with makeup?"

"I'd still know."

"How?" I demand, scowling now. "We're identical."

"That," he leans forward and boops me on the nose, "is for me to know."

I make a disbelieving sound. "Such confidence from a man who barely knows me."

"I've been looking at you and your sister for five days. Physically, I've learnt your differences."

"Sure, Jan."

"Look, I'm missing out on important facts because of you." He points at the TV.

With a huff, I turn my gaze back to the telly.

We watch in content silence for a while, only occasionally laughing at something one of the panellists says or answering a question and getting the answer completely wrong.

Once again, I'm struck by how easy it is to spend time with Myles, even when he's wearing so little. I realise this evening involved more flirting than I would usually partake in, which probably explains the giddy feeling in my chest. I don't think I've felt like this since I was a teenager.

I don't know how many episodes we get through before I fall asleep, but I know that I do so with my dog at my feet, a sexy, practically naked man by my side, and a smile on my face.

Chapter Thirteen

Too Cool for Me

MYLES

Such confidence from a man who barely knows me.

Like that observation hadn't been an absolute punt in the proverbial bollocks.

But I meant what I said. I *could* tell the twins apart, and not just because they dressed differently, or wore their hair differently. It was in their gait, and their posture, and that one mole just a millimetre shy of the crease of Sheridan's nose.

Yet I'd made myself seem like an arrogant twat.

Whilst wearing very few clothes.

Good one, Wilson. You dick.

Still, I don't think she minded too much. I noticed her looking, and while I hadn't purposely forgot to put more clothes on before I followed her to her room, I think she enjoyed the view. The smile on her face after she drifted off said it all. She liked my company, banter and all.

I'd turned the TV off when I was sure Sheridan had passed out, and like the utter creep I am, I watched her sleep for a little while. I couldn't help it—she was beautiful like that. Fresh-faced and serene. Happy. *Content.*

I couldn't stay with her all night, though. It wasn't even about Beau. I just didn't want the hassle of waking up in the morning and having everyone in the cabin talking about Sheridan and I sharing a bed. Especially now that I knew how little attention she liked. I wanted her, but I wasn't going to pursue her in front of all her siblings and friends. She deserved better than that.

So, like a chicken, I'd slipped out of her room at some ungodly hour and tucked myself back onto the sofa in the living room.

To absolutely nobody's surprise, I dreamt of Sheridan.

I should be embarrassed at how I jumped at the opportunity to spend more time with her, but I'm not. This holiday is somehow inexplicably nearing its end already. It simultaneously feels like I've been here mere hours yet also months. But in terms of getting to know the quiet Bennett sister, I've squandered my time away by pouting about Beau. So, I was keen to change that last night. Sue me.

She didn't seem to mind though, and I like that.

Did I learn anything from watching hours of *QI* with her? No. I hope the kids aren't too disappointed. Maybe I'll binge a season or three when we go home. I've still got a few weeks of freedom left.

I'm woken in the morning by a not-so-subtle bickering between Beau and Brinsley from the kitchen. At first, I think they might be talking about *me*, and I wonder how long I can get away with listening in before they realise that I'm not asleep. That just makes me think of Sheridan again, and the way she lurked in the shadows of the hallway last night because she thought I hadn't heard her door open. I don't think she'd have moved, either, if I hadn't put her out of her misery.

Bailey is suddenly mentioned in Beau and Brinsley's discussion, so I figure I'm good to make my consciousness known. I still refuse to speak to Beau, though.

"Sorry, Myles." Brin grimaces. "Didn't mean to wake you."

I wave her off wordlessly and tidy up the lounge before everyone else appears. I tuck the bedding into the empty double room—which we still haven't heard a peep about getting the bed fixed, despite our multiple visits to the help desk—then shower and dress for the day.

We're going kayaking this morning and heading out for a nature walk later, so after breakfast we head back down to the lake together.

It's hot again today, almost uncomfortably so, and I'm not sure how I feel about sitting in a plastic boat for hours without any cover.

At the docks, we're informed that we've got two-person kayaks, and that we need to pair up.

I rush a glance at Sheridan and find her looking thoroughly put out. I'm learning that anything remotely sporty or competitive is not her bag, which must be a nightmare when Beau is the main organiser of this holiday, and he must make *everything* a competition.

"How 'bout it, Shez?" Beau wraps a possessive arm around his sister's hunched shoulders.

Sheridan gawks up at him like he's gone mad. "What?"

"You and me? Team Beauridan." He grins down at her.

Even Nash is looking at him like he might've loosened a screw somewhere.

"You want to share a boat with me? *Me?*" She repeats.

"Yes. You." And then, as if I didn't already know exactly what his game was, he slides his blue gaze my way. Prick.

I almost let a growl slip. *Almost.* Instead, knowing he's looking my way, I scratch my cheek with my middle finger.

The sound of him choking on his tongue is oddly satisfying.

I wind up in a kayak with JP, who seems like the lesser of three evils. The girls split up between the four of them, leaving Stavros and Nash to pair up.

Rowing out into a quieter part of the lake, we start off with a few races. JP and I win two, Nash and Stavros win one, and Brin and Bailey win the other. Beau and Sheridan don't win any, which sees him looking pissy and her looking guilty, and I hate him for putting that on her, because this is his fault.

We swan around as a group for a little longer. Nash and Stavros capsize after trying to bait us into a fight. Em and Gemma do as well, but I think that might have been on purpose. It's so hot out today and tumbling into open water seems like a great way to cool off.

When our time is up and we head back to the dock, JP and I decide to capsize for the sake of cooling down, and tread water the rest of the way back to the stony shore.

We have lunch back at the cabin, and I decide to have a nap before we head out for our big walk later. The good thing about this activity, a bit like yesterday at the lake, is that Sheridan won't have to leave Hector in the cabin by himself.

I don't sleep for long—there's too much going on in the cabin for me to manage it, but when I do wake, I'm greeted by the sight of Sheridan tucked into the nearby armchair, headphones on and iPad resting on her thighs.

She must notice me stir, because she looks up from whatever she's working on and meets my gaze with a small smile. She shucks one of her earbuds free, "Good nap?"

I'm hit with another pang of longing for this girl I barely know. It's such a simple thing, but I imagine this is what a lazy Sunday afternoon with her would look like. A long dog walk with Hector; a stop at the local for a Sunday roast and a bottle of red; a nap for me and an escape for her through her art. I want it so bad; I actually get that tight, anxiety-like ball in my chest. I feel like I'm suffering from acid reflux, when, really, I'm just a fucking sap.

"Was alright," I say around a yawn. "Bit difficult with eight other people being noisy around me."

She frowns. "Eight?"

"You don't count, Birdie." I give her a lazy smile. "What are you listening to?"

"Oh, um, just a playlist I always have on when I draw," she mumbles, cheeks flush.

"What's playing right now?"

"Massive Attack."

I can't hide my surprise. "Wow. Alright?"

"What?"

"I think you might be too cool for me."

She snorts. "Yeah right. It's not all British indie alternative shit."

"No? What else you got?"

Her lips purse and it's freaking adorable. "I don't think I want to tell you."

"Alright, fine. We'll just go with the assumption that you're way cooler than me and I'm okay with it."

Sheridan points at me. "Deal. You made a friend, by the way." She nods towards my feet.

Sure enough, the canine embodiment of a snowball is curled up at my feet.

"Well, look at that," I muse and lean forward to stroke Hector's head. He lifts up, and I give him a scratch behind the ears. "He seems better now. More comfortable, I mean."

"I think he's used to everyone. Mostly, anyway. The first couple of days were overwhelming."

I meet her gaze again. "And what about you?"

"What *about* me?"

"Do you feel…less overwhelmed?"

Sheridan's lips press into a tight line as she keeps her gaze on me. "Nope. Only in certain instances."

"Like when you're drawing?"

"That…amongst others." She keeps her gaze locked with mine, and I don't know if it's because I'm a hopeless idiot, or because my ability to read between the lines has dulled, but I *think* she means me. That she's not so overwhelmed when she's with *me*, and fuck if that doesn't make me feel like a smug son of a bitch.

I know she's all the way across the room, but I want nothing more than to drag her into my lap and kiss that pretty mouth of hers. I want to feel her hips in my hands and the weight of her on my thighs. She's small but she's got curves in all the good places, and I just want to trace the lines of each of them with my index finger until she's shivering, mewling, and begging for me.

Yikes, that came out of nowhere. And now the little soldier in my underwear is at half-mast and Sheridan is *still* looking at me, like she knows all about my illicit thoughts.

Quick, Myles! Think of something else. Anything. Mrs. Burr from the foster home. That dead badger on the roadside last week. The taste of orange juice after cleaning your teeth.

I almost gag at that last one.

A shriek comes from the direction of the kitchen. I turn over my shoulder to see Brinsley standing in front of the fridge.

"Who ate my Babybels?!" Brin yells. "And my chocolate mousse!"

I've been in some precarious situations in my life, but I know better than to get between a woman and her food. And yet I've done exactly that.

Sheridan snickers as I sink into the sofa cushions, hoping I'll suddenly develop the ability to teleport away from here. Far, far away.

"You could've told me!" I mouth at her.

She gives the faintest shrug, mischief in her eyes, and the urge to drag her into my lap hits me all over again at full force. I give her my best glare, and all she does is stick her tongue out.

Then, she sits up straighter and clears her throat, "Sorry, Brin. I got hungry in the middle of the night."

Brinsley grumbles, "You owe me replacements."

Well shit, now I feel bad.

"You bet," Sheridan agrees, and then looks at me with a lifted eyebrow.

Translation: *I* owe Brinsley replacements.

* * *

Our nature walk at dusk feels like it lasts for hours, but I won't complain about it, because Sheridan decides—non-verbally—that she wants to walk with me for the majority of it. I don't know if she notices that Beau regularly sends dirty looks our way from the head of the group, but I do. I give him another subtle flip of the bird, but it doesn't make much of a difference.

Still, I generally keep my focus on Sheridan and Hector. I hold the pooch's lead for a stretch of the journey, which is nice because he's not a very demanding dog. He walks *with us* rather than walking *me*.

Our conversation is surface-level, and I keep the flirting to a minimum because I don't want to deal with what might happen if anyone overhears me. Plus, Brin and Nash regularly dip in and out of our conversation, and that alone is enough to keep things chaste.

By the time we get back to the cabin, it's pitch-black outside, the crickets are in full symphony, and the cabin actually feels cool enough to have a decent night's sleep in.

Bailey, Nash, Emma, and JP all decide to head to bed early. Apparently kayaking and a three-mile walk is enough to wipe them out. I wish I could say the same for me.

Brin has been fighting Beau all day under the guise that no one has noticed, and when she disappears down the hall, Beau follows her, which leaves me with Gemma, Stavros, and Sheridan.

Stavros and Gemma take an armchair each, while Sheridan and Hector sit in the corner of the sofa next to me. Someone suggests a nightcap, and I notice Shez fighting a giggle, because this is her second night on the trot. Together we share two fingers of Laphroaig each while silently watching old episodes of *Family Guy*. I don't imagine the program choice to be in Gemma's taste, but she doesn't comment on it. Beau and Brinsley don't make a reappearance, so I can only assume they've gone to bed.

After two episodes and only a sip of whisky, Gemma excuses herself for the night, too. Stavros decides to help himself to the glass, polishes it off in one and then tops his empty glass back up with another rough pour.

"Waste not, want not, aye?"

I don't grace him with a reply because I don't know what to say. I'm pretty sure I caught him taking hits out of a hip flask on our walk, so he's already suitably pissed. He didn't need the nightcap.

After he sinks the next one, he asks, "You tappin' that?" With a nod at Sheridan.

I scowl at him, glance her way, and notice she's fallen asleep, glass empty. Whisky really does seem to do the trick for her.

"Not that it's any of your business, but no," I tell him, then tip the amber liquid in my glass down my throat. I set the lowball on the table.

"Really? You've spent a lot of time together the past few days. I'd have had a go by now if I were you."

"She's not a fucking fairground ride, Steven. And I'd be careful how you speak about her when she's got two brothers nearby who're quite protective of her."

He scoffs. "Beau's a fucking hypocrite." Dammit, I hate that we're in agreement on something. "And Nash knows what I'm like."

"That's not an excuse."

He waves me off and I have to hold back a punch. He stands out of his chair, "Want help carrying her to bed?"

"No, I don't want to disturb her."

His grin is disgustingly wicked. "Bit of an exhibitionist, are we? Hoping to have your way with her out here where anyone might catch you?" His taunting is pushing my limits.

"Go to bed, Steven," I growl at him.

He simply laughs. "Sure, Wilson. Don't let me get in your way."

I don't watch him leave, but once the door to his and Nash's room is closed, I drag a hand down my face. Slimy prick.

I study Sheridan for a minute, the way her even breaths lift her chest, and her lids shine under the dim glow of the television. I'm struck again by how lovely she is and curling up next to her and Hector is all I want to do.

But I do the next best thing instead and retrieve our duvets from their rooms, and drape one over her. She must be pretty out of it because she doesn't move a muscle.

I lie on my side, perpendicular to her, with my head only a few inches away from her pink and blonde curls. I let her breathing and the single shot of whisky lull me into a satisfying sleep—one without any interruption.

Chapter Fourteen
Reckless, Philandering & Squandering

SHERIDAN

I wake up with a fuzzy head and a dry mouth. Then I open my eyes and realise I'm not at home. I'm not even in the room I've been sharing with Brin in this holiday cabin.

I'm on the sofa in the living room.

For the second night in a row, whisky has proven to be one hundred percent effective in knocking me out.

I grumble and roll over, burrowing back under the covers. But I catch a blur of dark blond hair, and I blink away the sleep in my eyes and try to focus. Sure enough, lying on his back with his phone screen angled at his face, Myles is stretched across the remaining couch space and reading an article on the Apex News site about our current holiday.

Of course, we've been sold out to the papers. Two Premier League football players are with us.

"Myles?"

He shifts where he lays, rolling his head to look at me properly, "Mornin', Birdie."

My stomach flutters at the nickname. It's such a stupid thing, but I'm obsessed with it. Well, the fact that he calls me it, anyway.

The only nickname I've ever gone by is Shez. It's nice to have a new one.

"Sorry for takin' your bed," I mumble. "You should've woken me up."

He tosses his phone aside and turns onto his front, resting his chin in his palm. Being the sole focus of his attention up this close is a little unnerving, but I can't bring myself to look away from his pretty green-gold gaze. "Why would I do that? There's plenty of room for both of us."

"You haven't slept in a bed all week. You should've taken ours instead."

"All your belongings are in there, it'd be inappropriate."

I can't help but roll my eyes, and yet he's such a gentleman, I'd swoon if I weren't already horizontal. "Did I snore?"

His face flickers with something akin to amusement, and I know the answer is yes, I did snore. But instead of admitting it, he says, "I don't know what they taught you at school, Shez, but women are physically incapable of snoring. It's been scientifically proven."

I think I might be well and truly gone for this man, and the giggle I let out at his jesting just solidifies that I am. "Thank you for reminding me."

He grins. "You're welcome."

"What time is it?"

"Early. Too early for the others, anyway."

I nod to myself for a moment. "Why is it always me and you awake at stupid hours?"

"Apparently early risers have more lust for life."

"That doesn't sound like me."

"No?" He tips his head, bed-head locks unmoving. "You're always the first one up and seem to be the last one in bed—with the exception of last night." The wink he gives me makes all my nerve endings tingle.

"I mean, I wouldn't exactly say that carpe diem is my mantra, as much as my mum and dad want it to be."

"Seizing the day is overrated anyway. Sounds hostile if you ask me."

There I go, giggling away again. "Aren't teachers supposed to be more optimistic than that?"

"I'm a realist, Birdie. I'm not gonna go tellin' a bunch of thirteen-year-olds to seize the day if it might land them in trouble. More like...proceed with caution but have fun while doing it."

With a flat hum, I say, "Doesn't quite have the same ring to it, though, does it? It's a bit wordy."

Laughter rumbles out of him, and I feel it in my bones. And my unmentionables, but we're not going to talk about that. Clue's in the name.

His beard is scruffy from where he's slept on it, and without thinking, I reach out to tame it. It's not difficult, considering there's maybe only five inches between us. He doesn't move away when I touch him, either, which lessens my inner panic. "Do you always get this...fluffy?"

Myles gives me a soft smile. "Not normally, no. I like a bit of stubble, and I'll have to neaten it up before the term starts." He just studies me while I graze my fingertips through the coarse hair. "What do *you* think about it?"

"Me?" I blurt. "Why does it matter what I think?"

A second's pause.

Two.

Three.

"Because you're the one looking at me."

I roll my lips together, then lick them. His gaze tracks the movement with no shame. "I think you're just as handsome either way."

He wraps his hand loosely around my wrist. "You think I'm handsome, Birdie?"

My cheeks flame again. I don't know where this confidence has come from, but I guess it's something to do with the knowledge that Myles is attracted to me, even if he hasn't verbalised it. But I see it in the way he looks at me.

My palm flattens against his cheek, thumb still stroking over his ginger-blond hairs. "Yeah, Myles. I do."

"That's good, 'cause—"

He's cut off by Hector barking. Loudly.

I sit up instantly, dragging my hand away from Myles's cheek. Hector leaps off the sofa, barking as he bolts down the cabin corridor.

"Bloody hell," I mutter, hauling ass off the sofa and following him. "Hector!" I hiss. "What are you doing?"

It's only now, as I stumble down the hall after my spooked pooch, that I realise I'm still in last night's clothes.

When I find the dog, he's scratching at one of the bathroom doors. I scoop him up and give his nose a light smack.

"What are you doing? Hey? It's too early for you to be making all this noise, mister."

The dog whines at me, and then the toilet flushes in the bathroom. Before I embarrass anyone, including myself, I march back down the hall.

"Shez?"

I whirl around to find Beau emerging from the en-suite. "Sorry. Don't know what's got into him."

"That's alright," he says, rubbing his hands vigorously across his face. "How come you're up so early?"

"I fell asleep on the sofa, and I woke up when the sun did."

Something unusual—something I instantly don't like—passes across Beau's face when I say it. He holds his hands out for the still whining Hector, so I wordlessly hand him over.

"You fell asleep on the sofa?"

"Yeah, I had a nightcap with Gem, Myles, and Stavros. I passed out about five minutes after I sat down."

"So, nothing happened?"

My gaze instinctively narrows on him. "I woke up with my duvet and still fully clothed," I tell him, and when he doesn't respond to me, I ask, "Is something going on with you and Myles?"

Beau looks away. "No."

"So why haven't you spoken to each other since you got here?" I fold my arms across my chest.

Even though he's not looking and is quite clearly sulking, he manages to absently pet Hector's head. Hector, who is now practically purring like a kitten in Beau's arms. "We just had a disagreement. It's nothing."

I narrow my eyes on him again. "I'm sure I don't need to tell you to get your head out your arse, but get your head out your arse, Beau."

"Why do you assume it's my fault?" He scowls, hitching Hector under his arm.

"Because it usually is. He's awake if you want to talk to him—I'm going to shower and change."

"Can I take the puppy for a walk?"

Assuming he wants it as an excuse to *not* talk to Myles, I frown. "Fine. Be on the lookout for paps. We're in the papers."

"I know. My publicist called—it's why I'm up so early."

I can't help but soften. Beau has always been a hot topic in the media, right from his practical crash into the professional footballing world. I didn't manage to read any of the article that Myles had up on his phone, but I'm almost certain it'll paint Beau the way they always do—to be a slacking, spoiled, self-obsessed striker with the inability to play on a team—with absolutely no mention of JP who plays on the same fucking team. Although, that boy gets into trouble all by himself.

"How dare we have a holiday, right?" I hedge.

"Yeah, right." My brother huffs. "I'll make sure Hector looks handsome if I see them."

I'm reminded of Myles then, and the fact that we'd just shared a moment that Hector had promptly ruined. "Thanks, Beau. His left side is better."

He snorts, and heads on his way.

I make my shower quick, and dress in the easiest clothes I can find—a white eyelet tunic dress and my Converse.

When I head back into the main room, Myles is still by himself, sitting at the rattan dining table on the patio outside. I notice that he's tidied the bedding away and changed into fresh clothes, too. There's a second mug of coffee in the empty place beside him. I make my way out and sit in that very spot.

"Hey,"

Myles meets my gaze with a warm smile. Good, he doesn't think I just ran off. "Hey."

"This for me?"

He nods, resting his chin in his palm again. "Did you manage to convince Beau to take Hector for his morning walk?"

"No, he made that offer all by himself. He's gone pap hunting."

"So, he knows about the Apex piece, then?"

"Yep. No rest for the wicked."

"Indeed. He's not done anything wrong, so I don't know why everyone's got their knickers in a twist. Well, not wrong for taking a holiday, anyway."

"Will the club say anything?"

"Doubtful. The manager might, but only if it gets seriously out of hand."

I sit back in my chair with a sigh. "I don't envy this part of his life."

"Me neither."

We sit in silence for a while, just soaking up the morning sun and our first coffees of the day. It's so domestic I almost feel winded when the others start to appear.

Beau doesn't come back until everyone is up and eating.

* * *

Our last night at Camp Bennett, we decide to get royally pissed. We eat dinner around the table on the terrace—which consists of basically anything we can find in the fridge as we need to get rid of it—and then start on the stash of alcohol we still have. I avoid the whisky knowing it has the potential to wipe me clean out.

There's a speaker system built into the cabin, and Nash manages to connect his phone to it. So, we have music. We have booze. And a bunch of twenty-somethings have been left to their own devices in a fancy cabin on a fancy holiday park with photographers lurking.

Am I worried?

Only a bit...

I spend the first half of the night observing everyone else from my favourite corner of the sofa while nursing a glass of wine. I think I've drank more alcohol this week alone than I did the year we turned eighteen. I'm not a massive drinker anyway, which surely explains my poor tolerance. I realise I should probably pace myself a little better if I want to last the night.

I talk with the girls for a little while, which mostly consists of Bailey showing us the social accounts her sister, Brandy, runs for the Crusaders, Coventry's ice hockey team. While ice hockey is nowhere near as big in the UK as it is in the States, they're having their best year yet and building a decent fanbase. I can only imagine Brandy's talent to garner attention on the internet is helping that.

After a while we split off. Someone finds a Twister game, which I decide to sit out on because my balance is horrendous on a normal day, without the aid of wine and boisterous men.

When that gets tired—in that Nash throws one of his infamous drunken tantrums because he keeps falling and losing—we start dancing. We put a queue of music on, although Beau promptly ruins it by forgetting, and we end up listening to Girls Aloud, followed by Westlife, followed by Take That, much to Stavros's dismay. Beau is drinking more than his usual limit and is getting clumsier by the minute. I can only assume it's to do with the article in the Apex this morning, but he's never usually this bothered by it. I still haven't read it, and I probably won't.

Beau is not what everyone thinks he is. He was once pegged as the 'Bad Boy of the Premier League', and I've never laughed so hard in my life. Never mind that he's the most organised sibling out of the four of us to a military degree, he's financially responsible, owns multiple businesses, launched his own charity last year, and regularly donates to others.

Yes, a real stain on the footballing world.

Somehow, *reckless*, *philandering* and *squandering* aren't adjectives that particularly fit right to the brother I know.

I dance with him for a little bit at his request, and he lasts three songs before he starts using *me* as something to physically lean on.

"Do you need to sit down, Beau?"

He responds with something that is completely incoherent. His eyes are glassy and drooping, and his posture is slumped. Something tells me he needs sleep.

When I suggest going to bed, he doesn't argue. With help from Nash, we manage to walk him to his room and get him into bed. It's not too late, so hopefully he'll be able to sleep off his hangover before we leave tomorrow.

Nash and I rejoin the party where dancing and singing still ensues.

"Is he okay?" Myles asks when I sink back into the sofa.

"He'll be fine. I think he just drank too much too fast."

Myles nods. It looks like he wants to say more, but he doesn't.

Ten minutes later a pack of playing cards appears, and we wind up playing three or four rounds—I lose count—of gin rummy. Stavros throws a fit when he continually loses every single game to me—yes, me—and stalks off to bed like a petulant child. He doesn't come back.

Gemma, who I think might be more drunk than I've ever seen her, smartly follows suit, with Brin right behind her. Emma starts tidying up and forces Nash to help her. JP heads to bed under the guise of checking on Beau, which leaves me and Myles. Again.

I start a game of solitaire because Emma refuses to let me help clean up. Apparently cooking six nights out of seven exempts me from any other household chores.

"Tag team?" Myles suggests as he perches beside me.

"Sure," I chuckle.

So, we take it in turns tidying the cards up by way of solitaire. We do it the traditional way—drawing three cards off the pile rather than one, just to make it a bit more difficult. We're still playing when Nash and Emma head to bed, stumbling on their way.

"I'm always surprised by how close they are," Myles admits once they're out of earshot.

I nod to myself because I've had the same thought many times. "They've always been like that, even when we were little. It's nice, I guess, 'cause she's our only cousin."

"Really?"

"Yeah. Dad doesn't have any siblings, and Aunt Sara and Uncle Steve only had Emma. One was enough, apparently."

"Nice that she's your age, though."

"Definitely. Mum and Sara were close growing up and they always said they'd want to raise their kids together. I don't think they were expecting to have *quite* so many."

"Yeah, you don't hear about quadruplets often. The house I was in when I was growing up, just down the road was a set of triplets—they were supposed to be quadruplets but one of them died during labour. That's the only other time I've heard of it."

113

"That's sad. I don't know if I'd cope knowing one of my siblings had died." *Knowing that, only ten years ago, it could've been me.*

Myles turns to me with a funny look. "It is sad. Can we pretend I said something witty or intelligent instead of just downright morbid?"

I giggle a little. I hadn't necessarily minded the conversation, morose as it was. "Sure, Einstein. I won't hold your ability to lower the tone against you."

He covers his chest with his hands. "Thank you so much."

"Anytime," I say as I pat the hands covering his chest.

Cards tidied up, I stack them in a pile and set them on the coffee table.

"What do you say…one more drink and a game of Snap?" Myles suggests.

"I've just tidied up!"

He grins. "So? Snap is fun. *Drunk Snap* is even better."

"Snap gives me anxiety—I don't cope well with the stress it causes. And I'm not that drunk."

"Easily fixed." He stands from his place and snatches my empty wine glass off the table and heads for the kitchen.

I stand too, but don't make any attempt to move. I just watch him.

He returns with a newly topped up glass for me, and an open beer for himself. He sets them on the table, then takes the cards in his hand. Circling my wrist, he pulls me onto the sofa next to him.

"Numbers or shapes?"

"I don't want to play," I insist.

"Of course, you do. Numbers or shapes?" He repeats.

"Shapes is too easy and there aren't enough numbers—we'll be here for hours," I moan, frowning. I really don't want to play Snap.

"Then I'll slimline the pack and we'll do numbers."

He separates the pack into four, then removes the numbers 6-9 from each so we've still got seven ways to match. I watch his slender fingers shuffle the cards with ease, like he's done it millions of times before. Then he starts splitting them between the two of us.

"Do you play card games a lot, Myles?"

"I did growing up," he says, gaze cast down. "Wasn't a lot to do at my house so we played cards to pass the time."

"I thought you'd be better at Rummy, then."

He smirks. "Rummy is a game of chance. Not a lot of strategy involved. I'm better at Poker."

"Why doesn't that surprise me?" I huff. Men love to say they're good at Poker. I'm sure it's something to do with wanting to seem intelligent, but what really concerns me is men who *are* good at Poker, because it means they're crap with their emotions—i.e., they don't show any ever. Beau and Nash were always rubbish at Poker because they wear their emotions on their faces for everyone to see.

Myles's grin widens, and he finishes splitting the cards between us. "I hoped I was less predictable than that."

"Yeah…aren't you supposed to be if you're an alleged seasoned Poker player?"

"No alleging about it," he says with a nonchalant sniff. "Ask Beau, we've played loads of times."

"Beau is a sore loser—he'll tell me you're shit either way."

Myles snorts. "True." Then he holds my gaze with such a playful intensity, my resolve at not playing this children's game completely crumbles. "Come on, Birdie. Play with me."

Chapter Fifteen

A Tool for Pleasure

SHERIDAN

This man is really testing my limits, but I'll bite, if not for any other reason than I don't think I'm currently physically capable of saying no. Pathetic, I know, but that's apparently my new state of being whenever Myles is in the vicinity.

Completely and totally pathetic.

I try to suck in a breath as subtly as I can. "Who's going first?"

His smile is blinding and beautiful. "Ladies first. Always."

I turn my first card over, placing it between us on the sofa cushion.

Queen of Clubs.

Myles follows suit, slapping his on top of mine.

Queen of Diamonds.

"Snap." He grins.

I let out a pained sigh. "Shit shuffle."

He sticks his tongue out at me while he collects the cards and adds them to his pile. He starts again, turning over the 3 of Spades. I cover it with a 5 of Clubs, and on and on we go.

Out of maybe ten pairs, I get two snaps in before him. It really is not my game, and my heart is rioting in my chest because of it. I'm not made for games like this. The anxiety practically slaughters me.

For some reason, I think downing a glass of wine will help me, but if anything, it makes me worse—my inhibitions are low, my reaction times slower.

And I'm pretty sure he's cheating.

"Snap!" I shout, as he does at the same time. "Fuck off, that was mine!" My heartbeat is thudding in my ears, mouth dry, fingers shaking.

"No, it was mine," He insists, trying to push my hand away from where it's quite clearly on top of the pile.

"Myles!"

"Sheridan," he says with the coolness of a freaking cucumber.

"You're cheating," I accuse.

"I'm doing no such thing."

As if I've forgotten I'm a grown woman, and not a scorned eight-year-old, I try to pry them out of his grip. "Give them to me."

"No chance, Birdie." He holds them high above his head.

Wine fully soaked into my bloodstream, forgetting where I am and who I'm with, I lunge forward in a farcical attempt at getting them back from him. Having seen him standing next to my twin brothers, I know Myles has an inch or two on them height-wise. Which means he towers over me. So, when he lifts his arm higher, I do the only thing I can do and use his shoulders as an aid to help me stand up on the sofa.

He starts laughing. "What are you doing?"

I grab his wrist and bring it to my chest, prying the cards free with my other hand. "These. Are. *Mine,*" I growl.

Suddenly my legs are swept from under me, and I fall back into the sofa cushions with a helpless yelp. "Myles!"

The culprit covers my mouth with his large hand, because I've lost the ability to control the volume of my voice now, as well. He hovers over me, his other hand on the back of my bare thigh. His thumb begins a lazy stroke of my skin.

Heat engulfs me like a burning flame. The intensity in his gaze now is severe, a complete contradiction to the way he touches me.

Lord, help me...

"I thought you weren't competitive, Sheridan."

The use of my first name like that, spoken all dark and silky has my insides ready to internally combust. I'm aware I must look like some kind of startled, deranged bird when he removes his hand from my mouth, and I'm staring at him with an open mouth and wide eyes. "I'm not. I don't like cheating."

"Birdie, that wasn't cheating." He tucks a strand—one rogue curl—of my hair behind my ear.

I can hardly breathe. "I won that round."

"I don't think so."

I can feel it—that calloused hand of his—moving north up the back of my thigh at a pace that shouldn't be legal. It's torturous. Cruel, even.

Goosebumps are rising all along my limbs.

His eyes never leave mine, not even when he starts stroking my cheek with the back of his index finger. His tenderness is debilitating, and I am no longer in control. At least my brain isn't. My body is because my fingers do whatever they want. Like, trailing the hem of his T-shirt.

"Mine," I mutter, but I'm not sure if I'm talking about the cards anymore.

He sucks in a breath. "Agree to disagree."

His touch on the back of my leg grows tantric, and my breath catches before I breathe out, "Myles."

"Yes, Birdie?"

I don't know what comes over me, but I do know I'm tired of waiting. "Kiss me, please."

His eyes flare with something carnal and joyous. In the next instance, he snatches the cards out of my hand, tosses them away, and grabs the backs of both my legs to yank me closer to him.

Then his mouth is on mine, and I learn what it's like to be kissed by a real man. By a man that really wants me.

Myles pulls no punches. He's eager and direct and downright punishing. His tongue plunders my mouth after barely licking the seam of my lips, and I let out the feeblest moan imaginable.

He growls in return like a kind of starved animal, and his grip on my leg tightens.

I wrap my arms around his shoulders and smooth my hands down his back, applying a light pressure so that he sinks his body onto mine. I want to feel his weight on me—to feel his strength and mass suffocate my own.

"You're unreal," he grunts, pulling my lip between his teeth. It hurts but I like it.

"I'm quite real," I assure him, pushing my fingers through his hair.

A shiver rolls through him, so I scratch his scalp with my nails. He produces a strangled whine, and God if that doesn't boost my ego a little bit.

"Sheridan, I'm pretty sure you're something out of a fantasy."

"Don't be ridiculous," I mutter and shove my tongue into his delicious mouth. He tastes like beer and chocolate—an interesting combination, but not totally awful. Definitely not a reason to stop.

"Is praise not your thing, Birdie?" His voice is like pure gravel, and I feel it straight to that sacred place between my legs.

"Not particularly," I admit. Because it's true—I don't need a man to tell me I take him well, or that *I feel good*. "But your voice is an aphrodisiac by itself." And I mean that. He could probably read a weather report and it'd make me wet.

Myles groans, and I feel his already stiff length get harder against the inside of my thigh. Shameless, I lift my hips a little to feel him against my core. He hisses, and I smile into our kiss.

"Baby," he chokes, and that is like a shot straight to my veins.

I can feel the slickness between my legs. I can't remember the last time I was this wet for a man. "I like that," I tell him.

"Like what?" His breathy question is like heaven to the ears.

I slide my hands beneath his T-shirt to feel his warm skin against my palms. "When you call me baby. And Birdie."

He starts moving his kisses south, and while I mourn the intimacy, my body lights up under the attention. "Anything else?"

Before I know it, he's lifted the skirt of my dress up and is sucking on the skin of my stomach.

Oh God, I'm so wet. "That," I gasp. "I like that a lot."

"This?" He asks, before leaving a new mark just below my belly button.

"Yes, that." I squirm, shoving my hands through his hair again. He practically purrs at the touch. "Anything with your mouth."

I see the smirk on his mouth. I see it when he lowers himself further and pushes my legs wider apart. And I watch him with rapt fascination when he pulls the seat of my knickers aside and stares at my glistening pussy with damn stars in his eyes.

"Even here?" His breath whispers *there*, and I almost choke.

"Fuck—*God* yes."

Once again, Myles saves any preamble for another time, and dives right in.

I sink into the sofa cushions, writhing with pleasure from the skill of his tongue. And what gets me even more is that he's clearly enjoying himself as much as I am. Plus, he's fucking good at it. I didn't think such a man existed, contrary to all those romance novels my sister has me read.

A real man is here and wants to eat my pussy.

"Yes, Myles," I pant, gripping his hair tightly. *"Yes,* that's so good."

He makes another growling sound as he feasts on me—dauntless and devouring. *"You* are good," he says into my core. "You taste incredible."

I squirm again, wrapping my thighs around his head so he can't go anywhere.

He doesn't seem to mind. In fact, it seems to spur him on. He readjusts himself and it's like his face disappears between my legs. His arms wrap around my hips. One hand playing with my clit while the other presses down on my stomach.

"Oh God," I whimper. "Oh God. Please tell me you have a condom."

He pauses with his work, head popping up. His mouth his covered in me, beard glistening, and yet doesn't seem to give a fuck. "I'm… You want that?"

"Yes, Myles. I want you inside me. Like, ten minutes ago."

He blows out a breath and my pussy contracts from the feel of it. He notices it, and a dirty smirk crosses his pretty features. "I don't know. I wasn't exactly planning on having sex this week."

He starts to lift after giving me a sharp nod, but before I let him run off, I drag him towards me again so I can kiss my mess off his face.

The look I'm met with when I pull away is dazed.

"Woman of my dreams," he mutters as he stumbles away.

I take my dress and my knickers off before he comes back, because even if he doesn't have one, he's not getting out of this now without both of us coming.

"Jesus Christ," Myles chokes at the sight of me.

I sit up straighter. "Have you got one?"

He flashes a foil square at me, and I could squeal with relief. I stand up, ready to strip him down, and he drags me toward him, my naked body flush against his.

Myles kisses me as I undress him, and then he sits back on the sofa and tugs me with him onto his lap. We both look down at the weapon he's carrying, and my mouth goes dry. It's *big*.

My breathing becomes laboured when he takes it in his hand. He's leaking from the tip, so he runs his thumb over the crease, and then he holds it up to me. I take it in my mouth without hesitation, which earns another groan.

"This is not how I pictured my week going," he admits as he watches me suck on his thumb with rapt attention.

"Me neither."

Myles rips the foil packet open. In one swift movement he rolls the condom on, and then he takes me by the hips. He gives me a look so determinedly confident that I'm soaked all over again. "Ride me until you come, Birdie."

I grip his shoulders and sink onto his length, choking as he fills me. "Fucking *hell*, Myles."

His grip on my hips tightens. "Baby, you're so tight."

I knew I would be. It's been a while since I slept with someone and I'm not one for dildos at home. I feel like I've been impaled. "Doesn't help that you're packing a fucking weapon of a cock."

He leans forwards, his arms wrapping tightly around me. "Stop stroking my ego and fuck me, Sheridan."

I'm still adjusting. "I don't think I can."

"Bullshit." He grips my hips and lifts me up, "Just like…" then slams me back down, "that."

He muffles my scream with a kiss but repeats the move like I'm some flimsy doll. He is the master, and I am his tool for pleasure.

Eventually, I get the hang of it. My hips move of their own accord, and Myles explores my chest, tits, and throat with his mouth. He worships me, and I am utterly here for it.

I drag my fingers through his scalp and down his back while he bruises my chest with his mouth and my hips with his fingers.

We're rough with each other—a side I didn't expect him to have, and yet it makes me like him just that bit more.

I bounce and bounce on him, until he lifts me up and turns me around to face the room.

I'm suddenly reminded of where we are and what we're doing, and yet I find myself not caring. *That's* not like me. But the thought of someone, anyone, coming in here and catching us, sends a strangely delicious thrill through me. I'm wet all over again.

Myles drops me back on his dick and slides an arm around me, the other hand still on my hip. He whispers filthy nothings in my ear—not praising but just delicious to listen to.

He lowers a hand to play with my clit again and wraps the other around my throat. When the slightest bit of pressure is added, paired with his lips on my shoulder, I come apart like a cheap tent.

I try to contain my cries as my body spasms in Myles's strong grip, and I feel him coming right along with me.

"Fucking hell, Sheridan," Myles pants, pressing his lips to my back, right at the top of my spine.

All I can do is nod.

He laughs breathily. "Forgotten how to speak?"

I just nod again.

He eases me up off him, legs like jelly, and stands behind me. He wraps his arms around my middle, hard dick nestled against my backside, and starts walking us through the hall.

"You're so beautiful," Myles whispers, his teeth nipping at the lobe of my ear.

I hum, because apparently good dick turns me into a useless heap, but I cling to him like a lifeline.

He chuckles again, his fingers delicately stroking my abdomen where he's left a litany of little purple love bites. "Let's get cleaned up, baby."

Chapter Sixteen
Back to Reality

MYLES

If you'd have told me a week ago that I'd be sharing a bed with Beau Bennett's sister after shagging her senseless on a communal sofa, I would have told you to get your head out your backside and go see a doctor. Yet here I am, sprawled on my back in the middle of Sheridan's bed, still half hard with her limbs draped over mine, her finger tracing the lines of my tattoos.

We'd used the en-suite shower together to clean up, gone for another round, wherein I shoved her up against the wall and feasted on that delicious heat between her legs—again—while tugging myself to orgasm along with her. I'm usually more ambivalent about oral sex, but Sheridan tastes fucking divine.

After drying her off, I thought she'd want me to leave—I wasn't really sure what this meant now, if it meant anything at all—but when I made for the door, she yanked me back and shoved me onto the mattress. Then she snuggled up to me like I was her favourite soft toy, and I haven't moved since. I don't think I ever want to.

"Why a bear?" She asks into the quiet room as her fingers trace the lines on my abdomen. It's the first time either of us have said anything since we got into bed.

My hand has been grazing up and down her spine for a while, and I pause at her question. "It's a bit of a long story." And likely one other reason Beau doesn't want me anywhere near her.

Sheridan rests her chin on my chest, and I tuck one of her curls out of her face. "Is it a sad story?"

"It's definitely not a happy one."

"Then you can tell me another time." She gives me a beautiful, impossibly soft smile, and I can't help but stroke the apple of her cheek. Something about those big blue eyes and that sated expression has my chest squeezing like it's trapped in a God damn vice.

"Why the birds?"

After a vacant pause, she giggles. "Um, no reason."

"None?"

"No. Just…really like birds. I like how colourful they can be. The fact that there's *so many* different types, breeds. Yeah… I just like birds."

"Well, that's okay. Not all tattoos have to have a meaning." I assure her. "Do you go to London a lot?"

She seems thrown off by the question, a change of subject. "More than I'd like."

"Have you ever noticed there's an unusual amount of these green exotic birds flying around at all?"

This perks her up. "No."

"Well, a few years ago, a zookeeper at London City Zoo accidentally left the cage open on the parakeet enclosure, and they all escaped. Rather than heading back to Africa or India they just spread out across the city and acclimatised. Now they're fucking everywhere." This hasn't ever been proven but it's definitely the version of the story I enjoy the most. It's easier to tell a fabricated story than *they just showed up one day and never left.*

"No way."

"Yes way."

"So, there's just parakeets knocking about all 'round London now?"

"Yeah. *Loads* of them."

Her gaze drifts off. "Damn. I need to keep an eye out for that."

"You're in North London when you go, right?" She nods. "Well, if you find time to go to Hampstead Heath, you're sure to see some there."

"Huh," she says, and then snuggles back into me. "Do you miss London?"

I wish I could say that I did—that I had something back there for me to mourn, someone to keep in touch with—but it would be a lie. "Nope."

"Not even a little bit?"

I shake my head even though she isn't looking at me. "Not at all."

Sheridan exhales heavily, and I feel her breath skitter across my skin. It raises goosebumps, but that's nothing compared to what my heart rate does when she presses her lips against my collar in a soft kiss.

I stroke my hand over her wild hair when she lays her head back down, and I fall asleep to the sound of her breathing.

* * *

The next morning, I wake early and sneak out of the room, but not before leaving Sheridan with a kiss she won't be forgetting any time soon. I make myself a coffee and sit on the sofa with it while the news is on at a low volume. This would be my routine if I were at home, sans the part where I leave a beautiful woman in bed by herself. Considering we barely slept last night, I'm not surprised that Sheridan grants herself a lie-in for our final morning.

Everyone else starts trickling in one by one, each with a sore head. Brinsley takes Hector for his morning walk—with a comment that she's going to visit the guest services to make an almighty complaint about the bed situation—and I'm surprised to see Beau up with a clearer head than one should when they drink as much as he did last night. He still refuses to talk to me.

Once everyone has surfaced, we have one final 'family breakfast' before we pack our things and start loading the cars ready to go home.

I watch with a clenched jaw as Beau intercepts Sheridan on her way to the car and hijacks her luggage and Hector's bed, packing them into the boot of his Range Rover. I half expected it anyway, but it still pisses me the fuck off. Yeah, *now* he wants the dog with anxiety and incontinence issues in his car. Just so he can get his sister away from me.

Never mind 'the Bear'—I feel like the big bad fucking wolf.

We each do one last sweep of the cabin to make sure we've got everything before we leave. Satisfied, we split up into the two cars.

This time, I'm carrying Brin, Bailey, Stavros, and Nash. How I ended up with the faux Greek on both journeys, I don't know. I must've pissed off a Greek God in a previous life. At least I can go home today with the satisfaction of—hopefully—never seeing that man again. Somehow, I think a week with Stavros was even too much for Nash. And they're business partners.

The drive is quiet, and I can only assume it's because everyone is still feeling the aftereffects of last night's 'farewell' party. I don't even bother putting the radio on. I'm just grateful it's not too long a drive back to Coventry.

We don't stop this time, either, which means Hector's travel tablets worked and there hasn't been any nervous urinating in Beau's car. Absolutely typical, considering I feel it would be almost justified if that did happen.

Maybe I'll mock up a quick comic strip about it later just to make myself feel better.

The troops rouse just as we get off the bypass on Beau's side of Coventry. They're practical chatterboxes when I pull into the driveway of his ridiculous sized home. Beau's house is a four-bed, three-bath detached monstrosity, complete with double garage, a gaming room, and surprisingly underwhelming back garden. And he lives here alone.

"Thanks for driving, Myles." Brinsley pats my arm as I help her unload her luggage from the boot.

"No problem. Glad you could get some rest."

"You should do the same." She gives me her sister's smile, and yet it doesn't have anywhere near the effect it would if it came from Sheridan, even though they've got near identical faces. *Near* identical.

"I plan on it."

I help the others with moving their bags around until everyone has what they need where they need it to be. And then we say goodbye.

The boys get handshakes, and the girls get hugs. Except Gemma, who I think is just awkward rather than frigid. I'm not one to push physical contact so I leave her with a polite wave.

Sheridan comes last, right on the tail of her sister. Even though we haven't spoken much this morning, our embrace is not awkward. It's comfortable. Almost *too* comfortable, and I know Beau is watching because I can feel his gaze on us from across the gravel drive.

"I guess I'll see you soon?" I pose it as a question, so quietly there's not a chance anyone will hear it. "Hopefully."

A hand slips low to my backside, and for a crazy minute I think she's copping a shameless feel in front of everyone. Then I realise she's slipping something into my back pocket. I try to keep my face neutral.

"Hopefully," she agrees, and then pulls away from me. I hate the absence of her body instantly.

I wander back to my car, pausing to look over the roof and watch Sheridan zip away in her tiny green Mini, her sister in the passenger seat. The other cars follow soon after, until it's just me left standing in the driveway, Beau hovering by the door. I cast him a look to find him hesitating.

He throws a thumb toward the house. "Want to come in for a cuppa before you go?"

It's an olive branch if I've ever heard one, and yet… "I'm good."

With that, I slide into my car again and drive off.

When I get home, the first thing I do is strip out my clothes and shove them in the washing machine, along with anything else out of my duffle that will fit and put it on to wash.

It's not until I've crawled into bed, ready to sleep the day away, that I realise I never retrieved Sheridan's note from my back pocket.

"Motherfucker."

* * *

SHERIDAN

I drop Brin off at her place and decline her offer to go in for a drink. I just want to curl up on the sofa and binge-watch something shit on the telly while stuffing my face and intermittently napping.

When I pull into the little space outside the cottage, I don't think I've ever been more relieved to be home. I take Hector inside first, still asleep and tucked into his bed, and put him down in his usual place in the living room by the fireplace. Then I retrieve the rest of my things, lock the car and the front door, and change into something comfortable and cool. I've already decided that I'm going to treat myself to a takeaway for dinner, which I haven't done for months.

I queue up the first season of *Friends*—because I really need a fill of '90s Matthew Perry—and sink into the oblivion of my sofa.

Though I laugh at the TV and keep an eye trained on Hector, I also keep peering at my phone, waiting for a certain unknown number to pop up. I didn't write Myles a crazy love note, if that's what you're thinking. I just wrote my number on an old receipt I had in my bag and shoved it in his back pocket. After what we did last night, I felt assured that he likes me and did the boldest thing I've ever done: gave a boy—a man—my phone number.

The only problem is that I'm impatient and want him to text me *now*.

I hear the clock ticking on the wall behind me and count the tocks. I reach 3,600 before I realise that I've wasted an hour waiting for it and missed three episodes and countless Chandler-isms.

To make myself feel less plaintive, I put my phone on silent and shove it between the sofa cushions.

Hours later, when I dig around for it to order my takeaway, I have messages from my mother, Brin, Emma, and Marina—my boss. But none from an unknown number and a certain sexy art teacher.

Chapter Seventeen
First Day of School

MYLES

My palms are sweating. I'm standing behind my desk in my classroom, glancing towards the door every five seconds as I watch the queue of eleven-year-olds grow and grow out in the hall ready to be let in. There is no reason for me to leave them outside, raucously waiting for their very first day as a high schooler to begin. The bell hasn't gone yet but there isn't a rule that says I can't let them into Form early.

Form. *Form.*

Such a funny term for what it is: a fifteen-minute period at the start of the day to confirm attendance and pass on any important information to twenty kids who probably couldn't care less.

My nerves are getting the better of me.

The classroom is a wall of windows on the hall side, so the children can see everything I'm doing—or rather *not* doing. I pretend to be doing something important for another minute when I'm really just rearranging my notes for the day and will have to arrange them back once this is over.

I finally move to open the door and plaster on a calm smile. "Good morning, everyone."

The noisy hustle silences at my appearance, and that is truly terrifying.

"When you come in, I want you to take a seat wherever you'd like, but choose wisely, because it'll be yours for the rest of the year."

Moving aside, the shuffle begins into the classroom. I haven't quite figured out how I'm going to police the seating arrangement, but they don't need to know that.

I have admittedly been fortunate with my Form group—a bunch of Year 7s experiencing their first day at Webster's right along with me. I know Brinsley hasn't been quite so fortunate, as she's taken over a group of Year 10s from her predecessor. Fourteen-year-olds are much less easy to control.

I know from the faculty induction we were given, new Year 7s are grouped in forms with at least one of their friends from primary school by request where possible. This is now glaringly obvious as a group of four girls sit together at the front, giggling any time they throw a look at me, and a good ten boys who gather over the back tables. The remaining students find seats where they can.

"Alright," I collect a sheet from my desk and hand it to the table of girls, "I'm handing out a blank table plan. You need to write your name where you're sitting and pass it on." I then collect the stack of school planners on my desk and leave them on the table on the other side. "Same premise with the planners. Take one and pass it on. When that's done, we're going to take the register. When I call your name, you need to come up to the front and get your schedule for the year."

The room becomes a hive of movement and murmuring. I take a seat behind my desk and wait for the table plan to come back to me. I tag it with '7WEB3'—the name of our Form group and slide it into the tray on my desk. Behind me, the whiteboard is turned on displaying my computer screen. The school's logo is at the top, my name underneath it, and the form group below that.

After the register is done, I play the video all the form tutors have been given, watching along with the kids as Eric Paulson, the head teacher, gives a stiff welcome introduction that looks like it was recorded about fifteen years ago. Knowing how long Paulson has been the head teacher here, that is entirely possible.

For the Year 7 students, there's an assembly in one of the halls tomorrow morning, so I make sure they write it in their diaries and mark the hall on their maps before they leave.

Given it's a Tuesday, after an inset day yesterday, my first class of the day is '9B', my secondary group of Year 9s. I have two groups of Year 7s, 8s and 9s, and then one group of Year 10s and 11s—my GCSE students.

I instruct them to sit where they please as I did with my Form group, and hand out a seating plan while I introduce myself and the curriculum this term. Thankfully, nowhere this year in the specifics does it mention 'A Study in Pink', which leaves no opportunity for any of the students to draw, or paint, or impression genitalia.

"Sir?" A boy at the back with dark tousled hair and a lanky frame sticks his hand up.

I quickly consult my seating plan. "Yes, Jamie?"

The teenager lowers his hand and leans forward. "My brother had Miss Rose last year, and he said they got to draw dicks and vag."

I close my eyes briefly, trying not to laugh. "Try not to use those words on school grounds, please?" A great start to my first day. I know they're trying to test my boundaries. I expected it.

"What, vag?" He's grinning.

"No, you know what."

"Oh right, yeah. Cocks, then."

I give the boy a withering glare. "Did you have a question or are you trying to fluster me?"

"Both?"

I roll my eyes but can't help my smile. Oh, to be fourteen again and discovering my body and the things it can do. "Go on."

"Well, are you gonna be doing that? 'Cause my brother's is up on the canteen wall and I want that, too."

"Which one is your brother's?" Another student asks—one of the girls. I try to hide my shock.

"The pink one."

I have to roll my eyes again. "No, Jamie, we will not be doing the same study this year. But whatever you end up with at the end of the year could still go on the wall. If it's good enough."

"I'm *really* good," he insists. "I just thought we'd be drawing penises and shit."

"If you're as good as you claim you are, you'll excel at whatever creative task you're given. Right?"

That shuts him up and sets a determined look on his face.

"We're not doing anything like last year, because this year you'll be narrowing down your own skills. You'll get to research a whole host of well-known artists, whittle it down to two you like the most, or feel most similar to creatively, and create a portfolio of works based on that."

The prospect of creative freedom seems to encourage them.

"There's a folder on each of your tables with a selection of artists and a brief bio. You're going to spend the first hour researching and the second hour coming up with theme ideas to do in their impression. And when I say theme, I mean something cohesive—animals, transport, a location, fashion, nature.

"Next week we'll do the same again, except the first hour we'll be going to one of the computer rooms so you can look a little further than what's in front of you. Any questions?"

"Can our theme be genitalia?"

"No. Keep it clean, please. I'll be consulting on all your themes before you start your workload in a couple of weeks."

A scruffy boy at the back of the room puts his hand up. I notice his polo shirt is far too large and heavily discoloured. Something tugs in my chest.

I check my seating plan again. "Yes, Sam?"

"What if we're not very good at art? At all?"

I study him for a moment—the shaggy hair, gaunt features, hollow cheeks, slumping figure. I feel him a kindred spirit to when I was at school—clothed in hand-me-downs and desperate for a haircut and a meal that hadn't come rationed out of the freezer. Bottling my anger and letting it fester into something it shouldn't. Avoiding the unwarranted wrath of a foster parent who considered me nothing more than a nuisance, who fostered for all the wrong reasons.

I shouldn't project onto an oblivious boy, but I can spot a child of the system as well as a hawk can spot a field mouse.

"It doesn't matter," I tell Sam honestly. It doesn't matter to me that he thinks he can't draw, or paint, or impress. Because not everyone can, and there's undoubtedly something else in another classroom that he *can* do. "We're not just drawing in this class. You find a style that you're *most* comfortable with and go from there. And if you're still not sure, then that's what I'm here for."

He doesn't look pacified by me, but he doesn't say anything else.

I tell the class to begin.

* * *

At half twelve the bell signals the beginning of lunch. On Tuesdays, the period between morning break and lunchtime is spent with my form group again for PSHE. I'm not entirely sure why it's not handled in science lessons but what do I know? I've had the training to teach it and so I must.

Once my classroom is empty, I lock it up and head to the staff room for lunch. There's a small selection of sandwiches, snacks, and drinks, so I take my pick and find a table. Within five minutes, Brinsley joins me with her pre-made lunch of some variety of tomato pasta.

"You. Are. So. Lucky," she tells me with a worn-out look.

"I am?"

"Yeah. Not only do you not have to teach a bunch of fifteen-year-olds about safe sex measures," I wince at the thought—my lesson plan covered bullying today, "but all your lessons are two hours long. I've had sixty kid's names to go through today, and I've still got another forty to go!"

I pull a face. "Sorry?"

Brin huffs. "I bet you are." She gives me a look, gaze scanning my clothes.

I glance down at myself. "What?"

"I'm used to seeing you in shorts or jeans… This is weird. I didn't expect you in this."

Perhaps my work wardrobe is somewhat eclectic, but I didn't want to cycle through black or grey trousers with plain shirts every day. Today I'm wearing a black dress shirt with light grey plaid suit trousers and braces.

I shrug. "I didn't want to be boring."

"When me and Shez were about fourteen, there was this new Geography teacher that started, and he always wore trousers like that, but with a white shirt and black braces. And he'd got a stretcher in one of his ears and these thick black glasses. *All* the girls fancied him."

"Except you, right?" I joke.

"No, I did fancy him. It was Sheridan who thought he was trying too hard."

I snort, even though the subject of Sheridan makes me a little angry. And only at myself. The day after we got back from our vacation, I went through every social media platform I could think of trying to find her and failed miserably. She doesn't even have a LinkedIn, and I don't know the name of the company she works for.

I could've asked Beau or Nash, but it would've ended up in a fight I don't want to have. I was too nervous to ask Brin or Shirley because it meant possibly letting on what had happened between us. There was the possibility that Sheridan had already told them but given the way the two of them spoke to me, I assumed that wasn't the case. There hadn't been a Bennett family gathering for me to attend since coming back, and with the animosity between Beau and I, I'm not entirely sure I'd go to one if the opportunity arose.

Still, I think about Sheridan—Birdie—and *that* night all too often.

"If he worked here now, would you ask him out?"

Brinsley looks horrified. "No, I have a boyfriend. Plus, he's at least ten years older than me, which I find a bridge too far. Add that he was *actually* my teacher once upon a time makes the whole thing a massive no."

"Fair enough."

"I was going to say, that's you now." Brin gives me a pointed look. "*You're* the teacher all the girls are gonna fancy."

"I can't see how that's a good thing." And I remember the French teacher saying a similar thing.

"It's fine if you don't do anything about it."

I can't keep the grimace off my face, and Brinsley laughs maniacally.

"Your face. Myles, you're too good for this world."

"I think not pursuing a student just makes me an average member of society."

"Bare minimum." She points her fork at me. "Valid."

Shirley, in a form fitting burgundy pant suit, suddenly appears and slides into a free seat. "I know this is just gonna make my Brinsley roll her eyes, but this is *so* nice."

I chuckle, and sure enough, Brin rolls her eyes like a teenager. "I'm glad there's familiar faces here," I admit.

"I agree," Brin says with a forkful of pasta halfway to her mouth, "even if one of them is my mother."

Shirley swats her daughter's arm. "Before I forget—Myles, our next family meal is the first week of October for Brian's birthday. It's the first Sunday, so make sure you keep the day free.

I mark it in the calendar on my phone to appear contrite. "Noted." I might have to be dragged to it by my ears, though.

"Good lad. How's your first day going? I didn't see you at break time."

I'd hidden in my classroom at break to give myself fifteen minutes to breathe. I'd also seen Emily the French teacher prowling the halls and wasn't mentally prepared to be hit on like she had done nearly every day last week while I was settling in. I'd shoved my earphones in and pretended to be deep in concentration when she ambled past. Didn't stop her from knocking the door, though. I pretended not to hear her.

"Yeah, fine. Good. Overwhelming, but fine so far."

"When don't you have any classes?"

"Tomorrow before break, Thursday after break, and Monday middle period."

Brinsley's mouth falls. "You have *six* free hours a week?"

Brinsley is an English teacher, which means she has *two* classes per year group, and multiple lessons with them a week. At least three hours, as it's a core subject. Art is not a core subject and is only an elective for GCSE students.

Shirley leans in and mutters something to Brin, which I imagine to be along the lines of the fact that I am undoubtedly paid less for the pleasure. When Shirley pulls back, Brin seems suitably scorned.

"I also have Thursday afternoons free, so if you ever want to stop by my office, feel free."

Given the lack of a mother figure in my childhood, I'm grateful for the offer and likely to take her up on it. "Thanks, Shirl."

Chapter Eighteen
The Weird & The Dull

SHERIDAN

My phone vibrates aggressively with an onslaught of text messages, and it gives me an instant headache. What's worse, is that I already know who they're from and what they're about without even having to look at my phone.

Brin
Oh, it's a good one today, Shez.
SO GOOD.
Are you ready?
White shirt.
Black tie (with tie clip).
MAROON trousers.
And a freaking BRUSHED WOOL GREY WAISTCOAT.
I REPEAT.
A FUCKING WAISTCOAT.

Me
The black tie ruins it.

Brin
Glaring emoji

Every weekday, Brinsley sends me a catalogue of what Myles is wearing, and every day I pick fault with it, just out of spite. We've been doing it for a month now. I'm not even angry at Myles for ditching my phone number and leaving me wondering. I thought I would be but I'm not.

Maybe I wasn't as into him as I thought I was. Maybe the bubble that came with being on vacation with him made him seem marvellous and handsome and special, and now that we're back in the real world, that bubble has popped.

And that's okay.

I pick fault with his outfits because I think Brin might finally get the hint that I don't care. Which I don't. I definitely don't imagine him in said outfit, and then peeling him out of it at the end of a very hard day playing teacher to bratty teens, while his pretty hazel eyes track my every move with heady lust.

See? Zero fucks.

Myles was good in bed for one night on holiday, and that's absolutely okay. People have one-night stands and say things they don't mean all the time.

I let my head fall against the table where I'm working and release a pent-up groan. It's high-pitched and petty and pitiful. Every day Brin reminds me of him, and every day I go through the same pathetic thought cycle.

Why didn't he text me?

I need to get out of the house.

I stretch when I stand and leave my study with a yawn. Hector barks when he spots me and heads for the front door. Walking the dog seems like a great idea.

Hooked up to his lead, we head outside and toward the village. It's warm still, even for early October, so I'm only wearing jeans and a long-sleeve T-shirt. We walk our classic loop—down into the village so I can pass by the shop for my essentials, and then down through the pub garden to the canal and back along the path to my back garden.

When we slip around the front, Nash is on the bench by my front door waiting. I didn't realise what the time is, and I forgot it's Wednesday. He said last week he'd come for dinner on Wednesday.

"Sorry. Forgot the day," I lament as we head inside. Once Hector is unhooked, he runs off out of sight.

Nash smiles. "Don't worry," he says.

I wander off to the kitchen and stick the kettle on. He's still in his suit so I know he's just come straight from work.

Nash and Stavros started a business together out of university—an online travel agent for elite clientele only, featuring luxury properties and first-class travel. Beau is a member. I *could* be a member if I wanted, but I rarely travel for pleasure, and I don't book luxury hotels for work, so it seems pointless.

When I come back with our tea, I find him not in the living room where he usually is, but in my study. *Oh shit.* I left the office door open in my haste to get out of the house earlier. I never leave the door open.

He's standing right in front of my storyboard for *Goth Frogs*, hands tucked into the pockets of his navy trousers. Sometimes, from behind, I can't tell him and Beau apart. The only distinguishing difference now is the length of their dark hair and their clothes. Beau rarely wears a suit day-to-day, and his hair is longer. Nash's hair is a neat undercut which he usually styles back with wax.

If I wasn't his sister, he would terrify me.

Nash is not only wealthy and attractive, but he's imposing, too. He's got a complex about being born last and being the least understood out of all of us, which I struggle to accept. He's built like a tank, and people who meet him for the first time are often afraid of him.

"What's this?" He asks, with a lazy finger pointed at the storyboard.

"Nothing. Come sit in the lounge."

He turns to face me, expression ambivalent. "Think you'll ever grow out of your weird drawing phase?"

I flinch at his words. I can't help it. Even as a grown woman with a well-paid job and my own house, my brother's obvious distaste for my hobbies—and some might say talents—always hit a nerve.

We've been doing this dance since we were practical babies. I have a weird brain and Nash doesn't want to understand it. I draw weird pictures and he thinks there's something wrong with me.

When I was a teenager, it'd upset the hell out of me. With him joining in on everyone's critique of me, I'd go home crying and we wouldn't talk to each other for weeks at a time. Until that one day that changed everything.

I'm thrown back to that version of me at fifteen, when I was unstable and going through the motions every day wondering what I was doing to draw such negative attention to myself. I feel a foot tall while my big scary brother crowds me against a wall in the school halls and all his friends call me a psycho. I see a bottle of antidepressants and then steam from the hottest shower of my life, my naked legs barely keeping me up. And then I see a hospital bed and my mother's sallow eyes and my sister's heartbroken face, Beau's rage, and Nash, in the corner of the room making himself as small as possible even though he was already pushing six feet.

I have no desire to go back to that place—that utterly destitute frame of mind. I'm not that girl anymore.

Out of all my siblings, Nash and I have the worst relationship. Or we did when we lived at home. As adults, he tries harder with me, and I do with him. But on occasions like this, it's quite clear he still finds me to be strange.

Now, I also don't let his words affect me so much.

"I hope not," I tell him.

He takes in a deep breath, and I can see he regrets what he said. "I didn't mean it like that, Shez."

I turn away, knowing he'll follow me. I hope he's chivalrous enough to close the door behind him.

"You did mean it like that, Nash, just like I know it's one thing you'll never understand about me."

"Perhaps not. But I didn't want to upset you. I find your imagination a little wild, that's all."

"Rather a wild imagination than one like yours. Grey, straight," he seems to hate that word, "linear."

"Alright, alright. I get it."

I leave our tea on the coffee table and sink into the sofa. Nash removes his suit jacket, drapes it across the armchair and then sits next to me, snatching my hand to give it a squeeze.

"You think I'm boring."

I roll my eyes at him. "I don't think you're boring. I just think the inside of your brain is incredibly dull."

"The weird and the dull," he muses.

I give a little chuckle. "Anyway, onto more pressing matters. I forgot you were coming, and I don't have much in the way of food."

"I'll treat us to a curry, then."

"You really do know how to make a girl forgive you," I jest.

"I'm practising for my future spouse." He grins.

* * *

After curry is consumed and our argument long forgotten, Nash departs and heads back into the city, leaving me alone for the night.

I hole up in my study, real work shelved for my wild imagination to take over. I picture a fae woman, with thick black hair that falls to her hips, dark skin, and glowing ember eyes. I start to draw her, dressing her in white furs with raven collars, leather boots and fighting armour. I imagine her with jewellery on her ears, her nose, her lip, her fingers, her neck, her head. A fierce warrior queen.

I call her Caerwyn.

She falls in love with a human boy—man—who doesn't believe in magic after she is cursed by a bitter hag of a high priestess. I draw a human man—handsome, obviously—but when I'm done with him, I realise he's wearing a brushed wool waistcoat and maroon trousers. And he's blond.

I clear the page on my iPad and start again.

And I draw for hours, making plot notes as I go, until the sun rises again from the back garden, and I have an entirely new cartoon to animate when I'm ready. But I've not slept.

"Bollocks," I mutter to myself.

I have an appointment at lunchtime in the city, so I set my alarm for an hour before I make my way up to bed.

I haven't pulled an all-nighter for a very long time, and it wasn't even on purpose.

Turns out, being insulted does wonders for the imagination.

***

On Saturday morning I wake up in a hotel room in London. It's not my ideal way to wake up on the weekend, but the restaurant and the hotel I'm working for both had work starting on them this week and I needed to be on-site for a day with them. Well, half a day.

I shove my face between the pillows and scream. I hate being away from home. I don't know why I chose a career that requires that so often. I just want to make my silly little web shows with my silly little drawings and take my silly little dog for walks whenever I damn feel like it.

After contemplating my life choices for another half an hour, I finally peel myself out of bed. I turn the kettle on as I pass the little desk on my way to the window, and I throw the curtains open.

It's a pleasant day outside, which hopefully means the drive back to Coventry won't be so bad—people tend to be more stupid on the road when it rains. And yes, I did drive this time, no thanks to the train strikes. Fortunately, this fancy ass hotel came with parking when I booked directly—a perk I know for a fact doesn't come included with a membership from Nash's agency.

I'm about to finish making my tea when I spot movement in one of the trees in the hotel's courtyard.

There, on a low branch picking at acorns, are three green ring-necked parakeets.

Chapter Nineteen
MORTGAGE ADVICE

SHERIDAN

When I collect Hector from my parents on Sunday, I'm dressed up for the occasion.

"Happy birthday, Dad," I say, giving him a kiss on the cheek where he greets me in the front hall.

Oh, yeah. That occasion, too.

Mum and Dad live in a five-bed, three bath detached red brick just a stone's throw from Walsgrave hospital, and only a five-minute drive from my village. I'm never sure why they haven't sold up and moved to something smaller since none of us kids live there anymore, and it is a monstrous-size property for just two people.

"We're not ready to let it go yet," I remember Mum saying once. "All our best memories are here."

Sure. I reckon they've buried a dead body in the garden and are scared someone will find it. Mum definitely has a murderous streak in her. That, or it's worth a fortune now and they're planning a massive fucking holiday. Or a caravan, apparently.

As with any family birthdays now, we don't do anything extravagant, we just have a big family dinner. Our week away this summer was just an exception—some of us (me) were bullied into it.

"Thank you, Shez." Dad wraps an arm around my waist and gives me a squeeze.

Beau is already here, smugly parading around the house after another win for the Rangers yesterday. The club now remain undefeated since starting the season back in the summer, and yesterday was all thanks to Beau's hattrick. The media don't call him Bionic Beau for nothing.

Brinsley and Andy are also here, lounging on the loveseat in our parents' front room. Brin is talking animatedly about one of the kids at school while Andy ignores her in favour of something on his phone. I 'accidentally' knock into him on my way by them, and his phone tumbles to the floor, like Alice when she fell down the rabbit hole, backside up and all.

"Oops," I bite, moving through the room. I don't bother looking at him, but I know he's glaring at me.

By the headcount, we're only missing Nash, but given Beau's peacocking and Andy's sheer presence, it's going to be a long afternoon.

In the kitchen, I pour myself a glass of wine and drink the whole thing in one go. I don't drink at home without company, so the alcohol goes straight to my head.

"Oh," Mum appears, taking stock of the empty room, save for me and a bottle of wine, "been a week, has it?"

"Something like that," I mumble.

She kisses my temple and helps herself to a glass before topping mine up. "How was London?"

I pull a face. "Same as always. Overcrowded and full of snobs."

Shirley snorts. "I think that comes with the territory you work in, darling. Speak to Myles about it and I'm sure you'd find him to believe the opposite."

He already told me as much when we were lying in bed together *that* night. I hate being reminded of it. I think of those damn birds and want to launch my wine glass at the wall. I know that's theatrical of me, but it's infuriating. I managed to avoid the man for five whole years without consequence. I spend a week and one night in bed with him and I can't seem to think of anything else. It's absurd.

"Did you get your work done while you were there?" Mum continues, oblivious to my internal crisis.

"Yeah, I'll have to go back before re-opening, and eventually to visit those houses I drew up plans for."

"Might be cheaper to buy a place there."

"Har har," I deadpan. "How's the pup?" I ask, desperate for a change of subject.

"Oh, fine." She waves her hand dismissively. "All he does is sleep and eat. The only time he's ever a bother is when the postman comes."

"Post-"

"Oh, yes, postal worker."

Being the deputy head of a secondary school, Mum is always hot on what is and isn't acceptable language nowadays—unless we're talking about that French teacher, in which case anything is fair game. She never needs correcting, and neither does Dad.

"I'm glad he wasn't a pain."

"Never. But I do think he's ready to go home and cuddle his mum tonight."

I smile at that. If one man loves me, it's Hector.

The front door opens, and voices emerge—more than one. Nash's is distinguishable, but the other... For a moment, a yawning chasm of dread opens in me that he's brought Stavros with him. Then I hear the second voice properly, and I realise it's much worse than the faux Greek.

"Oh, good, Myles is here," Dad says quite clearly, as if he wanted the whole damn neighbourhood to hear. "He can't deny joining my Beach Boys tribute band on my birthday."

I look on in horror, but I'm not sure if it's because Myles is *here*, or because my dad wants him to pretend to be Carl Wilson. Or maybe Dennis. Yeah, he's definitely a Dennis. No... Beau is Dennis. Myles wouldn't be caught dead in a cult.

My mother saunters off to welcome our guest and Nash, but I stay right where I am, staring at the marble countertop while swigging back my second glass.

I did *not* mentally prepare for this and I'm not sure how I'll cope sitting at a table with him for hours.

Brin appears, thankfully sans her idiot boyfriend, and tops up her own drink. "You not gonna go and say hi?"

"No, I think I'll wait." I refill my glass again.

Brinsley frowns. "I don't know *what* is going on, but between the cold shoulder Beau just gave him and you avoiding him, we are not being very hospitable towards Myles."

I shrug and come up with some utter crap: "You know I'm not the one to throw myself into a welcome throng."

Brinsley scowls and snatches my wrist. "Go and say," she shoves me out the door and hisses, "hello."

I stumble my way to a stop in the front room, only looking up when I catch my balance.

Myles is just a metre away talking to my mother, but he instantly turns his gaze on me.

My heart picks up at a gallop. Sadist.

He hasn't changed, save for that trimmed beard we discussed that morning on the couch. His eyes are still like honey, his stature impressive. He's wearing jeans and a plaid shirt, buttoned all the way to the top but untucked, the sleeves rolled up to his elbows. I want to say I'm repelled by him—or better yet, just completely ambivalent—but I'm just not. I don't think I ever will be.

Myles's gaze travels southwards, perusing me, drinking me. I send a thank you to the me of an hour ago for picking this dress. It falls just above the knees—a cream jumper dress that I've paired with woollen tights and black riding boots.

I take an unconscious step closer, and he does the same. Mum, offended by nothing, seamlessly moves her conversation to Nash. I'm also aware that Beau leaves the room.

"Birdie," is how he chooses to greet me.

Indignation spreads through me, and I see it in his eyes when he realises his error. Through clenched teeth, I say, "Myles."

"Listen, I–"

"–Excuse me."

I'm not ready for that conversation, and I'm sure he knows it. I mow past him and head for the stairs. If I'm going to have a breakdown, I'll at least have it in the privacy of a bathroom, or in the bedroom that was mine as a child. I still want to keep my dignity if my pride is going in the toilet. The bathroom is closer, too.

I lock myself in and pretend to relieve myself for the sake of it. After two glasses of wine, I refuse to break the seal.

When I'm done, I peer out, pleased to find the landing empty. I make my way back down to the party, where everyone is taking their seats around the dining table. I squeeze in between Mum and Brin, only to find that Myles is directly opposite me. I can't figure out if that's better or worse than if he were beside me.

Keeping my gaze down, I focus on filling my plate.

There's an obvious tension in the room, which I know is partially to do with me, but it's also very obvious that something is going on between Beau and Myles, too. Brin said they hadn't greeted each other, and Beau left the room when Myles came to talk to me.

Oh, fuck... Does Beau know what happened while we were away?

Andy, either with an inherent ignorance or a primal desire to stir the pot, asks, "How do you know the twins, Myles?"

"I went to uni with Nash."

"You're a money man, too?" Andy is a mortgage advisor.

"Er, no. Art History. We roomed together in halls."

"So...you work in an art gallery?"

All of us around the table turn a bewildered look on him.

"Andy, this is *Myles*," Brin tells him. "From the school."

"Oh, shit!" Andy laughs, but I'm a percentage shy of convinced he knows *exactly* who Myles is. "I don't know why I didn't put that together."

"You're so daft." Brin chuckles, rubbing his arm.

Yes, *daft* is certainly one word for him, amongst many others. Like *prick* or *massive fucking cunt*.

"You're a mortgage advisor, right?" Myles asks, proving that he actually listens to people when they talk. He just can't keep their phone numbers.

"I am," Andy preens.

"And how many mortgages did you give advice to this week?"

I fight back a snort. Dad, on the other hand, barks with his whole body.

"You do know that a mortgage advisor doesn't give actual mortgages advice, right?"

Myles squints and leans forward. "What?"

"I advise people—humans—about mortgages. Not…not…I'm not like a councillor for mortgages."

"I don't understand," Myles says.

"It's really not that difficult, mate," Andy snaps.

Beau, who is an eternal defender of Andy, looks positively furious. Nash looks baffled, as if he's found himself on an alien planet. Mum and Dad, who have only ever said nice things about Andy but remain generally neutral, are watching the whole thing raptly while shoving food into their mouths like they're enjoying popcorn and a movie at the cinema.

I take a gulp of wine. My face feels flush.

"Well, it's just that you said you're a mortgage advisor, yet you don't advise mortgages. Kind of contradictory, don't you think?"

"*I* think we should put this conversation to bed," Beau grits out, throwing daggers Myles's way.

"That seems sensible." Brin sighs. I know she's upset by the slump of her shoulders, but she'll never say anything. Sometimes I think Brinsley is of the belief that staying quiet when she's upset makes her stronger. I also worry that one day it'll break her.

Nash changes the subject to football, which seems like neutral territory for everyone.

I never go to the games because stadium crowds overwhelm me, and thanks to the FA broadcasting rules, league games aren't shown on the telly for three o'clock matches on Saturdays, which is usually when The Rangers play, so I listen on the radio when I can.

We talk while we eat, keeping the conversation neutral. Slowly, after cake and the Happy Birthday song, everyone starts splitting off. I'm five glasses deep at this point and starting to feel hazy. I've been talking to Mum and Brin about Christmas plans—apparently Andy wants to go to his parents' house this year and Brin isn't keen on the idea—and I've noticed that my ability to string a sentence together has become lax.

I politely excuse myself to get a glass of water.

Myles is in the kitchen by himself, reading something on his phone while picking at leftover bits of salad.

I'm suitably drunk so as not to worry about avoiding him, so I march straight to the sink and fill up a clean mug on the drainer with tap water. When I turn around, Myles is watching me expectantly.

"Did you enjoy that?" I ask.

I swear I see fear pass through his green-gold gaze. "Enjoy what?"

"Pissing off John?"

"Who's John?"

"Brin's boyfriend."

Myles frowns. "I thought his name was Andy?"

"His full name is John Andrews. Only his mortgage advisor friends get to call him John."

"He's a knobhead."

"I know," I tell him.

"And I think your sister could do better," he admits.

I glance towards the door because she's only in the next room. I dread to think what might happen if she heard us. Long tether she may have, but Brinsley Bennett's wrath is not one to get tangled up in.

"Is that you volunteering?" I'm loose-lipped now I've had enough to drink.

"What? No." Myles looks horrified, and I don't know whether to be comforted for myself or offended for Brinsley.

I stare at him for a moment—that sculpted face and capable body. I mourn the fact that I haven't seen it for two months, and yet that also hardens my resolve. "Why didn't you text me, Myles?"

He pinches his eyes closed. "It's dumb. I put my jeans in the wash before I took the paper out."

"That's not an excuse. You know my entire family."

"I can't ask your brothers. I'm already having a hard time with Beau, and Nash would probably be ten times worse if he found out. And I wasn't sure how you felt about…telling people. I knew you hadn't told your sister and she's not always subtle. If I asked her for your number, it would bring a line of questioning your way that you're not comfortable with. Same goes for Shirley. I don't want to put you in that position, no matter how much I like you."

Well. I wasn't expecting that.

Still, I can't help being petty while under the influence. "You should've put it straight in your phone as soon as you were in the car if you like me so much."

"I know." He's very agreeable, and it's grating on me. "But I was annoyed with Beau and just wanted to get home."

"I know he's a selfish pain in the ass sometimes, but you can't blame Beau for all your problems, Myles." I finish my water and leave the glass in the sink. "Suck it up, big boy."

When I turn around, he snatches my arm, a pen produced out of nowhere. "Here," he rolls the sleeve of my jumper up and writes his phone number on it between the ivy, "at least you have mine."

I gawk at him, at his unbridled boldness. "And you expect me to do something with it?"

"You can do nothing with it. You can make me wait another month, or a whole year. It won't change anything."

Butterflies take flight in my stomach, and I have to remember how to breathe. "You'd wait that long?"

"I mean, I wouldn't be opposed if you came around quicker. But at least I know you have it."

"What if I just scrub it off?" I'm just being difficult now, but I want to know how serious he is.

He smiles, and it's genuine and sweet and beautiful. "I'll hold it in good faith that you won't.

Chapter Twenty
FAIRY COTTAGE

MYLES

I've been avoiding the Bennett women at school this week. Mostly Brinsley, because I know she saw me and Sheridan talking on Sunday, and even though Sheridan didn't notice her twin lurking by the kitchen door, I did.

I'd bared myself to Birdie in that kitchen, and I have no idea if she's going to take me up on it. It's been five days since I wrote my number on the pale underside of her arm, and I haven't heard a peep.

Shirley is less the issue, unless Brin told her what she saw, in which case I'm Coventry's Number One Most Wanted by the Bennett girls. All three of them.

I dismiss my Friday afternoon Year 7 group, have a tidy up around the room so the cleaners don't have too much to do when they come in later. Then I sit behind my desk and finish a couple of bits of work.

I see Sam—the Year 9 student who believes he possesses zero artistic talent—trudge past with his head low and shoes squeaking along the linoleum as he heads home for the day. Something warm thuds in my chest, an ache accompanying it that feels far too familiar for my liking. It's a Friday afternoon and the kid looks like he'd rather be going anywhere but home. No child should feel that way about Fridays.

He was quiet this week, and last week if I really think about it. He wasn't really paying attention, but it wasn't like the other kids where they were lost in their work. It seemed like he was more lost in his head. I'd had a quiet word with him in the hopes of avoiding embarrassing him. I'm not the type of teacher to call out a kid for not paying attention when I used to have the same problem. If something's going on at home—which should be a safe space—it's going to take a lot of your attention. Something tells me there's always a lot going on at home for Sam.

Not long passes before I get a notification on my phone. For a second, I think it might be a text from Sheridan, but I'm not that lucky. It is, however, the next best thing: an announcement from BennyBetty with the release of a new *Goth Frogs* episode.

This girl has been on fire with the episode releases recently.

Forgetting where I am and what I'm supposed to be doing, I sink into the animated world of frogs in fishnets, black lipstick, and silly onyx toupees.

"*Goth Frogs*, aye?"

I startle, my phone clattering to the floor. My heart is thundering in my ears. "Fucking hell, Brin," I heave. "You scared the shit out of me."

She gives me a wry smile and swipes my phone up unscathed. Something about her is smug, and it's unnerving. "Sorry."

I shut off the video, feeling jittery, and place it face down on the desk. I glance up at her. "You know about *Goth Frogs*?"

She hesitates a moment. "Yeah, I know the creator."

No fucking *way*. Brinsley *knows* BennyBetty?! Fuck, this is cool. "Really?"

"Yeah, I…went to school with them for a little bit."

"It's a woman, right? The creator?"

She gives me a tight-lipped nod, which tells me Brin knows more about this than she's letting on. Knowing that BennyBetty is anonymous, I can only assume Brinsley is trying not to give too much away.

"That's so cool," I say, like a complete dork. "I've been watching it from the start. Probably sounds a bit lame to you, but it's my favourite series online. No, anywhere."

"Not lame at all, Myles. I'm sure she'd be flattered if she ever heard you say that."

"I, er, normally wait 'til I get home to watch new episodes, but she's been updating more often than usual, and I got excited. This must be what Harry Styles fans feel like when he releases new music."

Brinsley snorts. "Must be." She perches on the edge of a stool close to my desk. "Do you not want to go out with everyone tonight?"

I lean back on my chair and pull a face that's something between a cringe and a grimace. "I think if your mum found out I'd gone out with Emily, she'd probably disown me. And I quite like your family." One member, especially.

"Aw, we like you, too. But don't let my mother bully you into submission. If you like the French teacher, you like the French teacher."

This is not where I was expecting this conversation to go. Emily is harmless, constant flirting aside. And she is relentless, but I'm not really about sleeping with co-workers, and I have my sights set on a certain pink-tipped, curly haired pixie anyway. If she'd only text me. Going out with the other teachers probably will be uneventful, so long as Emily keeps her hands to herself.

"I *don't*," I clarify quickly. "Like Emily."

Brin looks taken aback. "Okay…"

I clear my throat. "I actually thought you might be here to interrogate me about Sunday. I've been waiting for you to corner me."

She laughs, the sound so similar yet so different to her twin's. "You make me sound like some kind of mafia wife."

"Is that not why you're here?"

She grins. "No, it is why I'm here. Sheridan has avoided me all week, and so have you."

"Great," I mutter.

"What does that mean?" She demands, defensive.

"I kind of already had the lecture off your brother on multiple occasions during our trip away. I'd rather not have it again."

"Lecture? What lecture? Why would I lecture you? And which brother? Beau?"

"Yeah, Beau. And the one about me staying away from Sheridan because I've got too much baggage, and she doesn't need any more shit in her life. Whatever that means."

Brinsley flinches. "Okay, ew. No, I'm not here to lecture you. And fuck Beau for even going there. I apologise on his behalf because that is straight up not okay."

"He doesn't seem to think so."

"Fuck him. Tell me what happened on Sunday."

"I don't know if I should."

"Why? Is it bad? If you've upset her, I hope you know I'll make your life absolute hell. Way worse than Nash or Beau could."

"I don't dispute that." And this is knowing that Nash can be a nasty son of a bitch if he needs to be.

"That's not what it looked like, though. If anything, it looked like you wanted to strip her naked and shag her right there on my parents' kitchen floor."

Not entirely inaccurate. I'd suppressed a boner when I first saw her in that soft dress and thigh highs. Then she got a bit lippy, and I remembered how much I like that side of her. And above everything she'd let me touch her. Only her arm, but it was good enough.

With a sigh, I say, "She gave me her number and I lost it."

"Well, that's silly. Why didn't you ask me for it.?"

I lift a brow at her.

"Right. The inquisition."

"I gave her mine instead hoping she'd text me, but she hasn't yet."

"Knowing my sister, she's only making you wait because she had to. She won't give you the silent treatment forever."

"Do you think she likes me?" I ask, then realise how pitiful I sound.

Brin snorts again. "You've been spending too much time around teenagers. But yes, I do. If she didn't like you, she'd have binned your number the second you gave it to her."

That's what I'd hoped for. "Will you give me her number now?"

Brinsley purses her lips while studying me. "No." At my protest, she holds up a hand. "Sheridan is a romantic at heart. Giving you her phone number now is too easy. You're gonna do one better."

I blink at her. "What…?"

"I'm gonna give you her address."

* * *

Brinsley sends me to an address in one of the small villages just outside the city.

On the way, I stop at a florist just about to close for the day and tell the lady I need a bouquet of peonies, dahlias, and carnations, if she can. She tells me that since it's the end of the day, I'll get what I'm given, and she's formidable enough that I don't argue. I don't even know what any of those look like—Brinsley just told me they're Birdie's favourites. The bouquet I'm given is a hodgepodge of blooms where no two are the same. I don't think, anyway.

I then stop by a Tesco Express and pick up a bottle of wine, condoms because I'm optimistic—and cautious—and a box of Lindor chocolate.

The cashier raises a suspicious brow at me. "Valentine's Day is in March, mate."

"No, it's in February," I retort.

"That's what I meant," he mutters, suitably scorned.

I pay the teenager and head back to my car.

I drive for another ten minutes before the sat-nav tells me I've arrived. I peer out the window, not convinced.

"This can't be right."

I'm parked in front of a cottage that looks like it's come out of a fantasy land. Or the house from *Tots TV*.

A thatched roof, red brick with visible timber foundations painted black. The front garden is picket-fenced with a small, raised porch, a bench outside the front door, and an iron bird pond in the centre of the front lawn.

It looks like somewhere my grandma might live. If I had one.

I decide to text Brin, just to be safe.

Me
Are you sure this is the right address?

Brin
Fairy cottage?

Me
Yep

Brin
Then you're in the right place!

I blink at my screen, and then out the window again. Fuck me. Either Sheridan got very lucky with inheritance, or interior designers make way more money than I realised.

Taking as many calming breaths as I can, I collect the flowers, wine and chocolate off the passenger seat and head up the path to the shiny black front door.

Steeling myself, I knock three times.

I hear the dog first—a kind of terrified yowling from somewhere near the front of the house. He quietens down soon enough, and a moment later the curtains in the front window rustle. It's too quick for me to see her, but I know she's seen me because the window is cracked open, and I can hear her hissing profanities.

I have to stifle my laughter.

Sheridan doesn't leave me waiting long, and before I know it, the front door eases open.

She's got Hector tucked under her arm, the poor sod shaking like a damn leaf in a light breeze. Her hair is piled atop her head in a mass of pink and blonde curls—the pink now faded to more of a pastel shade than it was in the summer—and she's wearing some grey leggings that show off her curves, a baggy T-shirt that's so old I can barely make out the print on it, and fluffy boot slippers. But best of all are the thick black frame glasses perched on her nose.

For the entire week we shared a cabin, I did not see her in specs, but fuck me do they suit her.

"Hi..." she says warily.

"Hi." I feel awkward. This was a rubbish plan—turning up at an unassuming woman's house without prior indication. People get arrested for this kind of behaviour.

"What… How did you find out my address?"

I swallow my nerves. "A woman who looks an awful lot like you gave it to me after seeing how sad and pathetic I am."

Sheridan's lips twitch, but only briefly. My appearance is clearly unsettling. "Sad and pathetic?"

"Yeah… But I'm now realising how weird and inappropriate this is."

"Don't tell me—my sister thought it'd be romantic?"

"Technically she said *you* would find it romantic. I'm starting to think Brin might be getting what you want mixed up with what she wants."

"I'm certainly not used to men turning up at my front door with flowers and…wine?"

"What can I say? I'm optimistic."

She sighs, placing Hector back on the ground—threat assessed. "You sure you're not here to murder me?"

"I think I would find very little satisfaction in murdering you, Birdie."

Her smile is bitten and cute as hell. "Fine," she says around a sharp exhale, and opens the door wide, "you can come in. Only because I can see those chocolates and I forgot to pick some up myself when I went shopping this week."

"There's a corner shop not fifty metres away," I say as I step over the threshold and into the cottage that looks like it came right out of a childhood fantasy of mine.

"I only leave the house when I absolutely have to, Myles. Which is rarely."

Sheridan takes the bouquet off me and shoves her face in the foliage. "Did Brin tell you I like carnations too?"

"Maybe, but I don't know if they're in there. The florist was a bit shitty with me."

She giggles, and I realise I've missed that sound. "You did good."

I shove my smugness back to the pits before my head can get too big. Praise from this woman is like a drug.

Birdie guides me through her fairytale cottage—all low ceilings, bright colour walls and exposed beams—to the kitchen at the back of the house. It overlooks a small, well-manicured garden and the canal.

The kitchen is modest, but not overwhelming, with pale green cabinets and clean white marble surfaces. It's cluttered in places with washed utensils still on the drainer, piles of post on the breakfast table and winterwear crowded in by the back door, likely for the rougher dog walks.

Sheridan leaves the bouquet on the counter and rummages through a cupboard, retrieving a crystal vase. She fills it up a third of the way with tap water, then transfers the tied blooms over. She then produces two wine glasses from a smaller cupboard and hands them over to me.

"Have you had dinner?"

"No, I came straight from the school."

I follow her as she weaves into the next room, which happens to be the lounge. It's smaller than I expected—a loveseat and an armchair, both assaulted with colourful woven blankets and throw pillows. A large TV sits mounted on the wall above the fireplace, a coffee table stacked with books, scraps of paper with scribbles on them and other items that she hasn't bothered to put away sits in the middle of the room.

"You have…a lot of soft furnishings," I blurt.

Sheridan laughs as she sinks into the sofa, the flowers now pride of place on the coffee table. "I have a friend. She makes a guinea pig product and I get the finished items when she's perfected it."

"That's cool." I set the glasses down on the table, take out the wine and chocolates, and start pouring.

"My boss *hates* my house."

"What—why?"

"It doesn't exactly scream interior designer."

"Who cares? You're the one living in it."

She pats the sofa when I hand her a glass of the good stuff, and I squeeze in beside her. "This is what I've always said. Just because I know how to make other people's houses look good—to societal norms—doesn't mean I want that for myself."

"It feels very *you* here," I tell her. "Of the two rooms I've seen, anyway."

"Does that mean you approve?"

"Not that my opinion means much, but I do approve, yeah. It feels like a home."

She studies me with a little dip in her brow, big blue eyes more intense than I'm used to, magnified by the lenses in her specs. And then the intensity clears, and she grins at me. "Thank you. Anyway, back to the matter of food—I also haven't eaten, and I use having company as an excuse to order a takeaway. So, what do you want?"

Chapter Twenty-One
Banking Material

SHERIDAN

We end up having fish and chips because it's Friday and we British people are stuck in our ways like that. I have a battered sausage, chips, and gravy, which Myles finds abhorrent by the look on his face— "Who has gravy on chips?" he asks with disgust — while he settles with the traditional battered cod, chips, mushy peas, and curry sauce. I'm too polite to slag off his food choices but I absolutely cannot stand mushy peas and spend most of my time trying not to gag while I eat.

When we're done, I clear away the plates and top up our wine before sinking back into the sofa. I was ironing out the final plot points for the very last *Goth Frogs* episode when Myles turned up and we ate in the dining room, so it's very quiet in the house. Hector is already asleep.

"Can I ask you something?" I say when Myles has resettled next to me.

"Sure."

"What's going on between you and Beau?"

He seems a little put off by the question, but he doesn't deflect, he just sighs. "He's been a prick."

"Not unusual. What did he do?"

"He told me to stay away from you because collectively we've got too much baggage and I'm not good enough for you. I'm probably *not* good enough for you, but it was shitty hearing it out of my best friend's mouth. Especially when Brin's boyfriend is such a colossal bellend."

For a second, I'm speechless. Beau and Myles aren't speaking because of *me*? "What? Why does he think *you've* got too much baggage?"

"Probably because I grew up in care." He shrugs.

"Oh." I didn't know that. "I'm sorry."

"Why are you apologising? It's not your fault my parents didn't want me."

I flinch and he winces.

"Sorry." He reaches for my hand, and I let him take it. "It just pissed me off that Beau used that against me, basically from day one, when it came to you."

"Day one?"

"Oh yeah. Literally when we were at the services on our way to the cabin, he pulled me aside and told me I'm not good enough for you. Apparently, I'm that transparent."

I scoff at him. "You did *not* like me that quickly."

"Birdie, I fancied you the second you got out of that little green car of yours."

A shiver runs through me from his blunt honesty. "Oh."

"That's it? Oh?" He nudges my calf with his foot.

"What else do you want me to say?"

"I don't know, maybe that you fancied me straight away, too?"

"I did."

His head rears back. "You did?"

"Yeah."

"Thank God."

I try, and fail, to fight my smile. "When was the last time you spoke to Beau?"

"Your Dad's birthday. And even then, it wasn't very pleasant." He pauses for a moment, shoving a hand through his gold locks. I track the movement and hate the way my mouth salivates.

"I haven't gone to any games, either. Stavros has been borrowing my season ticket."

This I find particularly interesting. Myles point-blank refusing to go to a game because he and Beau aren't talking. Diehard football fans with unlimited access would attend games come rain or shine, snow, or sleet. Which leads me to believe that maybe Myles isn't as hardcore a fan as I thought. Really, he's just there for Beau. "Are you going to ignore him forever?"

"I hope I don't have to, not least because he's my best friend but also your brother. But until he apologises, I don't want to know."

"He'll come around eventually."

"I don't know… He's stubborn as a mule."

"That's true. When we were kids—I reckon maybe nine or ten—Mum and Dad bought all of us scooters one Christmas. Beau played with his so much it broke so he started using mine. Eventually that broke too, and I was so upset the only thing I wanted to do was retaliate. So, I went up to his room and threw his Nintendo at the wall."

Myles laughs so hard it startles me. "Holy shit."

"I've never been in more trouble than when I did that, and Beau didn't speak to me for like a month. I never apologised either because I wasn't sorry."

"Remind me to never break anything of yours," Myles jokes.

"He was made to apologise to me for being careless with my stuff and that was that. He'll realise the error of his ways eventually."

"It's weird not talking to him or going to games, I will admit."

"I don't blame you for not wanting to go. What he said to you was rude and completely uncalled for. Also, it's not his place to dictate who I can and can't date." The more I dwell on that part, the more pissed off I become. "Or you, for that matter. Sister or not, he doesn't own me, and he doesn't own you. Fuck him."

"Exactly. Fuck him. So, what if we've got baggage? That's our problem, not his. And we work through it in our own time."

"Plus, my baggage is from years ago and stopped being a problem when I was like sixteen. How dare he put that on you. That's my story to tell."

"And you'll tell me when you want to," he assures me, his thumb stroking lightly across the back of my hand.

I think about my teenage issues and what I put my family through, and those insecurities rear up for a moment. Swallowing, I say, "It's quite heavy—my baggage. You sure you don't want to run now, while you still can?"

"Why? You a murderer or summat?"

I give him a half smile. "No."

"Then I'm not interested in bolting, Birdie. I'm interested in *you*. I saw some shit growing up in foster homes that I wouldn't wish upon my worst enemy. Whatever you've got going on, or are carrying around with you, I'll share the load. If you'll let me."

I blink at him once, twice. I neck my full glass of wine and abandon the empty glass on the coffee table, and then I use my liquid courage to crawl the distance between us and straddle his lap.

Myles's hands find my hips, and my mouth finds his mouth before my brain has the chance to second guess itself. I cup his face with my hands and lean all of my weight against him, and he lets out a satisfied moan.

Our kiss isn't rushed or frenzied. It's sensual and tender and exploratory. It's the perfect kiss for the moment. It makes sense. And I can't help but feel like Myles makes sense being here with me, in my house—my sacred space.

Beau can take his opinions and shove them where the sun doesn't shine.

Myles's tongue swirls with mine, his breaths deep and heavy. His hands have started roaming—up my sides, over my shoulders, in my hair, down my back. I feel consumed and I like it that way.

I scratch my fingernails over his neat stubble, and he growls, his touch growing heavier. I feel his length harden, poking against my thighs, and it takes everything in me not to just take it out and sit right on it.

I pull back but rest my forehead against his, breathing heavily. Myles slips his hands underneath my shirt, resting his palms just underneath my breasts.

"Is it stupid that I missed you?" I ask, still panting. "I knew you for seven fucking days and I missed you after we went home."

"Not stupid. I missed you, too." Myles rubs his nose against mine, and his thumbs skim along my breasts. He presses a kiss to the corner of my mouth. "I wanted to ask someone about you so badly, but I know how private you are. It was a lose-lose for me."

Rubbing my palms down his chest, I say, "Last weekend, after you scribbled on my arm—in ink that was annoyingly hard to clean off, by the way—I did this really sensible thing where I put your number in my phone and saved it."

He laughs, pinching my nipples with it. I swat him but he does it again. "Really? That's such a clever idea, I wish I'd thought of that."

I make a flat humming sound. "Yeah."

"What's my contact name?"

"Man Who Forgets to Check His Pockets Before Washing His Jeans."

That earns me a smack to the backside, and I gasp, leaning forward. He keeps his hand on my bum, squeezing it roughly, and I can't help my moan.

"You are cheeky," he says, his mouth hot against my cheek.

In response, I grind myself over his semi. He makes a pained noise and smacks my bum again.

"Myles!"

"You don't like it?"

Far from it. I like it a little bit *too* much.

Rather than answer him, I grip his shoulder and look him in the eye. "This weekend—what are you doing?"

"Nothing."

"Wrong. You're doing me."

He grins so big he could light up the Blackpool Illuminations with the wattage. "I'm forgiven?"

"Mostly. But we've gotta catch up on two months' worth of sex. Think you're up to it?"

"I'll certainly try my damn best."

I waste no more time and yank my T-shirt over my head, baring my tits to him. Before he can bury his face in my cleavage, I lean back and snatch his full wine glass off the coffee table and take a swig. I offer him some, but he shakes his head.

Before I replace it, I dip two fingers in the liquid and rub it over each of my nipples.

Myles's dick twitches between my legs, and he hisses, "Fuck me."

In the next breath, he's got his mouth around one.

His large hands knead each of my boobs while he licks the wine clean from each of my nipples. I shove my fingers into his messy hair, savouring the softness of it between my fingertips. He laps and laps and laps away at my breasts, *lick suck lick suck*, to the point my breathing is ragged and serrated.

I love the feel of his hands playing roughly with me. I didn't know I'd like it so much, actually. I can't help but touch them, encouraging them to squeeze harder, pinch tighter.

"Yes, Myles," I pant when he complies, "like that."

"You want it a bit rough, Birdie?" His voice is pure gravel, and it only encourages the slick between my legs.

Involuntarily, I roll my hips over him, and he groans loudly.

"I'll take that as a yes."

He persists with his heavy touches, using his teeth around my nipples.

I lean in closer, shoving my chest into his face while my mouth finds his. I feel my own tongue on my skin, paired with his, and shiver violently.

Myles claims my mouth in a punishing kiss, his tongue plundering, teeth nipping and lips sucking. It's the kind of kiss that renders you dumb, and I surrender to him like he's a lifeline.

We kiss and we kiss, and we kiss, time but a mere concept. Not important. Completely irrelevant.

The length of him hardens like a steel rod, surely, gradually, until I feel it pressing against my thighs, calling to me like a fucking beacon. I grind over it once, twice, three times, until I'm a moaning mess and Myles hisses like a panicked cat.

"Bloody hell, Sheridan," he grunts into my mouth, "you'll be the death of me."

I smile at this, and at the way his hands grip my posterior, encouraging my dry humping.

I tease him out of his shirt, undoing the buttons one by one and leaving kisses in a scorching trail down his torso as I go. His breathing is laboured, his warm honey eyes on me. I sponge my lips over every inch of him, paying special attention to that bear tattoo when I reach it while palming over the stiffness in his trousers.

Myles's hands find my hair, a makeshift tie keeping it all out of my face.

I find his mouth again while easing his trousers down. "Can I?"

"You never need to ask me permission to do that."

I grin, giving him a hard kiss on the mouth, then another, before completely sinking to my knees between his legs.

"Fuck, look at you." He breathes, "I know you're not a fan of praise, but the sight of you on your knees like this is banking material, baby."

I can feel the heat on my cheeks, but I ignore it as I take his cock in my grip. "Is it worth a lot in this bank of yours?" I ask, starting to stroke him up and down with both hands. And it requires both because he's big and my hands… aren't.

He makes a strangled noise. "The most."

Okay so maybe praise is a *little* bit my thing. I just like the idea of him using me in his imagination to get himself off.

I take him into my mouth, easing him in bit by bit as if he's working his way into my pussy. He's warm to the touch, filling my mouth with a delicious heat that has me salivating. I have to spit on him just to get rid of it.

The satisfactory noises he makes are like the best audio porn available. It sends a white-hot pleasure zipping down my spine straight to my clit. I'm not wearing any knickers and I know for a fact my leggings are soaked.

I take him all the way down, as far as he'll go until my body convulses, stroke him a couple of times, and then start fucking him with my mouth properly.

"*Fuuuck*, Sheridan," he grips my hair tighter, "who taught a quiet little thing like you to take a cock so well? Hm?"

I'm bobbing my head like a mad woman when he asks and decide to use answering him as an excuse to take a breath, "Maybe one day I'll tell you."

He leans forward and kisses me with such ferocity it leaves me dizzy. "Fine, keep your secrets."

He kisses me again, but I snatch myself away to return to my ministrations.

I give him everything I have from my mouth. I suck his tip; I use my teeth; I choke him down, down, down.

He holds my head still and fucks into my mouth, which serves to positively destroy my throat and tonsils. His cock is a weapon in size and my mouth isn't that big. Yet when my lips come away sore in the corners from being opened too wide too long as he eases off, I can't find it in me to feel mad about it. It just turns me the fuck on.

We give my poor lips a break while I lick up and down his shaft, and then I lift him up and suck on his balls a little bit.

"Baby girl, you're gonna end this before it's even begun sucking on me like that," he warns.

I just grin, drunk with pleasure, and carry on. I don't need praise, but I have to admit the power that comes with giving a man head is a heady, delicious thing.

I start rubbing my clit over my leggings, just to ease some of the pressure down there. It causes me to whimper, which in turn has Myles shuddering.

"Christ, look at you," he groans, one hand slipping to stroke my cheek, "I'm gonna come all over you if we keep this up any longer."

Shameless, I rub his wet dick across my cheeks as I say, "Maybe I want that."

"You want me to come all over you?"

"Kinda."

"Motherfucker," he hisses, then springs into action.

He helps me up, and, noticing the damp spot on my leggings, he brings my crotch closer to his face.

Those yellow-green eyes meet mine and I'm thrilled to find I don't have an ounce of embarrassment in me about it. He rubs two fingers into it, causing a dirty moan to tumble from my sore lips.

"This for me, Birdie?"

I nod, biting my lip.

He growls and buries his nose against it, and fuck if that doesn't only just make me a whole lot wetter,

He licks a stripe up from the seat to the top of my pubic bone, turning my legs to jelly.

"Something about you, Sheridan, turns me into some sort of feral beast."

I shrug, pushing my fingers through his sandy hair again. "I don't mind." *In fact, I encourage it.*

He growls, and I giggle when I find myself on my back and sprawled across the sofa.

"We're gonna get you out of these leggings, and then I'm gonna fuck those pretty tits of yours and paint you like a damn canvas. And once I've done that, I'm gonna bend you over the back of the sofa until you're screaming my name so loud your neighbours in the next fucking village can hear it." He's already got his fingers in the waistband of my leggings. "How's that sound?"

It's difficult to hide the excitement quite obviously glittering in my eyes, so I simply don't. "Sounds marvellous."

He growls, but he's obviously pleased with himself as he strips off my leggings and throws them over the back of the sofa. His eyes feast on my glistening pussy, taking two laboured breaths before he swipes a finger through my folds and tastes me with his tongue.

I can't help but groan as I watch, because it's so filthy yet so utterly sexy I don't care to fight the heat coursing through my body.

"Push those tits together, baby," he demands as he rids himself of his trousers properly.

I do as he says, and in the next breath he's leaning over me, all but straddling my waist, and pushing his dick through my cleavage.

He's imposing above me—a God made just for me. He looks incredible. Strong and masculine and all fucking male. I love his body. Stacked but not overly so. Lean but capable. His skin sheens with sweat, his shirt still hanging off his shoulders—the only garment left between either of us. Except his socks.

I've never had a man boob-fuck me before, but I'd let Myles do it every day until I die if this is the view I'll get.

"God, I love your tits."

For some reason, that compliment, of all things, brings a blush to my face.

He fucks and fucks and fucks my cleavage until I feel it chafing, and then I spit on myself, something else I've never done before.

Myles groans again, and apparently the sight of that alone is enough to get him off, because in the next breath I'm decorated, neck to navel, in ropes of his thick seed.

"Fuck," he pants, milking his cock to the very last drop.

I glance down at myself, somewhat startled. I feel like an oil painting. I don't know how to explain it, but I do. Before I can stop myself, I'm touching the come he's left on me, spreading it down the valley of my breasts.

Myles watches in rapt fascination as I continue to smear it all over me, until I decide I'm done. And I put my wet fingers in my mouth to taste him.

"Bloody hell," he says, but his voice breaks so many times it just sounds like a sharp rasp, "I think I like seeing that a little too much."

I smile around my fingers and sit up. I take his face in my hands and kiss him. He doesn't deny me, not even a little bit. Just continues to consume me, bit by bit.

His hands squeeze my waist, large and bruising, and then to my arse, where he gropes me until I might combust. He trails a finger between my cheeks and then through my folds and all that wetness collecting down there. The noise he makes when he eases one long finger into my heat is downright animalistic.

"God, I can't wait to be inside you again."

I kiss my way around his chin, his jaw, his neck as he finger-fucks me. "Find us a condom and you won't have to wait much longer."

He grunts, biting my bottom lip before pulling away, finger and all. He sucks on that finger while digging around in the back pocket of his slacks, producing his wallet. After some filing around, he finds one.

"Is that your only one?"

He gives me a funny look. "No, Birdie. I'm ashamed to say I was optimistic and there's a full box of them in the bag I brought with me."

I press my lips together in an attempt to stifle my giggle and fail. "Let's call it cautious."

"Rather that than assuming," he mutters. He rips the foil open and rolls it on, then finally rids himself of his shirt. "Come on, baby. Show me that ass."

Surprising myself with my own eagerness, I drape myself over the back of the couch and stick my backside in the air, completely forgetting I'd smeared his fluid all over my chest not two minutes ago. Oh well. This blanket can be washed.

Immediately, Myles's hands find my cheeks and starts squeezing. And kneading. And squeezing. Then he buries his face in my cunt and licks me clean like I'm a fucking passionfruit margarita.

"You taste…" he bites a cheek and I squeak a little, "*fucking divine.*"

He smacks my arse once, and I yelp, but I'm delighted by it. He does it again and the sound I make is just downright dirty.

"Like that, Birdie?"

"Yes," I say breathlessly.

He brings his hand down on my other cheek, and the sting resonates across my entire body, but it's not painful in a bad way. Oh, no. The slick between my legs is back, and I'm *dripping*.

"Fucking hell, you really did like that."

Then he shuffles, and before I have a chance to think about it, he's spearing me with his cock.

I choke around an expletive, because I forgot what it feels like to have him inside me, and I think I might die from the size of it.

Death by dick.

Not a bad way to go.

"Oh, Christ, that's good." Myles sighs like he's just entered the gates of heaven. His body drapes over mine, lips skating across the skin of my shoulder and neck. He nips my earlobe, "Forgot how tight you are."

I need him to move, because right now I can practically feel him in my throat and it's making me mute. I wriggle against him, urging him to move without my voice.

Myles coughs, "Oh, shit."

He pulls out, leaving just the tip in, and I take a deep breath before he slams back inside me.

"Myles!"

He nuzzles my neck as he pulls out again. "Like music to my fucking ears, baby."

Slam. Choke.

Jesus, I'm going to be split in half by the time we're done.

Over and over again he slams his cock into me with the force of a damn missile, and each and every single time I feel my organs rearrange themselves inside my body. The centre of gravity shifts around us. Ours is no longer the core of the Earth; it's where his dick joins my pussy.

As his pace evens out, Myles pulls his weight off mine, sponging kisses down my spine, and straightens up. His grip on my waist is bruising in its intensity, but I like it. I want his marks all over me.

I yelp again when his palm comes down on my arse cheek, immediately followed by another.

"I love your arse," he grunts, back to soothing the sting he created.

"I thought you loved my tits," I say breathlessly. I can feel said tits bouncing with each of his powerful thrusts, grazing the back of the sofa.

"I've got enough affection for both, baby."

His hand comes down on my backside again.

"Fuck, *Myles!*"

"That's my new favourite sound," he decides, voice utterly ragged.

His pace gets faster, more punishing, and I take it and take it because it feels *so fucking good.*

"Yes, Myles," I pant, "just like that. So good. So *fucking* good."

"You like that, Birdie?" He cups a breast, squeezing harshly, and takes my hair in a tight grip.

"Yes," I groan.

"You like it when I shag you hard and fast?"

"Yes!"

He releases my hair in favour of clasping my shoulder, and then finds my clit with his other hand. He pairs his powerful thrusts with flicking my clit with his fingers, and he absolutely fucking obliterates me.

My orgasm builds, crests, and detonates in the space of seconds, my tight heat suffocating Myles's dick for all its worth. "Fuck!" I scream, voice hoarse from the sheer volume of it.

"Oh my fuck." Myles leans over me, bites my shoulder, and then I feel him shudder and freeze.

He roars with his release, so loud it hurts my eardrums, but it's glorious and magnificent and wonderful to feel him come apart like this around me, over me, for me.

He buries his face in my neck, lips nipping and sucking at my skin as we catch our breath. I reach up to play with his hair, scratch his scalp, and he purrs like a damn kitten.

It feels different to when we were at the cabin. We were holding back, keeping quiet, because we had company, and we didn't want to get caught. There's no chance of that now.

We've been unleashed.

* * *

I'm spent and sore in more places than just one. Myles seems equally spent but is likely less sore.

He's currently lying on his front, starfish-ing, but with his head resting against my stomach. I'm idly pushing my fingers through his hair while I stare at the ceiling above my bed.

I came seven times. *Seven*. Myles Wilson—aka The Bear—spanked, choked, and fucked seven orgasms out of me. The man's libido is insane because we went four separate times: one on the sofa, one against the hallway wall, one in the shower, and then finally in my bed.

I am *exhausted*.

Myles hasn't moved for twenty minutes. He could be asleep, but something tells me he's staring into space like I am.

"Myles?" I mumble, pausing my grooming.

Silence.

"Myles, are you awake?"

"Dead."

I giggle, resuming my stroking. "We should probably go to sleep."

He grunts, and then he brings his arms in to wrap them tightly around my middle. Finding a morsel of energy, he sucks a love bite onto my midriff to join the ten others there.

Seriously, the man has given me so many I look like a damn Dalmatian. I gave him a few of my own, too.

Slowly, Myles crawls up my body until he's hovering over me, and he presses a slow, delicious kiss to my lips. "You, Sheridan Bennett, are the most incredible woman I've ever met."

Besides the absolute marathon we just completed, my blush comes up something fierce.

Myles pecks the tip of my nose, then my cheek, before he collapses onto his back beside me. Missing his warmth, I curl into his side. He slides an arm around my shoulders and brings my leg to hook over his with his other hand, leaving it to rest on the back of my thigh.

I peer up at him, and he meets my gaze with those warm green-gold eyes.

I don't think I've ever felt more content.

We engage in another kiss—this one lazy and unhurried. It could last seconds or hours. All I know is that it doesn't matter. I'm just happy he's here with me.

"I'm really glad you're here, Myles," I whisper when we finally break apart.

Still holding me tightly, he says, "I'm really glad I found you, Birdie."

Chapter Twenty-Two
Mighty Fine Myles

MYLES

"Tell me, Myles," Brinsley starts as I sit down in one of the chairs in the front of her classroom, "is the reason my sister has ignored me all weekend because of you?"

"No, it's because of you," I say with a smirk.

Brin narrows her eyes at me. "Touché, Mr. Wilson. Has she forgiven you?"

"I think so."

"When did you leave Sheridan's house?" She leans forward over her desk, gaze curious.

My mouth twitches. "This morning."

Brinsley gasps. "Wait, what?! You were there all weekend?"

"I was. I had to get up early so I could go home first. And that's the most I'll tell you. Sheridan can tell you the rest."

No, I never left Sheridan's cottage. We stayed in all weekend and cycled between eating, shagging and sleeping, and it was possibly the best two days of my entire life. I don't think my sex drive has ever been higher. I feel like I've been run ragged and yet I'm so rejuvenated I'm like a new man. I never thought a woman could do that to me, but Sheridan Bennett definitely does.

Leaving her in bed this morning was painful—the opposite of how it felt waking up in her bed on Saturday morning with her curled around me like a little bear.

Not going home to her tonight is also going to suck, but this is still new. I can't live in her pocket just yet.

"If she ever answers my bloody texts or calls. I should be so lucky." Brin sighs.

"Sorry." I wince.

"Meh, not your fault. Shez is a closed book on a normal day. She's probably going to be worse for a little while now."

I'm not entirely sure what to say to that, so I don't respond. Looking around Brinsley's classroom, it's so different to mine—unsentimental in its neatness. The displays on the walls don't breach the borders of their pinboards; the laminated quotes tacked up are all in a large serif font that's easy to read and not much higher than eye level. The walls are painted that generic magnolia colour which I quietly hate, and the pristine carpet is a worn and faded blue. Her student's desks have been arranged in two U-shapes rather than rows of paired tables.

"I'm glad you came to see me, actually." Brin is fiddling with her phone. "It means I can tell her what you're wearing."

"What?"

"Didn't she tell you?" Brin cackles like an utter menace. "I text her every day with a description of what you're wearing."

"You're joking," I accuse.

"I'm really not."

"Does she ever comment on it?"

"Oh, she comments." Brin snickers, typing away. "She always tries to pass it off that she's not interested in what you're wearing, but I know she is. She'll say she doesn't care, but then she'll make a single comment, like you shouldn't wear two different patterns, or the braces ruin the look. Like, sure, Shez… Not interested my arse."

Frowning, I say, "I thought my braces were cool."

"The braces are great, Myles. She was just being petty—she's good at that. In fact, I'm sure if you wore nothing but your trousers and your braces, she wouldn't have a problem with them at all."

I perk up at that. "Noted. Do you think my work attire will get her to finally text you back?"

"Probably not. But I'm due to go for dinner at hers tomorrow, so she'll have to break her silence."

"Tell me if she says anything negative?" I bat my lashes at her.

"No way." Brinsley scoffs. "Save the puppy eyes for Sheridan. Sorry, mate, but anything said about you between me and my sister stays between me and my sister."

I sigh. "That's fair."

The bell rings to signal the end of break time, and I stand from my seat ready to head back to my classroom.

"Oh wait, let me take a picture of you so I can send it to her."

I roll my eyes, even though the thought of Sheridan having a photo of me on her phone satisfies a very male part of me.

I lean against the tables while Brin snaps a couple of images, and then I head out the door. "See you at lunch."

There's already a queue of students waiting outside Brinsley's classroom, either eager or just in the right place at the right time, and I recognise a couple of them from my Year 9 groups.

"Hey, Mr. Wilson." One of the girls smiles up at me.

Think, Myles, think. What's her *name*? Not having my seating plans in front of me makes it hard to remember their names. She wasn't in my 9A group this morning which means she must be in 9B. Back row; sits on the left side of the table.

Erin?

"Good morning, Erin." I return her smile.

She seems delighted that I've remembered her name. "Bit far away from your classroom, aren't you? Are you and Miss Bennett going out?"

Going out. The term almost makes me laugh—we used to say that ten years ago at school as well.

I suppress a shudder at the passing of time.

"That's not an entirely appropriate question, but no, we're not. Miss Bennett has a partner that she's very happy with. We're just friends."

"Oh," Erin slumps a little, "that's a shame. You'd look cute together."

I have to refrain from snorting. Does that mean Birdie and I *do* look good together? Now I'm wondering how quickly I can get Sheridan to take a picture with me.

I say goodbye, pointedly, to Erin and her friend and make my way back to my own classroom for my free period, which will be filled with marking Year 11 coursework. I shut myself away and settle behind my desk, playing the radio through my computer on a low volume.

Just as I'm getting into a rhythm, my phone vibrates in my jacket pocket. It's a message from an unknown number, but the content makes me smile:

Unknown
Did you really let my sister take a picture of you???

Me
It seemed rude not to since it's for your benefit and all.

Birdie
Don't encourage her Myles. She's a heathen.

Me
But what did you think about my outfit?

Birdie
The outfit is fine.

Me
Fine??
FINE???

Birdie
Yep. Fine.

Me
Like...mighty fine? Like, DAMN, Myles is fine! That kind of fine?

Birdie
Sure.

Me
I'll take it.

What are you wearing?

Birdie
Shouldn't you be teaching young and impressionable minds right now rather than fishing for compliments and distractions?

Me
Free period so no kids in my classroom. I'm marking.

Birdie
Slacker.

She immediately follows her text up with a picture. Sheridan is sitting at her desk in her home office. I never went inside, but I can just about make out the garden through the window in the background of the image. Her hair is pushed back by a bandana, and she's in soft-looking grey loungewear—bottoms, vest, and matching cardigan. It's quite evident she's not wearing a bra and I want to shove my face in her cleavage. She's also got those sexy librarian glasses on again.

Me
Bloody hell. You're gonna get me in trouble.

Birdie
You asked for it.

Me
Do you want some company?

Birdie
You have work to do, Myles. And so do I.

Me
But you're so pretty :(

Birdie
You're pretty too.

Me
Stop flirting with me.

Birdie

Stop flirting with ME. I'm red as a tomato!

Me
Really cute tomato, I bet.
Text your sister back. She misses you.

Birdie
Yes, Daddy.

Good God, I have not flirted with a woman like this for a long time, but it's never given me the warm fuzzies the way it does with Sheridan.

Also, Daddy?!

I don't know if she's serious with that, but I might have to put a stop to it if she repeats it. Anything but Daddy.

Me
Can I call you later?

Birdie
Sure thing, Mighty Fine Myles.

Me
Is that my contact name in your phone now?

Birdie
Nope. Talk later x

I find myself staring at that single kiss until the bell rings to signal the start of lunch.

* * *

I stay at the school late so I can finish marking that coursework. Being distracted by Sheridan set me back and I hate being behind. I might have to be careful with that.

I don't get home until nearly seven o'clock, which is too late for me to be bothered about cooking anything particularly fancy, so I make a quick portion of Bolognese and put the rest in a plastic tub for lunch tomorrow.

I eat quickly, tidy up, and then switch the telly on. Beau's game is being shown on Prime tonight, so I queue that up and settle into the sofa.

Having not been to a game since the season started for the first time in about three years, I feel a weird pang in my chest as I watch Beau kick the ball around the pitch. He's easy to spot, because he's the fastest, and has the best hair on the team. Shirley keeps saying he's due a haircut, but I know he won't get one this season. It's long enough at the moment for him to get away with wearing it up, a la Gareth Bale.

About fifteen minutes into the first half, my phone starts ringing. My heart kicks up a right fuss at the name on the screen.

"Hi, Birdie."

"Hey…" Sheridan sounds wary, "I thought you were going to call me?"

I sit up straighter, surprised by the nerves in her tone. "I was. I stayed late to finish that marking and I've not long eaten. I'm just watching Beau's match. Haven't forgotten about you, I promise."

"Oh," she mutters, then sighs. "Wait, Beau's playing? I mean, I know he's playing, I just didn't know you could watch it."

"It's on Prime. Hang on." I quickly text her my log-in details. "Use my account."

"Okay…"

For the next five minutes I listen to the sounds of her shuffling, fidgeting, clicking, and cussing. She sets up a profile in her name—which I will be changing to Birdie later—and then she finally stills to watch with me.

"His hair looks stupid," Shez mutters.

"You don't like it up like that?"

"No, he needs it cut."

On the screen, Beau makes a long run down the wing towards the goal and passes the ball off to JP.

"You sound like your mum."

Sheridan scoffs. "There are worse things to sound like."

This is true. Shirley is an absolute gem of a woman.

JP passes the ball to the other forward, Connor Thatcher, just outside the box, who then wangs it back to Beau. It's onside.

"Go on!" Sheridan yells just as I shout, "That's it!"

Beau winds his leg back, strikes forward and sends it flying, but it's caught on the far post and ends up wide.

"Bastard," I grumble.

"Motherfucker," Sheridan says with a huff. "That would've been beautiful if it got in. Connor should've taken it instead of passing it back to Beau—he had the better angle."

Hearing her talk football is doing it for me big time. I'm half hard in my joggers. "Beau is one goal off thirty club goals, so they'll try and push 'em his way for that, I reckon."

"*Thirty?* I didn't know he'd got that many."

"I know. He'll be intolerable the next time we see him."

She goes silent, and I know it's because she's thinking about what might happen. We hardly spoke about Beau all weekend after our first discussion. It seems we both agreed he's made his bed and now he's got to lie in it, too. Until he apologises, I don't want to talk to him.

Our attention slowly drifts back to the game, which provides the team with multiple other chances to score that are all missed. Sheridan seems to be getting fed up with it.

"They're trying to force it and it's not working," she mumbles.

I hum in agreement. "Simmons will be absolutely dragging them for it, I'm sure."

"Well, he should. It's stupid, trying to win a goal all for some glory for one team member. I'd love for Beau to get his milestone, but it doesn't necessarily have to be today. It's not like this is his *only* opportunity, you know?"

She's so wise... I catch myself smiling at her words. "No, you're right, Shez."

"Can I ask... Do you only support the Rangers because of Beau?"

"Yeah, pretty much. Before I met your brothers I wasn't really into football."

"Oh, really?"

"Nah. Thought it was full of idiots." *Still think it's full of idiots.*

"What did you like?"

"I wasn't a massive sports lad 'cause I was trying to get into art, and I thought it was socially unacceptable to be into both." She laughs on the other end of the line and it's gorgeous and musical. "But I did like ice hockey a bit. NHL, though, it's pretty dead over here."

"No way! You know Bailey's sister, Brandy, does social media for the Crusaders?"

I know the Crusaders are Coventry's ice hockey team—I went to a game once—but that isn't the bit I'm stuck on. "Bailey's sister is called Brandy?"

"Oh, yeah." I can practically see Sheridan rolling her eyes. "Something to do with their parents' favourite drinks. Their family dog is called Bourbon."

"Interesting…" I muse, trying not to laugh at her obvious exasperation.

"Also, I'm pretty sure she's seeing the team net minder, who is quite frankly delicious."

"More delicious than me?"

"I don't think I've ever known a man dig for compliments more than you."

"That's not true—your brother is Beau fucking Bennett, and he is a freaking Labrador."

"God, I hate that you're right."

"I have probably seen him in action more than you with women. That whole thing with Bailey was very…unusual. For him, I mean."

"I don't want to think about my brother and Bailey, Myles. They're both free birds and can do whatever they want, but the whole thing was damn weird."

Not to mention that he's a complete hypocrite.

Thankfully the second half starts, and Beau is back to running up and down the field with his luscious locks blowing in the wind. For some reason he's taken his hair down.

"I think Mum legitimately texted Beau at half time to tell him to take his hair down." Sheridan giggles.

"This seems controversial, but I think it suits him when it's up," I admit.

There's a vacant pause, and then: "I think we should see other people."

My heart falters in rhythm and the tips of my ears get hot. "What?"

"Kidding!" She barks a laugh. "*God*, your voice. Sorry."

"Birdie, that was cruel," I whine.

"I know, but you're so wrong."

"It's an opinion." I huff.

"An opinion that is *wrong*."

"If we were in the same room, I'd smack your arse so hard right now."

That delightful laughter bubbles through my speaker again. "It's rude to tease a girl like that when you can't follow through, Myles."

"I assure you, I can follow through, baby," I say darkly. "The next time I see you, expect a good smacking."

"Bit aggressive, but sure."

"Sheridan?"

"Myles?" She mimics, and I feel so giddy that I'm able to do this with her that I have to sit forward and stick my head between my legs.

"*When* can I see you again?"

She goes quiet, and I imagine her chewing the inside of her lip like a little tease. "I have to go away for a couple of nights tomorrow. Might have to leave it 'til the weekend."

"I thought you were having dinner with your sister tomorrow?" As soon as I've said it, I realise that this was information Brinsley volunteered.

If she notices it, she doesn't say anything. "Yeah, Tuesdays are our normal day. I need to reschedule with her to Thursday. So does Friday work for you?"

Christ, that seems like a long way off. "I guess I'll have to wait. Friday works."

"Bring a change of clothes this time."

I grin at that. Not having any other clothes but my work clothes was my main excuse for not leaving her house this weekend. Although, it didn't seem to bother her. In fact, I'm pretty sure Sheridan wanted me to stay as much as I did.

"Sure, baby. Maybe I'll plan a date for us on Saturday."

"I'd like that."

"Anything else you'd like?" I ask with a jesting lilt to my voice.

"I can think of a few things, but I'm not going to tell you now."

"No? Why not?"

"Because they all involve your body."

The silkiness in her voice makes me groan. My dick likes it just as much. "Don't tease me like that. It's gonna be shit enough tonight without you as it is. I don't need to be having lewd fantasies on top of it."

"If *I* have to suffer lewd fantasies about you, then you have to suffer the ones with me."

I blow out a breath. "Friday can't come soon enough."

"The week will fly by in no time," she says, her voice suddenly softer.

I make a non-committal noise. "Where are you going tomorrow?"

"York. This couple have bought this gorgeous place—Victorian villa type, five bedrooms, massive garden. It just needs *a lot* of work done to make it liveable."

"Wow. Sounds amazing. How much do they want you to do?"

"All of it."

"Oh. Blimey, that seems like a lot."

"Not the biggest one I've taken on. I did a hotel in the summer."

I remember her mentioning it. Her nonchalance is intimidating but so fucking sexy. No big deal. Just flipping a freaking mansion.

"I need to see more of your work."

"I'll show you some on Friday. This is the initial meeting to view the house and go over their brief. When I come home, I'll work on all the design plans and go back when they're done."

"How long will that take?"

"Couple of weeks max?"

"And you drive up there?"

"This one I will. The house is in a village just outside York itself and not accessible by train. Easier to just drive."

"Okay, fair. Will you text me when you get there?" I don't know how that makes me sound, but I feel uneasy at the thought of her travelling in that old Mini such a distance by herself.

"Yeah, Myles. I can text you."

Chapter Twenty-Three

BLANK CANVAS

SHERIDAN

Brinsley pounces on me the second the door to her place is shut behind me. "Talk to me, baby sister of mine," I try not to roll my eyes—there was barely a minute between us, "why have you been avoiding me?"

"I haven't been avoiding you." I sniff indignantly through my bald-faced lie.

"Yeah, sure. My fifty unanswered texts and calls beg to differ."

"I've been busy."

"Busy fucking our brother's best friend," she mutters as we file into her kitchen.

"Not true. I haven't seen Myles since Monday. I only got back from York this morning."

"Bet you've had time to call and text Myles multiple times, though. And before you even try to deny *that*, I know for a fact that you have because I was sat next to him when you texted him to say you'd stopped at a services on your way home."

I lick my lips as if that'll help me avoid the inquisition that's about to hit me. "He asked me to give him an update whenever I could…"

"And what about me? Huh? I'm your sister. Your *twin*. We shared a womb!"

"You know full well that if I started updating you with my every move, you'd get irritated real quick."

"I still deserve a reply!"

I blink at her after her outburst, a little bewildered. "Er... Sorry?"

She blows out a breath. "Thank you. Sorry."

I can't help but eye her warily. "Are you okay, Brin? You seem a bit...stressed."

"I don't know, Shez," she whines, leaning over the kitchen island. "Andy has been super weird recently, work is a bit overwhelming, Mum won't leave me alone, Beau has been kind of awol, and now you won't answer a text!"

I close the space between us and wrap her in a hug. "I'm sorry, Brin. I just...didn't want to talk about Myles yet, and that's kind of all you texted me about. If you'd have said things are getting a lot, I would've answered." And I mean that wholeheartedly. Of all of us, I know best what it's like to be stuck in that dark place in your head. The thought of Brin on her way there unsettles me. "You know that, right?"

She pulls back but doesn't completely let go. I am looking in a mirror, except it's warped and not quite accurate. Sometimes it startles me how different we are in every way except our genetics. "I do know, Shez," she tells me. "I just wanted to talk about something *exciting*. Someone finally sees you for how awesome you are, and I wanted to gush with you. Also, Myles? God, that man is so lovely and I'm so happy you're getting to enjoy some real time with him."

I groan, head lolling back. "Now I feel like a twat for ignoring you."

"As you should," she says primly. "I was rooting for you from day one, as you know. Speaking to Myles on Friday about you gave me a distraction from all this shit."

"I guess we can talk about him after dinner," I concede.

"*Hell* yes. And I want *all* the dirty details. If only to distract from the fact that my own relationship is on rocky terrain."

I try not to turn my nose up at the mention of John Andrews. The only reason I agreed to dinner at theirs instead of my house tonight is because I've been assured that he's out of town. The flat is his and the decor gives me a migraine. It's so…white. Clinical. It reminds me of a morgue. He refuses to let me touch it.

"What's going on?"

"I don't know." She sighs, turning the oven on. She moves around the kitchen robotically as she speaks, prepping to start cooking. "Ever since we got back from Lerwick he's been getting more and more distant. He works late, he barely talks when he's home, always on his phone. I don't know what to do."

I chew on my lip thoughtfully. "You don't think he's… Christ, I hate to suggest it, Brin, but do you think he might be cheating?"

"It's not a ridiculous assumption, and I had the same thought originally, but honestly, Shez, he doesn't have the libido to cheat."

I wrinkle my nose. Information I could've done without. "Hm… Maybe you should just talk to him? Avoiding the problem won't make it any better."

"I know, he's just… You saw how he was with Myles at Dad's birthday. Sometimes talking to him can be like trying to get a conversation out of the God damn wall. He's a pig-headed bastard at times."

You don't say. "Has it happened before?"

"No, never."

I purse my lips. "I don't know then, Brin. I still say at least try and talk to him. You can't live with him not knowing where you stand."

My sister pulls a face. "Of course, you're right. I'm just whining."

"Hey, we all need a good whinge every now and then. Let it all out."

"Mum has been worse than usual." Brinsley doesn't even hesitate. "I don't know what is wrong with her, but she will not stop pestering me. Sometimes I have to wonder if working in the same school as her and doing the same subject was a smart choice. She's incessant, Shez. Now she's a deputy head she's got less classes, which apparently means more time to harass me. She sits in on my lessons! At least once a week! Honestly it was cute the first time, but now…"

Brinsley rants about our mother for the next thirty minutes, and I barely manage to get a word in.

I do feel guilty for ignoring her. She clearly doesn't have many other people to confide in when it comes to her stress. The fact that she doesn't even feel like she can rant to Andy about things is another strike against him. Currently, on the pros and cons list I keep of him in my head, the pros list is looking short. It might be awful to say, but I hope she dumps him.

By the time we've sat down and are eating, we've moved onto the topic of Beau, who is in the doghouse with both of us over the Myles thing.

"Does he know you're seeing each other?"

"Not as far as I know," I say, just before I shove my face full of spaghetti.

"Well, I haven't told anyone, not even Mum, so he can't know."

"I reckon he's sulking over not having Myles in his corner. Apparently, Dad's birthday is the first time they've seen each other since the summer, and we all know it was rather frosty between them."

Brin whistles, cringing. "All your fault, Shez."

"It's fucking stupid, is what it is. Beau is a grown man. I'm a grown woman. I'm allowed to make my own choices about who I do or don't see."

"Amen, sister." Brin raises her glass of water at me." But you're preaching to the choir. I do think you should tell Mum, though."

"She'll just run straight to Beau about it, though, and I'm not ready for that fight yet. I don't even know how serious this thing is between us—I just know we like each other."

Brin seems to have hearts in her eyes. "*God*, it's so fucking cute. I love the start of a relationship. Everything is just so new and nice."

"'Relationship' is a bit of a stretch. We're just…"

"Fucking?"

I roll my eyes. "No. Well, yes, but I meant more like…getting to know each other better."

"While fucking."

I let out a heavy breath. "Yes."

"Is he good in bed?"

Now I'm blushing. "Maybe."

"That's a yes." My sister cackles. "Good for you, Sheridan. Shit, do I miss the days when I was having really great sex every day," she says wistfully.

I can't believe I ask it, but I do. "Is Andy good in bed?" I've never *wanted* to ask before.

"When he bothers, yeah. But tell me more about Myles. I know I work with him, but I won't say anything, I swear. Stays between us."

I know she's good for her word. So, I take a deep breath, and I unload the goods on my sister.

* * *

Maybe it's cute. Maybe it's cringeworthy. Maybe it's eye-wateringly pathetic. But I don't care.

When Myles knocked on my door five minutes ago, I basically launched myself at him, and we've had our lips locked ever since. Somehow, we've managed to make it halfway down the hall and the front door is closed, but I'm pressed against the wall with my legs hooked around Myles's waist like I've never known the taste of a man before.

And I. Don't. Care.

"Am I crazy in saying I feel like it's been weeks since I last saw you?" Myles pants into my mouth.

I shove my hands through his sandy hair. "I missed you, too."

"I feel like a teenager. Being around so many has sent my hormones out of whack."

"You certainly don't feel like a teenager to me," I mumble, referencing the rather large erection currently pressing hard against my centre. Nope, he feels *all man.*

He groans, moving his hands from my waist and down to my backside, taking it in a tight grip. "I am so out of control around you, it's fucking embarrassing."

"I think it's cute."

He lightly wets my nose with his tongue as he pulls me away from the wall. "You're a terrible distraction, Birdie. I came here to see some interior designs."

I sigh, resting my head against his shoulder. "Fine, if we must."

"Where am I going?"

"My office." I tidied away all my web show stuff this afternoon, knowing he wanted to see my *real* work.

Myles carries me through the cottage with ease and lets himself into my most sacred room, with me still clinging to him like a koala, sponging kisses into his neck. He gently places me back on the ground when we're inside, and I don't miss the way he readjusts himself in his work slacks.

Going over my bookcase, I pull out two photo albums. "These are projects that are now all completed. Residential," I tap one folder, "and non-residential. Or commercial if you like."

Myles takes the heavy albums off my hands and sits himself down in the office chair at my desk to start flipping through them.

He's silent for a while, but he pays such great attention to each photo, I feel weirdly judged. And the pathetic thing is that I want to please this man more than anything right now. He spends a lot of time on one particular flip, leaning over the photos so closely that I debate asking him if he needs a magnifying glass.

"This one is really cool," he says, looking up at me.

It's the first hotel I ever did. Not massive—a twenty-bedroom boutique country place in the Cotswolds. They wanted a contemporary twist on traditional Edwardian decor, and every room had to be different yet cohesive somehow.

"That's the very first project I did that got me an award," I tell him.

"I can see why," he says with such earnest honesty, my chest tightens a little.

While he continues fingering through the albums, I dig around for the plans I'm sending out next week.

"These are my mood boards," I tell him as I set a couple down beside him. "When a client sends me a brief, once I've seen the property I come home and start digging around for all the elements I want to use. I go through a lot of changes before I'm happy, which is why I've got such a big whiteboard." I thumb the monstrosity over my shoulder, now empty until I need to start using it for the York house.

"When I've made a decision, I put together these mood boards," I take each board out of the box to show him. "This is for a small cottage in North Wales, right on the coast. I'm only doing the lounge and the kitchen, but I give them a visual," I point at the digital image of the lounge, "of how it's all going to look, and then I attach all the fabrics I want to use on another, and then furniture and accessories on another."

He paws through the boards as if they're some kind of delicate jewellery. "And you do this for every project?"

"Yep. It's probably my favourite part of the job—clipping it all together."

"Fucking hell, that's a lot." He blows out a breath. "Do you get a choice in the projects you do?"

"Mostly. Marina—my boss—tries to distribute the projects to the person she thinks it suits best, but it can be a lot at times. This has easily been my busiest year since starting. Not just because we've been a designer down, but also because I've been—" I grimace, hating to say it, "well, I've been requested a lot."

"I'd request you too." He winks, and I blush like a fool. "I'd love to know what you'd do with my flat."

"Well, I'd have to see it first."

"That can be arranged. But I have to warn you," he stands, and twiddles with one of the curls brushing around my ear, "it's very boring."

"Most rented places are. Are you allowed to do anything to it?"

"I can paint it. But I have to paint it back white if I ever decide to leave. Why, what are you thinking?"

I purse my lips. "Don't know. But it could be fun to see it, and then come up with something just for funsies."

"You want to see my flat?" He seems bewildered by the thought.

"Sure, why not?" I shrug.

*   *   *

"Oh, wow."

Myles looks at me as if to say, "I knew it". I'm not sure what I was expecting, but it wasn't this. Rental properties can be anything from mouldy, damp, leaking dungeons to clean and dry and bright bachelor pads.

Myles's flat takes clean and bright to the next fucking level.

First of all, it's whiter than John Andrews's flat. In fact, it's so white that my eyes are starting to hurt. It's a boring person's dream. A bachelor pad for the tasteless. Even the carpet is off-white, which is just a disaster waiting to happen.

"Well?" Myles prompts.

"It's got two bedrooms. That's good."

"We didn't come here to talk about the layout, Birdie."

"No…" I bite my lip. "God, it's so white. You really need some pictures or art or something 'cause it's starting to give me a headache."

He snorts. "I'll only take advice from you. I can't use nails or screws, though."

"Oh, *boo*." I huff. "I just want to lob buckets of paint at it—all different colours. Pastels or summat. *Anything* to make it *less white*."

"Is there anything you like about it?"

"Yes. It's a blank canvas. I have more ideas than I know what to do with."

"That must be good for motivation, right?"

"Oh, yeah. Fucking marvellous. Except I'm not allowed to touch anything. I'm itching to get my hands on a paint roller."

"It's fine to paint. But as much as I like the idea of you doing this beautiful mural for me, I'd have to paint over it eventually, which would not only make me sad, but it would also be hard work."

I stare at the large wall for a minute, chewing on my lip. "Okay, no murals. I don't have time for that anyway. *But* I'm thinking we paint this wall a nice pastel colour—like sage or duck egg. And then we find some nice artwork, or make some pieces ourselves, uniform sizes, nice black wooden frames and use those tabs to hang them up that just pull off."

My brain is running a mile a minute. "And we can do the same in your bedroom. Paint one wall, cover the rest in artwork."

"I love how your brain works, but how much money is this gonna cost me?"

"Don't you worry, handsome." I pat his arm. "I know all the right places to go to get a good deal."

Chapter Twenty-Four

Cuddles on Park Benches

MYLES

After Sheridan finishes making her plans for the light refurb on my flat, we head into the city. We go for lunch in the city centre at Antalya—the Turkish restaurant Sheridan did the interior design for—and then we stop by her friend's little sewing shop to pick up a few things she had on order.

The owner, Sarah-Jane, is a beautiful fiery little thing with copper hair that cascades over her shoulders and down her back in thick waves, and an eclectic fashion sense. Her dress is a patchwork of fabric, colour, and patterns, but it's clearly handmade and one of a kind. I immediately decide that I like her.

"What's going on next door?" Sheridan asks, which sets Sarah-Jane off on a tangent.

"Don't get me started, Shez. You know that hotel closed down just after I opened this place, and those awful bastard owners have left it to rot. It's awful behind those damn boards. *Now*, the owners have decided they want to sell the fucking thing. Now! After leaving it to fester into a shithole for three years!"

Sheridan winces, but whether it's at the situation or Sarah-Jane's volume, I'm not sure. "Yikes. Well, the good thing is it's got loads of potential. It was beautiful before… It can be again."

"I'll be sure to tell the idiot who buys it that you're the best interior designer in the world," Sarah-Jane vows.

"Bit of a stretch, but I appreciate the plug all the same. See you soon, Sassy."

"Bye Shez, and Shez's hot friend."

I have to laugh. "Can I put that on my CV?"

"*Shez's hot friend*?" Sheridan grins. "Yeah, quality skill to have in your arsenal."

"I think so." I wrap my arm around her shoulders. "How do we feel about mini golf?"

She ponders this for a moment. "I'm terrible at it, as I am at most sports, but I enjoy it."

"Wanna do that this afternoon? It could be our first official date…"

"And here I thought our first date was four months ago on the beach when we drew each other's faces."

"No, baby. That was just flirting."

"Were you flirting? I can't remember—I've slept since then."

"Flirting or not, that was not first date-worthy, cute as you are. Come on, let's trash mini golf."

"Okay, okay," she says around giggles, "mini golf it is."

* * *

Four days later, while I sit behind my desk during my free Wednesday morning, I'm still thinking about Sheridan's colossal loss at mini golf. And it wasn't for lack of trying—she put her heart, soul, hips, *and* ass into every one of those swings, and still managed to lose her ball on most holes around the course.

At least she looked cute as fuck while doing it, in her little pink dungarees and Docs. I'm not one for teasing either, but when we got back to the cottage, I made more golf innuendos than I care to admit. At least she found them funny. Making Sheridan laugh feels good—I love seeing that unfiltered joy on her face. I love a lot about her, actually, but that thought feels a bit too deep and premature for such an early period in our relationship. If that's what we're doing. Again, we haven't even discussed labels yet. I'm just glad she hasn't told me to fuck off yet.

While I'm reminiscing on our perfect weekend, someone knocks on my classroom door.

I glance up as they slip in—one of the other teachers. I think his name is Bradley, but we've never spoken, and I don't even know what he teaches.

"Hey, Myles," he says with an awkward little wave. The bloke is exuding some serious nerd energy—woollen button-down vest over his shirt in a dull blue colour, with a tweed bowtie to match. It's wrong to stereotype, I know—he could ride a motorbike and sleep with a different woman every week for all I know. But his demeanour doesn't suggest that at all. "I'm Bradley—I teach Physics."

Oop, there it is. I would've guessed Maths, but I guess he does have a bit of a *Big Bang Theory* vibe going on.

"Hi, Brad." I figure if I give him a nickname right off the bat, he'll loosen up. The tension in his shoulders can't be good for his posture. "How can I help?"

"Sorry for interrupting your free period, I just… I have the same one and Brinsley said you might be about."

Brinsley does seem to have this habit of adopting the nerds. There's me, for one. By week two she was having coffee every morning with a dorky looking Music teacher who went to Brit School, and last week she was talking shop with one of the History teachers about Henry VIII. It does not surprise me that she's corralled this guy into her little gang, too.

"Sure, what's up?" I offer him to sit, and he perches on the edge of a table rather than a stool.

Interesting.

"There're two things, actually. Um, first, I thought you might like this." He hands me a leaflet and then adjusts his collar, as if he's about to start choking. I give him a cautious glance and then read the leaflet.

It details a competition through various different media for kids in schools and colleges to win an art scholarship in London. I've never heard of the company before, but it sounds interesting. I'd be willing to bet some of the GCSE kids would be interested.

"How did you find out about this?" I ask him.

Working with kids, you can't just throw them into something if it's not legitimate. I'm sure Brad knows this as a teacher himself, but it's good to ask.

"Oh, the people organising the competition are uni friends of mine," he says with the most confidence yet. "They know I work in a school, so they asked me to pass it on. It's completely legit, authorised by the government. I'm sure you've got some talented kids who might be interested."

I do. Even Jamie from my Year 9B group would probably like it.

"Thanks, Brad. I'll look into it."

"Cool." He rubs his hands on his trousers as he stands.

Am I that intimidating, or is Bradley just nervous all the time? Do his students run riot over him? I'd love to be a fly on the wall in that classroom.

"What was the other thing?" I ask before he manages to escape.

Bradley blinks. "What?"

"You said there were two things. That," I nod to the leaflet, "and something else."

"Oh, right. Um…" He plays with his bow tie, then his vest, and then shoves his hands in his pockets, irritated with himself. "I'm sorry if this is weird, but I just wanted to put my mind at ease before I do anything."

What a way to start. "Okay…"

"Are you and Emily…like, involved?"

I stare at him. "Emily, the French teacher, Emily?"

"Yeah."

"Involved?"

"Yeah. Or dating, or f—" poor sod can't even say the word 'fucking' out loud "—I don't know, anything?"

"No."

"No?"

"No. Emily I are not involved, or dating, or *fucking*, or anything of the sort," I assure him. And I don't know why he thinks we might be.

"Oh." Bradley nods, his bushy brows furrowing. I've met supermodels who'd donate a spleen for eyebrows like his. "Have you...?"

"Mate." I splutter a laugh because this conversation is getting weird. "No offence, but I don't know you, and that's not the sort of question you ask a stranger."

"I'm sorry," Brad groans, "I promise I'm not a complete loser. Here's the thing: Emily is my girlfriend. Or, at least, I think she is."

I'm bewildered. "You *think* she's your girlfriend?"

"Yeah. So, in the summer, we were talking and flirting a lot. We went out a couple of time, did...you know."

"You've slept together?"

Bradley blushes, and it's kind of sweet. I didn't think I'd ever use the word 'sweet' to describe another man, let alone an older one, but here we are.

"Yes. Like I said, she's my girlfriend. When we came back to school, I *asked* her to be my girlfriend and she said yes. We were seeing each other regularly, sleeping over each other's places, doing couple-y things. And then the past few weeks she's just stopped talking to me. Like, will not answer my texts, calls, never even acknowledges me here. She's basically ghosted me."

I expect him to continue, but he doesn't. "Okay...where do I come into this?"

"Well, some of the guys said that you're her type and that they've seen the two of you flirting."

I try not to lose my temper. "And who are *the guys*?"

"The Science teachers."

I roll my eyes. Who knew science bros would be such gossips? "Right. Firstly, no, I'm not sleeping, and have never slept with Emily. Second of all, I have it on good authority that Emily flirts with *everyone*, not just me, and you should probably be having this conversation with her, not me. Thirdly, I *am* involved with someone else and am not in any position to jeopardise that with someone I work with, because I like the girl a lot."

Brad stares at me. "Oh, shit." I'm genuinely surprised the bloke has the capacity to swear. "I'm sorry, I didn't realise. If it's not someone you work with, then I guess it's not Brinsley?"

This guy. "You are incredibly nosey for someone so awkward. But no, it isn't Brinsley. It's her sister."

"Oh. *Oh!* Wait, isn't she a twin? Doesn't that get confusing?"

"They're very different," I bite out. I let loose a long sigh and drag my hands down my face. "Look, Brad, I don't want to talk about my personal life on school grounds, not least because her sister works here, but so does her mum, and I don't think Shirley knows yet. But I do wanna help you with your Emily problem, so how about we go for a drink later?"

"On a Wednesday?"

I give him a flat look.

"Right. Yeah, okay."

"Good. Did you drive here?"

"No, I walk to work."

"Good—meet me in the car park and I'll drive us. Also, you need to get better friends. Or tell them to stop gossiping so much, especially when it comes to your life. That shit can be hurtful, and considering we're in a school, they should know better."

Brad seems shell shocked for a beat. "Wow. Thanks, Myles."

"No problem."

Bradley leaves with a spring in his step, and I let my head fall on the table.

That poor bloke. I don't know if Emily is leading him on or she likes him and she's scared, but I don't know how I've got dragged into it.

Still, I want to help the guy. It might be good for me to have another friend at work, especially a male one, because I've been spending all my time with the Bennett women, and as great as they are, I need some variety.

* * *

"Mum said you made a new friend this week?" Sheridan says as I buckle up in the passenger seat of her Mini the following Saturday.

She woke up this morning and declared she wanted to go for a drive. Apparently, she's a much more confident driver than I am because I can't say I've ever had that urge myself. It might have something to do with growing up in London and the fact that I never really had it as an option, but according to Sheridan, it's one of the only times she ever *really* wants to leave the house.

To each their own.

"How does your mum know that?" I ask, even though I can probably work it out for myself.

"Well, Mum heard it from Brin and Brin heard it from Bradley. Bradley is the new friend, right?"

"Yeah." I sigh. "He's a strange one, but I like him. His science teacher friends are just a bit…out of touch."

"How so?" She turns the engine on and it's a lot louder than I expected.

"They're a little fantastical in their way of thinking. It was a big leap from the truth."

"What you just said doesn't make any sense."

"They told Brad that Emily and I had been sleeping together. Emily is allegedly his girlfriend."

"Emily the harlot?"

I give her a look and she laughs.

"How did they draw this conclusion?"

"Well, according to Brad I'm the most handsome faculty member so it made the most sense."

"Ah." Sheridan nods. "Seems like the men of the Science department have got a little man crush on you, Myles."

"Not if they're accusing me of stealing Brad's girlfriend."

She pats my knee. "It's kind of a compliment if you think about it. What does Brad look like?"

"Why—you interested?" I joke. "Maybe we can all do a swap. You and Nerdy Brad and me and Emily the Harlot." Sounds like a sit-com title.

She punches my arm and I laugh at the scowl on her face, but I can see she's fighting a smile.

I think about him outside of his fashion choices. "Boyish, I guess? Like he's obviously a few years older than me but he's got a young face. Like that kid from *Love Actually* and *Maze Runner*."

"Oh, yeah. I know who you mean."

"But he's stockier than that and his hair is darker."

"What are his hands like?"

I throw her a look. "What the fuck does that have to do with anything?"

"A woman like Emily might be conceited on some level, but she obviously slept with him multiple times for a reason. Dork or not, Bradley clearly knows *some* tricks in the bedroom, and I'm pretty sure it's nothing to do with reciting the periodic table or where certain foods fall on the PH scale. I'd bet he's good with his hands."

I stare at her, gobsmacked. I can't believe that just came out of her mouth, quite honestly. "What are they meant to look like?"

"They're not *meant* to look like anything. But slender fingers are a good start. The best people to talk to about male hands are the Scott sisters. Brandy especially."

I frown and look at my own hands. I don't know if they're adequate.

Sheridan pats my knee in that way again, throwing me a smile. "Your hands are perfect, bab."

Bab. I've noticed the Bennetts use that term of endearment a lot, especially with each other. It's definitely a regional thing because you wouldn't hear a Londoner come out with it. I know Brian in particular uses it a lot.

Alongside a compliment like that, I feel a bit bashful.

We drive out of the village and away from the city entirely and into the Warwickshire countryside. Sheridan tells me about her week, which sounds eventful and exhausting, and I listen like it's the best podcast I've ever heard.

She's got a playlist on, which she refers to as her driving playlist. There's all sorts going on, from country to pop to soft rock to hard rock. Every damn day I learn a new side of her, and her varying music taste is just one of them. As she sings along to Jungle, cruising the country lanes as if they're the veins on the back of her hand, I find myself smiling, and I find myself falling.

I tell her about the competition for the kids, which I did a bit more research on after speaking to Brad about it properly. His friend's company is bigger than I realised—it's for all kinds of art and media and has great links to various platforms for young people to get into all sorts of creative careers.

There's an art scholarship, but there's also music, photography, journalism, social media, film, and TV. It's a great company and a brilliant starting point for young people to launch a career.

It's not only for kids, though, and that's why it's important work. Even for adults who need a change in career, The Creation Coup is the best place to start.

Sheridan drives like she's been doing it since birth. Even though, because the car is compact and low to the ground it feels like we're constantly going 100mph, I feel safe with her driving. I think I might always feel safe around her, car, or no car.

We drive the country roads for hours, through villages and parishes with pubs and churches, until we circle around to Stratford-upon-Avon just in time for lunch. We park up for a nice gastro-style interlude, and then we take a walk along the river and back. While it would've been nice to have Hector here with us, he never would've stomached a car journey that long. He's spending the day with Brinsley instead.

It's a warm day for late October and the sun is floating in the cloudless sky.

We pick up a coffee for the way back and sit on the riverside for a second before we get going.

Sheridan cuddles into my side as we sip our hot drinks, and I wrap my arm around her shoulders, keeping her tucked close. I bury my nose in her hair, delighted with that apple scent she always carried.

"I never thought I'd be in one of those couples that cuddle on park benches," Sheridan mumbles.

I don't know if I want to shove off the joy that comes with hearing her refer to us as a couple. "Neither did I. I've been a bit of a whore until this past year."

She snorts. "I'm quite the opposite."

"You've had boyfriends before, right?" Anyone who gives head like she does must have had a boyfriend.

"One. With my lacking social skills, I've never quite had that finesse when it comes to relationships. And my one serious boyfriend was equally as awkward and lacked libido."

"Yikes. How long did that last?"

"A year. Then he told me he's gay and now he's married to a man."

"Oh, shit."

She sniggers. "Oh shit, indeed."

"You don't seem very…upset about it."

"What do you mean?" She peers up at me with that big cerulean gaze, and I just about melt into the Avon River.

I peck the tip of her nose. "I know a lot of girls who'd be scarred for life if their boyfriend dumped them for a man."

She rolls her eyes. "That's stupid. I'm not the *reason* he's gay. He was already gay before he met me. I don't hate myself so much that I think I have the ability to change a man's sexuality.

"We're still friends—he's one of the contractors I recommend for jobs. He invited me to his wedding!"

"That's cool. I like that you didn't let it bother you."

Sheridan scoffs and settles back into my side. "It is what it is. Unless it happens repeatedly, there isn't a problem."

"Can we go back to the other thing where you called us a couple?"

"We are a couple!"

"We haven't had that chat yet," I retort.

"Okay, fine. I'm not sleeping with other people. Are you?"

"No" I say firmly.

"Do you want to sleep with other people?"

"Nope."

"Me neither. I also say we skip the 'exclusive' stage because it's stupid."

"Is that you asking me to be your boyfriend?"

She seems to think about this for a minute, her gaze trained on the calm river. "Yeah, I guess it is."

I lean forward, blocking her view of the Avon, and smack a kiss to her lips. "I'll be your boyfriend, Birdie, as long as you'll be mine."

"You want me to be your boyfriend?"

I pinch her waist and she yelps. "Cheeky girl."

She makes a happy little noise that brings a smile to my face. "I really need to break the news to my mum."

"I thought you already told her?"

"No, not yet."

"But she told you about Brad."

"Yeah, Myles, people like to tell me shit about your life now. Like Brin texting me every day with what you're wearing. Mum likes to keep me up to date on your social life, for some reason."

"You're gonna make her the happiest mum on the planet."

"Yeah… I just need to figure out how to convince her not to tell the boys."

A horrible but valid point. "We'll cross that bridge when we get to it."

Chapter Twenty-Five

ROOMIES

SHERIDAN

Today is a sad day. The end of the line. The closing of an era.

I've just posted the last ever episode of *Goth Frogs*, and I find myself a little overcome. I didn't expect to be this sad, but as soon as I hit *Post,* I burst into tears. Apparently, I'm more sentimental than I thought. I didn't even cry when I finished animating it.

Now what am I going to do? *Goth Frogs* has been my main project for close to two years. I suppose I have that fae story I started when I was pissed off with Nash, but I don't know if it has any real merit. Although, I didn't think *Goth Frogs* had any merit, and now it's up for Toonie awards, so what do I know?

Hector twitches in my lap. He curled up there after the floodgates opened and he hasn't left since. I'm too scared to move. I don't want to wake him when he looks so comfortable, but it's getting late, and I need to eat. Plus, I need a distraction from my misery over *Goth Frogs* ending.

As delicately as I can, I collect him into my arms and slip out of my office into the lounge. The radiator is on, so I nudge his bed closer and lay him down so he's still cosy and warm.

In the kitchen, I start prepping some dinner with my music on a low volume. I have a cooking playlist, which is quite the contrast to my Drawing playlist and my Driving playlist. There's a lot more country and pop on this one, to help keep me motivated.

I'm humming along to Morgan Wallen's One Thing at a Time when it abruptly cuts off.

I half expect to find my mother calling me, but I'm wrong.

"Hey," I answer Myles's call. He usually calls me a little later in the evening, but I don't mind hearing his voice now. It's a comfort these days.

"Hey, Birdie. You busy?"

I shiver at the nickname like a complete saddo. I hear it almost every day now, but it still sends goosebumps along my arms. "Just started making dinner."

"Okay... Are you in a place you can hold off for a while? Or does that have the potential to burn the house down?"

I pause in my prepping. "Why, what's wrong?"

"Er, there's been an accident in the flat above mine and now my flat is kinda leaking. And flooded."

"Oh, shit. Are you okay? Is it bad?"

"Well, the walls look like they're crying in some places. And there's an inch of water in all the rooms."

"Christ, okay. You want to stay here until it's sorted?" I offer before really thinking about it.

He sighs. "As long as you don't mind?"

"No, of course not. I'll come out to you now, alright? Give me fifteen minutes."

"Thanks, baby."

I hate how sad he sounds. "See you in a sec."

I tidy everything up so that I can easily pick it up when we get back and close all the kitchen doors so that Hector can't eat anything he shouldn't while I'm gone.

A minute later, I'm in my car and on my way to Myles's place.

When I get there, his patio doors are open and he's trying to scoop water out with a bucket.

"Hey," I announce myself.

Myles looks up, face flushed and hair a stressed, tousled mess. "Hi, gorgeous."

There goes my stomach and my heart, fluttering away. Again.

"I brought my wellies," I tell him, accepting the light peck he gives me.

"Good girl. The landlord is sending someone tomorrow to pump out the water, but it could be a week before it dries out completely," Myles explains as he shows me the inside.

There's definitely more than an inch of water now. At least three. The walls are staining with wet streaks, and some of the light fittings are somehow leaking.

I notice that the TV is still turned on when it's dangerously close to being an electrical hazard. I make for the wall switch, but not before I notice what's on the screen.

Goth Frogs. The last episode.

I glance Myles's way to find him arranging a couple of bags on the dining table.

"What were you watching?" I ask, as nonchalantly as I can manage.

"Just a web show I like," he says, without any indication that he knows I'm the creator. "I'll have to finish it some other time."

"You can watch it when we get back to mine?"

He meets my gaze then, but the look in his eyes suggests he's not interested in my silly web show anymore. "Maybe."

I spend an hour helping Myles bucket water into the drain outside, and then pack his essentials into a suitcase.

Then we drive back to the cottage in our own cars.

It gives me just enough time to have a miniature meltdown over the fact that *Myles watches my fucking web show. Because he likes it.*

I let out a scream as we drive through the city. I'm not sure what I'm screaming for, but it feels good. Of all the shows in all the world he could've picked to enjoy, it had to be mine.

It's wonderful, obviously. I've never been so hot for a man, and the best part is he has no idea. I'll have to tell him eventually, obviously, but right now I can keep my little secret to myself, just a bit longer. I kind of want to watch it with him. I want to know what he's like when he watches it. Does he keep his cards close to his chest? Or does he put it all out in the open?

We haven't really done the sit down and watch a movie thing yet, because whenever we're in the privacy of my house, we're usually sucking face, cooking, or shagging. Sometimes all three. We did that last Saturday night after we got back from Stratford, and it was incredible.

Right there on the breakfast table in the kitchen.

I need to repaint the wall.

I shove all illicit thoughts away as we enter the village outskirts. I've had my meltdown and my hot flush. Now I need to concentrate on looking after my man.

First, I help him unload his things.

In the entry hall, Myles sighs and falls back against the front door once it's closed. I sidle up to him, wrap my arms around his middle, and rest my head on his chest. "You okay?" I ask as he reciprocates the embrace.

"Yeah, just one thing I didn't want to have to deal with on a random Wednesday, you know?"

I nod, peering up at him with a sympathetic smile. "I know. But you can stay here as long as you need to."

"Thank you, baby."

We share a kiss, one full of kind promises and genuine affection. He strokes my cheek and I rub his back.

Something tells me I wouldn't mind if he never had to leave.

I peel myself off him and head for the lounge to check on the dog. Myles smacks my ass as I retreat, and I yelp.

A head appears above the back of the couch, and I'm about to scream that an intruder has managed to get in. The head turns before I can open my mouth, and a pair of familiar blue eyes greet me, bloodshot above a snotty nose.

"Brin?"

My twin sniffs, wiping her wet eyes. "Sorry for just turning up."

I run to the sofa and bring her into a hug. "Don't ever apologise for that."

"I'm still sorry. I didn't realise Myles was staying tonight."

I peek at Myles, who is hovering in the doorway, likely unsure of what to do with himself.

"Shall I go?" He mouths.

I shake my head with a scowl. He points upstairs and I nod. A second later, he's gone.

"He wasn't supposed to be, but he had an emergency of his own," I admit.

"God, I should go." Brin pulls back, sniffing.

"No, you should stay. Talk to me. What happened?"

"Fucking Andy. That's what."

"You had a fight?"

She makes a dull sound. "Could say that, in the sense that I fought him, and he just called me insane."

Bastard. "Did you confront him, then? About his recent behaviour?"

"Oh no, Shez. I didn't have to. I was supposed to be staying at the school late today because the English, Maths and Science departments had an important meeting about exams for core subjects, but it got cancelled at the last minute and moved to next week. Andy apparently had decided that because I was going out for dinner with the faculty after, he was going to have his *other* girlfriend over for dinner and sex on the sofa."

I stare at her for a second, unsure if I heard her right. Then the white noise starts and I'm positive I did. "Excuse me?"

"Yeah. When I said he didn't have the libido to cheat on me, I was talking out my arsehole apparently, because it turns out he does have the libido, but he spends it all on the girl who sits at the fucking reception desk in his precious fucking bank!"

"What a cunt," I huff.

Brin wipes her wet cheeks indignantly when the tears start falling again. "I'm in shock, Sheridan. I think I must've lost my damn sanity if I thought he was faithful. Months this has been going on. Since, like January. He didn't come away with us in the summer because he took her on a four-day break to Lake *fucking* Como! I've always wanted to go there!"

The more hysterical she gets, the more I want to drive into the city again just to punch him in the face. And then kick him in the dick.

"Right. You're moving in here, okay?" Another decision tonight I've made in a second. "I don't care how long it takes you to find a new place. On Saturday, we're going to that bastard's house and getting all your stuff out of there. Myles will help, too."

"Shez, you don't have to do that," Brin whines.

"Yes, I do. You're my sister and I love you. I have two spare rooms. Plus, no one wants to move back in with their parents."

She manages to splutter out a laugh, and I take that as my win for the day. Two wins, really, since my boyfriend loves my web show. "Thank you, Shez. You know, you're my favourite person."

"You're mine, too." I bring her hand to my lips.

"Yeah, well... Looks like I'm soon to be replaced by Myles."

"Never," I insist. *"We shared a womb."* She giggles again. "Do you want a drink?"

"An alcoholic one?"

"Obviously. I also need to finish making dinner, so if you've not eaten, I've got you covered, sissy."

"Isn't it a bit late for you?"

"Yeah, but Myles called, and I had to rescue him first."

"Poor bloke." She sighs. "I've probably ruined his night."

"No, I think the leak in his flat probably did that."

Brin cringes and then lets out another sigh. After a pensive second, she says, "I really like Myles, Sheridan. For you. He looks at you the way you deserve to be looked at."

"I really like him, too."

With that, I head into the kitchen to pour her a glass of wine and turn the oven on again. I tell Brin to find something to watch on the telly, and then I head upstairs to check on Myles.

I find him staring out the window overlooking the canal, hands on his hips. I wrap my arms around his middle, burying my face in his back. His posture relaxes, arms coming to rest over mine.

"Is Brin okay?" He asks, stroking his hands along my forearms.

"She will be as soon as I get her out of that bastard's flat."

"I heard what he did. I could murder him for that."

The warmth radiating off him is sleep-inducing. "So, could I. But please don't. I'm not cut out to be a prison wife.

That makes him chuckle, leaving me two-for-two. "You'd be the sexiest prison wife around, though. Endless bragging rights about my fit wife waiting for me on the outside."

"I'd still rather you didn't kill a man, even if it was for being trash to my sister."

He turns in my hold to face me, but in the next breath he has me lifted up with my legs wrapped around his waist. "I have no plans to go anywhere without you, Birdie."

Then we're kissing again, tangled together like this is how we're always meant to be. I've never felt more wanted than with this man.

"Will you keep Brin company while I make us dinner?" I ask when we've collected ourselves again.

"Sure thing. I already ate, so you don't need to worry about me."

"Thank you, Myles." I peck his mouth again. "It's about to get very cosy in this house."

* * *

Later that night, after the kitchen is tidy and Myles and I have made quiet, slow love, I'm still wide awake thinking about my sister and her piece of shit boyfriend. Myles is wrapped around me like a protective bear, but I know he isn't sleeping either, probably thinking about his flat and what it means for his tenancy. He's more fidgety than usual.

I roll onto my side to face him, and he brings me flush against his body. "Are you okay?" I whisper.

"Yeah. Today was a lot, I guess," he mumbles, his lips grazing my hairline.

In the dark, I trace my fingertips over the lines of the bear tattoo on his abdomen. I still don't know what it means. "I know. I'm sorry about your flat."

He shrugs. "Not the end of the world. I'm just glad we hadn't decorated it yet."

"Me too. I would've been devastated."

There's a quiet moment, where neither of us speak but we can't help touching one another. My lips trail his chest while his fingertips brush and tickle the expanse of my back.

I love these moments with him. I love the intimacy he gives—that he doesn't shy away from touching me. That he seems to want to be around me as much as I want to be around him.

"Do you think Brin's alright?"

"I think I've heard her crying," I admit.

"Me too."

I search for Myles's gaze in the dark, and he's easy to find—already looking at me. He licks the tip of my nose, and then meets my mouth again.

"I don't mind if you want to keep her company tonight, Birdie," he mumbles against my lips. "She probably needs your comfort more than I do."

I fight off a groan and fail. Why is being considerate such a turn on? "I hate how good you are sometimes."

He rumbles out a laugh that vibrates deliciously against my chest. "Want me to be a bit of a prick tomorrow?"

"Yeah, can you, like, talk shit about my mum or summat? Just don't cheat on me."

"I only have eyes for you, baby."

I snort and push him onto his back before mounting him again. "Do you want some bread with that cheese?"

I can see the beautiful grin on his handsome face. "No. But I wouldn't mind if you came on my dick one more time before leaving me for the night." He lifts his hips, emphasising his arousal.

"I think I can do that."

***

Ten minutes later, I slip into the room my sister is staying in, and tuck myself under the covers behind her, spooning her. She sniffles but rests her arms on top of mine.

"You and Myles aren't very quiet," she tells me.

"Sorry," I say after a vacant pause filled with cringing. "Not used to having company."

"Cover his mouth next time."

I snigger. "Noted."

"I don't mind it, by the way. It's like being back at home when Beau discovered his sex appeal."

"A time I'd like to forget," I grumble.

"He was really bad. How Mum and Dad let him get away with it, I don't know."

"First born, favourite child."

"Prick."

I giggle again and snuggle in closer to her. "I love you, Brin."

"I love you too, Shez."

We fall asleep cuddled like spoons, with only the sounds of the countryside for the soundtrack.

Chapter Twenty-Six

SOULMATE

MYLES

Brinsley and I have carpooled to work together since we're living in the same house. It's nice, actually, not having to drive so much. Especially since I'm still a relatively crap driver. Both Bennett sisters have repeatedly teased me over it.

"How did you even pass your test driving like this?" Brin had asked me on Friday morning and followed it up with a squeal terrifying enough to disturb a flock of birds when I clipped the pavement. An overreaction in my opinion, but I know I'm no Jensen Button.

I've been roped into helping Brin move her things out of Andy's flat. Not that I find it a chore, but I do worry that I won't be able to control my temper if I see the bastard.

We've taken all three cars, and the plan is to have two of them loaded up with things to store at Brian and Shirley's until Brinsley finds her own place.

"He usually goes golfing on Saturday mornings," Brin tells us, with all the optimism of Charlie Brown.

Golf on a Saturday? What a wanker.

John Andrews's flat looks like a pathologist could bring in a dead body and perform a post-mortem at any second. It smells like Dettol and vinegar, with the odd hint of bark.

I fail miserably to hide my distaste for the place when I drop the moving boxes in the middle of the living room floor.

"I'm so glad you never have to come back here after today," Sheridan says, already getting to work.

"I can't believe you ever lived in a place like this," I mutter.

"Yes, well," Brin has a hand on her throat, "it's not my preferred choice of home either."

"It's like a fucking morgue."

We work quickly, and I'm grateful because, honestly, the entire place makes me itchy. The twins fill up boxes and label them according to their location, and I take them down to the cars and put them in the right ones.

My Polo is mostly filled with Brinsley's clothes, beauty products and her other essentials. I split the rest between Birdie's Mini and Brin's Ford Fiesta.

By the time we're done, it's quite obvious that Brin was the one bringing life into the place, because now the apartment looks like a wasteland of bachelorhood.

Brinsley leaves him a note with her key, dutifully placed on the kitchen counter ready for when John comes home. We vacate the sparse apartment by lunchtime, with the twins clutching each other like adrift otters.

"Thanks for helping, Myles," Brin says when we reach the cars again.

"No worries. I'm just pleased you don't have to live in that," I wave a dismissive hand at the building, "anymore."

"Me too," Sheridan agrees, gravitating towards me.

Brin turns one last look at the place, then flips it the bird. "Good riddance."

Sheridan turns to me, and I leave a light peck on her lips when she steps into my space. "I'll see you at home?"

I nod once. "Yep. Take your time, though. I can entertain myself for one afternoon."

Sheridan kisses me again, innocent enough but with more fervour this time. "Thank you for being so good. I appreciate you."

"Any time, baby."

Sheridan and Brinsley are going to a spa after dropping everything off at Brian and Shirley's. Brin just doesn't know it yet.

When I find the will to let Birdie go, I slip into my car and head off back to the cottage. I unload Brin's belongings and leave them in her room ready for her to unpack, which I imagine she'll do tomorrow.

I head into the kitchen to make a cuppa, and then situate myself in the living room.

I feel strange being in Sheridan's home without her. Like an intruder. I realise that this might be quite a large step—her feeling confident enough about me to allow me here without supervision. Obviously, I'm not some unruly child with the potential to destroy the place, but her faith in me boosts my ego a little.

I turn the TV on, already on Amazon Prime, and realise that Beau's game is being televised again. I stick that on and get comfortable.

About five minutes after kick-off, I get a text off Brad with a picture of a blurry football player in a sea of pixelated green. This is followed up with a second photo of the Rangers pitch, and a packed stadium. I'm hit with an instant pang of longing, even though it's on my screen.

Brad
Brinsley lent me her season ticket for today's game. Is no. 71 her brother?

Brad is quite obviously not a Rangers fan, and I'm sure he's told me before that he finds football tedious. I imagine this has something to do with the Emily situation.

We've started going to the pub on Tuesday evenings and I actually quite enjoy the guy's company. He's just so incredibly nerdy.

Me
He is. They're quadruplets. He's a good friend of mine, too.

Saying that feels weird considering I've barely spoken to him for months. If he had the sense to pull his ginormous head out his arse, we might be able to talk again.

Brad
And you're dating their sister?

Me
That I am.

Brad
We need to unpack that later.

As if he knows it's messy as shit right now.

Brad
OH
OH!!
GOOOOAAAAAL!!!!!!!!!!

Sure enough, thirty seconds later on the screen, the Rangers get a corker in from the right wing.

Me
Enjoy the game bud. We can discuss on Tuesday.

The game finishes on a score of 3-1 to Coventry, which nestles the Rangers nicely at the top of the league. Part of me is somewhat relieved that I don't have to listen to Beau gloat, because his competitive side can be utterly unbearable, but at the same time I wish I was celebrating with him, too.

The Rangers have never been top of the league while Beau has played for them, and I know that he and JP at least will use it as an excuse to have a bit of fun tonight.

I decide to send him a text.

Me
Congrats on the league position, mate. Now you just need to hold that shit down for another six months.

Beau answers quicker than I expect him to.

Beau
Thanks bro. Come out for a drink with us?
We're going to Pink Skunk.

The Pink Skunk is a massive bar and nightclub in the city centre that somehow manages to attract every type of crowd imaginable, from hen dos to sports bros to the LGBTQ+ community, and still owns the reputation of being an overpriced shithole. I haven't been for a while but when Nash was at university and I was painting the town with the brothers, it was one of our frequent haunts. I'm not sure if I could stomach it today.

Me
Can't tonight, sorry. But I'm proud of you and the boys. Have fun.

Beau
Thanks. Is Brin okay? You see her more than me these days. Is she out of that bastard's place?

Oh, *now* John Andrews is a bastard? I shove the indignation down, because this conversation is going well and I don't want to ruin it, as much as he pisses me off.

Me
I think she's been better. She said she's living with Sheridan until she can find a place.

A little white lie. I don't need to mention that I am also temporarily living with Sheridan, or that I helped Brin move her shit *into* Sheridan's house.

Beau
Yeah, Dad said. I need to call her. Can we catch up soon? I think we need to air our shit out.

He's not wrong. But I know he isn't going to like what's changed.

Me
Yeah, soon.

I don't dare indicate when, and in turn Beau doesn't reply. I can't work out if that's a good thing or not but dwelling on it seems pointless.

It starts to rain outside, so I stand up and head to the kitchen to make a fresh brew and watch out the window. Droplets paint the view in a dreary, glistening light, and the downpour is obnoxious against the surface of the canal at the foot of the garden.

For the first time in years, I feel an itch to draw. I don't think I've *wanted* to draw since I was in uni.

I text Birdie.

Me
Don't suppose you've got any charcoal and an empty sketchbook knocking around? X

Part of me doesn't expect her to answer knowing she's at a spa, but it only takes her a couple of minutes.

Birdie
No charcoal, but there's an unopened set of pastels in the bottom drawer of my desk that I won't use and an A4 sketchpad in my paper tray on the top. X

I wander into the office that Sheridan almost always closes the door on and head straight for the desk in the corner. I dig to the bottom of the paper pile and find the A4 pad, flicking through to find it completely empty. Then I open the bottom drawer and pull out a pristine set of pastels that call out to my finger-smudging little heart.

I perch on Sheridan's luxury office chair, open the pad to the first page and unwrap the unused pastels. I decide to do a test-run first, because I haven't drawn something freely outside of lessons at work for a long time.

I conjure up an image of Sheridan in bed this morning and sketch the lines of her in pink—her favourite colour—until the page is full. I turn to the next page and draw another—her messy-haired and sleepy-eyed while we played cards with Brin last night. I draw the Mini, and Hector in his bed, and the cottage, and when I'm satisfied, I've got my groove, I stand and start to head for the kitchen.

Before I make it to the door, something catches my eye. I don't know how I missed it before, but I see it clearly now.

On Birdie's armchair is a storage box crammed with loose bits of paper. *Sketchpad* paper. Written elegantly on the side in sharpie is the word *Frogs*. And on the sheet most visible to the room, is a loose drawing of green legs in fishnet tights.

It might be absolutely absurd that my heartbeat starts thundering in my chest, and that I feel heat on the back of my neck. But as I abandon the pad and the pastels and delicately finger my way through the sheets in the box, I realise something.

I keep going because I can't help myself. There are loose sketches, and essays worth of notes, and detailed plots which I know almost by heart, and pencil storyboards, and letters from voice actors, and from the Toonies. The fucking *Toonies*!

I panic when I realise what I'm doing and step back. I drag my hand down my face, inhaling deeply.

This is crazy. *Crazy*.

Sheridan—*my* Sheridan—my Birdie, created my favourite show?

I take my phone out and look through the BennyBetty Instagram page to find the image she posted in the summer—the one of her desk—and make the comparison.

It's the same fucking desk!

I'm having heart palpitations.

This is, quite possibly, the best day of my damn life.

* * *

Brin and Sheridan return home just before I've finished making dinner.

Brinsley is puffy-eyed and red-cheeked but still has that post-spa glow about her. She doesn't say much before she excuses herself upstairs.

Sheridan, on the other hand, looks positively ethereal. Her skin is shiny with oil, curls piled atop her head with a few strays stuck to her neck. Her blue eyes are clear and bright, and her cheeks look utterly pinch-able. I feel a warmth spread through my chest at the sight of her, so deep I feel it in my cockles.

"Dinner smells good," she tells me, leaning into my side.

"*You* smell good," I reply, and lean down to kiss her deeply. When she pulls away, she looks a little light-headed. Glad it's not just me. "How was the spa?"

"Fine. Bit busy, but generally fine."

I make a contemplative sound. "Don't imagine a spa to be very relaxing if it's busy."

"It wasn't. I had a massage and even that was difficult. Wasn't anywhere near as good as the one at Lerwick."

I rub her back soothingly. "But you still look pretty."

The tips of her ears turn pink, just like her hair. "Thank you. Did you draw much?"

Ah. "A little." I didn't draw anything after my revelation. "I actually wanted to ask you something."

"Oh?" Sheridan leans back against the counter, her arms folded across her chest so they push her tits up. "Don't tell me the art teacher needs advice."

"No." I pinch her waist in favour of shoving my face between her cleavage, and she yelps, smacking my hand away. "Nothing like that. I just wanted to confirm something."

"Okay…"

I lick my lips, suddenly nervous. "Did you, by any chance, create the web show *Goth Frogs*?"

Sheridan stares at me for a second, the colour quickly leaching from her face. "Er–"

"Birdie," I take her face in my hands, stroking my thumbs across her cheeks, "it's not meant to freak you out, I'm sorry."

She looks so pale, and I feel like a complete bastard. "Well, um, I, er,"

I bundle her against me when I realise that she's shaking, pressing her body tightly against mine. "Baby, I'm sorry," I whisper. "I saw some stuff in your office. It's my favourite show and I got excited. I didn't mean to freak you out, alright? I just wanted to make sure I wasn't leaping to conclusions."

She mumbles something I don't quite hear.

"Huh?"

Birdie pulls back and peers up at me, eyes damp. "Yes."

"Yes?"

"Yes, I created *Goth Frogs*."

I blow out a breath and stroke my hands over her oily hair and face. I can't seem to stop touching her. "I'm not exaggerating when I say it's my favourite show. Brin caught me watching it at work once."

"That's kinda cute." She makes a blubbering, giggly noise. "Only Brin and Beau know about it. Not even the voice actors know who I am, or the site hosts, or the Toonie organisers. Aside from Beau and Brin, and now you, I am completely anonymous. And I kind of like it that way."

"So, you're not going to these awards?"

She shakes her head. "Absolutely not. I'm not going to win, but I don't want to be seen. I like my secret life."

I study her for a moment, and she looks set on her decision, as sad as it makes me. This woman deserves to be celebrated. But I suppose, even if she doesn't go, she still might win. And regardless of whether she does or doesn't get anything out of it, I'll still celebrate her in my own way. "Alright. Then I'll keep my mouth shut."

Birdie smiles up at me as she leans forward, pressing her front against mine. "Thank you, Myles.

I bend down to give her another deep kiss, which she melts into like butter.

"Are you working on anything else?" I ask her when I return to the cooking.

She hesitates, nervously chewing on her lip. "I have an idea but it's in the very early stages. It needs a bit more body and thought before I'll be happy to move forward with it."

"What is it?"

"You really want to know?"

I scoff. "Of course, I do. I want to see everything you've ever done."

She blushes again, and I can't believe how lucky I am to have her. "I can show you after dinner, if you like?"

"I do like, Birdie. I like very much."

Chapter Twenty-Seven
SECRETS

MYLES

On Tuesday when I start my Year 9 lesson with the B group, I notice that Sam—who continues to insist he possesses no artistic talent but is always the first one to arrive and engages more often than I expect—is absent. I only see these kids for two hours every week, but some of them still leave an impression—like Jamie who always has to be the loudest in the room but backs it up by being an amazing cartoonist, even at the age of fourteen. Or Erin, who flirts with anyone who will pay her a lick of attention but still gushes over the idea of me and Brinsley from time to time.

Sam sticks out not only because he looks like a pubescent Shaggy from *Scooby-Doo* most days, but also because he *tries* with me. Across all my Key Stage 3 groups, my favourite students have become the ones that *try*.

It's almost ten o'clock by the time he appears. I'd checked the daily bulletin where the admin team posts the absent or sick kids with an excuse, but he wasn't on it. Assuming my hunch that Sam is growing up in a care home, his tardiness is concerning. I was only ever late when something bad happened at home.

The morning passes by quickly after Sam's mumbled apology. As with most of my classes, it's a flurry of activity and vibrant chatter. Jamie is still talking about the Rangers result from Saturday and drags me into a conversation about Beau's style. Trying to appear neutral on that one is difficult. Erin loudly announces that the boys in Year 9 are immature and stupid and that any future prospects of boyfriends will be taken from Year 10 or above. I have to keep myself from lecturing her on how 'above Year 10' amounts to sixteen-year-olds and would be a massive problem for a lot of people.

I notice that Sam, while not the gobbiest of students, hasn't said a single word since he arrived. I ask him to stay behind when the bell goes.

"Am I in trouble?" He asks when the room has cleared out.

I study him for a second—his demeanour is hunched, and he trembles occasionally. I notice a nasty bruise on his wrist where his sleeve has ridden up, and he's quick to pull it back down again when sees me assessing it.

"No, Sam, you're not in trouble," I assure him with a flash of a smile. "I just wanted to make sure you're alright. You're never late."

He gives a shrug that's been the subject of adult skits across the world. "I'm fine."

"Can I ask why you were late, then? Since you're fine."

"I had to take my sister to school."

"Do you do that every day?"

"No, Helen does."

I know my eyebrows are joining my hairline.

"She's my foster mum. And Pip is my foster sister."

"Ah." Sometimes, having a foster family is worse than living in a care home. "I see."

Sam laughs in such a bitter way that it adds ten years to him. "Do you?"

"Do I what?"

"*Do you see?*" He bites, and the anger rolls off him like a crashing wave. "Everyone, especially adults like you, behave like you *know* what the fuck is happening in my life when I mention foster, or care. You don't *know*, and you don't *see* shit."

I wait a second to see if he's going to continue, because the worst thing I think I could do in this instance is talk over him. When

I'm sure he's done, I gesture to the closest table and sit at it. "Sit with me for a sec. I wanna tell you something."

He scoffs. "Tell me what? Are you gonna compare your lower-middle class upbringing in some random North London borough to mine right now? 'Cause if you are, I am not interested."

His dismissal stings a little, and yet I completely get it. I, too, used to walk around in my teen years with a chip on my shoulder the size of a small country, wondering when the world would be put to rights.

I gave him a placating smile. "When I was seven, I got sent to my very first foster home. A family. I was so excited I wet myself on the way there, but it didn't matter. I still didn't really understand the difference between fostering and adoption, but this was it, you know? A family—a real one.

"They were good people, but they were old. Maggie and Brendan O'Hare. Irish, retired, practically on death's door. They'd had their own child who caught a terrible disease years before and died as a teenager. They never wanted to replace her, so they decided to foster instead, and they did it their whole lives until me. I was the last one."

Sam, who has been gawping at me slack-jawed for the entire period, finally sits opposite me. I take that as a cue to continue.

"Turns out our Brendan had dementia and Maggie had severe arthritis. Six months after they fostered me, I was shipped back to the care home and waited for the next one. They both died by the time I was ten, and yet they were the best foster family I ever had.

"I'll be honest—the next ten years or so were not fun. I was in and out of that house like it was a hotel. Some of the foster families were okay, and others were awful. And I've seen shit *no one* should *ever* have to see." Sam grins at my cursing, and I give him another tentative smile. "I never got adopted and my entire childhood was spent being passed from family to family like a joint at a uni party. That sticks with you, Sam."

"I'm sorry I snapped, sir." He appears genuinely guilty and that bothers me.

"I get it. You and I are in this little boat surrounded by everyone else in their big boats. You were never gonna know I've had that life, too. And I know why you would assume that—because I had the same experiences. People love to pity the kids in care, but they don't want to do anything about it."

"I stopped telling people I was in care when I came here. You get treated differently, and I just wanted to feel normal for once," Sam mumbles, staring at the fake wood laminate on the table.

"I get that. But like recognises like, Sam. I knew the first day you walked into my classroom."

He grimaces. "Am I that obvious?"

"Only to me. Can you do something for me?"

Sam looks at me with wariness. "What?"

"That anger you're feeling—you're entitled to it. It *is* justified. But don't let it consume you. Don't let it make you stupid because you'll regret it."

He narrows his gaze. "Sounds an awful lot like there's a good story there, sir."

"There's a story, but it definitely ain't good."

"Will you tell me?"

I check the clock and sigh. "I was probably your age. Maybe a year older. I'd been living with this big foster family for a while, and they were the worst kinds of people. Proper London scum—dad was a drug dealer and the mum used to sleep around. With a penchant for underage boys, I should add. House was always a mess. Their actual kids were, quite frankly, arseholes. It was definitely the worst house I'd lived in.

"One morning I got into it with the dad. I'd spent the night batting off the advances of his wife and was angry by my lack of sleep. Then when I got up in the morning the dad was still drunk and getting nasty. After a bit of back and forth, I called him the less pleasant version of a waste of space, and he hit me in the gut in response.

"I took my anger with me to school. Some of the kids learnt I was in care and used that against me. They saw the state of me that morning and started gobbing off. I was getting pretty tall at this point, and I'd been doing the heavy lifting around the house, so when I reached the end of my tether and snapped, I caused a lot of damage. One of the boys ended up in hospital."

"Oh, shit." Sam is gaping again.

"Oh shit, indeed. It didn't stop there, either. Any time anyone pissed me off I'd lash out. I didn't stop until they sent me back to the care home. By that point I had a bit of a reputation and a nickname to go with it."

"What was the nickname?"

"They called me The Bear."

Sam laughs, delighted. "Sick."

"Well, no, not really." I wince. "Look, Sam. I don't want you to end up like that, alright? I was messed up as a kid and you're way better than me already. I'd hopefully like to keep it that way. That being said, I want you to know you can come talk to me if it ever gets a bit much."

"Thanks, sir."

"Also, please don't repeat any of this to anyone. My girlfriend doesn't even know about the Bear thing, and I'd rather tell her myself."

"Isn't your girlfriend Miss Bennett? The English teacher?"

I roll my eyes. "*No*. It's her sister. But keep that to yourself, too," I say as I stand.

"Woah," Sam laughs again, "sir. Is she as fit as Miss Bennett?"

"They're twins."

"That's a yes, then. Nice one. Is it true they're related to Beau Bennett, the footballer?"

I stare at him as I hold the door open, and I realise I've just given this kid enough ammunition to absolutely destroy me if he ever needed to. "You've had enough personal details out of me today."

"Also a yes, then," he says cheekily, and then he sobers some. "Thank you for talking to me, sir. Sorry if I was a dick earlier."

"You're forgiven. Just keep your head up and keep talking to me."

"I will, thanks." He turns to leave and then pauses, "You should tell your girlfriend about the Bear thing, though. I feel like that's something she probably needs to know."

And I know for a fact the kid is absolutely right. As soon as the door is closed, my head falls to the table.

***

Later that night, after we've eaten and are tucked up in bed, I share my secrets with Sheridan.

She is attentively quiet and asks questions when she thinks of one. But her body language never changes—she stays in my arms, her fingers skimming the lines of my face and neck throughout, and I love her for it. I think I *am* in love with her and I'm not afraid to admit that to myself.

"Thank you for telling me, Myles," she whispers when I'm done, still stroking my face. "I hope you know that I don't judge you for what happened and I'm proud of the man you've become despite it. You might be my favourite person."

I hold her body closer to mine and press my lips to hers. "You are absolutely my favourite person, Birdie."

I could follow that up with an 'I love you'. It's on the tip of my tongue, like the words might crawl out of my mouth if I open it wide enough. But I don't know if she's ready to hear them yet and I don't want to overwhelm her. I think I do enough of that already.

We kiss for a little longer and then she burrows into my chest like it's the only place she wants to be, and I feel that warmth, that love, for her spread through my body like medicine. I think this woman has cured me from something I didn't know I was suffering.

It's quiet for so long that I think she might have fallen asleep, and am about to do the same when she speaks again:

"When I was sixteen, I tried to commit suicide."

I freeze like I've been tasered, and then my arms instinctively tighten around her. "What?" I croak.

"That's why Beau is so protective of me."

I pull back to look at her, and find her staring blankly at my chest, at the bear tattooed on my abdomen. "That's... I don't know what to say."

Sheridan hums a little laugh, and I think she finds me genuinely amusing. "Most people don't." She looks up at me. "I had very unstable emotions as a teenager. I was on contraception long before I lost my virginity in attempts to balance my hormones. I started puberty when I was seven."

"*Seven?*"

"Yeah… I was a handful at home sometimes. I had these bipolar tendencies where I'd go from quietly brooding and sulky to a screaming lunatic. Sounds like any teenager, I guess, but I was seven, nearly eight. And then I had my first period in the middle of P.E and everyone thought I was weird.

"I spent a few years in and out of hospital before they learned I had a cyst on my ovaries that needed to be operated on. I could've become barren, and it could come back. I was on medication all through school and college for various things.

"In amongst all this, I started to draw a lot. The kids who already thought I was psychotic used my strange drawings as ammunition. Nash, going through his own complexes, often joined in, and encouraged bullying.

"I got to sixteen and couldn't bear the thought of going on in life being made to feel shit about myself or knowing there was a possibility I wouldn't have kids of my own, or even just constantly being in and out of the hospital. I felt like I was drowning in self-hatred and the hate of everyone else.

"So, I took all my tablets at once and got in the shower. Next thing I know, I'm at the hospital again."

"Jesus, Sheridan." I squeeze her tightly, and she hugs me back.

"I know. When I got the clear to go home, I went through several rounds of therapy. Nash backed off. I found something I was good at while I studied at home. The girls—Emma, Bailey, and Brin—rallied for me. The summer after school finished, they were at our house all the time. I learned to accept that I couldn't change the things about my body that failed me, and that none of it was a reason not to live.

"I stopped all my medication just over a year ago and I honestly have never felt better. I just don't think Beau has learnt that yet. I never got over my social anxiety but it's easy enough to live with. I got better with it over time, if slowly." She laughs despite herself. "Maybe one day I'll finally cross that bridge, maybe I won't. But I know I'm happy right now and I don't need to change anything. Well, maybe Beau, but…"

God, this woman. *This fucking woman.* "You're incredible, Sheridan Bennett. I hope you know that. I'm so lucky I met you."

She gazes up at me with a cerulean smile that utterly does me in. "I'm lucky I met you, too."

I meet her mouth with mine, and we kiss, and we kiss, and we kiss some more until I'm on top and inside of her and there isn't an inch of skin untouched, until there is no space between us, until we are linked together, and I have all of her and she has all of me.

This woman—this delicate, strong, *beautiful* woman is mine, and I love her.

I love her.

I love her.

I love her.

When we're done and I'm once again holding her close to me, cocooning her into the protection of my body, I whisper all the praise I have for her until she tells me I'm utterly ridiculous.

"Utterly ridiculous I may be, Birdie, but it doesn't change that I'm right. You are marvellous and you can do anything."

"Except handle big crowds," is her attempt at a joke.

"I think you could do that too, if you wanted to."

"Your faith is misguided, handsome, but I appreciate it nonetheless."

I preen at her compliment and make gobbling noises into her neck. "I'd be with you every step of the way if I needed to be."

"I know you would. Something tells me you wouldn't ever let me down."

"It would in no way benefit me to do that. Why would I jeopardise moments like this with you?"

"Stop with the charming words or I will pounce on you."

"You say that like it's a bad thing," I murmur into her neck, my hands making the most of her exposed backside.

"Myles," she breathes.

And just like that we are together again, moving our bodies as one to extinguish the constantly reigniting flame between us.

In the silent moments after, Sheridan asks, "Do you think I'm a fool for not going to the awards next month?"

"I've never once thought you're a fool, Birdie."

"But do you think it's a mistake? Not going?"

I turn my head to look at her, and the little crease between her brow has me worried. I reach out and smooth it away with my thumb. "The decision is yours, baby. It's your show, your characters, your anxieties, and your feelings. If those feelings tell you not to go, then don't go."

"Myles, I don't know what to do. Part of me thinks I should."

"So go, then," I say simply.

"But I'm scared."

"So don't go."

"But it's a really big deal to even be nominated. And they sent me a reminder today because I haven't RSVP'd and it got me thinking about it all and that, actually it might be fun to go considering I might never get nominated again... And I did something I never do and looked at the comments on the show, and on the Toonies site, and... People were so nice about it."

"Because it's awesome, baby," I whisper, brushing my lips against her forehead. "Go."

She sits up and turns to look down at me, nervously chewing her lip again. Like a greedy bastard, I eat up the sight of her nakedness and graze my hands over her side and front.

"Would you go with me?"

"I would go anywhere with you." I don't think I've ever said something and meant it as much as I do right now. Again, those three little words are on the tip of my tongue.

Iloveyou.

"You'll come to the awards with me?"

"Absolutely." *Because I'm in love with you.*

"I'll buy you a new tux for the occasion."

I can't help but laugh. "Shez, you don't need to bribe me—I already said yes."

"Right." She covers her face with her hands. "I guess we're going."

I pull her on top of me and kiss her firmly, chaste. "You can't change your mind now. I'm committed to seeing you in a sexy dress and all dolled up."

"I admittedly can't wait to see you in a tux." She giggles.

"I look good in black tie."

"You look good in everything," she grumbles, and I pinch her bum cheek just to hear her squeal.

One last time tonight, I completely devour her.

Chapter Twenty-Eight

I'm Not Irish

SHERIDAN

I'm aware that all the girls are already here at The Pink Skunk, and that Brin and I are late. I'm aware that while Brin eagerly leaps from the car to join in the birthday festivities, I linger behind to give Myles a kiss goodbye and a promise to text him when we're ready to go home. I'm aware of my sweaty palms at the thought of going into this bar and sitting in a crowded space for an unforeseeable number of hours.

I am *not* aware, however, that all the girls—with the exception of Brin, of course—are watching us with slack jaws until I turn around and find them all gawping at me like a school of fish.

I turn a look over my shoulder in case they're actually looking at something else and I'm being self-conscious, but the street is practically empty save for Myles's car. He pips his horn with a wave and cruises away. I'm not ashamed to say I already miss him.

"Was that Myles?" Bailey demands.

Ah, right. I clear my throat. "Er, yeah."

"Did you just kiss him?" Gemma asks, horrified.

"Yep."

"Are you together?" Emma follows up.

"Considering I'm not one to usually go around kissing my brothers' friends, I'm gonna go with yes to that, too."

Brin sniggers, squeezing my arm.

"Damn," Brandy, Bailey's older sister whistles appreciatively, "well done, Sheridan."

"I told you he was fit," Bailey says to her sister under her breath.

I give Brandy a blushing smile, whilst being reminded just how gorgeous she is. She's tall, made taller yet by knee high stiletto boots, with glossy dark hair that falls straight down her back to her waist, deep brown eyes, and an olive complexion. She's beautiful in a sharp and striking kind of way—she always has a male's attention whether she wants it or not, and right now, with her suede mini skirt and halter top, that is every man in the near vicinity.

Brin and I used to go for sleepovers with Gemma at Bailey's house all through school, and when we were younger Brandy would often bring her own friends, too. Then, as we got older, she started going out instead. Being three years older than us, staying in with your younger sister's friends probably wasn't seen as very cool. Amongst all this, the Scott sisters' parents seemed to develop an alcohol addiction around the time we started high school, and sleepovers became few and far between.

Bailey and Brandy don't talk about their parents much anymore.

I hand Bailey her birthday present and give her a hug. "Happy Birthday, Bay."

"Thanks, chica." She grins, hooking her arm through mine. "Tell me how this thing with Myles happened, then."

With a small sigh, I reluctantly explain how Myles and I came together. Bailey is suitably scandalised and delighted by the tale of our sofa sex, appalled by the lost phone number, and swooning when I recall how he showed up on my doorstep with flowers. I admit to her I've been somewhat romanced by him these past weeks, and she seems genuinely happy for me.

We snatch a table towards the back and decide to take it in turns to do the rounds at the bar. Brin and Brandy go first, returning with a tray of multi-coloured shots and an assortment of fruity cocktails. We *cheers* to the birthday girl with a shot each and down it in one. Mine tastes like sour apples and regret. I chase it with a second one, if only to curb my anxiety at being in such a packed bar.

It's rowdy and full of large groups of men—stag dos, I assume. I'm hoping if I drink enough my nerves will ease up. This is supposed to be my 'soft launch' into busy social scenes before Myles and I venture out to London in a couple of weeks for the Toonies. I'm still terrified by that.

While we each drink our first round, we catch up on each other's love lives—Bailey is seeing some middle-aged solicitor she claims is the best sex of her life. I'm just secretly glad it's not Beau. Brandy is still with the sexy goalie from the Crusaders team; Gemma is suspiciously coy about her relationship status; Emma is single, along with Brin. When all eyes land back on me, I politely ask them to keep the news regarding my relationship with Myles to themselves until I manage to speak to my brothers. I do not need one of them accidentally spilling it to them that I've been having fantastic sex with their best friend.

"Fantastic, aye?" Bailey nudges my side with a smirk.

"If you heard what I can hear on a nightly basis, you would *only* assume it's fantastic," Brin grumbles.

"Or she's just a really good actress," Gemma says, voice void of much emotion.

I try not to roll my eyes at her. "If I had to fake an orgasm, I wouldn't be sleeping with him."

"Amen, sister." Brandy lifts her glass in a mock toast.

"Lots of people fake orgasms," Gemma retorts in an oddly defensive tone.

"Well, I don't," I snap. "I don't want a partner I'm not sexually compatible with."

"I once slept with a guy who had two kinks in his dick," Bailey admits, I'm assuming to diffuse the tension between Gemma and me.

I nearly spit my drink out. "Jesus, Bailey."

"What? I did." She shrugs.

"Did you have to fake your way through it?" Brin asks, darting a cautious look at Gemma.

"Well, yeah. It was uncomfortable to be honest, and he was trying too hard."

Brandy snorts. "Ew. The only time I've ever faked it was when some guy asked me to role play with him."

"What was the scenario?" Emma asks, leaning forward.

"He wanted me to be an alien, which could've worked if he hadn't been so…technical."

I burst out laughing. "Wow."

"Yeah, his vocabulary was *super* specific, and while I'm not opposed to a hot nerd or dressing up in silver PVC and deely-boppers, it turned me off a bit. Like, yes, please use dirty science puns, but don't mansplain protons and neutrons to me."

I am fully cackling at this point. Looks like the sour apple shots are doing their job.

* * *

I think I've reached Raving Lunatic territory on the Drunk Scale. I can't remember the last time I was this drunk. I feel like I've been taken out of my body and thrust into the ether that is the sticky dance floor of this shitty bar. I didn't drink this much on our little summer holiday, so *that* is saying something.

I can't remember why I'm here. I can't remember why I was using alcohol as a crutch. I'm not sure I can even remember my own name.

Shirley? No, that's my mum.

Sh…antelle? That doesn't sound right, either.

Sh… Siobhan? Nope. Not Irish.

Huh. Oh well. I'm sure it'll come to me.

I've been throwing myself around the dance floor for an indeterminate amount of time. The girls have come and gone intermittently, whether for a bathroom break or to rehydrate, but I haven't left since the DJ played Chaka Khan. I've become that person who screams when I like a song that comes on.

We've hit that run of songs club DJs always play that are slower, more sensual. All of a sudden everyone around me is in a couple. Bailey is grinding her arse against a man's crotch who looks twice our age, and it's not the solicitor she showed us a picture of earlier. Emma is playing tonsil tennis with a pretty woman with an afro and ebony skin, and I am flooded with love for her in a way that is a little more than just familial.

I am crowded from behind by a solid chest, and for a short, blissful second, I'm reminded of blond hair, honey eyes and a bear tattoo.

Hands find my hips, and I just *know* it's not him. Engulfed in the scent of cheap cologne mixed with sweat and stale beer, I know this is not my man. My Myles.

I don't have time to lecture this stranger on touching things that don't belong to him.

"Sheridan!"

Right, *that's* my name.

Brinsley is by our table waving me over.

I smack the man's hands away and throw him a dirty glare before sauntering back to the table.

Taken away from the bubble of the dance floor, I realise how unsteady I am on my feet, and how blurry my vision is. This, for some reason, makes me start to giggle. And then I'm laughing uncontrollably.

Brin just shakes her head with a fond smile and hands me my bag and coat.

"Is Myles here?" I ask, like a lovesick idiot.

"Five minutes. We just need to say bye."

We make the rounds quickly. Even as inebriated as I am, I'm astute enough to recognise that Brin is eager to leave, and I relate to the feeling so much I'm not going to let her suffer.

Myles pulls up just as we're exiting the bar and seeing him so relaxed at a late hour like he is—in jogging bottoms and a fleece, hair mussed and a little greasy—something wicked and wonderful expands in my chest.

He leans over and pushes the passenger door open for me. Brin slides into the back seat, and I settle into the front.

"Hi!" I say brightly, grinning like it's the best day of my life.

"Hi," Myles greets around a chuckle. "Did you have fun?"

"I think Sheridan had more fun than the birthday girl," Brin says.

"I drank *a lot*," I admit, positively beaming.

"*No*, really?" Myles jokes, and I smack his arm. "I'm glad you had a good time."

I babble the whole way home, about how grumpy Gemma is, about how pretty Brandy is, about the music, and the dancing. Brin occasionally chips in and Myles plays the good sport and asks questions he deems relevant.

I love that about him—my attentive listener.

His hand is on my bare thigh and I'm trying my best not to think about how much I like it. Occasionally he squeezes it, and it reawakens the familiar fire in my belly. I try not to think about how I want him to slip it a little higher, under the fabric of my skirt and into my knickers.

When we get home, Brin yawns her way around a goodnight and heads to bed.

I am still a stumbling mess when the bedroom door closes behind us.

Myles produces a glass of water and a paracetamol when I collapse onto the edge of the bed. When he got them, I have no idea, but I'm so grateful for his foresight because I would not have even thought about it. I pop the tablet in my mouth and wash it down with the water, then finish it off. He takes the glass off me and places it out of reach, which is probably sensible, and I'm not offended by it.

I clumsily pull off my shoes one by one and toss them at my open wardrobe. Then, when trying to undress, I get stuck in my shirt.

"Myles," I whimper.

He snickers, but when he reaches me, his touch is warm and attentive. Once we've manoeuvred me out of it, I'm met with the sight of his bare chest. Without much thought—none at all, actually—I start tracing the lines of his tattoos, starting with the bear on his abdomen.

His breathing is even, and he smells like pine and chamomile. He is steady, sturdy, constant, consistent. He is both equally, I think, what I want and what I need.

And I think I might have fallen in love with him.

"Myles," I say, completely paralytic and unfiltered, "I think I'm in love with you."

He pinches my chin and lifts it to meet his gaze. With all the confidence in the world, he replies, "That's interesting, Birdie, because I think I'm in love with you, too."

Chapter Twenty-Nine
The Toonies

SHERIDAN

The Toonies are held at the Park Plaza Hotel in Westminster, London, on the third weekend of December. Due to its proximity to Christmas, the festivities are all but shoved down our throats from the second we arrive in the capital city, and it doesn't wear off even after we leave.

Myles and I decide to treat the event as our first weekend break away as a couple, so we pack our bags and head down on the train the Friday night, leaving Hector with Auntie Brin at the cottage.

Myles's flat is now liveable again, so he is back to staying there in the week and only visiting me on the weekends. I'm sure Brinsley is thrilled not be listening to us shagging multiple times a night, not that she's ever said anything more about it.

On Saturday morning, I ask Myles to show me where he grew up, so we get on the tube outside the hotel, and ride it all the way to Morden—the very last stop on the Northern Line.

I feel like we walk the entire town, and he somehow manages to have an anecdote for everything—the shop on the corner where someone stole his scooter; the cinema where he kissed a girl for the first time; the house where his driving instructor lived; three of the *five* foster homes he lived in growing up, as well as the care home he was almost always sent back to.

I fall in love with him a little bit more with each story he tells me, and in between he tells me about Sam, a kid at school who is going through a similar thing.

As we ride the tube back into the city after our tour is complete, I realise that Myles could've become an absolute liability after leaving school. He could've got himself into trouble, continued feeding off his anger in a negative way. But he didn't. He stuck his down and managed to take everything he learned and turned it into something he can give back.

By the end of the morning, Myles becomes the man that I admire the most.

* * *

We eat lunch at The Ivy where we share a bottle of champagne—because we're celebrating, duh—oysters, and beef wellington. Myles spends the entire meal looking like he thinks he's about to be thrown out and tells me more than once that he feels out of place.

"You're not out of place, Myles," I assure him as we mop up beef jus with crusty pastry. "You're exactly where you need to be. With me."

We pay the bill and head back to the hotel, where I spend two hours showing him exactly how I feel about him and what he means to me, with my mouth and my body.

When I finally find it in me to drag myself off him, we share a long shower and get ready for the evening.

I've never been to the Toonies before and given the possibility it could be full of a bunch of incels and nerds, I'm not sure how formal the whole thing is going to be. I've bought a new outfit for the occasion—a rust-coloured velvet jumpsuit with a cowl neck and wide legs. I fashion my curls into a low bun, add a golf pendant necklace and matching bracelet. It's the most glamorous I've ever felt.

Myles manages to match with me in burnt orange and brown plaid trousers, and pairs it with a pale blue waistcoat over a white shirt. He's put a comb and some wax through his hair to neaten it up, and when I walk out of the bathroom and spot him standing by the window scrolling through his phone, I almost combust.

"Wow," he says as I approach him, his gaze trailing downwards in a sweeping assessment of me, "you look amazing."

I rest a hand on his chest, still dwarfed by him even in my heels. "You scrub up pretty well too, handsome."

He grins and bends to press a light kiss to my lips.

We take a number of what he refers to as 'obligatory couple selfies' and then head down to the lobby to find the function room.

We're directed to a lower ground lobby, where near one hundred people are mingling in their finery while sipping bubbly from branded flutes. It's loud, dark, and crowded.

My palms start sweating and I feel the skin on the back of my neck prickle with heat.

I flag down the nearest staff member with a tray and hijack two just for myself. I knock the first one back down in one.

The girl stares at me wide-eyed, and Myles is snickering just behind me.

"I'm so sorry," I mumble, abandoning the glass on her tray. Unconsciously, I wipe my hands down the sides of my dress.

"Are you okay?" The server asks, her gaze wary, and I am almost certain she is a student working part time just to earn some cash.

Myles rests a hand on my back and takes a glass for himself. "We don't do big crowds very often."

She looks twice at Myles—a double take, visibly interested in his face—and then her attention returns to me and the fact that I'm now pressing the cold glass to my cheek, even though it's December and the air conditioning is on down here.

"Are you having a panic attack?"

I shake my head. "Not yet."

She gives me a sympathetic smile. "I get them too, before interviews and exams. Can I give you some advice?"

"I'll take whatever you can give."

"Alcohol is a stimulant, not a relaxant, so it'll only make it worse. The best thing you can do is stand outside for ten minutes, and then when you come back in, talk out loud about what's going on around you. What you can see, what you can hear."

I blink at her. "Wow, okay. Are you some kind of therapist?"

"Not quite." She grins. "I get it, anxiety is a bitch."

"Thank you…" I squint at her name tag, "Cass."

"You're welcome. I hope you get to enjoy yourself."

I leave the second glass on the tray, and Myles tugs me up and outside the front into the bitter December air. Even though it's cold, I must admit it feels good on my skin.

"You alright, Sheridan?" Myles asks quietly, squeezing my hand.

I meet his gaze and nod once. "You're not allowed to leave my side all night," I tell him sternly.

"What if I need the loo?"

"I'm coming with you."

He chuckles and wraps himself tightly around me. I fall into his warmth easily, comforted by it. "I'm not sure the other men would appreciate that. The scenes at the urinals might permanently scar you."

"I am permanently scarred by things far worse than men at urinals."

That green-gold gaze studies my face intently, a small crease appearing in his brow. "Having the opportunity to meet you and love you is the best thing that ever happened to me."

I wasn't expecting him to get so deep, but hearing the words come out of his mouth make me feel buoyant. "I'm not going anywhere, Myles."

"I really hope not."

We share a kiss, right there on the pavement in the centre of London so the world can see.

This man is mine.

"You're the best thing that ever happened to me too, by the way." I say against his mouth, "Just don't tell Hector."

Myles's responding laugh is throaty and dirty. "I think it would be in poor taste to gloat to a dog."

I snort shamelessly. "God, I love you."

"Good, because I love you, too."

* * *

When we finally head back inside, we've been called to sit for dinner. After the lunch we shared I'm not particularly hungry, but I eat what's put in front of me and don't manage dessert. Myles, who is apparently a gannet, eats everything, and mops up each plate afterward.

When the noise levels feel just a bit too loud, I close my eyes and count to ten, then back down to one, and then I turn to Myles and tell him five things I can see, five things I can hear, and five things I can feel. My favourite is his warm palm against my thigh. The anchor.

The awards ceremony starts after tea and coffee has been served and is hosted by a YouTuber who I've never heard of and barely looks the legal drinking age. He reads the list of categories, which feels immense and time-consuming. We're going to be here for hours.

Like any ceremony, they start with the subcategories: -
- Best Horror
- Best Thriller
- Best Sci-Fi/Fantasy
- Best Comedy
- Best Drama

Fortunately, there's no fannying about with different readers or speeches—we just go up and collect the award, take a photo with someone, and then head back to our tables.

Sitting and waiting for the Comedy category feels like it takes hours, and when it finally rolls around, I feel like I might be violently sick right here in front of all these strangers, all over the nicely decorated table. I stare at the black linen and try to calm my breathing as they read out the nominees. I've never been to a show like this before. With my interior design work, Marina would always go on our behalf, even if it was one of our projects that was nominated.

Why did I decide to do this?
Why did I come here?
Why did I ask Myles for this?

Suddenly I'm being shaken, and the room is in whistling applause.

"Birdie," Myles says to me with his hands on my shoulders, "you won, baby."

Fuuuuuck.

Somehow, I manage to stand, and looking out across the vast, packed function room, my ears fill with cotton wool and my vision blurs, like I'm underwater. I navigate my way to the front of the room blindly, up the steps without tripping, accept the award that looks like a glass cock ring, and take a photo with a man who's easily pushing sixty-five and can't take his eyes off my cleavage.

I'm dismissed with a pat on my back that's dangerously close to my arse, and I stumble my way back to the safety of my Myles.

"Congratulations, baby." He beams with a peck on my cheek when I sit down.

I just about manage to smile at him, but I know it doesn't touch my eyes.

"How much did you hate that?" He smooths his hand up and down my back and it eases some of the tension.

"If it were on a scale of one to ten, with ten being the highest, it'd be about fifty."

Myles pecks my cheek again, and then my shoulder. "I'm proud of you. Although, I have to say these awards look very…"

"They're like designer sex toys," says the man sitting on Myles's other side, apparently having heard us.

"Yes! That's exactly it."

And this makes me smile, because even if today had me in a mental headlock, at least I know I got a designer cock ring out of it.

They announce the technical awards next, and I lose out on the *Best Animation* category to a pair of forty-year-old men with *Red Dwarf* T-shirts and big beards. I don't know what their show is, but from the clips they show of it, I'm not surprised I didn't win.

It's late by the time *Show of the Year* gets read out. I'm ready to call it a night, I'm drunk, and would rather let some other nerds win just so I don't have to walk up to that stage like a zombie again. My wish comes true when they announce the winner as a girl who can't be older than fourteen with bright purple hair, black makeup, clothes, and massive stomper boots. I think I love her.

Myles leans over, arms slung across the back of my chair and murmurs, "Is it time to leave so I can celebrate you in my own way?"

I heat up in an instant like a damn Bunsen burner. "I think so."

Chapter Thirty
Confrontation & Hypocrisy

MYLES

"What…the fuck is happening right now?"

Brinsley's question makes my head snap up after scrolling on my phone in the back of her car. She picked Sheridan and I up from the train station to take us home after our weekend in London.

I lean sideways to get a good view out the front windscreen.

Beau's Range Rover sits in a guest space at the back of the car park, the man himself leaning against the driver's side with his arms folded, and Nash standing right next to him.

Oh, fuck.

Sheridan laughs—a bubbling, hysterical sound that's completely at odds with the feeling in my gut.

This isn't going to end well.

As soon as Brin has her car pulled up, I slide out the back and head towards the Bennett brothers, because there's no getting out of it now. D-Day has arrived.

"Care to explain what's going on, Wilson?" Beau demands, shoving off his precious car.

"Sure. I'm returning home from a nice weekend away."

"With my sister?"

"Beau." Sheridan's voice brokers no argument.

"I told you to stay away from her." He's stalking towards me now, shoulders rigid with wound up energy.

"Excuse me," Sheridan, all five foot two of her, squares up to the oldest sibling, "you are in absolutely *no* position to dictate who I spend my time with."

"You're not just 'spending time'," Beau air-quotes around the words, "with him, though. Are you?"

"So? It's none of your damn business!"

"It is my damn business when you're so—"

"Finish that sentence, Beau," I warn.

"You're behaving like a bloody child," Brinsley adds, scowling at her brothers.

"I can't believe this. *My sister*."

I kiss my teeth. "Pipe down, Ross Geller."

"I'm my own fucking person, Beau. You do not get a say in my personal relationships."

"He could've picked anyone, Shez," Nash says, quietly seething. "*Anyone.* And he had to pick you."

"So what if he picked me?!"

"Never mind the fact that I had to find out about your fucking relationship through a picture from the God damn *Toonies website*." Beau scoffs. "I didn't even know you were going! I just followed along because I wanted to know if you won."

"How the hell could you expect me to tell you about my relationship when I knew you'd react exactly like this? Like a fucking arsehole," Sheridan seethes.

Beau barks, "He doesn't deserve you, Sheridan! No one does!"

I ignore that pang in my chest that feels let down. I already know that's what he thinks about me, but to hear it out loud is still gutting. This is supposed to be my best friend.

"*Myles* doesn't deserve me?" Sheridan looks feral. "Yet you let John Andrews fucking ruin Brinsley and have barely said a word about it to her. *He* was a goddamn cunt from start to finish, and yet you're here going off about your own *best friend* not being good enough for *me*? You're a prick, Beau Bennett. Do you expect me to live by myself forever? You want me to die alone?"

"Brinsley isn't unstable!" Beau argues.

Rage like I haven't felt in a long time surges in me at Beau's nasty words, and I feel Sheridan stiffen beside me. I can't help it; I instinctively move closer to her.

"Hey!" Brinsley yells, marching forward. "*Do not* talk about her like that."

"Have you even considered the fact that maybe, *just maybe,* I really care about Sheridan?" I'm incredulous now, subtly touching Sheridan where I can. "Do you think I'd really want to just fuck about with your sister, even though that's exactly what you do with *their* friends?"

"And believe me, none of us wanted to watch you and Bailey ship off together for a quick fuck in the woods, Beau," Brinsley growls.

"That's completely different, and you know it is."

"Yes!" I explode, "It is completely different, because I am not just spending time with Sheridan only for the outcome of getting into her knickers! I love her!"

Before I have a chance to defend myself, a fist makes an uppercut to my nose. The pain is somehow unexpected, the crunch ear-splitting, and I stagger backwards, holding my face.

"Nash!" Brinsley screams.

"What the fuck is wrong with you?!" Sheridan is incandescent, but I can't see her face because I'm too busy keeping my head tilted back and my eyes squeezed shut.

I can feel the blood pooling in my palm and white noise fills my ears.

I never thought someone else would throw the first punch. It's always been me—I've always been the instigator.

"Are you a fucking idiot?" Brinsley shoves her brother. "He's a teacher—he can't go to school like that!"

"I'm sure Mum will give him a free pass," Beau grumbles.

I feel a dainty hand on my arm and the essence of apples around me.

"You're damn right she will because I'm gonna tell her who did it." This side of Brinsley is a little terrifying, but I like it.

"Both of you fuck off," Sheridan bites. "Go home, seriously—I am so fucking upset with you. I hope you've broken your finger, you absolute dick."

I can think of a few other words to call her brother, but I'm not exactly in the market for another broken body part. 'Dick' seems relatively tame.

A gentle hand wraps around my wrist while the other cups my face. "Let me have a look, Myles."

"You're not seriously picking him over your own family, are you?" Beau demands.

"Are you dense, Beau Bennett?" Sheridan snaps, her gaze whipping back to her brother's. "Did you take too many balls to the face and head recently, or have you just suddenly lost your fucking mind?"

"This isn't about choice. It's never *been* a choice between you and Myles, because you're my brother, and believe it or not, we can all exist in each other's lives without things being so black and white. He can be your friend while also being my boyfriend. That is a thing that can happen.

"And don't even *think* about using my mental health problems as a reasonable excuse to behave the way you are. We've had our conversations and neither of us have run away. And regardless of that, it is still not up to *you* whether that has to be an issue or not. It's up to us." She gestures between us.

Beau stares at us, frowning like he's still a stroppy teenager. Nash is cradling his hand against his chest, not used to bare-knuckling anything, which hopefully means he's broken it, too.

"Fine." Beau shrugs. "Whatever. But I don't like it or condone it." I'd roll my eyes if I didn't think it would hurt. "And you may think it's not a choice Shez, but I'll always pick you."

"I don't need your permission to date someone, Beau. You're not Dad, or Mum. In fact, you've behaved more like a child the past few months than when we were actual kids. We're adults. You need to grow up."

He scowls and storms to his car without another word, Nash hot on his heels.

My head starts throbbing a painful rhythm and I squeeze my eyes shut.

"I think we should take Myles to the hospital," Brin mutters.

Sheridan sighs. "Agreed. Come on, handsome."

"So much for an early night, aye?" I joke in a pathetic attempt to lighten the mood.

Sheridan helps me back into Brin's car and then sits behind me in the back seat. Beau and Nash have already peeled out of the car park so it's thankfully not too embarrassing.

At the hospital, the A&E nurse looks at me like I'm some kind of thug. It's not the first time someone's looked at me that way, but it's been a while since I've felt so…common.

"How did the injury occur?" She asks sceptically.

I clear my throat, using the feeling of Sheridan's hand in mine to ground myself. "I was punched. It was just a misunderstanding."

"Do we need to involve the police?"

"Absolutely not. Like I said—it's a misunderstanding," I insist. The thought of Nash spending overnight in a shitty local police station cell is sobering enough.

"My brother is an idiot. That's all you need to know," Sheridan adds, and Brin snorts behind us.

The nurse's gaze flicks between us, then drops to our joined hands. "I see."

Brin leans forward conspiratorially, "He's our brother's best friend."

Something passes across the nurse's face, and I know in that instant that underneath her stoic exterior, she loves the drama. I'll be hot gossip at the nurse's station when we sit down.

* * *

"What happened to your face?" has been the question of the day, and it's only eleven o'clock.

I've been telling people I walked into a door, which somehow feels more shameful than the truth—that I was punched in the face by my girlfriend's brother. My nose is swollen black and blue, and I'm on so much medication I'm not entirely sure it's sensible for me to even be at work. But I can't afford to miss a day so here we are.

Some teachers have given me a wide berth because I apparently seem to look prone to fighting, and others have outright sneered at me. Is this seriously the price I have to pay for falling in love with my best friend's sister?

Worth it.

Shirley slides into the seat opposite me and gives me a look that is both sympathetic and questioning. "What happened, Myles?"

"Walked into a door," I mutter.

"Uh-huh," Shirley nods, thoughtful, "and was that before or after my son hit you?"

I meet her gaze, alarmed. "What... Which one told you?"

Shirley laughs, a lovely sound. "The one who tells me everything."

Brin appears with a grin. "Hi. I'm the one who tells her everything."

I try—and fail—not to sigh. "Are you mad?"

"At you? God no." The Bennett matron shakes her head. "With my sons? Absolutely. Brian is appalled. Christmas is ruined and I was looking forward to it this year. I had big plans for my turkey, but obviously one of the boys just had to go swinging his fists and fucked it all up."

"Sorry," I mutter, feeling somewhat scorned even though Shirley has said she isn't angry with me.

"What are you apologising for? You didn't hit yourself, did you?" Shirley scoffs. "Besides, Nash and Beau are clearly dumb idiots if they can't see how good you are for Sheridan. I should be thanking you, if anything, for making my baby girl so happy."

"She deserves to be happy. I *want* to make her happy."

Brin rubs my arm. "You do, Myles. Trust me."

"I wish I knew sooner," Shirley says wistfully.

"That's my fault," I admit. "I was worried about Beau's reaction, and... Well, he proved me right."

"That boy." Shirley shakes her head. "You'd think he'd be delighted. He knows you're a good lad. I think he's reluctant to share—he never was very good at it."

Brin pulls an incredulous face. "You don't say."

My phone lights up on the table with a text from Sheridan:

Birdie
How are you feeling? Xxx

Cooing noises ensue around the table, and suddenly Shirley is standing behind me, her hands on my shoulders.

"Take a picture of us, Brin, and send it to her."

Before I can protest, Brinsley has her phone up and Shirley is planting a smacking kiss on my cheek. She shows it to us then sends it off.

"She'll love that." Shirley beams.

"You should send it to Beau," I joke.

"Oh my God, great idea." Brin cackles.

A moment later, I have another text come through.

Birdie
Glad you're being well looked after... The shiner really gives you a dangerous, rugged sort of look xxx

Me
The Bear has made his return xxx

Birdie
If you shaved your beard would you look like 17 y/o you? Xxx

Me
Probably. I'll see if I can find some photos later. Miss you xxx

Birdie
Yes please. Miss you too. Call me later xxx

"Have you got any plans for Christmas Day, Myles?" Brin asks me quietly. Shirley is already talking to a faculty member on another table.

"No." Christmas is the one family event of the Bennetts' that I refused to go to—and is probably part of the reason it took me so long to meet the girls. Something about it felt sacred and I didn't want to tarnish that. "No plans."

"Well then we need to fix that, don't we?"

* * *

It turns out that Nash and Beau have apparently refused to come over for Christmas if I'm going, and Sheridan and Brinsley refuse to go if I'm not there, even though I'm not family. Clearly, the girls weren't having it.

Instead, the plan is that Sheridan will host Christmas for Brin and me, Brian and Shirley are having Christmas by themselves, and Beau and Nash are doing whatever they want.

This is all my fault. If it wasn't for me, the Bennetts would be having their Christmas together the way they should be, and I would be spending it alone like I'm used to.

I argued with the girls over it for hours last night, but they wouldn't listen. Sheridan insisted she would much rather spend it with me than with people who don't appreciate the good in their life, and if that didn't do my damn ego the world of good. I stopped fighting after that.

"What's wrong with your face?"

I look up from my lesson plan, startled into the present. Sam and Jamie, the unlikely duo, stand in front of my desk with matching expressions of concern. "Of all the ways I've been asked that question the past two days, that has to be the worst yet."

"Oh, we don't mean your nose, sir," Jamie says, shoving his hands into his pockets. "We know all about that."

I raise an eyebrow at him. "Do you now? Please share because the rumour going around yesterday was that I'm in an underground fight club."

"Jesus, sir," Jamie hisses, throwing a cautionary glance at the classroom door, "keep your voice down. Everyone knows the first rule of Fight Club is you don't talk about Fight Club."

Sam shoves him. "Mate, shut up. That's not it. And we know you didn't walk into a door, either."

"We actually just meant that you look a bit miserable, but anyway. There's a video." Jamie produces his phone and pulls up an app I don't recognise.

He taps a few buttons, and then there I am. There we *all* are—me, Sheridan, Brin, Beau, and Nash—in the car park outside my flat, and there Nash goes, clocking me right in the face.

"Oh, fuck," I say without thinking.

"I know!" Jamie seems more excited than anything, even though a yawning pit of dread has opened up in my stomach. "You've gone viral! Like, that's *Beau fucking Bennett*. And you! And... Miss Bennett?"

"Jamie," I say in my most stern teacher voice. "This is really serious." More serious than worrying about Christmas arrangements. "I could lose my job. Beau's career could be in the toilet if this isn't handled properly. And my neighbours are obviously absolute dickheads."

"Wait, why should you get in trouble?" Jamie frowns. "You didn't do anything wrong."

This is why I love teenagers. "That may be, but it's now an even stickier situation than just me dating my friend's sister and him being upset about it."

"You're dating your friend's sister? Woah, sir, that's gross." Jamie's nose wrinkles.

"It's Miss Bennett's twin," Sam mutters.

"Wait, seriously?" Jamie looks between us. "I take it all back, Miss Bennett is fit as."

The sigh I let out is deep and long. "I need to rectify this before it goes totally wrong. Can you send me that please?"

"Oh, sure..." Jamie texts me the video, and I tell him to delete my number immediately afterward. "You don't look too good, sir."

"I'm about to offer my testicles on a silver platter to Paulson. Put yourself in my shoes."

"First of all, if I was in your shoes, I wouldn't call them testicles. *Bollocks* is much better."

I give the boy an incredulous look.

Chapter Thirty-One
THE NAME OF THE GAME

SHERIDAN

I'm in that place again.

It's dark yet warm. Cool yet comforting. Reachable and somehow completely untouchable, a cosy ether I'll never *really* get to brush my fingertips against. But I'm a force of my own creativity and I grasp onto this feeling, keep myself in my own mind for just that bit longer, because I haven't been here for so long and the fruits of my labour are becoming undeniably rewarding.

Once again Nash is the cause of my sudden motivation. People used to say it was a coping mechanism—a way to avoid the real world and all the problems it brings. But how can creative motivation be an issue? It's not, really. Maybe I should fight with my brother more often. His constant disregard for my actual feelings and the things that bring joy to my life is apparently the greatest encouragement of all. My way of silently pushing back.

The biggest Fuck You of all.

My little faerie-tale has gone from a seed of an idea to a full-blown plot with a storyboard in the space of two days. Caerwyn and her mortal are coming to life before my very eyes, and I feel somehow more powerful than when I verbally demolished my brothers.

I barely see daylight on Tuesday. I neglect all my work to focus completely on this queen and the journey I want her to take. I expect a part of me to feel bad for ignoring my actual responsibilities, but all I do feel when I put my art supplies away is immense satisfaction. I let my imagination run wild and it's turned into something beautiful.

This is what I want.

I stretch in my seat before rising on my shaky legs. I think I heard Brin get home a few hours ago but she hasn't come to see me. She knows what I'm like when I get into a zone and to leave me to it.

I catch a glimpse of the leaflet Myles's cute nerd friend gave him a few weeks ago and I debate actually *doing* something with it.

It's a big deal, putting myself out there like that. So many things could go wrong if I'm not careful. People talk. Commercialising my work to a new network of watchers could break my otherwise solid opinion of my abilities, and humans are especially cruel.

I like my job well enough, but it's not what I want to do forever. Not really. I want more than that, and I think winning that Toonie was just the tip of the iceberg.

I decide there's no harm in trying.

* * *

It takes me two hours to go through the application, so by the time I'm done I'm starving and knackered.

If I were a Sim, I'd be dead.

I check my phone for the first time in hours and find two notifications from Myles, which automatically brings a smile to my face.

Yep, I'm that girl now. I smile at the sight of a boy's name on my phone. Although this particular boy is all *man*.

It's short-lived, however, when I open the texts and read their contents:

Myles
Im sorry Sheridan.

Myles
You don't deserve this.

"Don't deserve *what*?" I ask the empty room.

Me
What does that mean? Xxx
Is everything okay? Xxx

When I don't get an answer after a minute, I try calling him, but it goes straight to voicemail, and that anxious ball that's been growing in my belly finally drops and the nausea hits.

I leave him a panicked voicemail. "Myles, I don't know what your texts mean but can you call me back, please? I'm worried."

I move out of my office, yanking the door open, and stalk into the kitchen where I find Brin sitting at the breakfast table nursing a glass of wine while she stares at an untouched plate of food.

"What's going on?" I demand, my tone ruder than I'd intended.

Without missing a beat, my twin says, "Someone filmed our argument outside Myles's flat on Sunday—one of the neighbours—and posted it online. The kids have seen it and shown it to Myles, who gave the footage to Paulson. Myles and I have been suspended for two weeks pending investigation. *Beau* has been suspended from his next two games, which happen to be home games, and has been pulled from the England draft. And Nash has gone awol."

I stare at her for a long minute, slack-jawed and nonplussed. "What the *fuck*?"

"Mum is raging, obviously. I've never seen her so mad, and it was all aimed at Paulson."

"Well, I'm not surprised—you didn't do anything wrong!"

Brin just shrugs. "But we were involved."

I slip onto the chair opposite her and take her hand. "Why didn't you come and tell me? I've been home all day fucking around with a goddamn cartoon."

"Honestly, I was embarrassed." She sighs, resting her head in her hand. "I've been a teacher less than a year and I've already been suspended over something. I just wanted to put off my shame a bit longer."

"Brin, this is not your fault. Anyone with a brain knows it. Please don't beat yourself up. I'm sorry you got dragged into it when it should've been between Beau and me. It's all been blown completely out of proportion, and you've somehow been punished for it."

"Well…done now, innit?"

I scowl. "We'll sort it out. If Mum has *any* say in it, she'll rip Paulson a new one and get you working again soon."

"I really hope so," she mumbles.

I help myself to a glass of wine too and rejoin her. "What was Myles like when you left? I had a cryptic text from him, and his phone is going to voicemail."

My sister grimaces. "He wasn't great. He was all tense and quiet—barely said a word before he left."

I feel my chest squeeze painfully. I know he's going to be beating himself up over this and it's all because of me. "I wish he'd speak to me."

"I think he just needs to wallow, Shez. I know if I wasn't in your house, I'd be sulking by myself, too. Just give him tonight and try again tomorrow."

I know she's probably right, but I still utterly detest the idea of leaving him by himself. He's been by himself forever; I want him to lean on me.

I stick Brin's dinner in the microwave and help myself to a portion, then call Marina while I wait.

"Sheridan?" She sounds perplexed, and I only then realise it's almost eleven o'clock.

"Are you going to sack me? And sorry for the late call." No point in beating around the bush.

"What?"

"Are you going to sack me?" I repeat.

There's a pause. "Is this about that video? Because I was going to call tomorrow rather than harassing you at this hour. But no, I'm not, as disappointing as the whole thing is."

"You're right, it is disappointing. My brothers are a pair of overgrown morons stuck in the 1800s."

"Do I even want to know?"

"My boyfriend is Beau's best friend."

She scoffs. "Men. Say no more. Take a day off, Sheridan. Or five. You'll give yourself an aneurysm soon."

That does make me laugh. "Thanks, Marina. Have a good Christmas."

"And you, my love."

I end the call and look at Brin, who manages a flat smile.

"Let's eat and get really drunk," I suggest.

"God, you read my mind. It's like we're twins or something."

I peck her temple. "I love you, Brin. I'm sorry you got dragged into this."

And I really was sorry, because *how* had my relationship with Myles come to involve so many other people?

If 'ridiculous' was the name of the game, I'd be winning it by a landslide.

* * *

I wake in the morning with a painful throbbing in my head, a dry mouth, and a crick in my neck from sleeping at a stupid angle on the sofa instead of in my bed. When I look up, I find Brin in a similar state, although she's still catching flies and snoring away.

God, I haven't drunk that much in a *long* time, and I was really just trying to keep up with Brinsley who has always had a higher tolerance for alcohol than I have. She drinks like a fish, whereas I drink like a slightly wet seal. And sleep like one, apparently.

The room is a mess. Half empty crisp and biscuit packets lay strewn across the coffee table and mantelpiece, along with a variety of glassware filled with rank-looking concoctions. So, we went *uni student* hard apparently. I can't remember much except screaming as loud as we could to early noughties music as if we had any right to be that rowdy that late at night on a Tuesday in December.

Stumbling into the kitchen I find it in much the same state and wince at my own neglect. I'm not the tidiest person but this is, quite frankly, disgusting.

Apparently two people can cause utter chaos in the space of a few hours. I'd almost consider it an achievement if I wasn't so horrified by it.

I decide that before I tackle the mess, I'm going to take Hector—who has been following me around and grumbling like a scolding old man—for his morning walk and pick up something for breakfast. And when I say *something*, I mean full of fat and so unhealthy my veins might clog with it.

Thankfully the morning is mild if a little cold. I've got a hat and gloves on, but my big coat is a little too heavy and I find I'm overheating in places when I reach the corner shop.

God, is this early menopause?

I shove the irrational thought into a box along with all my others, like do my parents secretly hate me, or was I rude to that random corner-shop cashier in Manchester last year who looked at me funny when I bought tampons from him?

After I've picked up the makings of a well-worthy full English, I start back home by slipping through the pub car park to the canal. The weather feels a little murky and I'm sure a good rain-pour is coming imminently.

Somehow, by the time I get home again I haven't checked my phone once, even though the thought of Myles has been wriggling around in what I like to refer to as the 'garden shed' of my mind. Within reach, good for storage.

I know he hasn't replied to me yet or even called. I always have this strange inkling when he's about to pop up on my phone, but that mystical tether has been dead since Monday. Not even a mild vibration. Like it's been snipped with oversized shears.

Brin might have said he'll come to me in his own time but that doesn't fill me with much comfort. He might never be ready, and I'm not about to soak myself in a love that lacks communication.

If I don't hear from him by tomorrow, I'm going over there.

My sister is still passed out when we get home, so I quietly work around her to tidy up the carnage we created. On a normal day

I'd blast some music, either through the speakers or my earphones but my head hurts a bit too much for that.

I don't see Brin until I'm halfway through cooking our breakfast of—not quite—champions.

"Have I ever told you you're the best?" She says around a groan as she enters the room, hair like a haystack, and wraps herself around me.

"Not nearly enough, sissy."

"Consider it your daily reminder." She gets to work drying the things on the drainer. "Have you heard from Myles?"

I do my best to ignore the squeeze in my chest at the thought of him. "Nope."

She sighs. "Poor sod. This is worse on him than it is on me."

"Perhaps. I just wish he'd talk to me."

And I continue to wish it all day, to no such luck.

We spend our entire Wednesday on the sofa with Hector, bingeing rom-coms and snacking on anything we can get our hands on. It's the laziest day I've had since the weekend Myles appeared on my front doorstep.

I wish more than anything he'd do that now.

My fingers twitch to text him or call him again, but that invisible tether between us is still dead. Part of me debates shoving my phone under my cushion again like I did the last time he vanished, but I don't want to miss a second if he reaches out.

I never realised how dependent I was on him for my sanity until now.

I miss him, which is ludicrous considering I only spoke to him two days ago.

By the end of the day, when I crawl into my cold and empty bed, I'm despairing.

I sleep like shit.

I refuse to look at what people are saying online because the consensus is that only idiots express their opinions on the internet and the sensible ones get swept under the rug.

At three a.m. I find myself crying because my chest hurts so much.

I revisit Myles's texts and realise there's an undertone of finality to them I hadn't picked up on the first fifty times I read them.

I'm sorry, Sheridan.
You don't deserve this.
That's not an apology.
It's a goodbye.

Chapter Thirty-Two

Rangers vs. Athletic

SHERIDAN

When Boxing Day rolls around the following week, I still haven't heard from, or seen, Myles.

I spent all day on Friday trying to reach him by text and phone call to no avail. And then I burst through my tolerance levels, got in the car, and drove to his flat in the city. My anger didn't subside when I found he wasn't home. And because I was so angry, I kept looking in the direction of the flat where the video was taken, but that window was quiet, too.

I'd never felt this way over a boy before. And I don't mean disgustingly in love with one. I mean incandescent with rage that he had the nerve to ghost me after everything he said to me—after everything we said to *each other*.

Who does that? Who disappears without an explanation except a vague few words and a bruised ego?

Myles Wilson does, apparently.

My rage eventually subsided after I realised that I was freaking Brin out to the point she was debating going to Mum and Dad's for a few days, but that just made way for self-pity. In my fury's stead, I wallowed like an adolescent whose crush got a new girlfriend. I slept all day and cried at night. Brinsley comforted me as much as she could, but I knew I was being a hindrance. She was being sisterly, but she wanted to slap me all at the same time.

I spent all yesterday, Christmas Day, hoping he'd just turn up. I had enough food to feed all of Jesus's disciples and my fridge was overflowing with Christmas niceties, so the least he could do was come and help us consume some of it. Of course, he didn't. No sign of him at all. Not even a whisper or a text. And stupid me had texted him Happy Christmas, as if that was going to get me anywhere.

I had been completely rejected, and that stung more than what my brother did.

I'm sitting with Hector in my lap and a *QI* Christmas episode marathon on the telly—with a box of tissues within easy reach—when I hear the front door open.

"Brin?" I call out. "Where you goin'? If you're going to the shop, can you get me some more tissues? And a box of Maltesers? The big one."

When I don't get an answer, I turn over my shoulder towards the door, and a second later my dad, of all people, strolls through.

"I know you've both got half my genes, flower, but Brin doesn't look *that* much like me," he jokes.

I frown and turn back to the TV. "I want chocolate," I mutter.

"No, what you need is to get out of the house," Dad says brightly, perching beside me to stroke Hector's sleeping head.

"Hard pass."

"Sheridan, it's Christmas," he reminds me. "Stephen Fry in a Santa hat aside, you should be with your friends or family—and Brin doesn't count. Not sulking at home over a boy who doesn't have his head on straight."

I feel my eyes water again, because my first instinct is to defend Myles even though he doesn't deserve it. I just hate the thought of my parents forming a poor opinion of him when they've loved him for so long.

"Come on, poppet." Dad takes my hand and squeezes it a few times. "Let your wizened old dad take you out for a few hours."

After a rigmarole of back and forth for another fifteen minutes, I finally give in, because I'm a pushover and I love him for making the effort to come and get me.

I take a quick shower and dress in comfy clothes—black cargo trousers, white Reebok classics, and a cream cable knit cardigan over a white t-shirt with the words *if you can read this, you're too close* printed on the front. I shove my hair up in an untamed bun and keep my glasses on because I can't be bothered with contact lenses today, and then bundle myself into a big coat and slide into Dad's car.

He makes small talk about work, and I play along because he's the last person I'd ever want to upset. I don't know where we're going but I have an inkling, and the closer we get, the tighter my chest becomes.

When Dad pulls into the filling car park at the Rangers' ground, I feel sick.

I stare out the window at the crowds building and try to keep myself from hyperventilating.

"You're alright, flower." Dad pats my leg and waits patiently.

He's been with me during so many panic attacks he knows when to leave me be and when to step in. He hasn't had to do this for a while, though. I managed to keep myself away from crowds like this.

Until recently, anyway.

"Five things you can see?" He prompts, taking my hand.

I take three or four deep breaths and look out the window. "Football fans. Merch vendors. The stadium. Um, security teams. And the shopping centre behind the ground."

"Good girl. Four things you can hear?"

"I think you're pushing your luck with that one."

He chuckles and squeezes my hand. "Try for me."

"Er...the cars on the bypass." I roll the window down a little. "The Athletic fans chanting." I leave out the mention of Beau, who they're chanting obscenities about. "The home fans telling them to fuck off, and...my heartbeat in my ears."

Dad grins. "Ready to go?"

"No."

He rolls his eyes. "Come on, Shez. It's early enough that this is tame. Leave it any longer and it'll only get worse."

Well, that gives me the kick up the bum I needed to get going. I'm out of the car like a bullet.

Since I've never been to the football ground before, I have to wait for Dad to catch up so he can show me where to go. He's here every home game so the staff seem to know him well and even refer to him by Brian rather than Mr. Bennett. I find this inexplicably cute.

We reach a floor with tall ceilings and partitioned rooms with various bars and signs on them. Dad leads us to one right in the middle, our surname tagged to the wall beside the door, and he knocks twice before entering.

I don't know why it didn't occur to me sooner that he'd be here, but I stall when I see Beau standing in the doorway to the private box that leads out to the seats. I guess I assumed because he's suspended, he wouldn't be allowed anywhere near it. Apparently, I'm wrong.

He looks over his shoulder before turning fully, a tentative expression on his face.

I throw Dad a glare. Traitor.

"You two need to work out your issues." Dad shrugs. "We're family—you can't avoid each other forever."

"I owe you an apology," Beau says straight off the bat, and it throws me for a loop. "I behaved poorly, and I hate that it's had an impact on you."

Indignation spreads through me. "Don't for one second think I'm under any illusion that if you hadn't got caught and thrown under a very public bus, you wouldn't still be off sulking in your mansion, Beau Bennett."

He winces, and I'm pretty sure Dad does, too. "Perhaps. But I'm glad it got put out there."

"You're *glad*?!"

"I needed a reality check! I'm an arsehole, I know that."

"Oh, I'm *so* glad that your reprimand has given you some fucking clarity, Beau. Meanwhile our sister and Myles have been suspended from their jobs pending an investigation! They could get sacked! All because you couldn't keep your ego in check!"

He winces again. I wonder if I came at him, he'd do it a third time. "Right, yeah."

"*Right, yeah,*" I mock, scoffing. "You really are a selfish prick at times. You've been vile. Fucking *vile*. You insulted your best friend. I can't say a word on his behalf, but I hope he bins you off like he has me because it's the least you deserve."

"I just thought I was looking out for you, Shez."

"I don't need you to do that! I can pick my own battles, Beau. Just like I can pick my own damn romantic partners. I'm *sorry* I fell for your best friend, but I did. And stupid me fell hard. I honestly can't remember the last time I was as happy as I am with Myles, and you've gone and completely fucked me over because your fragile ego can't take it. You're an arsehole. A selfish, self-centred, tactless prick."

"Come on, Sheridan, don't be like th—," he stops himself. "Wait. Did you say he binned you off?"

Unbelievable. "Congratulations, Beau. You actually listened to me. Yes, he's completely vanished and cut off all contact like a thief in the night. Poof. Gone. And part of me doesn't blame him, as messed up as I am over it. I blame you. Because if you hadn't started swinging your dick around like some territorial dickhead, Myles would still be here, and I wouldn't feel so fucking sad."

My voice breaks on the last word, and I have to take a deep breath, but it does nothing. Before I can stop it, my vision blurs and I'm crying in the middle of this stupid private box. I take my glasses off and hide my hands in my face and try to stifle my sobs to no avail.

No sooner than I start sobbing is Beau wrapping himself around me in comfort. For all his flaws he's always been a good hugger, and I hate him for it right now.

"I'm sorry, Sheridan," he says, voice gravelly. "I've fucked up. I'm so sorry."

I don't answer him. I just continue weeping until his shirt soaks through and I'm hyperventilating. My chest is tight, and my head hurts and my breathing is more like panting. I feel like I've run a sprint.

I'm manoeuvred to a sitting position and Beau pulls my hands away from my face, keeping hold of them. He's talking to me, but I can't hear him over the white noise in my ears. He imitates deep breaths and I try to follow along.

I'm a certified mess.

I somehow manage to get a hold of myself, and by the time I've calmed down I feel hung out to dry.

"I know I'm like your least favourite person," Beau says quietly as he hands me a glass of water, which I sink in one gulp, "but I am genuinely sorry for making you feel this way. I was out of line and I'm gonna fix it. I'll talk to Myles."

"Good luck," I mutter, taking another long drink.

"I mean it, Shez. This is my mess to fix, and I will."

The noise in the stadium intensifies, which I take to mean the game is about to start. We all look towards the door.

"I don't even have a shirt," I say around a pout.

"I'm sure we can find you one." Dad says, the picture of calm.

"Go splash some water on your face and I'll find you a shirt, yeah?"

I nod, making to stand on shaky legs. "Yeah."

Fifteen minutes later we're sitting in the seats outside the box with beers—and sparkling water for Beau—snacks, and a great view.

Without Beau playing, it's obvious that the team is trying twice as hard to get a win just to prove that they can. Thirty minutes into the game, though, we're two-nil down.

"This is awful," I find myself saying just as the half time whistle blows.

"It's not because we're shit," Beau insists.

Dad barks a laugh.

"You have to say that," I retort.

"But it's true. Their defence has always been stellar."

When the teams come back on and play starts, Coventry seem to have a fire lit up their arses, because they make attempt after attempt, shot after shot, mostly on target, and yet they just can't seem to get the ball in the net.

I study S.L. Athletics' goalkeeper—currently just a speck of neon pink amongst a sea of green and white—and notice that he's *massive* compared to the other players.

"Who's their goalie?"

"Roberts," Beau mutters. "He's a beast but he's an utter prick. Like a big growly bear."

"Didn't you play fisticuffs with him once?" Dad ponders.

I get my phone out to look him up.

"Yeah, couple of seasons ago. He accused me of fouling their left back and got physical when I denied it. Guy's temper is on a real short leash."

My search results tell me he's Ashley Roberts, and his fight with Beau is one of the top videos under his name. I imagine it's resurfaced after the recent debacle.

Another thing I spot is multiple articles about the death of his wife and daughter three years ago in a car accident. Roberts was in the car with them and the only one to survive with barely a scratch. They were T-boned by a lorry on a blind junction, hit on the passenger side. No wonder he's a growly bear—I think anyone would be if they'd been through that, and still managed to go back to playing a sport he loves professionally.

A small, evil little part of me is glad he had a little tiff with Beau once. That same part hopes Roberts got a really good hit on him.

I peek at his pictures and find he's quite good-looking when he's not scowling—dark skin, dark eyes that seem to glitter if he's caught smiling, big round cheeks, straight white teeth, trimmed black hair that curls tightly. And he is truly stacked, and tall at well over six foot. A really hench bastard. No wonder we can't get a goal in, he barely has to lean to stop the ball.

By the end of the second half, we've lost spectacularly. Four-nil.

"I don't think I should come to another game if you're just gonna lose when I'm here," I joke.

"You're not the problem, Shez." Beau wraps an arm around my shoulders, and I'm surprised to find I simply let him.

He made a mistake, but I can tell he genuinely means his apology. The man hates making people sad, or angry—especially his own family.

I don't believe that he'll fix it—it might be too late for that—but I do wholeheartedly believe that he'll try.

Chapter Thirty-Three
Four Rounds

MYLES

The incessant buzzing from my phone isn't helping my headache. I know who it is, too, and it's not the woman I've been avoiding. It's her dickhead brother.

Beau started texting me three days ago and he hasn't stopped since with messages, calls, and voicemails. I don't know what he wants since I gave him what he wanted. And I took the chicken's way out, too. I'm not proud of myself but I couldn't face Sheridan knowing how fucked up everything had become.

I wince again when my phone buzzes with Beau's follow-up voicemail. One more vibration and I might throw it at the wall.

"I know you're in pain," Brad says delicately.

He has no idea.

"But I think you might need to stop with the fighting."

I eye him from where I'm sitting on his sofa, head back to stop my nose from bleeding. Yeah. I've broken my nose. Again.

Well, someone else broke my nose for me. I didn't realise how much pent-up rage I had until I found Nash in the dodgy gym he trains at and unleashed myself on him.

Yep, I finally let the caged animal inside me loose, and we've been on a rampage ever since.

Like any good drug, the first hit felt good, and every punch after that felt even better until we were completely battered and bleeding in the middle of the sparring ring. And I've gone back time and time again knowing he'll be there waiting to go. It's never been as satisfying as that first fight, but I'll keep going until he apologises.

I know for a fact that he isn't talking to the other Bennetts. I think it's a mixture of shame and pettiness, but I'll continue pushing with him until he admits he was wrong. Knowing how stubborn he is, it might never happen.

He broke my phone in our first year of university and has still never admitted it was him or said he was sorry for doing it. As if it wasn't the only thing of value I had to my name at the time.

It's memories like that—his unbridled selfishness and ignorance—that keep my anger at a continual simmer until I see his stupid face.

"I will when he apologises," I say to Brad, my voice nasally like a ventriloquist. I might've permanently damaged something up there.

"I don't think he's going to apologise, mate." He scratches his cheek then pushes his glasses up his nose.

"Then I'll keep fighting him."

Brad sighs and leaves me alone again.

It's been two weeks and I've had four bouts with Nash. This is the second time Brad has tried to talk me out of it.

I've been hiding out at his house so no one can find me. I can't believe he hasn't tattled on me to Brinsley quite honestly. I thought she'd be the first person he told when I turned up on his doorstep that Tuesday night after my suspension.

It's been a slow downward spiral ever since then.

I appreciate Brad for that alone. I needed another friend in this town that isn't completely linked to the Bennett family, and I found one. For all his dithering and debate over a woman who clearly doesn't appreciate him—Emily the French teacher has been here one singular time since I've been crashing and was a walking red flag in that she incessantly flirted with me the whole time—Brad is a good bloke, and I'm glad I have him.

Twenty minutes later Brad is back with his car keys in hand, which I know means it's time to go to the hospital. I haven't needed to go since the night Nash punched me, but breaking your nose twice isn't going to look great.

We're at the hospital for hours, unsurprisingly, because A&E is overrun with patients but distinctly lacking nurses and doctors. Fortunately, my nose stopped bleeding some time ago, so I don't have to stare at the ceiling anymore.

When I'm finally seen, it's by a pretty nurse who might have a penchant for men with bruises and broken noses from the way she flirts with me. I try not to be rude with an obvious dismissal, but how do I tell her I've just given up the only woman I want, and I'm in far too much pain to even be concerned about the advances of other women.

Finally, about four hours after we arrived, we get to leave. I realise I owe Brad a big something to say thank you for putting up with my fucked-up self and plan to rectify that soon.

A mop of brown hair catches my attention as we're passing through the waiting room on our way to the exit.

Sam is sitting by himself in a secluded corner quite clearly trying not to draw attention to himself. The sight is so startling that my shoes skid and squeak against the linoleum with my abrupt halt.

"What?" Brad asks cautiously when I grab his arm.

"That's Sam."

Brad's gaze sweeps across the room to the dishevelled boy in the corner and widens with concern at the way he cradles his arm. "Do you think he's by himself?"

It's likely. Knowing what his home life is like with his foster family I wouldn't be surprised if he is here alone.

"Probably." I face Brad, determined. "I'm gonna stay with him. I don't know the procedure for helping minors without an adult and I don't want him to suffer. If you want to go, I get it. I can take him home."

Brad shakes his head. "I'll come back. I'll just go shopping down the road while you wait."

"Thanks, mate." I pat his shoulder and head towards Sam.

He doesn't notice me at first, too busy fiddling with his phone. I tentatively sit in the seat beside him, not oblivious to the way he curls in on himself. He's playing some version of Candy Crush one-handed. He makes the wrong move and fails.

"Should've gone for the yellow," I say with a nudge to his good arm. "You'd have passed."

Sam's eyes widen as he looks up at me. "How did you-," he *really* looks at my face, "Holy shit, sir. What happened to you?"

I shrug, even though it hurts. "Got into a bit of a barney with someone." I probably shouldn't be passing off fist fights with disgruntled brothers as nothing but I'm more concerned about the boy. "What happened to *you*?"

He echoes my shrug. "Fell off my bike. I think my wrist is fucked." He lifts it up and flinches at the effort.

"Fell off your bike, aye?" I challenge with a raised brow. I point at the bruises around his wrist. "What's that then?"

"Nothing," he mutters.

"Hmm. Did you also fall onto something hand-shaped when you fell off this bike?"

"Maybe."

"Come on, Sam. I'm not stupid. You need out of that house."

"I'm *already* out of the house."

"What? Since when?"

"Last week. Shipped me off back to the care home just in time for Christmas."

Fuckers.

Sam rubs his face and groans. "I thought I left something there, so I went back to check. Turned me away at the door and when I tried again the bastard shoved me off. I fell on my arm funny and when I got up it hurt like a bitch. So, I came here."

"How did you even get here?"

"Bus."

I sigh and lean forward on my knees. "Do the guardians at your care home know?"

"No. But it's gonna be pretty hard to hide it." He's silent for a minute, and then, so quietly I nearly don't hear him over the bustling waiting room racket, he asks, "Are you gonna tell anyone?"

"Do you want me to tell anyone?"

He hesitates, and then shakes his head. "No."

"Then I won't tell anyone," I promise.

I get it, because I've been in his position, and I never wanted anyone to know either. It's damaging to your pride as a young boy to have a bigger man knock you about.

"Why weren't you at school last week?" He asks after a quiet few minutes.

"I've been temporarily suspended."

"Over that video?" Sam seems baffled. "That's not fair, *you* got punched, not the other way around!"

I can't help my laugh. "Unfortunately, it doesn't work that way."

"So, what happens? Do you get to come back?"

"Depends. I have to talk to the school board and tell them. Nash—the guy who hit me—will have to submit a statement, too. Then it will be up to them."

"Can you get sacked?"

"Possibly," I admit with a cringe. "Shirley—sorry, Mrs. Bennett—doesn't think that'll happen but it's not great with it being my first year teaching and all. So, I could be."

"That's bullshit, sir."

I smile at his defence of me. "Not much I can do about it."

"What will you do if you get sacked?"

"Don't know, to be quite honest. I've always wanted to be a teacher, so I don't have a backup plan. But I don't think I can stay here. I'll probably move to another city. Fresh start."

"What about your lady?"

My smile saddens. "I, er, don't think she's technically my lady anymore."

"She left you?!"

"Er, no, not quite."

Sam's gaze burns the side of my face for a long time. "Can I come with you? If you do go? I hope you don't. Like, I hate art but you're my favourite teacher easily."

My face feels hot. And my eyes feel wet. Fucking hell. "Thanks, bud."

"So, can I come with you?"

I hastily wipe my face before I embarrass myself. I never thought a kid would take to me like that. Growing up the way I did, it seems far-fetched that another boy would be in almost the exact same position and look up to me because of it. I'm no idol, no role model. I've spent the past two weeks willingly getting into fights, for crying out loud. But I'd be better for the sake of an impressionable kid, because I never had that person myself.

The very last thing I want Sam to become is the bad version of me.

My laughter is wet. "Sure, mate. You can come with me."

*　*　*

It takes us an hour and a half more to be seen by someone, where they X-ray Sam's wrist and arm and decide to put him in a cast up to his elbow. It's midnight by the time we leave, and Sam's phone has been going bananas with calls and texts.

Brad graciously takes us to the group home Sam has been cruelly returned to and lingers while I deposit him through the door.

"What happened to you?" A harried-looking woman in her early sixties gasps when she opens the house up.

"Broke my wrist," he murmurs, looking sheepish while he toes the doormat.

"How on earth did you manage that, Sam? And who are you?" She turns a glare on me.

I realise that with my face the state it's in, I probably should've let Brad take him in. Sam and I share a conspiratorial glance.

"He's my teacher. And I fell off my bike."

"*This* man is your teacher?" Her tone drips with disbelief, and honestly, I don't blame her. I'm a mess.

"Yeah. He got jumped on his way home from the gym and saw me on his way out the hospital." Sam shrugs.

His ability to lie easily is terrifying.

The woman sighs. "Fine. Whatever. Just text me next time or *something*."

"Yeah. Sorry."

"Say goodbye and go to bed. I'm exhausted," she orders with a withering look and abandons us on the porch.

Sam turns to look at me with an awkward grin.

"Stay out of trouble, Sam," I warn him. "But use that number I gave you if you ever need it. Hopefully I'll be back in school by the end of Feb. I'll tell you what's going on."

"Thanks, sir. And thanks for staying with me through that."

"I'd be a rubbish adult if I didn't. Just try not to make it a regular thing, alright?"

"Yeah, alright."

I head back to the car as he dips inside and wait until all the lights are off before we pull off. I'm so tired that when we get back to Brad's, I pass out on the sofa within seconds of being horizontal.

Chapter Thirty-Four
WANTING TO BE WANTED

MYLES

"Fuck," I hiss at my phone, the text I just opened by accident glaring up at me. My thumb was in the wrong place at the wrong time. "Fuck, fuck, fuck."

Beau
I don't know where you're hiding but this is getting daft mate.

Now that I've opened it, I decide to read the entire thread of grey messages I've neglected. He can see I've read it anyway.

Beau
I think we need to talk.
I said some shit I don't mean and want to apologise. You've been my best friend for five years and I'm not about to throw that away because you fancy my sister.
Or love her, or whatever.
I've been a dick about it all and I'm sorry, okay?
Dude answer your phone.
This is so dumb. I feel like the scorned lover.

I hope you know Shez is raging. Mostly at me because she thinks you left her because of what I did. That probably is the reason you've buggered off but that's not cool, mate. I made her cry in the middle of the box at the game yesterday. And I promised I was gonna fix it and I intend to uphold that. So answer me fucker.

Myles!
ANSWER YOUR FUCKING PHONE
istg if you're dead in a ditch somewhere I'll never forgive you.

I think I'm getting repetitive strain injury in my thumb joints because of you.

Fortunately I don't need my hands to play football.

This is so fucked up mate. Please just talk to me. Shez will never admit it to me cause she's weird and private and whatever but she's devastated about all this mate. I can see it all over her face. She tries to hide it with whatever but she's really sad. If you wanted to say fuck you to me you should've stayed with her.

She's the best thing to ever happen to you. Best girl in the world. Well, on par with Brin and Mum obvs. Can't show favourites. But you've fucked up by leaving. Brin said she's incandescent. Whatever that means.

We're gonna fix our bro mess and then I'm gonna make you grovel on your fucking knees for abandoning her. Be prepared to look like a tit. A bigger one than you already do.

oh my god you stubborn prick just ANSWER ME
Never mind Nash and his poxy left hook, I'm gonna beat you senseless when I see you.
GET YOUR HEAD OUT YOUR ASS MAN
You're a royal arsehole Myles.

That was the last text he sent before this morning's attempt. Another comes through as I reach the bottom.

Beau
I SEE YOU READING YOU BASTARD

I decide to reply with the first thing that comes to my head.

Me
She's not weird.

The little grey dots start pulsing.

Beau
HE'S ALIVE
What??

Me
Sheridan. She's not weird.

Beau
Seriously??? Out of all that, THAT'S what you focussed on? You dickhead. You're so whipped, and yet you left her. Idiot.

Me
This coming from the man who made her feel like crap for dating his friend. Yeah, sure. I'm the idiot.

Beau
I AM TRYING TO APOLOGISE

Me
YOU ARE NOT DOING A VERY GOOD JOB AT IT.

I don't get a reply. Instead, my phone starts ringing obnoxiously in my hand with Beau's stupid face filling the screen.

"What?" I snap, accepting his first call in months.

"I'm *sorry*," Beau whines.

"You are such a prick, Beaumont," I tell him.

"Oh, fuck off, you know that's not my name. And I *know* I'm a prick, okay? I have had the sentiment relayed to me repeatedly over the past two weeks, you really don't need to remind me."

"I could lose my job because of you and your insane brother! I never thought having feelings for a girl would somehow wind up with a broken nose and a suspension from my job!"

"If I could get hold of Nash to tell him how much of a moron he is, I would! But much like you, he's off the grid somewhere. Probably beating some poor sod senseless."

"I know Nash is off the grid because *I am* the poor sod he's beating senseless."

Beau finally takes a breath. "Oh shit. What state are you in?"

"I've definitely been better."

"Mentally?"

"I'd say about sixty-five percent stable."

"Emotionally…?"

"Oh, like two percent."

"Fuck, Myles."

"Fuck indeed, Beaumont."

His exhale is weighted. "Can we meet up? Go to the pub or something? I want to fix this."

My chest squeezes painfully with nerves. I've been avoiding going out in public, although I'm supposed to be taking Sam bowling later. He texted to say he was bored so I said I'd take him out for a few hours and get some dinner. I'm about to tell Beau that when I realise that he'll have no idea who Sam is. And that is a tragedy.

"How about bowling?"

"…What?"

* * *

"Sir." Sam aggressively slaps my arm with his good hand. "Sir, look. Sir, that's Beau Bennett."

"I know it's Beau, now stop freaking hitting me." I bat him off with elbows and hips.

"What's he doing here?"

"Going bowling, I'd imagine. Unless he's got a real hankering for air hockey." Which he is also a beast at.

"He's looking right at us."

"I know."

"*Why?*"

"I don't know, maybe he thinks you've got a funny face."

Sam turns a look on me that is so devastated I actually feel a bit bad. "I don't have a funny face."

"If you say so, mate." I give him a patronising pat on the head.

"I *don't*. Erin said puberty is doing good things to me."

Jesus. "We are not going there right now."

"This the lad?" Beau asks as we reach him at the bowling kiosk, glancing between Sam and me.

"Yeah. This is Sam. And Sam…well you know who Beau Bennett is. I just call him Beau, or Beaumont. Or stupid prick depending on the day."

"Woah," Sam says wide-eyed. "Which one do I call you by?"

Beau smirks. "Just Beau is fine, mate."

"Okay, Just Beau." Sam shrugs.

Now it's my turn to smirk.

We pay—Beau pays—for a lane and three games at the kiosk and change our shoes, then find our lane and program our names in.

Naturally, when we start playing Beau can't rein his competitive streak in and bowls a strike every throw. By the fourth round, Sam is gawking at Beau like he's the best thing since sliced bread. I'm sure to certain members of the Ranger's supporters he is, but I know better.

"Are you trying to impress the kid or what?" I mutter when Sam takes his next turn.

"Come on, Myles. You know I have to have every new person's approval when I meet them. That includes fourteen-year-olds with jokes."

I roll my eyes. "Fine. But I didn't put you on a pedestal with him."

"Neither should you."

"Oh, come on!" Sam shouts, bent over with his face in his good hand. "That was so close!" He points to the aisle, and the singular skittle sitting at the bottom.

"You've got another throw, mate. Get it on a spare," I say encouragingly.

"I want a strike, not a spare!"

I give him a wide look. An image strikes me in that instant, of Saturday afternoons in autumn with Sam and Sheridan and harmless games at the shitty bowling alley. Sam losing his temper and Sheridan not making an effort because she hates sports, but we're here for Sam so it doesn't matter. The longing hits me hard and I feel it right in the chest like I've been impaled.

I shake it off.

"Alright," I exasperate, and stand to meet him, "you're too old for a tantrum over bowling."

Sam eases up. "Sorry."

"Get your spare and next throw I'll get Beau to chuck one down for you."

"That's cheating!"

Beau snickers from his seat.

"Alright, fine. I'll help fix your technique. You throw like you're bowling on Wii Sports."

"What's that?"

I share a horrified look with Beau. "Never mind. It probably doesn't help that you've got a broken arm."

"I want Beau to help me."

"Excuse me?" I blink at him.

"You've only bowled one strike. And your left arm isn't even broken."

Beau is fully cackling now.

I give up, raising my hands like a white flag. "You know what, fine. Have the footballer help you, I don't care." I sniff indignantly, but I'm laying it on thick. "But just so you know, he'll sabotage you the first chance he gets."

"I will not!" Beau retorts.

"He will," I whisper. "Your choice."

* * *

"So, are you gonna tell me what's going on with the kid?" Beau asks with a raised brow.

Sam has just excused himself from our table in Nando's to use the bathroom. We've finished eating.

"He's one of my Year 9 kids. *Was* one. Maybe. I don't know. He's also in care, so I kind of…well, we talk to each other about it. His foster parents were horrible, and they've just sent him back to the care home. I ran into him in the hospital a few days ago and stayed with him while he got his arm sorted. Gave my number to him just in case."

"He's a good lad. Hopefully his next foster family are better."

"Yeah… I've been doing some research into fostering," I admit.

You never think about the other side of it when you're a child. You just want someone to want you.

"You want to foster him?" Beau looks surprised.

"Maybe. I know what it's like to be a teenage boy in care and I don't want him to turn out the way I did."

"Might have to stop getting into fights for that to happen, mate."

"I know. I need to watch the job situation first. When it levels out, I'll put a bit more thought into it." My chest is aching again, and I rub it with my fist. "He asked to come with me if I move and I don't think I could ever say no, because everyone said no to me."

"Fuck, Myles." Beau sits back and rubs his face. "You can't leave."

"I don't want to stay here if I lose my job, Beau. With you, and Sheridan here… Hell, all of you frickin' Bennetts, it's painful."

"Brinsley does want to murder you, to be fair."

"Comforting."

"You brought that on yourself, mate."

"I know." I wave him off. "Everything is fucked. But right now, I'm thinking about Sam and that's my priority."

Beau nods thoughtfully. "I get that. I do. I'm sorry I fucked everything up, though. And I'm working on Nash."

"You can't force someone to apologise," I say. "I'll take it if and when it comes, but I don't want one if he doesn't mean it."

Beau continues nodding away, but he remains quiet for a minute. After a while, he says, "Are we good?"

I give it some thought. "I think we're getting there."

Chapter Thirty-Five
Coercion, Reconciliation, Redemption

SHERIDAN

I'm greeted by skittering paws and gentle ruffs when I get home from three nights away in York. The second the front door is closed, Hector barges around the corner and leaps into my waiting arms.

"There's my handsome boy," I coo, scratching around his ears and under his chin, my fingers disappearing amongst his soft, fluffy white coat. "Did you miss me?"

Hector licks up my face, and even though I've had him over two years now, it never gets any less gross. But I'll take the affection because it's the only kind I'm getting.

"Brin?" I call out, placing the big puppy back on all four paws.

"Kitchen!" She calls back.

I head straight there, nervously fidgeting. She had her hearing today with the school board and I spent the majority of my drive home trying not to stop at every single service station so I could either have a nervous wee or vomit.

She's leaning against the counter dressed in her PJs, hair a nest atop her head, but her eyes are clear, and she smiles at me when she spots me.

"Are you clear? Going back to work?" I ask, crossing my legs so I don't have to use the bathroom for the twentieth time today.

She bites her lip and nods furiously. "I'm all good. Back to work on Monday. Although I don't know how I'm going to explain it away to the children."

I wrap her up in a hug, squeezing and shimmying and making excited little squeaking sounds. "I knew you'd be alright. You were practically an innocent bystander. And hate to break it to you, but the kids probably already know."

"So much for discreet, aye?"

I snort. "No such thing in our family apparently."

I pull away when I hear the toilet flushing in the upstairs bathroom. "Who…" I glance at my sister, who is suddenly sheepish. "Who's that?"

It's then I notice two mugs of steaming something on the kitchen side and my brain starts whirring like an overheated fan.

"Don't be mad. He was there today and wanted to see you and I couldn't say no, Shez. He's a damn mess."

My heart starts beating wildly at the prospect of Myles being in my house. Of seeing his perfect face again. Brinsley can forgive easily, and I try to shove away my frustration.

The stairs creak and I feel sick all over again.

And then Nash enters the kitchen, in one of his many smart suits—though his shirt is untucked, and his tie is mysteriously absent—and my disappointment that it *isn't* Myles is palpable. And that tells me everything.

Nash's face is a canvas of colours. Fading green and yellow bruises, nearly healed pink cuts, and a new purple splotch under his eye. Brin's right…he's a freaking disaster.

"Hi, Shez," he manages, throat hoarse.

I stare at him for a minute, a little dumbfounded. It's the end of January. I haven't seen him since the day he punched my boyfriend in the face. And he's a categorical shamble.

"What the fuck happened to your face?" Is the first thing I ask, a lot less elegantly than I wanted to.

Nash, who has never been nervous in his entire life, hesitates, throws a look at Brin, and scratches the back of his head. "Er, it's a long story."

"I've got time."

I can see Brin's head spinning in my periphery. She clears her throat. "I'll leave you two to it."

Nash and I watch her leave, and then we go back to staring at each other.

"You were in York?" He asks tentatively.

"Yeah, finishing a house."

He nods. "Go alright?"

"Always does when I'm there."

His lips twitch with a smile. I'm never arrogant like that unless it's about work, as opposed to him who is just always arrogant all the time. "Good."

"I'm gonna go get changed. I've been driving for hours." I promptly turn on my heel and leave him alone in the kitchen.

I change into a large T-shirt and a pair of fleece-lined leggings, adding bed socks because the stone floor in the kitchen is enough to freeze anyone's toes off in the winter.

Back in the kitchen, Nash is sitting at the breakfast table nursing his coffee. Anyone who drinks coffee after midday needs to be studied, because my legs would be bouncing all night if I did.

"Why were you at the hearing today?" I ask him as I pour my own tea.

"Mum asked me to, for Myles's sake. As an outsider I don't think they ordinarily would but…well, I did it for Brin more than for Myles."

I lift my head, but I'm still confused. "What did you say?"

"The truth. That Brin was just a bystander and her presence during our…altercation," I guess that's one descriptive for it, "didn't impact any of my decisions."

"Right."

"And then I said Myles didn't coerce me into hitting him, it was just a culmination of things that happened, and him saying he was in love with you made me snap. I said it was a mistake and I shouldn't have done it. Myles didn't deserve it and I've accepted I'm completely at fault."

"Does Myles know you've said this?"

"He wasn't there today. I think his hearing is next week, but I told him I was gonna take responsibility for it."

"You've seen Myles?" I ask, somewhat surprised.

"Yeah... He, er," Nash points at his face, "helped with a lot of this."

"*What?*"

"I know." He manages to laugh. "Known the guy nearly six years and I did not know his right hook was that strong."

"That new one is from him too?"

"I gave him a free hit. After he and Beau made up, he came to see me again and I said I wasn't fighting him anymore. I'd gone through four bouts with him and I'm tired. Also, he's trying to foster that kid, so I figured a man that committed to doing something good needs his livelihood back. I can give that to him."

There is so much to unpack in all that I think I might get an aneurysm. Nash and Myles had *four* rounds with their fists? Myles wants to foster a child? Nash has admitted defeat?

"I...am so lost," I admit. "You've been fighting each other?"

"He just kept turning up, and I guess being his punching bag might not repent my sins or whatever, but I knew he was itching for a fight, so I hit back."

"Jesus Christ."

"I broke his nose the last time we fought."

I drag my hand down my face. "Again."

"Yeah...not my proudest achievement."

"He wants to adopt a kid?"

"No, foster. That one from his art class."

I don't know what to say for a minute. Somehow this man who disappeared on me is still worming into my broken heart and making it better and worse simultaneously. I hate him yet I still love him. It's only been six weeks and so much has changed.

"Sam."

"I think so, yeah." Nash shrugs, and I see him as a surly, stroppy teenager who thought the world was against him, even though he wasn't the one bullying his own sister.

"Well, besides a few bruises and scratches, you seem to have come away from this the best of all of us." Perhaps it's a cruel thing to say but considering he's the one that hit someone and had them suspended, it still rings true.

He gives me a sad smile. "Stavros bought me out of my half of the company."

"Oh."

"He said my behaviour was damaging to the business and he didn't want to be associated with me if I was going to bring that kind of attention."

"This coming from a man who has made regularly scheduled misogynistic comments? Sure, okay."

Nash shoves his hands through his hair, messing up the gel holding it all together. "I know he's an arsehole at times, but he's been a big part of my life for a long time. Cutting ties with him like that is…harder than I thought it would be."

"Maybe I'm missing something, Nash, but from my side of things, you've just got a shit load of money out of selling off your business, and you've cut a frankly toxic bellend out of your life. I call that a win-win."

My brother stares at me for a minute with a look that's so confused it's disconcerting, and I feel like I'm missing something. "You haven't got a clue, have you?"

Bile rises up my throat at his tone. "Excuse me?"

He lets out a heavy breath and buried his face in his hands. "I don't know how you and I got like this. We're so…far apart from each other."

"I mean…you spent a good three years encouraging bullies towards me, so I have a pretty good idea of how we got here. You're my brother and I love you, but sometimes I really don't fucking like you."

"Sheridan…"

"What? Maybe you think I'm being unreasonable, I don't know, but I don't think you ever really understood how much your taunting and egging on others to do the same affected me. It fucked me up a lot. As if I wasn't worried about my thoughts myself, you had to go and make me look like I was seriously mentally ill. And, yeah okay, hurting myself the way I did probably didn't help matters, but at the time no existence at all felt like a far better alternative than being hissed at all day for being a fucking psychopath. You helped that, and you never took responsibility for it, either.

"You and Beau like to live in this world of deniability where if we don't talk about it, it's not happening. I've never confronted you about this before because it was years ago and I'm better now. *Much* better. I have a life I *love* and every day I thank whatever freaking ethereal entity I have to that I failed at hurting myself enough that day to end it all. Because imagine if I had? I wouldn't get to see Beau play football every week. I wouldn't get to spend time with Brin like this now that her toxic wanker of a boyfriend has fucked off.

"Which, by the way, how you couldn't find a single issue with that cunt in three or so years but have the nerve to hate Myles enough to hit him just for being with me, is the biggest head fuck I've ever had. John Andrews had his dick in another woman for months and broke Brin's heart, but you never touched him. Myles treats me like a fucking queen but because he's your friend and I've been a bit delicate in the past, he deserves a broken nose? It doesn't make sense, Nash. I've had six weeks to try and understand it all, and I just don't."

I've been venting so long I don't realise until now that Nash is crying, although pretending like he's not.

He wipes his wet cheeks and sniffs. "Fuck, Shez, you really know where to hit a guy's sore spots." His voice is choked so I push his mug closer to him and watch him take a sip. "And that's not a criticism, it's a compliment. I admit I'm terrible at being accountable for things when I fuck up. And I also know how much my behaviour affected you when we were at school and I'm ashamed you ever wanted to take your own life because of something I encouraged. I was the worst type of bastard back then and I've tried to do better as an adult. Although apparently not well.

"I'm sorry. We'd be here for a long time if I sat and apologised for every bad thing I've ever done to you, but I'll do it if you want me to. I think I've been on a bit of a downward spiral recently and seeing you with Myles at that awards ceremony I knew nothing about tripped me over into completely unhinged territory. It shouldn't have. I know Myles is a good bloke. No one will ever be good enough for you, Sheridan—you deserve the world. But I will admit Myles comes pretty close to the best. Or at least he had been pretty close before he ran off and broke your heart. Pretty sure he's still in love with you, though, if that helps at all."

"It doesn't," I say.

"Okay." He laughs, wiping his face again. "But I really mean it when I say I'm sorry. It was wrong of me to take out my frustrations on your relationship. On your partner. If I'd have found out any other day, I probably would've been pro-Meridan. I *am* pro-Meridan."

"What's Meridan?"

"Your couple ship name, according to Brin."

"Oh my God." I manage to laugh. "It's awful."

"The alternative is Shyles which is just atrocious, so I think Meridan sounds comparatively better."

I wave my hands dismissively. "This has gone off the rails. What's going on with you that's so bad you ended up punching your best friend?"

Something crosses over his face, and he's serious all over again. Stern lines and unforgiving creases. "You're not the only one with secrets, Shez. I learnt a lot about myself when I went to university, and I'd like to think I came away a better person. But there are some things I've kept completely to myself. Brin worked one out because she's annoyingly intuitive. But there are other things I probably won't tell anyone."

"At all? Like not even your future wife?"

He smiles at me in that sad way of his. "I don't think anyone will ever like me enough to want to marry me, Sheridan."

"I don't know, some women like the broody thing."

"I'm bi."

"Okay, some men like it, too." I shrug. "Do *you* even want to get married?"

Nash blinks at me like I'm some kind of alien. "Wait, what?"

"What, what?" I frown.

"That's all you have to say? Okay?"

"Why, were you expecting me to call the police, and have you arrested? This isn't the fifties, Nash. Lots of people enjoy everyone. Also, I'm kind of not surprised. You have an air about you."

He looks bewildered. "I can't believe you're not making a bigger deal out of this. Brin spent the following three days sending me potential candidates for boyfriends."

That makes me cackle. "Not me, bro. Find your own boyfriends. Or girlfriends. Was that your secret?"

"Kind of."

"I'm sorry, Nash. I just... I'm in a community where pretty much everyone is bisexual. I don't mean to take away from it for you because it's important, but when you hear *I swing both ways* once a week it kind of becomes the norm. But thank you for telling me."

"It's okay, I get it. Unfortunately, I'm the opposite, where everyone around me is so...masculine and ignorant that if everyone knew about it, I'd be kind of shunned."

"Seriously? That's bad, Nash. Like, that's not normal or even okay."

"So... Stavros. I'm always in two minds about him." *Fucking Steven.* "In uni we were close, as you know, and I told him how I was feeling and my inclinations and he just kind of shrugged it off and said it was cool and he didn't care. Then a few years later we launched the business and when we celebrated, things changed between us, in that we got *closer*. More intimate."

I blink at him. "You slept with your business partner?"

"Yep. Silly mistake and yet it didn't happen just once. We've never had any chat about it or anything, we just occasionally used each other to let off steam if the gym wasn't doing it for us. So anyway, summer while we're away he wouldn't touch me and I didn't think much of it, like we've only ever been like that in private and we were in a cabin with eight other people. I just brushed past it. We come back home, and he starts initiating it again.

"At this point the business is going so well that we're so busy all the time and I've not slept with *anyone else* for months. I mentioned this to him, and he freaked the fuck out."

"Freaked out how?" I ask because I have to, even though I know that whatever is about to come out of Nash's mouth is only going to make me hate Stavros more.

"I can't remember all of it; I actually think I blacked out a little bit I was so upset. But he basically said I was trying to make him gay, which is utterly ridiculous. Apparently, I've been 'slowly coercing him into a gay relationship' for years. And then apparently to prove he isn't gay; he took our brand-new receptionist into my office and made me watch him fuck her."

I'm lost for words for a second, because I'm not sure which part to focus on. "Is the receptionist okay?"

"I mean, I'm pretty sure she's still working there and they're probably still shagging. Stavros, as I'm sure you've worked out by now, lacks a lot of decorum."

I gasp. "What? No. No way. Not my Stavros. Take it back."

Nash snorts. "Right? Anyway, that was the day I found out about you and Myles. And your secret life as a cartoonist. Is that what it's called?"

"It's an animated web show. I don't know what my title is."

"Okay, well, yeah everything happened on that day. I kicked Stavros and the receptionist out of my office, Beau turns up in a fiery rage and shows me this photo of you and Myles together at some awards ceremony, and the next thing I know, we're all in the car park outside Myles's flat having a fight."

"Yeah…busy day for you."

"Busy day for all of us." His laugh is humourless.

"You're better off far away from Stavros. It's a blessing in disguise, trust me."

"I hope you're right."

"I am right." I say confidently, giving him a smile. "What are you going to do now you've not got a business?"

He purses his lips. "I've been looking at that old hotel in the city. The empty one."

"The Godiva?"

"Yeah, that one. I might buy it. Get it up and running again."

I squeal. "Yes! Can I do the interior design?"

"Abso-fucking-lutely."

"I can't wait to tell Sarah-Jane." I think of her, red hair and overalls and coffee, and grin. She'll be so happy.

"Who is Sarah-Jane?"

"She owns the shop next door. She's been waiting for someone to bring it back to life. Oh my God, Nash, please do it."

"Maybe. I need to do a lot of research, but it's the only idea I've got."

I think it's the best idea he's ever had.

Chapter Thirty-Six

HOMECOMING

MYLES

I hear the shoes squeaking on the linoleum outside the classroom before I see him. Sam bursts through the door, eyes lighting up when he sees me standing behind my desk, and if that isn't something to be proud of, I don't know what is.

"I fucking *knew it*!" He shouts, beaming.

"Language, Sam," I scold him.

"I *knew* you'd be allowed back; the whole thing was *dumb*."

I laugh at his tone. "Dumb is certainly one word for it."

"Why didn't you tell me?" He demands, folding his arms over his coat. "You said you were gonna text me when the result came back."

"Maybe I wanted to surprise you."

"Sir, I thought you might be in hiding! That's what you did after you dumped your girl, so why would I be any different?"

"Those situations are slightly different, Sam."

"They're literally exactly the same. About the same thing."

"Yes, well you've never been my girlfriend. And abandoning a foster kid seems like a pretty shitty thing to do when I know how it feels."

Sam mutters something unintelligible. "Anyway, have you spoken to your lady yet?"

"No, and I'm probably not going to."

"What, why?"

"Because I'm not good enough for her and she deserves better than a flake like me."

"You're not a flake. Yeah, you might have skipped out on her, which was a terrible mistake, but you're not a *real* flake. And you can still fix it, which would make you even less of a flake."

"This is all very flattering and encouraging, but I'm pretty sure Sheridan doesn't want to talk to me."

"How do you know if you don't even *try*?"

I give him a perturbed look. "What is with you this morning? Did you stay up past your bedtime watching motivational speeches or something?"

"No, I'm just obviously way more intelligent than you."

"Obviously."

"Will you do it for me?" He bats his eyelashes at me.

"No. Now go to form before you're late."

Sam snorts. "Sir, you know we've got ages before form. Stop trying to get rid of me."

I have to laugh. The kid is observant. I haven't told him that I've started the fostering process. It's a long one and will likely take a few months. But if I do get approved to foster him then he'll be the one trying to get rid of me, not the other way around.

"I have stuff to do before form starts and you are distracting me. I haven't been here for months, and I want to see the status of all my classes, so unless you can be quiet, I really need to concentrate."

He sighs. "Fine, I'll leave you alone."

"Come and see me at break time if you're so desperate for my company."

"No, that's lame."

"Thought as much. Behave. I'll take you home later if you want."

"Yes! No bus," he shouts on his way out. "Oh, hi Miss Bennett."

I think my soul has left my body. I knew seeing Brinsley again was inevitable given we're colleagues, but I didn't expect her to hunt me down the second I got let back into the building.

"Morning, Sam."

I glance up again at her voice and she appears in the doorway, watching the teenager head off down the corridor. Then she turns to face me with a scarily calm expression.

"Myles." She may seem calm, but her voice is tighter than Paulson's leather belt.

"Brin."

She shuts the door behind her and crosses her arms. "I thought I'd come and see if the rumours were true."

"What rumours would they be?" I remain as still as possible. I don't want to fight her but I'm sure she's looking for one.

"That you're here. That your face is messed up." *That you're not hiding anymore* is what she doesn't say, but I know it's implied.

"I'm here, and my face is messed up. But it's better than it was."

"You did a pretty good job with Nash's face, too, I noticed."

"Yeah, well…we talked it out and we've forgiven each other."

"I don't think there was much talking involved."

Her voice has gotten sharper, and I don't blame her. "No," is all I can think to say.

She nods, her lips pressed tightly together as she scans the room. "I just want to be clear about something, Myles, so that we're both on the same page. I don't condone what Nash did, and Beau is an idiot. I'm not on their side of any of this, even if they have both apologised and Sheridan has forgiven them. But if you think *I've* forgiven *you* for running off and breaking my sister's heart because you were scared, I can assure you I have not. You're a coward, and you have a lot of grovelling to do before we're anywhere close to being friends again."

"I know," I say through a rough voice. "I think I convinced myself that I'd be let go, and it did scare me. I was terrified, and I know I've never been good enough for her. This whole thing just kind of cemented it for me, and I panicked that maybe one day she'd leave me again like everyone else always has."

"And you left first," Brin concludes. "I get it, but your first mistake is grouping Sheridan in with a bunch of people who failed you, when she's never done that. Even now, after you abandoned her, she's still Team Myles. She still defends you. I don't know much, but I know my sister and I know she's still in love with you."

The wooden desk creaks and I realise it's because I've got a white-knuckle grip on it. My knees are weak, and I need to sit down but that feels rude. "Yeah, I'm...still in love with her, too."

"Then *fix it*, you idiot. Stop feeling sorry for yourself and *fix it*." In the next breath Brinsley is standing right next to me, glaring up at me with those same eyes as her sister's. And then the blue in them softens and she says, "All this aside, Myles, I'm really pleased you're okay and I'm glad you're back at work. Beau said you'd mentioned moving, and I'm gonna be really selfish here and say I don't want you to because we need you. All of us. You might not be blood but you're family, and none of us—not even Sheridan—want to see you disappear."

Fuck I think I'm crying again. "Thanks, Brin. I'm sorry I hurt you."

Taking me completely by surprise, she wraps her arms around my waist. "I'll break your testicles if you ever do it again."

"I think that's fair."

She laughs and pulls away. "Start grovelling, Myles. My favourite flowers are tulips. And you already know Sheridan's."

Peonies, dahlias, and carnations. I'm surprised I remember that.

"Noted."

A second later she's gone, and I'm left alone for all of thirty seconds before the first kid from my form group arrives.

"Oh," she startles, offering a gentle smile, "welcome back, Mr. Wilson."

* * *

SHERIDAN
I'm a bit lost.

I don't know why I bothered getting out of the car when Brin texted to say she was going to be a while, but I didn't want to sit in silence for half an hour, so I thought I'd try and find her classroom. Turns out I don't actually know where that is, or where Mum's office is, and so I'm aimlessly wandering the halls and reading the displays of the children's works as I pass.

This is probably illegal. Or, not illegal, but definitely frowned upon. It's after school hours but there are still students milling around the corridors and whispering when they think I'm out of earshot. Maybe now they'll think Brin's got an alter ego as someone with curly purple hair—I dyed it last week—and wears a lot of purple denim.

I turn a corner and find myself in the canteen, open plan with the hallway carrying on straight through the centre, kitchen on one side and rows of benches with plastic stools attached on the other. There's a horrendous art display on the walls that I'm pretty sure is all vaginas.

"That can't be legal," I mutter.

"Woah," a newly broken voice says from nearby.

I look towards the voice, finding a boy with a messy mop of hair and creased uniform staring straight at me.

I lift an awkward hand, "Hi."

"Are you Sheridan, by any chance?" The boy asks.

"Yes…"

"I'm Sam." He grins, and it all makes sense. *This* is Sam. Myles's favourite pupil—the boy he wants to foster.

He holds out a hand, which I don't hesitate to shake. "I've heard a lot about you, Sam," I admit.

"I've heard a lot about you, too. And it makes sense." This kid is practically glowing with excitement, and I have to say I find it oddly charming.

"What makes sense?"

"Why Mr. Wilson doesn't shut up about you."

"Myles talks to you about me?"

"All the time. And to be fair to him, if I had a girlfriend who looked like you, I wouldn't stop talking about her, either."

I have to laugh. This lad is going to make some girl very happy one day. "Thank you."

"He really likes you, you know." Sam suddenly grows serious, a crease appearing between his bushy brows. "He's a twat for running off, but he likes you a lot all the same. Probably scared you'd abandon him for someone way cooler and better looking. Don't get me wrong, he's not ugly, but he was punching with you."

I'm in full on hysterics at this point. I can't find it in myself to be sad at the topic of conversation because this boy is a delight. I want to foster him, too. "Thank you."

"Seriously, you're way too cool for Mr. Wilson."

"Sam?" A painfully familiar and smooth voice calls from down the corridor.

I baulk and nearly make a run for it. I don't know if I can see Myles now. Am I ready? Probably not. I'll be a sad little mess by the time I find Brinsley and her classroom, which is apparently located in fucking Narnia.

"Sam?" His voice gets louder, and I get sweatier.

"Here!" He calls back.

And then Myles is there, dressed in green tweed trousers, a white shirt, and brogues, with a grey wool coat over the top. His face is still a little battered but it's cleaner than Nash's. A couple more days and no one would know.

But beneath all the bruises and the cuts is my man. *My* man. I can't deny that I'm still head over heels for him, even though he vanished. My head is at war with my heart. I want to forget everything that's happened over the past month or so, but I also want to verbally rip him to shreds for the damage he did to my heart.

He's gone very pale in the two seconds he's been standing there. "Sheridan?"

I do my awkward wave again. "Hi."

He looks at Sam, who is still smiling, either oblivious to the tension or just delighted by the reunion. "What did you do?"

"Nothing! I was just going to get my stuff like you asked and she was here. She's way too cool for you, by the way."

"I know she is," he mutters, and I pretend not to hear it.

"I'm looking for Brin. I've never been inside before, and I got lost."

"Oh," is all he says to me. Then he starts jiggling around in his pockets and produces his car keys, holding them out to Sam as he comes closer, "Sam, can you go wait in the car, please?"

Oh no. I'm definitely not ready for whatever this is.

Sam's gaze flits between us. "Are you getting back together?"

"*Sam,*"

"Right, not my business. Sorry." He lifts his hands in surrender then turns that grin back on me. "Bye, Sheridan. He's very sorry, by the way. Feels an utter fool."

"Sam!"

"Alright, I'm going!"

He takes off down the corridor and we watch him go. I'm still smiling after him when I blurt, "You're really good with him."

Myles looks at me as if I'd spoken in a foreign language. Then he relaxes. "He's important to me."

"I know he is."

He rubs the back of his neck which stirs the position of his coat and tightens the fabric of his shirt across his torso, highlighting the lines of his muscles, and my mouth starts watering. Jesus, how little does one girl need to be teased with before she turns into a thirsty bitch?

"I promised I'd take Sam home today, but are you free tonight? I'll make us dinner. I feel like I owe you an explanation. An apology."

My heart squeezes like it's in a vice. "That depends, will you actually be there?"

He nods. "I deserve that. I promise I'll be there."

I let out a long breath. "Yeah, okay. I need to take Brin home and walk Hector, but I can come after."

"Thank you. Whenever you can, I'll be home all night."

I nod once. "Okay."

Chapter Thirty-Seven
Whole Again

MYLES

The buzzer goes off at an eerily punctual seven o'clock on the dot.

When I open the door to the flat, I'm relieved to find Sheridan in the same clothes as she was at the school earlier—a matching, purple-stained denim jean and jacket combo with a black turtleneck and black hi-top Converse. Her hair has been put into those space buns, the newly dyed purple tips peeking through each little twist.

Time apart hasn't dulled my attraction to her. If anything, it's worse. She looks incredible, if a little tired.

And I'm a bastard.

"You came," I state, like a complete moron.

She's pulled the sleeves of her jacket right over her hands, hiding them. "I said I would."

"I know, I just…wouldn't blame you if you didn't," I admit. When she doesn't say anything, I take a step to the side, opening the door wider. "Come in."

"Thank you."

She takes her jacket off and I mourn the co-ordination of her ensemble, but I take it from her and hang it on the hooks in the entryway. Wordlessly, she follows me into the kitchen.

"Can I get you a drink?"

"Water is fine. Please."

I nod, and silently fill a glass with water from the kitchen tap. She gulps half of it down in one.

"Are you hungry—did you eat?"

She gives me a long look that feels something between pity and scathing. "I didn't come here to eat, Myles."

"Right, yeah. Um," I absently scratch the back of my head, "shall we sit down?"

We migrate to the sofa, where I sit at one end, and she sits at the other. As far away from me as possible. That seems…fair.

"I, er," I clear my throat, "don't know where to start even though I've been thinking about it for…a while."

"Why don't you start with why you just disappeared with nothing but a two-line text message?" She suggests, with only the tiniest hint of hostility.

Alright. "I panicked. I've been in a position like that—in trouble, in the crossfire—so many times it's normal. But the difference is, this time, you were there, too. I've always been by myself with these things, Sheridan. If I ever got myself in any kind of trouble, I was alone, so it didn't matter. The only person getting hurt was me. But you were there, and Brin was there, and it got way out of hand.

"Then to make matters worse, it got filmed and put all over the internet because your brother happens to be a celebrity. I've wondered every single day since Sam and Jamie showed me that video, if it wasn't Beau involved, would it have been filmed in the first place?

"If *Brinsley*, who, apart from a few choice words for her brothers, was a practical bystander, got suspended, what might happen to you if your boss caught wind of it? And if it escalated?"

"But, Myles, nothing happened," she says with a little frown. "*I* called Marina and asked her outright if she was going to sack me, and she said no. Adamantly. And if you'd have answered any of my calls or texts, you would've known that.

"Also, so what if I was? None of it was your fault. You didn't hit anyone. You *got hit*. The school board is frankly ridiculous for suspending the two of you in the first place. And I can just get another job, but I would never have blamed you if I did get sacked."

"I'm sorry." God my throat feels awful. "I just couldn't handle the thought of being responsible for anything bad happening to you, and I thought the easiest way to do that was to leave."

"Well then, you're an idiot," she says simply. "You're so caught up in all the 'ifs' you don't look at the actuals. You need to stop living like that, Myles, it's not healthy. You're such a good man and anyone with two brain cells to rub together would be able to see it. I wouldn't have blamed you and I wouldn't have left you. Because I love you. And I don't say those words to just anyone."

Christ, my chest hurts. To hear Sheridan say she loves me in present terms is like taking a defibrillator to my still heart.

"Unfortunately for me, I'm not in a position to look at another man ever again," she says with a sigh. "You've ruined me for other people so if you don't want me anymore then I'm destined to a life alone. With my twin for a roommate."

I shake my head adamantly. "No. No, Birdie, that's not true at all," I insist, the nickname slipping off my tongue without thinking. "I hate that I ever gave you that impression because it's not the case. I want you. Always. I just about choked a lung when I saw you at school because time apart has done literally nothing to temper the effect you have on me. I'm so in love with you it's pathetic—"

"It's not pathetic," she interrupts with a frown. "Don't say shit like that."

"I never thought I'd be beholden to anyone, Sheridan. But I am to you because you're like oxygen. You're not a drug—something to enjoy. You're a necessity. And I let you go because you deserve better than me."

Sheridan stares at me for a moment, and then says, so quietly, "I really wish other people would stop telling me what I do and don't deserve." Then, with determination, "Here's the black and white of it, Bear. Even though you left me and made me feel like a fool, I still love you. That's not gonna stop any time soon, either, because you are easily the most selfless person I've ever met."

I'm trying not to repeatedly trip over the fact that she called me *Bear* without a hint of disdain, but rather as some term of affection. "Even though I've physically battered your brother on more than one occasion? Doesn't seem very selfless to me."

"I'm going to choose to ignore that over the fact that you are, according to hot gossip, fostering a boy out of the system because his shitty home life is relatable to you. I don't know many people our age who would do that."

"You're painting me like a martyr," I grumble.

"I am not. Don't know many martyrs who go four rounds with their girlfriend's brother."

I sigh and cover my face with my hands, and I'm pretty sure Sheridan is laughing at me on the other side of the sofa.

"You're so fucking daft, Myles. I don't know what you want. You asked me here to apologise which gave me a terrifying injection of hope, and now I'm here you're just stressing why you don't think you're good enough for me to stick around. Are you pushing me away? 'Cause if you are, can you just tell me so I can go on with my life?"

Fuck, fuck, fuck. "I don't want you to go anywhere, Birdie. I'm quite clearly rubbish at this, but of course I fucking want you. I do love you; I'm just petrified of fucking it all up again. I'd never do it on purpose, but I'm a man, and I think we've established that all the men in your life are stupid."

"Maybe if you talk to me instead of running away, you'll fuck up less," she deadpans.

"Christ, I—," I stop myself from telling her I don't deserve her again because she clearly doesn't like it. "I'll take anything you give me. If you'll still have me, I'll be happy with whatever you let me have from you, and I'll work my arse off to make sure I'm good enough for you."

"Right, well," Sheridan scratches her head, hands still covered by her jumper sleeves like little paws, "good."

I blink at her. "That's it?"

"Yeah, I guess. I'm not gonna do a Brin and demand flowers every day."

I narrow my eyes. "Is that what you want?"

She abruptly stands. "Can I use your bathroom please?"

Her question startles me. "Er, sure."

She breezes off, and I stare after her wondering if I've finally lost it.

I remember that my mouth feels like cat litter and head to the kitchen to make myself a glass of water. My stomach rumbles at the sub-par sustenance, so I peek inside the fridge for something to pick at while I wait for her to come back.

I don't know what's happening. Sheridan seems to have accepted the fact that I'm an idiot and still wants me anyway, but now that we've established that I'm still obsessed with her, is behaving like a skittish feline, and hiding in the bathroom.

Where do we stand?

What's going on?

Is she talking herself out of forgiving me?

I wouldn't blame her because Brin is right. I was a freaking coward ghosting her.

Sheridan reappears while I'm shoving grated cheddar out of a bag into my mouth like a caveman. I didn't hear the system flush so she can't have used it. She stands close to me—much closer than we were on the sofa a minute ago—and watches me swallow like I'm the most fascinating thing she's ever seen. Her body heat is delicious, the minute space between us vibrating.

"I lied earlier," she says quietly, and my stomach sinks.

I knew it. She's talked herself out of it.

But then she says, "I didn't eat at home and I'm absolutely fucking starving."

I practically choke on a shred of cheese with my relieved exhale, and white-knuckle the counter while I recover. And when I do recover, I'm laughing. I laugh so hard my ribs ache and my eyes weep. The sound of her laughter is infectious too, and a minute later I've got my forehead pressed against the cool kitchen work surface because I can't stand up straight.

The small hand with delicate fingers that starts stroking through my hair doesn't help the fact that I'm overheating, but it does subdue me enough to take a real breath. When Sheridan's nails scratch my scalp I shiver violently, but she carries on. She's pushed her entire front against me, her other hand smoothing along the length of my forearm.

I twist my head slightly to find her watching me with a small, innocent little smile, and my guilt eats away at me all over again for having behaved like such a prick about everything.

"I'm sorry, Birdie," I say gently. "I've been such an arsehole, and I'm so sorry."

The hand in my hair lowers to the back of my neck and rests there. "I know, Myles. I know you are."

She doesn't say it's okay, or that she's forgiven me, because it isn't okay, and she hasn't forgiven me yet. But we're making progress, and I'm going to keep that progress going, keep being better, until she does forgive me. Even if it takes years.

I finally straighten up, but she doesn't stop touching me, and eventually she's standing with her chest flush against mine while standing on her tiptoes, her arms looped around my neck.

"Can you tell me about Sam?" She asks, gaze warm with curiosity. "He seems like such a good kid."

"He's a great kid. His foster parents sent him back to the care home at Christmas like heartless animals, and then I found him in the hospital with a broken wrist on New Year's Eve. He was all by himself, and I kind of just...saw *me* in him. How many times had I done the exact same thing—got on a bus or the tube and ridden to the nearest hospital—because some horrible people managed to get permission to look after a child that they were only using to get money out of?"

"Is that a thing?" Sheridan is quite clearly horrified.

"Oh yeah. That's the thing with fostering. You get financial support to raise a child. As long as you have a spare room and can put up the front of a healthy lifestyle for a child, they'll give you one and a bunch of cash to help raise it." I shake my head. "Some people—and way more than you'd think possible—don't use that money towards the child. They use it towards themselves."

"Fucking hell." She sighs, leaning closer somehow. "What a shitty world we live in."

"Tell me about it," I mutter. "Anyway, I mentioned to Sam that everything had kind of gone tits up and that I was thinking of moving if the board decided to sack me. And the scrawny little fecker asked if I'd take him with me."

"That's because he can see you for who you really are, Bear. Not this version of yourself you've created in your head."

I don't know what to say to that, so I turn my head away from those pretty blue eyes of hers.

A second later she slips her hands to my face and coaxes my gaze back. Her thumbs stroke my cheeks as she talks. "Sam sees you the same way I do. You're *good*, Myles. Prior reputation be damned, you've earned another as a good teacher. A *great* teacher if he's asking you to take him with you. When are you going to realise that you're not this monster you think you are?"

I can't help but study her face intently while she's this close, back to praising me as if I have any right to her affection. The freckles on her nose have faded with the winter weather but are still there, lingering like water droplets on dried glass. Her little upturned nose. Her full lips. Her big blue eyes. I don't think I'll ever meet another woman as beautiful as this one. And for some reason she wants to be mine.

"Maybe if I hear it enough times from people who regard me as highly as you do, I'll start believing it," I say hoarsely, and turn my face to kiss the palm of her hand.

Then, without giving myself time to hesitate, I snatch her by the waist and lift her up onto the counter, where I settle between her legs.

"Now," I mumble, pressing a kiss to her forehead, "I think you told me you're *absolutely fucking starving* a minute ago, so can I please cook you some dinner?"

"That depends," she pecks the underside of my chin, "will it involve an entire bag of pre-grated cheese?"

I pinch her hip and she yelps, the noise somehow delighted by its own shock. "I *was* going to whip up a curry that cheats the marinating system, but I think I've changed my mind."

She gasps in mock horror, "You would deny me a hearty meal?"

I purse my lips, tap them twice, and study her again—the roundness of her face, her slender neck, her slim waist and wide hips, her thighs. God, her thighs. I could suffocate between them and die a happy man. It's that thought that has me dropping my bravado.

"You know what, Birdie, I don't think I could ever deny you anything again."

Sheridan's gaze softens, and then sparkles with something more mischievous. "Even if I asked you to fuck me on your kitchen counter?"

Sweet baby Jesus. "That is…not where I expected this conversation to go."

"But would you?"

"Right now?"

She hums seductively.

"Would I fuck you on my kitchen counter if you asked me to?"

"Yes, Myles."

My eyes glaze over, and I'm harder than a fucking lead pipe in my jogging bottoms. And I think Sheridan knows it, too. "Yeah, I probably would."

Her grin is triumphant. "Myles, baby," she bats her lashes at me, "*please* put me out of my misery and fuck me, right here, right now, on your kitchen counter."

At her pretty little beg, I am unleashed.

When I sink my way inside her, I am home.

And when we fall apart together, I am whole again.

Epilogue

SHERIDAN
8 Weeks Later

"Shez, post!"

I startle at the sound of Brinsley's voice out in the hallway.

"Yeah, coming!" I shout back from my office.

I've been very unproductive today, and I blame Myles. The second I sat down at my desk to start illustrating for the day, he appeared in the garden and started...gardening.

It's the first Monday of April and the weather is unseasonably warm.

Myles started in a light T-shirt and old, well-worn jeans. After half an hour he caved and changed into shorts. When he started getting really sweaty—which was no eyesore to me—he took his T-shirt off. Again, this was no bad view, but it has been incredibly distracting. I have done *nothing*. N. O. T. H. I. N. G. Other than stare at him and his naked back and the tattoos painted on him while drooling like a woman starved. I don't know how many times I've wondered if my neighbours would mind me mounting him right there in my little garden.

A trowel has never been so sexy.

At some point Beau, who is on a day off—and has done nothing but complain—arrived and trampled all over my sexy gardener/lonely housewife fantasy, but then I learned to tune him out and refocus on my man.

My man.

I moved Myles in last week. His tenancy was up sooner than he realised while we were looking into Sam getting fostered and decided to adjust the application slightly to include me and the spare room in my house rather than Myles's flat.

It's a big responsibility, taking on a child when the relationship is so new, but after speaking to my parents and Brin, everyone was supportive of the idea. Plus, having such a big family was a huge positive on our part in the eyes of the care system. Sam will have a support network—a family that loves him. And that love will be unconditional.

My relationship with Myles feels even stronger than it did the first time. It definitely helps that my brothers aren't a constant rain cloud over our heads, a lurking threat to our happiness. It's the total opposite, actually. Sometimes I can't get rid of Beau.

Our application to foster Sam was approved on Friday, and we're telling him tonight. We've told him he's coming for dinner—which is not the first time we've done it—but the difference is that we'll all be there to break the news. Family dinner at the fairy cottage.

I've never been so nervous and excited in my entire life.

In the hall, I take the stack of post off the side table and sift through it. Most of it is crap, obviously. There's a reminder to renew Hector's insurance, a letter from Myles's bank, and from the DVLA which is likely his new driving licence.

And then there's a big A4 envelope with my name and a big fat purple T on it. The *ToonStream* logo.

Oh God. The pitch I sent back in December. The same day my life upended. They finally came back to me.

I amble through the house in a daze as I open the letter, finding a wad of printed white paper and a brochure inside. The first page has CONFIDENTIAL stamped on it in giant red letters.

My heart is going a mile a minute. What is happening? Are they rejecting me? This seems like a very big letter to deliver just to say they don't want me and my work at their company.

I barely notice anything else going on around me when I flip the page to read the first few sentences.

Myles has appeared in the kitchen and is drinking from a glass of lemon juice as he leans casually against the kitchen sink. "You alright, Birdie?"

I don't answer him.

Dear Miss Bennett,

We are writing to you with regards to the submission you sent to us on the 18th of December last year.

We apologise for the delay in contacting you, but we take any submissions very seriously and take the time to review them in detail, which brings me to your submission for ALL_IS_NOT_ALWAYS_FAIR. *We greatly appreciate the time you took to put forward your talent, and we are extremely interested in taking the project forward with you—*

I start screaming before I finish reading.

Myles is across the room in seconds, his glass smashing against the stone floor where he abandons it. "What's the matter? What happened?"

"Oh my God!" I shout, my hands shaking violently. "Holy fucking *shit!*"

"What, Sheridan?" He's fussing over me, touching my face, and checking my pulse and searching my eyes.

"Myles!" I'm incoherent apparently.

"What?!"

"What's going on?" Beau appears in the threshold of the back door, looking surly and concerned.

"Why are you screaming?" Brin joins us all then, decidedly more cautious than Beau. "Was it a spider again?"

"No, it wasn't a fucking spider!" I squeal and turn the page around to show them. "Look!"

The three of them close in on the letter, reading in sceptical silence, before utter chaos erupts.

"Holy fuck!" Beau shouts.

Brin gasps, "Sheridan!"

And Myles sweeps me off my feet so that I have to cling to him like a damn koala. I'm being spun around, kisses littering my face, and I can't help my delighted, squeaking giggles, joining the soundtrack of my siblings' joyous excitement, praise filling the room.

"I can't believe it," I say when Myles stops moving. "I sent it on a whim *ages* ago. I forgot about it, to be honest."

"I told you you're awesome." Beau takes his turn to sweep me into a hug. "And this proves it."

"I'm shocked. *Shocked.* I'm getting an actual TV show." I pull back. "Oh fuck, you can't tell anyone. It says confidential."

"I'm pretty sure you can tell whoever you like."

"Considering you're someone with a PR agent, you should know better than anyone that is not true," Myles scolds him.

"We won't tell anyone. Not yet," Brin promises.

"I'll tell Mum and Dad. And Nash," I decide. "Fuck, and Sam. But no one else."

"No one else," Myles agrees with a nod.

I turn my face up to him, smiling helplessly, and he leans down to press a soft kiss to my lips. "I'm so proud of you," he says against my mouth.

"Thank you." I peck him back. "Can you put a T-shirt on please? I've managed to get sweet fuck all done all day because of you."

Beau snorts when Myles flexes. Brin just looks uncomfortable.

"It's nearly time to get Sam, anyway." Myles shrugs, leaving one more kiss on my mouth. "Sure you don't want to come with me to get him?"

"I'm sure." I wrap myself around him, easing into his body heat like a lizard on hot sand. "I want you to have five minutes with him before he comes into this madhouse and everything changes."

I'm not sure when Beau and Brin decided to leave, but I know that when Myles kisses me again, deeply, and sincerely, we're alone in the kitchen again. I savour the taste of him—this man who makes me feel secure and loved and cherished—sink into his warmth and the safety of his touch.

"You and me, Birdie," his voice rumbles.

I smile into his mouth. "Me and you, Bear."
"And Sam."
"And Hector."
He chuckles, and the sound is like liquid smoke. "Always."
"Always."

Acknowledgements

Writing my first acknowledgement section feels a little surreal!

Anyone who knows me well knows that I've wanted to publish a book for some time now—pushing on five years, if not more. For a while I never thought I'd get here, but I did. I actually finished a book!

Firstly, I'd like to thank my parents for never telling me I can't when it comes to my own capabilities. Writing a book comes hand-in-hand with a lot of self-doubt and occasional imposter syndrome, but J&K have always supported me, and I owe them a lot for that alone.

Secondly, my bestie of coming up on eight years, Emma. Thank you for accepting my weirdness and strange quirks, and for reading Sheridan and Myles's story as soon as I was happy with it. I appreciate you, and I love you!

Thank you to one of my OG internet girlies, Sarah, for being an amazing beta reader, picking me up on my waffle, correcting my nonsense, and helping me bring this book to be the very best version of itself. I hope I haven't scared you off with my intensity to read the next one!

I'd also like to say a big thank you to Alice for bringing my visions of Myles and Sheridan to life. If you don't follow my Instagram, hop on over if you'd like to see my very talented friend's incredible interpretation of Meridan, and share some love.

Thank you to a small corner of Tumblr who adopted me and my stories five years ago and encouraged me to keep writing. I'm here because of you.

And lastly, thank you to YOU for reading in the first place. I appreciate it endlessly and will keep going so long as you keep coming back for more!

About the Author

Kate Vikki lives in the South West of England with her two cats and an ever-expanding library. A native of the Midlands, when she's not reading or writing, she's daydreaming the day away or helping create the perfect day for brides and grooms.

Follow Kate on Instagram - @authorkatevikki
Follow Kate on TikTok - @kate.vikki

You can listen to The Bird & The Bear playlist on Spotify!

Don't forget to leave a review!

Printed in Great Britain
by Amazon